HIBERNIA

Book two of the Veteran of Rome series

By: William Kelso

Visit the author's website **http://www.williamkelso.co.uk/**

William Kelso is also the author of:

The Shield of Rome

The Fortune of Carthage

Devotio: The House of Mus

Caledonia - Book One of the Veteran of Rome series

Hibernia - Book Two of the Veteran of Rome series

Britannia – Book Three of the Veteran of Rome series

Hyperborea – Book Four of the Veteran of Rome series

Germania – Book Five of the Veteran of Rome series

The Dacian War – Book Six of the Veteran of Rome series

Armenia Capta – Book Seven of the Veteran of Rome series

Hibernia – Veteran of Rome Series

Published in 2014 by FeedARead.com Publishing – Arts Council funded

A CIP catalogue record for this title is available from the British Library.

To Mum and Dad

Chapter One - The Stone Merchants

Spring AD 86

Corbulo stood in the prow of his ship and silently cursed the fog that hung over the Thames. His chin and cheeks were covered by two days' worth of stubble and his hair was completely white. He looked tired. It was late in the afternoon and the dull grey skies had not changed since he and his crew had left the stone quarry that morning. Somewhere in the mist a sea gull screeched as it hunted for food but in the ship the rowers were silent and the splash of their oars in the river was slow and methodical. Corbulo peered into the fog but he could see no more than a dozen yards ahead. Where the fuck were they? The river was nearly a thousand yards wide at high tide and he could see neither the north or south bank, but they couldn't be far from the port. He lifted his nose, sniffed and caught the faint smell of human sewage. Yes, they weren't far from home. He grunted, opened his mouth and ran his finger over his remaining six teeth. The fog was dangerous. He would need to be careful that they didn't strike one of the multitude of sand banks, mudflats and small gravel islands that made up the south bank. If the boat sank and he lost his cargo it would be a catastrophe and he was a poor swimmmer.

He turned sharply to look at his crew and the cargo of Kentish rag stone that they were transporting. The rowers, all of them local men, Britons, looked exhausted. He would need to give them some extra rest and maybe a bonus when they reached Londinium. He had timed his return journey up the river to coincide with the sea tide so that the tide would help push them upstream, but the rowers had already been dog tired from the extra shift he'd demanded from them the previous day. He was pushing them too hard he knew, but such was the demand for stone in the fast growing capital of Britannia that he had not dared say no to his clients. There were plenty of merchants in Londinium who would leap at the chance to snatch his government supply contract from him and destroy his little business, for which he toiled so hard. He couldn't allow that to happen. At forty-eight he was too old to learn a new trade and too old to be a soldier again. The Legions were not short of willing recruits and they could and did choose the best and fittest men. No, he would be damned if he allowed his business to go under. It was all he had. He had invested everything in this venture. When he had first come to live in Londinium with his new wife some eighteen months ago, he had sold the amber stone he'd taken from the sea cave in the far north of Caledonia and bought himself a house and a boat. There had been just enough money left to bribe the Procurator's officials into giving him a contract to supply stone to the burgeoning capital and so his business had begun. But he still only had one boat. Tensely he picked at one of his remaining teeth and suddenly he felt it move. Abruptly he shut his mouth. Another one was coming loose. His face darkened. Soon he would be eating soup and milk every day like a newborn baby. He gestured to the helmsman who was standing at the back of the ship.

"Take her to the right," Corbulo yelled.

A moment later the ship started to veer away on its new course and Corbulo felt the oarsman apply some extra strength to their oars. The rowers too had sensed that they were nearly home and they suddenly seemed in a hurry to finish their long journey and get ashore for some well-earned rest. Anxiously Corbulo peered into the mist. It would not do if they overshot the harbour and sailed straight into the bridge. Then he heard it. Men's shouts, the bark of a dog and the noise of sawing and hammering. He turned to his men but the rowers had heard it too and were already scrambling to lower the sail from the solitary mast. Then without warning the dark solid wooden-fronted quayside loomed up out of the mist. Corbulo watched it draw closer as his helmsman expertly manoeuvred the craft alongside the harbour jetty.

"Priscus, Priscus, are you there? We're back! Where are you?"

Corbulo shouted looking up at the waterfront.

A group of labourers paused and turned to stare at him from the quayside where they were mending an upturned boat. Corbulo ignored their inquisitive glances.

"Priscus get your lazy arse down here!" Corbulo roared as his ship gently nudged up against the harbour wall. The massive, solid squared oak beams had been hammered into the riverbed in a perfect straight line and were covered in green moss. Corbulo was about to shout again when a small timid figure of around twenty with jet black hair came limping hastily up to the edge of the quay.

"Sorry I am here Sir, I am here now. Throw me the rope and I will tie you up," Priscus shouted in his west-country accent.

Corbulo muttered something under his breath and flung the mooring rope up towards the young man on the waterfront. Priscus always liked to call him Sir even though Corbulo had made him his business partner six months ago. It was, Corbulo had concluded, probably because Priscus had originally tried to enlist in one of the auxiliary cohorts but his limp, a consequence of a childhood disease, had prevented him from passing the medical. The young Briton was fascinated by the Roman Army. Corbulo waited as Priscus hastened to secure the ship to the quayside. His wife was always telling him off for being too hard on his young business partner and maybe she was right, for Priscus was a good, trustworthy and educated man with a genius for maths and accounting which Corbulo knew he himself was no good at. But the young man could also be easily distracted and intimidated and twenty-five years service in the Twentieth Legion had taught Corbulo that being distracted, even for a few moments, could cost a man his life. Competition amongst the merchants in Londinium was tough and violent and his rivals were always on the lookout for an opportunity to steal a man's business.

"What have you been up to?" Corbulo cried.

Priscus lowered the ladder into the ship. "I was over in the Forum speaking to the Procurator's staff. They want you to go out again tomorrow morning on the first tide. Full load of stone, same price as always."

"Tomorrow on the first tide?" Corbulo's exclaimed in surprise. "Tomorrow is a fucking festival day, no one works on a holiday."

Priscus shrugged. "That's what they told me. I don't make the rules."

Corbulo shook his head in dismay and turned to look at his crew. The rowers were resting on their benches and all of them were looking up at him. They had all heard Priscus's words and the news had not gone down very well. For a moment Corbulo was seized by indecision. He couldn't piss off his clients, but if he forced his rowers to work on a holiday they may well tell him to go fuck himself. The rowers after all were not slaves but freeborn men. The ship fell silent and for a moment the only noise was the gentle lapping of the water against the side of the boat and the creaking of the deck planks.

"Allright," Corbulo exclaimed in a resigned voice as he looked at his crew, "We will do another run tomorrow morning and I will pay you double the going rate. Does that sound fair?"

The rowers glanced at each other sullenly.

"That sounds fair," a huge oak of a man at the back growled at last.

Corbulo nodded satisfied. He was giving up all the profit he would make from the run but at least he would be able to deliver the stone and keep his clients happy and the rowers decision confirmed something else which had always intrigued and impressed him. The native Britons didn't mind hardship, even extreme hardship as long as they were confident that everything had been handled fairly. To try and swindle them, as Corbulo had seen some of his competitors try to do, would only ignite in them a rage that was truly frightening.

"There is another matter, Sir," Priscus whispered loudly. Corbulo turned to look up at his young business partner and there was something in Priscus's voice that put him on guard. The young man looked uneasy.

"There are some men here," Priscus said quietly as he cast a glance to one side, "They have been waiting to speak to you all afternoon."

"What kind of men?" Corbulo frowned.

"The worst kind," Priscus hissed, "bounty hunters Sir. They say they are acting on the Governor's orders."

Chapter Two - "No Hard Feelings"

Corbulo clambered up onto the quayside. To his left London bridge disappeared off into the mist and along the waterfront to his right ships, lay drawn up along the massive box-like quays, where they unloading their cargoes of Gallic wine, Batavian pottery and olive oil from Hispania. Cranes were hoisting the cargoes out of the galleys and dumping them onto the harbour front, where a steady flow of labourers with carts were whisking them off into the massive timber wharves and warehouses that lined the river. Londinium and its port were thriving and the harbour was full of activity and noise. Further along the river, beside the quays reserved for export business, ships were being loaded with copper, tin, silver, corn and oysters, all destined for the hungry masses who populated the great metropolitan areas in Gaul and Italia. Corbulo glanced around him and laid a hand on Priscus's shoulder.

"Unload the stone and make sure you get the right price from the Procurator's office," he said quietly. "Then take the boat across the river and moor her in the usual spot. I will join you later. Now tell me where I can find these men?"

Priscus turned to look down river.

"They are hanging around outside Lucius's shop," he muttered. "They are a rough lot and they are armed. I don't like the look of them Sir, why don't you take some of the rowers with you?"

Corbulo shook his head. "No, I will be alright," he replied as he set off along the quayside. The smell of fish mingled with the stink of raw sewage and the noise of hammers, rattling wagons, sawing and the voices of a dozen different nationalities. Corbulo picked his way through the throng of labourers, carpenters, merchants, boats men and slaves. What did a group of bounty hunters want with him? Could it be something to do with the amber cave he had discovered in Caledonia some two years ago? His face darkened. If Falco the banker, to whom he had sold the amber stone had talked, he would cut the man's balls off. He had sworn the banker to secrecy about the amber stone. Corbulo stirred uneasily. Had something happened to Marcus, his son? Marcus and he were friends now but that had not always been the case. There had been a time when his son had hated him. There had been a time when Marcus and he had been estranged. Corbulo sighed. He had not always been a good father or husband but he had managed to put those days behind him now. But what could bounty hunters want with his son? Marcus was an auxiliary cavalryman and was with his unit, the 2nd Batavian Cohort at their base in Luguvalium, *Carlisle*. Had he deserted? Had he run into debt? The last time Corbulo had seen him had been during the Saturnalia festivities, a few months ago.

Lucius's shop was a fast food outlet, a narrow ramshackle wooden hut wedged in between two enormous warehouses. The smell of cooking pig and chicken greeted Corbulo as he noticed the six men lounging around outside. The men were clad in long, grey, muddy travelling cloaks with hoods and they were eating strips of pork and chicken legs, whose bones they kept throwing into a nearby well. Corbulo paused to watch them carefully. They were young and fit and looked like they knew how to handle themselves.

"I am Corbulo. You wanted to speak with me?" he said stepping towards the men.

The bounty hunters turned to look at him with hard, unfriendly faces and their conversation ceased abruptly. For a moment no one spoke. Then behind him Corbulo suddenly heard a voice and as he recognised it, a tremor ran right down his spine.

"It's been a while hasn't it Corbulo," the voice chuckled. "The last time that I saw you, you were surrounded by Caledonian tribesmen, fighting for your life, but I always knew that you would manage to escape."

Corbulo whirled round and stared into the face of a small, tough looking man of around forty. The man chuckled again but there was nothing friendly in his voice or in his manner.

"Bestia," Corbulo muttered as he struggled to overcome his surprise, "The last time I saw you was when you abandoned your master and fled like a coward. So the Caledonians didn't roast you alive after all. That's a shame."

"They tried," Bestia shrugged, "But I too am not so easily caught."

"So have you come to try and kill me again?"

Bestia shook his head.

"Not this time Corbulo," he replied sheepishly, "I am working for the Governor now. It's all legitimate business. No hard feelings eh."

"Fuck you," Corbulo snarled angrily, "I have not forgotten what you are. Does the Governor know that you are a deserter? Or do you suck his cock to keep him quiet?"

Bestia smiled and glanced away along the quayside. For a moment he said nothing. Then he turned to Corbulo.

"Like I just said," he muttered patiently, "I am here on the Governor's orders. I work for him now and he has business with you Corbulo, so shut the fuck up and listen to what I have to say."

Corbulo struggled to restrain himself. It was all he could do to stop himself from smashing his fist into Bestia's face. The man's presence had vividly reminded him of his long journey north into Caledonia in search of Marcus his son and the two separate occasions upon which this small but highly dangerous ex soldier had tried to murder him.

"I am looking for someone," Bestia went on, "The Governor is keen to speak with this man. His name is Quintus, recently retired Centurion from the Twentieth. He and you, I understand, go back many, many years." Bestia paused to study Corbulo. "I understand he was your best friend. So have you seen him recently? Do you know where I can find him?"

Corbulo looked genuinely surprised but instead of replying he stubbornly folded his arms across his chest.

"Come on Corbulo," Bestia growled. "You are his closest friend. Quintus and you spent over twenty years together in the Twentieth Legion. They tell me that you two were like bread and salt. Just tell me where he is and I will leave you alone."

Corbulo cleared his throat.

"No," he muttered, "I haven't seen him recently but he has a farm some six miles due south of Londinium..."

"We have already been there," Bestia interrupted, "It's all locked up. He's disappeared. Do you know where he is gone?"

And as he said the last sentence Bestia took a menacing step forwards. His eyes glinted darkly and behind him Corbulo sensed movement amongst the six bounty hunters.

"Don't lie to me," Bestia said quietly, "I know when you are lying. Just tell me where he is and we will leave you and your family alone."

At the mention of the word family, Corbulo froze. For a moment he glared at Bestia. Then he half turned to look at the men behind him.

"I last saw him about two, three weeks ago," Corbulo replied, "He was in the Forum buying supplies for his farm. I have been busy so there hasn't been much time. If he is not at home then I have no idea where he is." Corbulo paused. "Why do you ask? What has he done?"

Bestia was studying Corbulo carefully. For a moment he didn't reply. Then he gestured to his men.

"Allright, I believe you," Bestia replied, "but if you see him or hear anything about his whereabouts you are to inform me right away. Go to the Governor's palace and leave me a message. And Corbulo, if you hold back information and I find out about it, you are going to be in trouble, you, your little business, your business partner and that sweet wife and daughter of yours. The Governor wants to speak with Quintus urgently and you don't want to annoy the Governor!"

***

Corbulo watched Bestia and his thugs disappear into the throng of people along the waterfront. For a while he just stood there running his thumb over the stubble on his cheek. Bestia was the worst kind of man, a deserter, a killer, a hard, violent man without a shred of pity for others but Corbulo had sensed that he'd been speaking the truth this time, when he'd said he was working for the Governor. He shook his head and sighed. What had Quintus got himself into? What had he done to get the Governor of Britannia so worked up that the man had resorted to hiring bounty hunters to track him down? This couldn't be good. Corbulo sighed again as he pushed through the crowd and headed for the bridge.

"What have you done Quintus?" he murmured. The thought of Quintus being a wanted man troubled him. When he'd last bumped into him in the Forum Quintus had seemed in good spirits and there had been no hint of trouble. Quintus was his oldest and closest comrade. They had been Brothers in Arms. The two of them had joined the Twentieth as teenagers and for over twenty years they had fought, bled, starved, whored and drunken themselves silly across the length and breadth of Britannia. They had saved each other's lives on more than one occasion. It had been Quintus who had revived him and coaxed him back to life at Inchtuthil, the great northern Legionary fortress in Caledonia, when Corbulo, wounded by an arrow and searching for his missing son, had come riding into the camp. It had been Quintus, who the following spring, had helped him rescue Efa and Dylis from the Crannog, the artificial island in the Caledonian lake. Efa was Corbulo's new wife now and he had adopted her daughter Dylis. It was Quintus too who had persuaded him to settle and retire in Londinium. The former Centurion had bought himself a plot of land on a wooded hill some six miles due south of the city, which he had intended to farm. Quintus had said that one day Londinium was going to rival the city of Rome in size and importance. Corbulo's face soured and he muttered to himself. If his old friend was in trouble he would need help and if Quintus came asking for it he would give it despite all of Bestia's threats. There was no question about that. Loyalty to his old comrade in arms came before everything else.

The fog still hung across the river and he couldn't see the south bank. The low wooden bridge disappeared eerily off into the mist. The timber piles had been driven into the soft riverbed at an angle and upon them the engineers had constructed a flat wooden deck, the width of a Roman road. Close to the bridge entrance stood a marker stone proudly proclaiming that the first cohort of Thracians had built the bridge and the waterfront. As Corbulo approached, he noticed the duty detachment of Legionaries from the Second Augusta guarding the entrance. Another detachment would be guarding the southern exit. The soldiers had piled their large oval shields and spears against the wooden railings and were sitting in a circle on the ground gambling on a game of dice. A solitary member of the unit stood guard beside the customs men, who were collecting taxes from the merchants and traders crossing the bridge. Corbulo grunted in relief. Perialis was on duty today, that was good. The officer was not corrupt. Unlike that arsehole Cato who was known to force merchants to give him a little extra before they and their goods were allowed to leave or enter Londinium. Corbulo strode past the eagle-eyed customs officials, but as he started out across the water one of the soldiers glanced round and called out to him.

"Eh Corbulo, where's that friend of yours, Quintus? Did you know that the Governor has just announced a reward for anyone who brings him in?"

Corbulo paused in mid stride and slowly turned to look at the soldier. It was Perialis. The officer was young, in his mid twenties and there was an intelligent gleam in his eyes.

"No, I hadn't heard," Corbulo lied, "What has he done? What have you heard?"

Perialis shrugged and grinned. "Fuck knows, thcy dun't tell that to the likes of me You haven't seen him recently though have you Corbulo?"

Corbulo shook his head, "Not for a while and I don't know where he is either. So don't bother asking me again."

Perialis studied him shrewdly and for a moment the officer did not speak. Then he broke out into a friendly grin.

"Well I have orders to arrest him if he comes across my bridge. Seems that he has done something rcally stupid to piss off the Governor. The old man has been in a violent rage ever since. They say he's smashed up his own palace."

"Sounds bad," Corbulo muttered.

"Well it will be worse for Quintus if he comes across my bridge," Perialis called out as he turned back to his gambling.

Corbulo's eyes narrowed. Was it his imagination or had Perialis just tried to warn him? For a moment he stared at the young officer's back. Then abruptly he turned and started off across the bridge. Soon the fog enveloped him. The traffic on the bridge was light. He passed an ox-drawn cart, loaded with amphorae going north. It was followed by a few solitary figures, labourers returning home from a hard day's work. At the deepest part of the river a group of women were praying to the water spirits and throwing votive coins into the brown water. The

15

Legionaries guarding the southern end of the bridge looked bored. They clustered together chatting and ogling the women crossing the bridge. Corbulo stepped ashore onto the island that made up Southwark. Watling Street, the Roman road leading all the way to Rutupia, Richborough, vanished off southwards into the fog.

Southwark had its own small quayside but it was tiny compared to the port on the northern bank and only a few small ships lay alongside. It was here though, that the Garum ships unloaded their cargoes and the stink of rotting fish sauce never seemed to go away. Corbulo however had become so used to the smell that he hardly noticed it anymore. He turned upriver and strode along the gravelly riverbank. The Thames was at its highest point and the dirty brown water lapped gently against the wooden revetments that were supposed to protect the growing town from the periodic floods that had so troubled and threatened the early settlement. The land was lower here than on the northern bank and Corbulo had to weave and pick his way across the water channels and the marshy ground. A patrol of four fully armed soldiers of the city guard passed him heading in the opposite direction. Corbulo ignored them. The patrols had begun a week ago after the native Britons had tried to destroy the revetments and flood defences. The Britons had claimed that the revetments were altering the course of the channels and the waterways and that this was angering the water spirits who lived in them.

A couple of grazing sheep watched him pass and somewhere along the shore he heard a creature splash into the river. When at last he came to a broad channel that cut deep into the island he paused and grunted in satisfaction. His boat lay moored and secured at its usual place. Priscus had done as he had asked. He hadn't expected anything else but for some reason he just couldn't shake the old habit of checking that his orders had been carried out. It was an old routine he'd picked up in the army when as a Tesserarius, watch commander, his job had been to make sure that the sentries were alert and knew the daily password.

He retraced his steps and as he emerged onto the hard-packed gravel road he caught the delicious smell of a meat stew. His wife made a fantastic stew and at the thought of hot food and seeing her and his daughter his mood suddenly improved. His house was the third one along from the bridge. The Roman strip houses, long and narrow wooden framed buildings with mud brick walls and thatched roofs stood packed together lining Watling Street. Here and there the terraces were separated by narrow alleys and at the rear there were small backyards with outhouses in which he could hear pigs and chickens. Southwark may stink and suffer the occasional flood and local riot but it was quieter here than in the city and the land prices were cheaper and it was this that had finally persuaded him to bring his family across the river and settle them on the south bank. Corbulo crossed the street, stamped his feet at the entrance to his house and entered with a cheerful cry of greeting.

Efa, Corbulo's wife appeared in the doorway that led into the second room. She was young, half Corbulo's age and of Celtic origin and her long black hair fell to her shoulders. She was clad in a simple brown tunica and she looked like she was in a bad mood. As Corbulo approached to peck her on her cheek she picked nervously at her fingernails.

"What's this?" Corbulo grinned, "No welcoming smile for your husband?"

Efa looked tense and Corbulo felt a sudden tug of alarm.

"What's the matter? What's happened?" he said hastily.

"You are late," she scolded, "I am going out into the city. I have an appointment with Marcella. Her son is ill and needs my healing potions. Your dinner is in the pot over the fire."

Corbulo, who was at least a head taller than her, sniffed and glanced hungrily in the direction of the hearth. Then he turned to his wife and reached out to give her arse an affectionate squeeze. Normally this kind of behaviour was enough to get a

17

strong reaction from Efa, for she was a proud and fierce woman who didn't take kindly to being teased but instead of the retaliation he'd expected, she just brushed him away with an irritable twist of her body before moving away into the room. Corbulo sighed wearily. What was the matter with her? Puzzled he shook his head. Women and their mood swings was something that he was never going to understand. He glanced around at the amphorae, sacks and barrels and other junk that littered the front room. Then he undid his mud caked boots and stepped into the main living quarters of his house. To one side in the hearth a fire crackled and spat, and over it on a metal spit hung an iron pot.

Efa was stuffing herbs and potions into a leather satchel as Corbulo took off his Pallium, travelling cloak and hung it on a hook that protruded from one of the solid oak beams that held up the roof. He turned to warm his hands over the fire and as he did so Dylis, his seven-year old adopted daughter appeared in the doorway to the back room. Quietly she crossed the timber floor and wrapped her arms around him. Corbulo grinned in delight and lifted her off the ground.

"Hello Dylis," he said. "Did you know that you are my favourite daughter?"

The little girl looked bemused.

"That's because you only have one daughter," she replied rolling her eyes.

Corbulo looked surprised. Then he turned to look around the room in mock disbelief.

"Damn, I think you are right," he said ruffling her hair and lowering her to the ground. "But you are still my favourite daughter. That's why when I go to meet my ancestors I am going to leave you my business and all my money."

Dylis folded her arms across her chest.

"But maybe I don't want to be a stone trader," she protested.

"Of course you do, everyone wants to be in the stone trade," Corbulo grinned glancing at Efa. His wife had finished packing her satchel and was reaching for her cloak.

"Efa," he said quietly, "I will come with you into the city. Just give me a few moments to eat."

Efa sighed irritably and refused to make eye contact.

"It's better if I go alone," she retorted, "I don't need an escort."

Corbulo nodded.

"I know, I know," he muttered, "But something has happened to Quintus. The Governor is out looking for him. They have even placed a bounty on his head. I am going to go to the Mule for a drink and to try and find out what has happened. If there is anywhere in the city where they may know something, it will be there."

Efa's face drained of colour at the mention of Quintus's name. Abruptly she turned away so that he could not see her face.

"Well I hope they never catch him. Quintus is a good man," she murmured, "He is a very good man."

Chapter Three – Londinium

It was dark when Corbulo and Efa left their home. A gentle breeze was blowing in from the west and the mist had lifted. In his left hand Corbulo was holding an oil lamp from which a fragile flickering flame emitted a little light. He glanced up at the stars as he laid his right hand on his wife's shoulder. Something was troubling her. There was something she was not telling him but when he'd asked her again what the matter was she had evaded the question. From experience he knew that it was pointless to persist for she could be a very stubborn woman when she wanted to be. He sighed. He would have to be patient. She would tell him once she was ready to do so, she always did.

The night sky and twinkling stars suddenly reminded him of that autumn night, eighteen months ago, when he and Quintus with his hand-picked group of Legionaries from the Twentieth had freed Efa and her daughter Dylis from a life of slavery on the Caledonian Crannog, the man- made island in the lake. Efa and her daughter had been kidnapped from their coastal village north west of Deva a couple of years before by Caledonian raiders looking for slaves and they had ended up in the household of two brothers. Corbulo had cajoled Quintus into aiding him, for without Quintus and his soldiers, he could never have been able to help Efa and Dylis escape. The expedition to free Efa had been dangerous for the crannog was located in a remote and hostile part of Caledonia, well beyond the vicinity of any Roman forts but it had been the right thing to do. Corbulo had not forgotten that it was Efa who had saved his and Marcus's life by warning them about her master's intentions, when during that summer, he and Marcus had passed through on their desperate flight south. During the raid to free her, Corbulo had killed the younger brother but the older one, Sceolan had managed to escape. After the escape Efa had flatly refused to be parted from Corbulo's side.

Perialis and his men were still on duty at the northern end of the bridge but the young officer ignored Corbulo and Efa. There was no wall or gate to mark the boundary of Londinium and the two of them strode straight up Watling street towards the Forum and the heart of the city. It was a short walk from the river side and there were few people about at this time of the evening. The wooden framed strip houses with their narrow frontages were packed tightly up against each other as they lined the street on both sides. Now and then the terraces were separated by a narrow alley from which a drain would protrude to merge with the drainage ditches on both sides of the main street. The whiff of sewage and rotting garbage from the alleys mingled with the scent of freshly baked bread, rotting fish soup, the stale smell of urine and the heady pong of pig manure. Up ahead Corbulo could hear the Forum before he could see it. The noise of laughter and of music drifted towards them. He glanced at Efa. Her eyes were on the road. She had not said a word since they had left their house.

At the intersection with the road that led westwards towards the Governor's palace and the Wallbrook they halted and Corbulo turned to his wife. In the glow of the oil lamp he could see she looked tense. Once again she refused to meet his gaze.

"How long will you be?" he asked.

"I don't know, it depends on how sick the boy is," she muttered.

Corbulo nodded. "Well I am going to the Mule. I will come over to Marcella's house in an hour or so to pick you up."

"There is no need," Efa hissed irritably. "I can find my own way back. It's not far." And with that she broke free and vanished off into the darkness.

Corbulo watched her disappear and then rolled his eyes and sighed. What was the matter with her? Was it something he had said or done? He shook his head. He had been with many women during his life but he couldn't claim to understand any of them. His face darkened as he had a sudden thought. Was his wife having an affair? Were all the long hours in which he was away on business making her lonely? He stared at the spot where she had disappeared and for a moment he struggled with the urge to follow her. Then with an effort he turned away and started up the road that led to the Forum.

As he approached the Forum the sound of laughter and music abruptly ceased. It was followed moments later by a single high-pitched female scream. Corbulo froze. Then he heard it again, a piercing scream. The woman sounded terrified. It was followed by loud angry shouting. Then silence. A man came hurrying past Corbulo heading towards the river. He looked nervous. He was followed by a couple carrying a young child. They too seemed in a hurry to get away from whatever was happening further up the street. Corbulo blinked. The woman could not have been his wife. The noise had come from a different direction. He grabbed hold of the man's arm as the couple drew level with him.

"What's going on?" he said holding up his lamp.

The man angrily wrenched himself free. "The Procurator and his staff are looking for someone," the man snarled, "They are searching people's homes. They have killed three already. They are coming this way."

The couple vanished into the darkness as Corbulo slowly turned to look up the street. What the fuck was going on? The Procurator was the government official in charge of overseeing and managing the province's financial affairs. The man was a senior government official, second only to the Governor in the hierarchy of the provincial administration. What was he doing searching people's homes and murdering people in the street?

"Who has been killed?" Corbulo cried turning back to the couple but the street behind him was silent and deserted. It was as if the whole city had suddenly shut themselves up inside their homes.

For a moment Corbulo was torn by indecision. Then he grunted in disgust and started up the road in the direction from which he had heard the woman scream. As he moved up the street he heard angry voices and shouts. To his right the door to a house had been kicked in. Corbulo halted and lifted his lamp up to get a closer look. The entrance passage to the house was stained by a large pool of blood. He turned away. The voices were close by now and coming towards him. He moved across the street. Here too the door to a house had been broken down and as he drew nearer Corbulo nearly tripped over the corpse of a man. Another corpse, that of a woman lay in the doorway. She had been stabbed in the neck. Corbulo straightened up as several torches appeared in street ahead. The torches descended upon him and in their glow he caught sight of the men holding them. They were armed with knives and clubs and they looked unfriendly.

"What are you staring at? Get the fuck out of here," one of the men cried.

Corbulo stood his ground. Slowly his eyes moved from one man to the next.

"What the fuck are you doing," Corbulo bellowed suddenly and there was real anger in his voice. His hand shook as he gestured at the corpses in the street. "What did those people do? Why did you kill them?"

The fury in Corbulo's voice seemed to take the men by surprise. For a moment no one replied.

"What's it to you?" one of the men shouted at last, "Do you want to join them?"

"I am a Roman citizen," Corbulo roared taking a step forwards. "Just you try and touch me you prick."

At the mention of his Roman citizenship the men seemed to hesitate. Corbulo glared at them. Roman citizens were after all at the top of the social hierarchy and enjoyed the full protection of the law.

"They are followers of Christus," a voice replied from the darkness beyond the torch light. "and I hate Christians. Nero was right to kill them. He should have burned every last one of them."

A moment later Classicus, Procurator Augusti, chief financial officer of the province of Britannia stepped out of the darkness. He was a small bald man clad in a fine woollen tunic. He paused and Corbulo felt the man's quick, intelligent eyes sizing him up. Classicus was well known to everyone in Londinium. He was an accountant by training and infamous for his highly suspicious nature. The lengths to which he would go to uncover fraud and corruption had become widely known throughout the province. It was a safe bet that if there was fraud or corruption on the government books he would find it. The accountant had the eyes of an owl and nose of a dog and when he caught corrupt officials he could be ruthless too. It was no wonder that Emperor Domitian had appointed him to manage the imperial treasury in Britannia. The man had been born to do the job.

Corbulo lowered his lamp. "Followers of Christus," he muttered. He had of course heard about this obscure eastern sect. Nero had executed Christians by the hundreds in Rome but he had not expected that their religion had spread to Londinium. It took him a moment to recover from his surprise. Then he looked the Procurator straight in the eye.

"I am no follower of Christus," Corbulo said slowly, "but I do know this. I know that the law says that all religions are tolerated. That is the Emperor's will and everyone knows it. So why are you killing these people? This is nothing but murder. What crime did these people commit?"

The accountant's eyes gleamed in the torchlight. "This is state business," he snarled. "These Christians are dead because they refused to answer my questions. I gave them a fair choice."

"Without a trial?" Corbulo muttered.

The accountants' sharp intelligent eyes flashed dangerously.

"Do I know you? You look familiar," Classicus exclaimed taking a step forwards as he peered closely at Corbulo.

Corbulo cleared his throat uneasily.

"I have a contract with your office to supply stone. We met when you signed the deal."

"Ah yes," Classicus exclaimed with a nod, "I remember you now. Corbulo isn't it, ex Legionary of the Twentieth with a house across the river." He paused and a little crooked smile appeared. "Now fuck off citizen and do not interfere with state business again."

Corbulo glanced at the armed men holding their torches. Without another word he started up the street towards the Forum. Classicus may be a complete dick and all the merchants and businesses along the waterfront may be afraid of him but he did keep corruption and fraud to a minimum and his efficient management meant that taxes did not need to rise.

Corbulo had only gone a dozen or so paces when he saw another corpse. The man had been nailed to the front door of his house and his head was resting on his chest. A small wooden cross dangled from his neck. Close by a child lay in a pool of blood. Corbulo took a deep breath and carried on walking. State sanctioned pogroms happened now and then for beneath the veneer of the Roman peace, Britannia was a lawless, violent place. If it wasn't Christians it would be the Jews or some other religious sect that had fallen out of favour. Corbulo had seen religious persecution before and it filled him with disgust. The officers who commanded the Legions and who were tasked with maintaining the peace only cared about threats to the state. They didn't give a shit about the daily dangers faced by the populace such as rape, murder and extortion. The Legions couldn't care less whether the strong and powerful stole from their weaker neighbours. The only way a man could protect himself was to place himself under the protection of a powerful patron. Corbulo muttered something under his breath and carried on walking. The actions of the Procurator may be distasteful but whatever that man was looking for it had nothing to do with him. He needed to be careful. The accountant could cancel his contract at any time and then how would he feed his wife and daughter?

Corbulo's boots crunched over the gravel. The Forum loomed up out of the darkness. The rectangular stone building with its elegant stone columns and red roof tiles looked out of place amongst the lines of densely packed wooden houses with their thatched roofs, that crowded around it. The Forum was the second centre of Londinium after the harbour, and in the central courtyard the farmers and craftsmen would come to sell their wares. The whole lower floor of the Forum was taken up by banks and lawyers offices. It was here too, in a long beautiful hall on the second floor that the city council would meet to manage the running of the town. Only a month ago these councillors had announced that a new much larger Forum was to replace the old building. The plans for the building were rumoured to make it the largest Forum north of the Alps. Corbulo had been delighted for it would guarantee an insatiable demand for stone. But now in the darkness the Forum looked deserted and forgotten apart from a single armed Legionary on fire watch duty outside the front gate.

The Mule tavern was just off to one side of the Forum. A sign above the door read Cum Mula Peperit but Corbulo had always known the place as The Mule. It was a repository for his life for he had been drinking in this tavern on and off for nearly twenty-five years. The place was full of memories, of good and bad times, of friends found and lost long ago. He pushed through the

door and entered a warm dimly lit room. A fire was crackling in the hearth and a few men were sitting at crude wooden tables. They looked up anxiously as he entered and then slowly turned back to their conversations. Against the far wall a narrow staircase led up to a second floor and a young prostitute was leaning against the wall beside the stairs examining her finger nails.

Corbulo caught the eye of the fat woman behind the bar. She was serving another customer and for a moment he hesitated. Against the far wall the prostitute glanced at him but her gaze did not linger long and as she looked away Corbulo felt a pang of dismay. He had noticed this before. The whores had stopped seeing him as potential business. He opened his mouth and touched his tooth. It was definitely loose and his shoulders slumped. His body was beginning to fall apart.

The fat woman had finished with her customer and Corbulo greeted her silently as he came up to the bar. The woman was old with grey hair, which she had tied into a ponytail and fixed with a fibula. She smiled and he pecked her on the cheek. He'd known her for over twenty years. The woman was the owner of the tavern now that her husband had died. She and her husband had been running the Mule for as long as Corbulo had been drinking in it.

"Did you come across the Procurator and his men?" she exclaimed glancing warily at the doorway. "We heard the screams. They say he is searching people's homes. What's going on?"

Corbulo nodded.

"Yes I saw him," he muttered lowering his eyes, "He's killing people too. He's gone after the Christians. Fuck, I didn't even know we had any in this town."

The woman raised her eyebrows and for a moment she looked thoughtful. "That's probably because you spend all your time on

27

that boat of yours." She turned to look at him. "Efa allright? You want a drink?"

Corbulo glanced at the barrel of wine behind her. Then he shook his head. "You know I don't drink anymore," he replied with a sheepish smile.

The woman nodded. "You aren't a very good customer are you," she replied, "but I will let you off. How are Efa and Dylis?"

Corbulo ignored her question and leaned towards her.

"Listen," he said quietly, "I ran into a bounty hunter today, a real arsehole called Bestia. He told me that the Governor is looking for Quintus. He told me that Quintus has vanished and that there is a price on his head." Corbulo gave the woman a questioning look. "Is Quintus in trouble, have you heard anything? Have you seen him recently? They say his farm is all locked up."

The woman straightened up and glanced around her tavern but no one seemed to be paying them any attention. Then slowly she shook her head.

"I haven't seen him for a while," she said quietly, "but I bet you that his disappearance has something to do with what the Procurator is doing out there."

Corbulo was staring at her intently.

"What are you saying?" he replied with a frown.

The woman sighed. "Don't you know," she whispered, "The last time that I saw Quintus he told me that he had become a Christian."

Corbulo froze in surprise and for a moment he seemed lost for words.

"What?" he exclaimed.

The woman smiled. "Yes he told me. He converted after his retirement. He said the teachings of Jesus had given him a new perspective on life. He was very serious about it all."

"Well fuck me," Corbulo muttered looking away in confusion. "I served with him for over twenty years and I never suspected." Corbulo paused and then shook his head in disgust. "A Christian? What a load of bollocks. That is no faith for a soldier. No the only thing that a man should care about is Jupiter, greatest and best and the fucking honour and dignity of the Legion. Everything else is just superstitious crap."

"Well Quintus has become a Christian," the woman replied firmly, "and if you ask me they aren't all that bad. The Emperor seems to tolerate them."

Corbulo muttered under his breath and glanced at the prostitute.

"Well if you see Quintus let him know he needs to be careful. There are a whole load of bad people out to get him. What the fuck has he done anyway?"

A sudden glint appeared in the fat woman's eye. "I don't know," she said, "but I remember now, when I last saw him, he said something strange. He said that he may be going away."

"Where to?" Corbulo said sharply as turned to stare at her.

"Hibernia," the woman whispered.

***

Corbulo stumbled out of the Mule and into the fresh, cool night air. There had been a time when he'd liked to drink until he would throw up but those days were long gone now. He hadn't touched a cup of wine in over three months, ever since the feast of Saturnalia that marked the start of the New-Year. He strode passed the solitary guard on duty outside of the Forum and headed up the main street that led to the eastern edge of the city. Londinium was quiet and there were few people about. A stray dog padded past him and in one of the alleys he could hear a drunk singing to himself. He paused at the intersection with the street that led to the bridge and peered into the darkness but there was no sign of disturbances. The Procurator and his men must have called it a night.

He moved on up the street holding his oil lamp before him. The drains on either side of the road smelt of stale urine, rotting garbage and shit and here and there the town's folk had laid wooden planks across them so that they could reach their front doors without getting their feet soiled. Corbulo blew the air from his cheeks as he tried to make sense of what he'd learned and the more he thought about it the more uneasy he began to feel. Maybe the woman was right, maybe the Procurator's pogrom against the Christians was connected to Quintus's disappearance. The Procurator had been looking for something or someone. But why? What the fuck could be so important to arouse both the Governor's and the Procurator's wrath. Quintus after all was just a retired soldier, a small farmer of no consequence. Corbulo looked baffled. And why Hibernia, why of all the places in the world would Quintus want to go there? The island lay across the western sea and beyond the imperial frontier. There was nothing there apart from rain, poverty and hordes of miserable inhabitants who were as hostile and treacherous as any he'd come across.

He shrugged and turned left into a side street. It was time to pick up his wife from Marcella's house and in the morning he would need to be up early for the run down to the stone quarry. The houses along this road looked smarter than the ones along the main street. He grunted as in the dim light he saw that some were made of stone. Only the wealthy could afford stone. Marcella's house was in a well to do neighbourhood where the rich lived, away from the traffic, noise and smells of the main thoroughfares. Finally, close to Aldgate and the earth embankment and ditch that marked the outer boundary of Londinium he halted in front of a stone house and raised his lamp to make sure he had the right place. A stone statuette of Diana, the huntress holding her bow glared back at him from where it stood on its plinth just beside the door. Corbulo knocked on the door and waited.

It took a while before he heard movement inside the house.

"Who is it? What do you want?" an irritable sounding male voice cried out.

"It's Corbulo. I have come to pick up my wife," Corbulo replied.

There was no reply from inside the house. Then Corbulo heard the metallic noise of sliding bolts and a moment later a man's face peered out into the street. As he recognised Corbulo the man sighed and opened the door wider. He was dressed in his night clothes and it looked as if he had just been woken up.

"I have come to pick up Efa," Corbulo muttered.

A woman clad only in her under garments suddenly appeared beside the man. She looked startled.

"Efa is not here," Marcella replied. "We have just gone to bed."

Corbulo's face grew pale. "I don't understand. She told me that she was coming here to give your son some of her potions. She said he was ill."

But Marcella shook her head. "No my son isn't ill and I didn't ask your wife to come round. She hasn't been here tonight, Corbulo. I haven't seen her."

Chapter Four - The Nine

It was dark and in the clear night sky the stars blazed brightly. Corbulo's boots crunched across the gravel as he strode up to the front door of his house. He looked furious. Efa had lied to him. Why? Was she having an affair? Had she run away? Had he not been good to her? Did he not look after her daughter? The gratitude of women he thought derisively. Did he not provide? What had he done to deserve this? His hand clenched into a fist but mingling with his rage there was anxiety. Efa never lied to him. She had never been afraid of telling him the truth even when he didn't want to hear it. Maybe something had happened? Had some drunk attacked her and dragged her into an alley? He had searched the streets around Marcella's house and retraced his steps to the Forum. Then he had spoken with Perialis and his soldiers but no one had seen her cross the bridge. There had been no sign of his wife. She had vanished. Eventually, exhausted and dispirited he had decided to go home.

He wrenched open the door to his house, stamped his feet on the earthen floor and stepped inside. The hearth was still alight and in its flickering light he saw someone standing in the doorway between the front and central rooms. Corbulo felt a surge of anger and relief. It was Efa. His wife stood blocking the doorway with her arms folded across her chest. In the gloom he could not see her face.

"Where have you been?" Corbulo roared slamming the door shut behind him. "I went to pick you up at Marcella's house but she said that you never came to see her. You lied to me. What's going on?"

Efa did not reply and did not move.

"Well," Corbulo bellowed angrily, "Explain yourself woman?"

"Keep your voice down," Efa snapped and there was no mistaking the tension in her voice, "You are scaring them."

Angrily Corbulo strode towards her but as he bore down on her Efa refused to budge, blocking his way into the main part of the house.

"What are you talking about?" he snapped.

In the flickering firelight he could see his wife's face now. She looked tense, nervous and defiant.

"Promise me Corbulo," Efa whispered, "Promise me this husband, that you will not turn them away, for if you do I shall leave too and I shall take Dylis with me. I mean it, I really do."

Corbulo stared at his wife. "What are you talking about?" he growled.

"Promise me," she hissed.

Corbulo looked perplexed. "Who? Who are you talking about?" he cried.

Efa was staring at him and there was no mistaking the defiance in her eyes. She had meant every word she'd said. Slowly she stepped back into the living room allowing Corbulo at last to enter the long narrow room. Against the wall the wood in the hearth glowed, crackled and spat and huddled around the fire were nine children. They looked frightened. Corbulo grunted in surprise as the nine children stared back at him in wideeyed silence. They had been eating soup from wooden bowls and some of the children looked soaked whilst others had blankets wrapped around their shoulders. A little girl with tangled blond hair and pale blue eyes had a leather satchel strapped across her back from which protruded the head of a crude straw doll. She looked around seven years old. The youngsters around her all seemed to be aged between seven and twelve. Dylis was standing close to the fire holding a large pot of soup, which she had been serving to the children. She gave her father a brave little smile.

"They are Christian children," Efa said hoarsely, "I had to save them. If they had stayed with their parents they would be dead by now. The Procurator would have murdered them along with their families. You must have heard the screams. You must have seen what he and his men were up to?"

Corbulo was staring at the children. The room fell silent. Then he noticed the small wooden crosses around their necks. Every single child seemed to have one. He grunted and turned to Efa. He had never seen her look as tense and determined as she looked right now.

"Is that what you were doing?" Corbulo muttered.

She nodded. "The Christians knew that trouble was coming. They knew that the Procurator was out looking for them. The parents refused to flee but they told me that I should take their children and get them out of the city. I promised to help them and I have." She paused. "I am going to hide these children in our house. I am going to keep them alive. The Procurator will not have them," she said fiercely.

Corbulo took a deep breath as he remembered the corpses he'd seen in the street and the brutality of Classicus's men.

"Why did you not tell me the truth?" he growled.

"I didn't know whether you would agree with what I was doing. You told me so many times that you didn't like Christians," Efa retorted.

"Oh for fuck's sake," Corbulo said quietly shaking his head. "What kind of man do you think I am."

The room fell silent as Corbulo turned to look at the children again. They looked terrified and most of them seemed close to breaking into tears.

"It's a noble gesture Efa," he said at last with a reluctant voice, "But how are we going to feed them? What are we going to do with nine extra mouths? What are they going to do? They cannot stay here forever. It's only a matter of time before someone gets suspicious. By morning there will be a bounty on the head of every Christian left in the city."

"We have no choice," Efa snapped, "If the Procurator finds them he will kill them all. You know what that man is like. He hates Christians. He is out to kill every last one of them. If we don't hide these children they will die."

Corbulo took a deep breath. "You are asking me to risk my family for these children," he said, "We do not know these children. Is that fair Efa? I have worked hard to give us a decent life here in Londinium. You are asking me to put all of that at risk. If they find them with us, the consequences will be..."

"I know the risks," Efa interrupted, "but I am doing it anyway. If you don't want to be part of it then walk out of that door and don't come back."

Corbulo sighed. Efa was in a mood but before he could reply one of the older boys of around twelve with jet-black hair rose to his feet and stretched out his hand.

"Sir, I have money," the boy muttered as he looked down at his feet, "My father gave me money, I will pay you to look after us, please Sir, we don't want to die."

Corbulo stared at the youngster and the small bag of coins in his hand. In the hearth the fire spat and crackled.

"Allright, allright," Corbulo said raising his hands in defeat, "I am not walking out on my family and I don't want any money." He turned to Efa. "They can stay until we find them permanent homes but they stay indoors at all times and they will make no noise and they will do exactly what I tell them to do. I don't want the neighbours getting suspicious. You know what they are like."

Efa was staring at him with her large dark eyes. Then silently she came towards him and gave him a kiss on his cheek.

Corbulo glanced at her carefully. "Anyway, how did you get them across the river? The soldiers at the bridge said that they had not seen you."

Efa's eyes gleamed triumphantly. "Priscus brought the boat," she replied.

"What?" Corbulo exclaimed, "Priscus knows about this? He knew before I did?"

Efa smiled.

"He is a good man. He will say nothing."

"Damn right he won't," Corbulo growled in alarm. He turned and glanced at Dylis. His daughter had started refilling the wooden bowls with soup.

"Great," Corbulo muttered to himself, "This is just great."

Beside the hearth he suddenly noticed that the little girl with the tangled blond hair was watching him curiously.

"Why are they looking for us?" she asked in her childish voice. "Why do they want to kill us?"

"It's because of who you are little one," Efa said quietly.

Chapter Five - Enemies of the State

In the forum the farmers market stalls lined the edge of the open courtyard and behind them their owners were doing a brisk business. The Forum at Cornhill was packed with people and the sound of advertising cries mingled with the noisy chatter of the shoppers. The stink of pig manure was overpowering. It was just before noon and it was a beautiful day with a bright sun and clear blue skies. Corbulo picked his way carefully through the crowd clutching a leather bag that hung around his neck. A sword, a Legionary Gladius was strapped to his belt and he looked alert. He'd learned the hard way that it paid to be on one's guard against the gangs of pickpockets that operated in the Forum especially when he was bringing a month's worth of company profits to the bank. He stopped as he caught sight of a gang member whose face he recognised but the girl ignored him. Maybe the gangs had learned their lesson and had decided to leave him alone he thought sourly.

Two days had passed since Efa had brought the nine Christian children into his home and they had already managed to drive him crazy. He'd instructed Priscus to take the boat out and pick up the stone while he himself had remained at home sorting out his new guests. He'd set them to work cleaning, scrubbing and repairing his house and even though some jobs were unnecessary he'd made them do them anyway. The army had taught him that. Never let the men get bored or restless, make sure that they always have something to do, even if it's a pointless exercise. If they are too busy they will have no time to cause trouble. Corbulo grunted. He had certainly dug his share of pointless holes during his time.

The bankers had their offices inside the Forum's eastern wing. Corbulo squeezed in between two market stalls and stepped into the shade of the stone paved and covered walk way that separated the atrium from the offices and shops. A line of wooden posts, driven into the ground at regular intervals, stretched away along the side of the Forum holding up a sloping roof that was covered in red roof tiles and ended in an open lead drain. A series of doors set in the stone-wall led to the offices beyond. Corbulo paused to look around him but everything seemed normal. He turned and strode along the covered walkway until he came to a door with the sign above it that read

"Argentarii Britannia, Owner Gaius Valerius Falco, authorised money lender and foreign exchange dealer, good rates for all."

Corbulo muttered something under his breath. Falco was not one of the large sophisticated banking companies that operated out of the Forum and who lent to big businesses or managed the wealth of the rich. He was just a one-man bank who catered to the lower end of the banking market, lending money to desperate and poor people and the occasional legitimate business. Corbulo had sold him the amber stone, which he had taken from the sea cave in Caledonia because Falco had a reputation for not prying into his client's affairs. The man was discreet and that suited Corbulo just fine. The less people who knew about the amber the better. But that didn't mean that Falco wasn't interested in his client's affairs and as Corbulo had learned, the banker's discretion only continued if his profits continued. Corbulo had always suspected that Falco knew much more about what was going on than he would admit to. Information was power as Falco liked to remind his clients. There had been times when the banker had hinted that he knew about the affairs of Corbulo's business competitors but Corbulo had always resisted the bait - there would be a price to pay for such information.

Corbulo stepped through the doorway into a cool square room. A pair of big thuggish looking men with shaven heads and tattoos running down their arms rose to their feet as he entered. They gave him a hard-suspicious look, which he ignored. Falco was sitting behind a table counting a large pile of copper coins. The counted coins had been stacked in neat columns and on the table lay an opened wooden writing tablet and a stylus. On the corner of the desk a cup of wine perched precariously on a stack of wooden tablets. Falco looked up and a broad grin appeared as he recognised Corbulo.

"Always good to see you friend, always a pleasure Sir," Falco beamed rising to his feet and extending his arm. The banker was small with thick bushy eyebrows and a fat belly. He looked around forty.

Corbulo took the arm in greeting and glanced cautiously at the two thugs. Falco kept them around just in case someone was foolish enough to try and rob him. But what was stopping them from stealing from their master? Corbulo had often worried about that risk but trusting the banker was still a better option than keeping his money at home. For an ordinary man who could not afford his own protection, the banks in the Forum of Londinium represented the safest and most profitable place in which to invest one's money. It was here in the Forum, the financial and legal heart of the province of Britannia that the great and powerful mercantile business interests were concentrated and these interests would not tolerate a threat to their reputation. If the thugs were to steal from their master their chances of survival were slim. The banker's guild were ruthless and would kill them just as easily as they would take into slavery any debtor who failed to pay their debts.

"What can I do for you today Corbulo?" Falco exclaimed.

"I have come to deposit some money into my account," Corbulo replied as he undid the leather pouch from around his neck and placed it on the table.

"Ah yes, this is good," Falco's eyes gleamed hungrily as he looked at the bag. "Business must be going well. I like it Corbulo. One of these days you must come and visit me at my home and I can show you my new Carrus, wagon and horses. I bought them just two days ago. How is Priscus, well I hope? He usually deposits your cash doesn't he?"

"Not today he doesn't," Corbulo said.

Falco scratched his cheek. "Allright, no problem, no problem," he said hastily. He reached for a wooden writing tablet. "Are you good to wait whilst I count the money?"

"Of course I am," Corbulo replied, "and I want a receipt and I want to know how much is in the account?"

Falco nodded. "Certainly," he said as he took the bag and emptied its contents onto the table. Corbulo watched him closely as the moneylender started to count his coins.

"I suppose you have heard about the trouble a few days ago," Falco said smoothly as he began to stack the coins. "The Governor is furious with the Christians. He has thrown all their remaining druids into prison. The Christians have been declared official enemies of the state. Now anyone is allowed to kill them, enslave them and take their property without fear of retribution or the law." Falco said. "It's bad business if you ask me. Some of those Christians were good clients of mine. This money here," Falco said gesturing at a pile of copper coins, "belonged to one of them poor fools. Now the Governor's officials want to get their hands on it and if none of the owner's relatives come to claim it soon, I will be forced to hand it over. Greedy bastards. The State wins every time."

"Enemies of the state," Corbulo murmured. "Well the Governor is a prick. He doesn't compare to his predecessor Agricola. Agricola was a good man, an honest man, he would never have allowed this to happen."

"Yes," Falco nodded, " Agricola was a good Governor but he is gone now."

Corbulo grunted. "Well you are right. This trouble is bad news. When the mob gets excited they may start to attack non-Christians as well." He paused. "What did these Christians do anyway?"

Falco looked up and there was a sudden gleam in his eyes.

"Well," he said carefully, "I have just heard an interesting story." He leaned forwards and raised his eyebrows. "Apparently it all started with one of the Governor's freedmen, a man called Alexander, a Jew who worked on the Governor's staff. The rumour has it that Alexander stole something from the Governor. Something that was very precious to our dear and most respected commander."

"What did he steal?"

"A letter, apparently he took a letter," Falco nodded carefully.

"A letter?" Corbulo said with a puzzled look.

"Yes and now the Governor is desperate to retrieve it," Falco said shaking his head. "So desperate in fact that he has signed the death warrant for an entire community. The city guard has searched every Christian house they know about. But they haven't found the letter. They must have gone through the whole city but it's still missing. They say that the Governor stalks around his own palace smashing everything in his rage because they can't find it. Now isn't that an interesting story. That must be one valuable letter. I wonder who wrote it and what it says?"

Corbulo looked confused.

"But what has this Alexander and the letter got to do with the Christians?"

Falco smiled coyly.

"Alexander was a Christian," Falco said. "He was one of their druids and the first to die. He killed himself before they could interrogate him."

"So the Governor thinks Alexander may have passed the letter on to someone in his community for safe keeping?"

Falco grinned again and started counting the coins. "You are smart Corbulo. Yes, I believe that is what the Governor thinks. A tough determined bunch though these Christians. They refused to say anything. Many of them died without defending themselves. They seem to have such faith in their one God."

"So did the Governor catch them all?" Corbulo asked.

Falco raised a finger in the air as he counted the coins. "They are a small community these Christians, only a handful of families we think. The adults are dead or in prison but most of their children have not yet been found. They must be hiding somewhere in the city. The Governor is searching for them."

Corbulo leaned back against the wall as he allowed what he'd just heard to sink in. Was this why they were looking for Quintus? Was this why his friend had vanished? Had Alexander given him the letter?

Falco looked up, "Strange thing is," he muttered, "that the Procurator has now decided to get involved as well. Everyone knows that Classicus hates the Christians, but the ferocity with which he is hunting and killing them is truly shocking." He paused. "I don't particular like these followers of Christus but this violence and disorder is scaring away business and investment. It must stop. My clients don't like it."

Corbulo was staring at the far wall. The banker was right. Why had the Procurator got involved? It was odd. Why would the chief financial officer of the province be interested in a stolen letter?

"Unless," Falco said suddenly in a quiet voice, "Classicus suspects that the letter incriminates the Governor in some way. If that were the case I can understand why he would be interested."

"I don't understand," Corbulo muttered.

42

Falco raised his hands in mock despair. "You have been spending too much time on that boat of yours," he exclaimed. "Don't you listen to the gossip?"

"I haven't got any fucking time, I have a business to run," Corbulo replied in an annoyed voice.

"It doesn't matter," Falco said hastily, "Anyway, the point is that Classicus and the Governor hate each other. They truly loath each other. It's highly entertaining to see them together in public, the fake smiles and shows of unity." Falco chuckled. "You see," he said in a patient voice, "the Procurator, as chief financial officer of the province is in charge of collecting taxes and he is appointed by Domitian himself. Classicus reports directly to the Emperor. He's the Emperor's man, he's Domitian's eyes and ears here in Britannia." Falco chuckled again. "He is the only man on this island over whom the Governor has no authority and our beloved Governor must resent that immensely."

"So the Governor hates Classicus because he can't tell him what to do?"

"Well yes," Falco eyes gleamed like gold coins in the sunlight, "and then there is also the rumour that Classicus fucked the Governor's wife and daughter, but that's just a rumour, I can't confirm anything, so don't quote me."

Chapter Six - The Governor's Palace

Corbulo strode down the street that led from the Forum to the bridge. Up ahead a party of workmen were working on a construction site for a new house. A huge pile of stones lay to one side, waiting to be used and Corbulo grunted approvingly. The construction rate in the city was increasing rapidly and it was stone buildings that were replacing the old wooden constructions. He had chosen the right business allright. If he could just survive for a few more years the money he would make would be enough to set up Dylis, his adopted daughter for life.

The street sloped gently down towards the waterfront and as Corbulo approached the river he caught sight of the usual detachment of soldiers and customs officials guarding the entrance to the bridge. A queue of people had formed and were waiting to cross and Corbulo suddenly noticed that the soldiers were searching everyone wanting to cross the bridge. He stopped in his tracks. Something had changed. The Legionaries had not been doing that when he had crossed a few hours earlier. As he stood staring at the crowd a figure detached itself from the mass of people and came towards him. Corbulo stirred uneasily as he recognised the man. It was Perialis. The Optio was wearing a rough civilian Pallium, cloak over his armour. He looked worried as he hurried towards Corbulo.

"What's going on?" Corbulo said stiffly.

"I have been waiting for you," Perialis gasped, "I have some bad news Corbulo," he said laying a hand on the older man's shoulder. "Efa your wife has been arrested. She was caught trying to smuggle a Christian child across the bridge. Cato was on guard duty. He caught her. They have taken her and the child to the Governor's Palace for interrogation."

Corbulo's face turned pale. For a moment he was unable to say anything.

"The child was wearing a wooden cross around her neck," Perialis continued. "That's how Cato knew. By the Gods Corbulo, what was your wife thinking? Everyone knows that the Christians have been declared outlaws."

Corbulo was staring at Perialis in dismay. Then his dismay turned to anger.

Without a word he wrenched himself free and started off in the direction of the Governor's Palace but Perialis caught him by the arm.

"Don't be a fool," the Optio hissed, "You will never get into the Palace, the place is far too well guarded. The Governor commands a thousand men. They will kill you if you try to force your way in."

Corbulo's breathing was coming in short sharp gasps but he paused. Then he nodded.

"You are right," he said in a tight voice.

Perialis tightened his grip on Corbulo's arm."Listen," he said quietly turning to glance at the queue before the bridge, "If you want to help your wife, I know how you can get into the Palace but you must wait until its dark."

Corbulo turned to stare at the soldier.

"Why are you doing this?" he said slowly, "Why have you come to warn me? I am not your friend, you barely know me."

Perialis sighed and looked away.

"Come on," he muttered, "You are a veteran, you were a soldier once like me." Perialis shook his head in slight embarrassment. "Everyone in the barracks knows about you Corbulo. Twenty-six years ago you were one of the men who fought and defeated the Barbarian Queen. You are fucking legend Corbulo and there aren't many veterans left like you. If you came to the barracks one day, I swear, you could make a fortune from telling the men about the day Governor Paulinus and the Twentieth destroyed Boudicca and her rebellion."

***

The narrow log boat nudged into the solid manmade waterfront and Corbulo tensed as the hull scraped gently along the wooden piles. It was night and the Thames was quiet except for the occasional splash of a river creature somewhere off in the darkness. Corbulo grasped hold of the wooden piles and began searching with his hands. Perialis had told him it was here somewhere. The piles were wet and slippery and covered in soft moss.

"Can you see it?" a voice whispered behind him in the darkness.

Corbulo said nothing as he pushed the log boat along the side of the wooden waterfront. Then he found it; the ladder leading up the revetment. He grunted and looked up. High above him in the night sky hung a blood red moon. Mars, the God of War was watching him. It was dangerous to go out when a blood red moon was visible. Everyone knew that but right now he couldn't give a fuck. His anger was etched into his face. He was going to take his wife home come what may. He turned his head.

"Stay here and wait for me," he grunted.

In the darkness he couldn't see Priscus but as he clambered up the ladder he knew his young business partner would do as he was told. Carefully he raised his head above the waterfront and paused to listen. The night was quiet. He scrambled onto the deserted quayside and crouched peering into the darkness. A gentle breeze was coming in from the west. Where was the guard who patrolled this part of the Governor's palace? Corbulo waited ready to slip back down the ladder but there was no movement or noise from the darkness. Once more Perialis was right. The officer had told him that the guard on the waterfront had a habit of sneaking into the kitchens to snack on the

46

Governor's leftovers. Corbulo rose to his feet and started boldly across the open stone paved embankment. The doorway into the kitchens was somewhere to his left. He stepped over a short wall and cursed as he nearly fell into a long rectangular swimming pool. To his right the massive stone palace of the Governor of Britannia loomed over him. He could make out some of the windows from the glow of oil lamps in the rooms beyond.

Straight ahead of him he could see a dim light coming from a doorway. He crept towards the partially opened door and crouched against the wall. The smell of freshly baked bread filled his nostrils. Inside the building a man was laughing. Corbulo closed his eyes and his fingers touched the pommel of his Gladius. It had been difficult waiting for nightfall. The thought of Efa and what the Governor could do to her had haunted him. Would they have tortured her? Had she already cracked and told her captors about the nine Christian children in her home? If she had then he Corbulo was a dead man and so were the children. He opened his eyes. No, she was a tough woman, his Efa, she wouldn't say anything without a fight. She would be allright. She had to be allright.

The man was still laughing. Corbulo rose and risked a quick peek through the partially opened doorway. Something was cooking in a closed oven and two oil lamps bathed the kitchen in a reddish light. The guard had his back to the door and a cook was sitting at a table chopping away at something. She was smiling. Corbulo leaned back against the wall and took a deep breath. It had to be done. Quietly he slid his sword from its scabbard and stepped quickly and calmly through the doorway. The guard had no chance as Corbulo came up behind him and slit the man's throat in one fast and smooth movement. The soldier gurgled as the blood gushed down his chest. Corbulo lowered him to the floor. The cook was staring at him in utter shock and horror. Then loudly she rose to her feet but before she could scream Corbulo was at her side and had clamped his hand over her mouth. He raised his bloodied sword to her neck. The woman looked up at him   with terror stricken eyes.

47

"He was a fool," Corbulo whispered, "He was on guard duty and he left his post. That's what happens when a sentry is not alert."

The woman was trembling now. Corbulo snatched a quick glance down the corridor that led into the palace but all seemed quiet. He took another deep breath and turned to the cook.

"I won't harm you," he said quietly, "if you tell me where they are keeping the woman they brought in today. Tell me where they are holding her?"

The cook looked terrified. Slowly Corbulo peeled away his hand.

"The woman was with a child," he snapped. "Are they still alive?"

The cook's upper lip was trembling and there were tears in her eyes now.

"Don't hurt me," she whispered in a foreign accent, "I am just a cook. I am just a slave Sir."

Corbulo slapped her across her cheek.

"The woman and the child, where are they being held?" he growled. It was the only piece of information that Perialis had been unable to provide him.

"They are down in the cellar where the Governor keeps his wine," the cook sobbed.

Corbulo felt a surge of relief. Efa was alive. He examined the cooks face but the poor woman didn't look like she was lying.

"Show me," Corbulo whispered forcing her towards the doorway. He touched her back with the tip of his sword. "And if you make a noise you will be dead before you hit the ground," he muttered.

The cook did not reply. Her whole body was trembling. Corbulo nudged her into the long dimly lit corridor. As they moved deeper into the palace they passed darkened doorways on either side and Corbulo suddenly remembered that these were the offices of the officials and bureaucrats on the Governor's staff who helped administer the province. He had been here before when he had come to sign his government contract with the Procurator to supply stone to Londinium. Suddenly his foot crunched on something lying on the floor and he looked down. The stone floor was covered in shards and broken pieces of pottery. Corbulo froze whilst with his free hand he jerked the cook to a halt. What was this? He peered down the corridor. The fragments of pottery were everywhere.

"The Governor smashed his vases today," the woman sniffed.

Corbulo said nothing as he remembered. Of course, Perialis and Falco had mentioned that the Governor had taken to breaking everything in his own palace in his impotent rage against the Christians. He gave the cook a little shove and they started off down the corridor. The crunching noise of the shards and fragments sounded horribly loud under their feet. At the end of the corridor he forced the cook to a halt and snatched a quick glance around the corner but saw no one. The new corridor was lit with oil lamps that seemed to cast shadows upon the walls. Without a word the cook turned left and after a few paces she halted beside a flight of narrow circular stone steps that led downwards into darkness.

"They are being kept down there," she whispered.

Corbulo peered into the darkness. He could hear nothing. He gave the woman a little push and they started down the stone steps. The circular staircase didn't go far and he emerged onto a narrow hall that led into a dark and damp tunnel. At the end of the passageway an oil-lamp had been fixed to the wall and in its light Corbulo suddenly caught sight of the figure of a man slouched on a wooden stool. Corbulo jerked the cook to a halt. For a moment the two of them did not move as they stared at the figure. Then Corbulo heard it. The guard was snoring. He was asleep. Corbulo pressed the tip of his sword into the woman's back and brought his head close to hers.

"Not a sound," he whispered.

The two of them ducked into the low tunnel and started towards the guard. The passageway was too small for them to stand up in. Corbulo could see the man's spear leaning against the brick wall. In the dim light he caught sight of a large number of keys hanging from the soldiers belt. Corbulo tensed. As they drew closer to the sleeping guard they passed doorways on both sides and behind the doors he heard little noises, a whimper, a cough, a quiet voice uttering a prayer. These cells must be where the Governor kept his Christian prisoners. As he reached the end of the tunnel Corbulo suddenly shoved the cook forwards, grabbed hold of the soldier's hair, yanked his head backwards and slit his throat. Blood spurted over Corbulo's hands and arms, splattering his face as the man died. Corbulo lowered him to the ground. The cook had pressed her hands to her mouth and was staring at him with renewed horror.

"He would still be alive if he hadn't been sleeping on duty," Corbulo hissed. Without waiting for an answer he crouched and unhooked the keys from the dead man's belt. There were eight in total. He rose and lifted the oil lamp from its holster on the wall. Then he grabbed the woman by her arm and pushed her down the tunnel in the direction from which they had just come. The first cell was occupied by an old man. The second by two women. Corbulo said nothing as he left the doors unlocked. Then as he opened the third door and shone his oil lamp inside the tiny space he saw her. Efa was slumped on the floor her back leaning against the wall. She raised her hand as if to fend off a blow.

Corbulo pushed the cook into the tiny space and crouched down beside his wife.

"Efa, it's me, your husband," he whispered touching her face, "I have come to take you away. Are you hurt?"

Efa gasped but said nothing. In the dim light it was hard to see whether she was allright.

"Come on girl, we have to get out of here," Corbulo whispered. He slipped his hand around her waist and lifted her up onto her feet and as he did so he heard a clinking metallic noise. He lowered his lamp and groaned. Efa's ankles were locked together by an iron slaver's chain. She couldn't walk. Corbulo placed his lamp on the hard cold stone floor and fumbled around with his hands. Then he cursed with relief. At least the chain was not fixed to the wall.

"Climb onto my back, I will carry you out of here," he said quietly. For a moment he wasn't sure if his wife had understood. Then he felt her fingers grasp his neck as she heaved herself up onto his back. Corbulo grunted as he went down on one knee and adjusted himself to take her weight. Thank the gods that his wife was not overweight. He rose and carefully backed out of the cell. The cook was pressed into a corner of the tiny space. She looked frightened.

"Stay here and do not make a sound or I will come back and finish you off like I did with those two men," Corbulo said sharply.

The cook said nothing. Corbulo turned and started off towards the circular stairway.

"The child," Efa suddenly whispered, "We must rescue the Christian child."

Corbulo shook his head. "No, it can't be done," he muttered, "We have to get out of here. I am sorry."

"The child," Efa whispered, "we can't leave her here. They will kill her. She is only a child. Please, we must go back for her."

Corbulo said nothing. There was nothing more he could do. He made it to the staircase and was just starting up the steps when a high-pitched female scream shattered the silence. Corbulo froze in horror as the woman screamed again. It was the cook. Corbulo cursed and stormed up the staircase, puffing and heaving as Efa clung to his back. The two of them staggered out into the corridor, turned left and then right. From inside the Palace Corbulo could hear men's voices. They were close. In the tunnel below his feet the cook screamed again. Up ahead he could see the doorway leading to the kitchen. The corpse of the soldier lay on the floor amidst a large pool of blood. Corbulo felt Efa's nails digging into his neck. The kitchen doorway was just a few yards away when he heard a noise and saw something move. A man stepped out of one of the office doorways just ahead of him. Corbulo's eyes bulged. It was Bestia. The bounty hunter was clad only in his undergarments and he was unarmed. Without pausing Corbulo raised his leg and kicked Bestia in the groin. The blow caught the bounty hunter completely by surprise and he went down with an agonising hiss. Fear lent Corbulo a savage strength and without hesitation he lashed out again and his foot caught Bestia on the side of his head sending him crashing backwards against the wall. Corbulo pushed passed him and had reached the kitchen when he heard a shout behind him.

"There he is, get him, stop him!"

There was no time to look behind him. Corbulo skidded through the blood on the kitchen floor and banged his head against the door but he didn't feel the pain. Then he was out into the dark night. Efa's weight was slowing him down and he was gasping for breath. There was no way he was going to outrun his pursuers. He heaved her higher up onto his back and felt her muscles clamp onto him. Watch out for the pool, watch out for the pool he thought as he scurried through the darkness. Behind him his pursuers were closing. Their shouts of alarm seemed to be everywhere. He nearly tripped head long over the short wall. He had forgotten about the wall. With straining muscles, he forced himself over it. Not far now. The river had to be straight ahead. High above him in the night sky he caught a glimpse of the blood red moon. Mars was watching. Corbulo staggered up to the waterfront. He was exhausted. Where was the log boat? Where was Priscus? He had told the young man to wait but in the darkness, he could see no sign of him or the small boat.

"Priscus, Priscus, where are you?" Corbulo hissed furiously.

The shouts of his pursuers sounded horribly close by. They would find him within seconds. Out on the dark river nothing moved. There was no sign of Priscus.

"Oh fuck it," Corbulo cursed taking a couple steps backwards. On his shoulder's he felt Efa tense as if she had guessed what he was about to do. Then before she could say anything he launched himself forwards and leapt out into the river. Efa managed a small cry of panic before they crashed into the water. Corbulo gasped at the coldness of the Thames as he went head under. For a moment the dark and cold were utterly disorientating. He thrashed around with his arms. Then he surfaced gasping for air. Efa was still clinging to his back, her arms and thighs locked around him so tightly it was as if their two bodies had become one. From the embankment he heard angry cries and in the red moonlight he could make out figures. Corbulo spluttered as he took in a mouthful of river water. Efa's weight was becoming too much, she was going to drown him if she stayed on his back but there was no way she could swim, not with that heavy iron chain around her ankles.

"Priscus," Corbulo cried out taking in another mouthful of water. "Priscus."

For a moment the dark river seemed utterly peaceful. Then something moved. A shadow against the red moonlight.

"I am here, I am here," a voice suddenly whispered loudly in the darkness. Corbulo spluttered as he caught sight of the shape of a log gliding towards him. He raised his arm and tried to swim towards it but he had no strength left. Startled he suddenly realised that the tide was taking him towards the bridge. Close by something splashed into the water. It was an oar. Corbulo made an attempt to grab it but missed. His head went under and he coughed and spluttered as the river water surged into his mouth. On his back he felt Efa shift her weight. He surfaced and cried out. Then suddenly he was being dragged through the water. Efa had caught hold of the oar. The low hull of a boat appeared and Corbulo felt Efa being lifted from his shoulders. The release felt wonderful. Exhausted he caught hold of the hull but he lacked the strength to haul himself over the side. For a moment he clung to the side of the boat. Then a pair of hands were pulling him out of the water and after a short struggle he rolled over the side onto the middle plank of the craft.

"Sorry Sir, I had to move the boat," Priscus whispered apologetically.

Chapter Seven - All Change

Corbulo lay on the bottom of the narrow log boat staring up at the red moon as he struggled to regain his breath. Then he turned on his side and vomited, bringing up a mass of river water and bile. As he wiped his mouth on his sleeve the boat drifted under the bridge and to his left he heard voices and saw the torches of the soldiers guarding the northern entrance. He turned to look behind him and in the moonlight caught Efa staring back at him. She was shivering.

"Do you know what you have done?" Corbulo hissed furiously. There was no stopping his pent up anger now. It came flooding out of him like a great unstoppable tidal wave. "I told you to stay at home and you disobeyed me. I told you. You foolish woman. Do you realise what you have done?"

Efa had started to cry. Her shoulders shook as she raised her hands to her face. Her tears however did nothing to placate Corbulo's rage.

"We're finished here," he snapped, "We will have to leave Londinium. We can't stay here, not after what has happened tonight. We're going to have leave everything behind, our house, my business, my boat, everything. Damn you Efa, you have ruined us, you have ruined everything that I had built up. I am too old to start from scratch again. Where will be go? How will we survive?" There was a note of desperation now in Corbulo's voice. He had never expected this. He had not been prepared for this but now the looming realisation that they would have to go on the run was making him feel sick.

"You put everything we had at risk by trying to rescue that child," he hissed, "You had no right to do that Efa, you should have told me, damn you!"

"I am sorry," Efa sobbed, "I am so sorry."

Corbulo shook his head in dismay and looked away into the darkness. For a long moment no one spoke. The log boat bobbed up and down on the water as Priscus tried to steer her towards the southern bank. Corbulo ran his hands over his face and took a deep breath.

"We will leave tonight," he growled. "We will pack what we can carry and we will leave before light. That man, the one I kicked, he knows me, it's only a matter of time before they come for us and they will show no mercy Efa, no mercy. I know these men, no law or custom is sacred to them."

Efa's soft weeping was all that he got as a reply.

"Priscus," Corbulo said quietly, "I am going to have to ask you to look after my house and the business whilst we are gone. Will you do this?"

"Ofcourse Sir," Priscus said without hesitation. Corbulo twisted to look at him but in the darkness it was impossible to see the young man's face.

"If I do not return by Saturnalia, at the end of the year, then it will all belong to you," Corbulo murmured.

Behind him there was no immediate answer. Then Corbulo heard a gasp.

"That is most generous Sir," Priscus said, "Most generous but I cannot accept it. We are partners, you and I, so I shall keep things going until you return Sir."

Corbulo sighed and turned to stare into the darkness. His anger was fading. The goddess Fortuna was playing with him, watching to see how he would react to her games but the goddess could fuck off; he wasn't here for her amusement. Suddenly he felt in charge again, his decision was the right one. He knew it in his bones. He raised his hand to his mouth and cursed. When he had banged his head in the kitchen the blow had loosened a tooth.

"Where will you go Sir?" Priscus said from the back of the boat.

Corbulo shook his head. He hadn't had time to think about that.

"What about the children?" Efa sniffed, "we can't just leave them behind. They will die if we leave them. The Governor is bound to find them. He will kill them and if he doesn't then the Procurator will."

Corbulo groaned. He had forgotten about the nine Christian children hiding in his house. Efa was right, there would be no one to look after them if he left. The boat fell silent and for a while the only noise was the gentle lapping motion of the waves against the hull. Corbulo looked up at the blood red moon as he struggled with the decision that he had to make.

"Fine," he said at last in a quiet dignified voice, " We shall take them with us, all nine of them. Those children deserve a fighting chance I suppose."

Behind him he heard Efa cry out in relief. Then he felt her hand on his shoulder and a moment later her head was resting against his back.

"Thank you," she murmured wearily. "The Christian God says that the strong must protect the weak. You would make a good Christian, Corbulo."

"The Christian God can fuck off," Corbulo snapped irritably. "I have heard that these followers of Christus claim that they and they alone are just and merciful but I have known many good men who were not Christians. These Christians think that they are better than me, they think that they know something that I don't. Well I will tell you something, if those children are strong, they will survive but if they are weak they will die and there is nothing that we or Christus can do about that."

"So why do you want to take them?" Efa murmured.

"Because I am not a complete arsehole," Corbulo growled, "Now shut up woman and let me think about what we are going to do."

In front of him tall river reeds suddenly loomed up out of the darkness and without warning the bottom of the log boat scraped over stones. Their momentum carried the narrow craft on and straight into the reeds where it finally came to a shuddering halt. Close by a river creature vanished into the water with a loud plopping noise. Corbulo scrambled over the side and lurched onto a sand bank. A quarter of a mile away he could see lights and the torches of the soldiers guarding the bridge. He turned as Efa and Priscus waded ashore.

"Look at Londinium," he muttered, "What a fine city and here I was hoping that I would live long enough to see her all clad in stone. Now wouldn't that be a sight. Wouldn't that be something." Sadly Corbulo shook his head and in the darkness no one saw him smile.

"Where will you go Sir?"

"We will go west," Efa replied firmly, "We will take the children to my people and the village where I was born. My family will protect them. We will be safe there."

Chapter Eight - The House on the Fleet River

Anxiously Corbulo glanced up at the dark sky as he made his way along the bank of the Fleet. Dawn was not far away. He would have to hurry. To his right, beyond the timber revetments and flood defences, the Fleet glistened in the red moonlight as its waters flowed south into the Thames. On the opposite eastern shore of the Fleet, where two small islands jutted out into the river, he could just about make out a massive warehouse and the adjacent construction site for a tidal mill. He had been supplying stone to that site. He wiped the sweat from his forehead. None of that mattered now. He had to forget about his business and concentrate on the task at hand. He was exhausted but there was urgency in his movements as he picked his way across the boggy uneven ground. He was fairly certain that Bestia had recognised him and if that were the case then the Governor's men would already be out looking for him. There was no time to waste.

He cursed as his boot disappeared into a muddy puddle. To his left, stretching away into the darkness were the urn fields and Columbaria, the cemeteries where the ashes of the dead were brought and interred. It was a depressing place and the closeness of the dead seemed to weigh on him. Nine children! What had he been thinking when he had agreed to this? If it was only himself, Efa and Dylis it would be fairly straightforward for them to disappear but with nine children in tow it was going to be hard if not impossible. For a start the children would slow them down and then he had to feed them. In the few moment's he'd had to himself since their escape he had worked out a rough plan. They would need to get north of the Thames as soon as possible and then get away from Londinium as fast as they could. The fastest route north and on towards Deva was via Watling Street and despite the risk of running into Bestia or the Governor's patrols this was still there best option, provided they could move fast. With a bit of luck the Governor and Bestia would waste their time concentrating their search on Londinium. If he and the children could slip away chances were that the

Governor would lose interest and give up the search. But before all of this could be accomplished, there was something that he had to do.

Falco had built his house close to the banks of the Fleet, a hundred paces south of the bridge that carried Watling Street into the city. In the red moonlight the building looked deserted. Close by stood a large wooden barn with double doors inside which Corbulo knew Falco kept his brand new Carrus. Corbulo clambered over the low wall that marked out the banker's property and paused to listen but in the darkness the only thing he could hear was the gentle movement of horses inside the barn. Falco had better be at home he thought. He wiped the sweat from his face and his fingers closed around the tooth he was holding. It had been dislodged during the escape from the Governor's Palace. He was down to five. He found his way around the side of the house and banged on the front door.

"Falco, Falco, it's me, open up," he whispered loudly.

From inside the building there was no reply. Corbulo waited and then knocked again and this time he heard a muffled noise. A little while later he heard movement from inside the house.

"Who is it?" a suspicious voice snapped, "Do you know what hour it is?"

"It's me," Corbulo growled, "Listen Falco, I need my money, I need it now. I need all of it."

From inside the house there was no immediate reply. Then Corbulo heard bolts being undone and a moment later the door swung open. Falco stood in the entrance holding up an oil lamp. He was dressed in his white night clothes. He glared at Corbulo.

"Can't it wait until the morning?" he said irritably.

Corbulo shook his head. "I need it now. I am going away."

Falco raised his lamp and peered at Corbulo with sudden interest.

"Away," he muttered, "At this hour? Where are you going Corbulo?"

"South towards Rutupia, I have some urgent business there," Corbulo said smoothly. He glanced over his shoulder into the night. "I am setting out this morning. Priscus will be in charge of the business whilst I am away. Treat him well Falco. When I return I don't want to hear that you have given him a hard time."

Falco was staring at Corbulo and for a fleeting second Corbulo thought the banker had seen through the lie. Falco's eyes gleamed in the torch-light and for a moment he remained silent.

"Your money is at the bank in the city," he said at last.

"Come on," Corbulo interrupted, "I know you keep some here in your house. I don't have time to go to the Forum. I need all of it now. Don't make me wait Falco or else you and I will no longer be doing business. I mean it."

The threat seemed to leave Falco unruffled. The banker rolled his eyes and sighed.

"Wait here, I will see what I have got," he said.

Corbulo waited as Falco vanished into his house. A minute later the banker was back holding two leather bags. He handed them over to Corbulo who peered at them suspiciously.

"This is all that I have, it covers about two thirds of your deposit. If you want the remaining third you will have to come with me to the Forum," Falco said. "Or do you want to count it here first?"

Corbulo was weighing the bags in his hands. There was no time for counting. He looked up.

"No that won't be necessary," he said clearing his throat, "but how about you sell me that wagon of yours, the Carrus and your two horses. I will give you the money that you still owe me for them."

Falco looked surprised. He turned to glance in the direction of the barn where the four-wheeled carriage was kept.

"That's a bit short," he murmured at last, "the wagon is brand new and the horses are in excellent condition. I wasn't planning to sell them but if you really want them it will cost you another bag like the one you are holding."

"Done," Corbulo said quickly handing back one of the leather bags.

Falco stared at the bag in his hand. Then cautiously he looked up at Corbulo. "It's none of my business of course," Falco said quietly, "But I just thought you should know, when we were talking about those Christians, your friend, Quintus the retired Centurion, the one who the Governor is looking for. The rumour is that he's fled to Hibernia. That seems to be the place where all wanted men flee to these days."

Corbulo avoided the banker's gaze. Falco had never inquired into his personal or business affairs but that didn't mean he could trust the man or tell him the truth. If, as was likely, the Governor placed a bounty on his head Corbulo knew that Falco's loyalty to his client would be severely tested. At the most he would have a couple of days before Falco gave in to temptation and alerted the Governor. Corbulo cleared his throat again.

"So I have heard," he muttered as his fingers came to rest on the pommel of his sword. In the darkness Falco did not seem to have noticed the movement.

"Well it's a good thing that you are not heading north," Falco sighed, "There is trouble around Verulamium, *St. Albans*, some sort of local rebellion. They say a druid is stirring up the Britons against the local landowner. The Governor is despatching a company of the city guard to restore order. They are leaving at first light. You wouldn't want to be riding into that mess with a brand-new wagon and a bag of silver now would you."

Corbulo was silent. Then his hand moved away from his sword.

"I will be back shortly to collect the wagon, goodbye Falco," Corbulo said as he moved off into the darkness.

***

The log boat was where he had left it drawn up along the river-bank. As Corbulo approached he heard an urgent whisper in the darkness.

"It's me, I have got the money," he called out softly. A moment later two figures rose from where they had been hiding amongst the tall reeds. It was Priscus and Efa. Priscus had armed himself with a pickaxe. They approached with Efa trailing a broken slavers chain that was still clamped to one of her ankles. The metal rattled and thudded across the ground. She touched his arm.

"Are they allright?" Corbulo said gesturing towards the log boat where he could just about make out some of the children.

"They are frightened and they don't know what is going on," Efa said quietly.

Corbulo grunted and turned to Priscus.

"Well we are all set," he growled. "Falco has sold me his wagon and horses. We will place the children onboard and take the road north. With a bit of luck we will be miles away before its light. I know these wagons, with a good road and strong horses we will be able to do fifty miles in a day, maybe more."

"That's good Sir, that's good,"   Priscus murmured.

Corbulo stretched out his arms and clasped Priscus by the shoulders.

"Farewell then friend," he said softly, "I will be back one day when matters have settled down. Look after our business and the boat. You are the best business partner that I have."

In the darkness Corbulo could not see the smile that appeared on Priscus's face.

"But you only have one business partner," the young Briton whispered.

Chapter Nine - The Rebellion

Wearily Corbulo rubbed his eyes. Gods what would he do to get some sleep. He was exhausted. The noon sun had come and gone but he could still feel the heat and glare of it on his cheeks. He slapped his face and shook his head. It was all that he could do to stay awake. In his hand's he held the 'horse's reins and at his side Efa's head was slumped against his shoulder. She was fast asleep. The Carrus, with it's four large spoke wheels and pulled along by the two horses, rolled, rocked and creaked along the straight paved road. The wooden sides were up and he had managed to erect the cover to give the children some protection from the dust of the road. He glanced over his shoulder. The children lay on the bare wooden planks of the wagon. They looked like they were sleeping.

On both sides of the road the green and fertile looking meadows and fields seemed peaceful. The only other travellers he'd seen so far had been a trader and his wagon heading in the opposite direction Here and there the gently rolling landscape was interspersed with woods and apart from the road that cut a line across the land, he could see no sign of human activity. He sighed and felt his eyes close. So much had happened in the past few days. Part of him could not believe he was leaving behind everything for which he had worked so hard in order to save a group of children who he didn't even know. The thought depressed him. Efa was demanding a lot. He had already spent two thirds of his savings on buying the Carrus and the horses, an investment that he didn't need. Maybe when they reached Deva he would be able to sell the damn thing and recoup some of his investment? The thought of seeing Efa's family again didn't exactly fill him with joy either. He hardly knew them for he had only met her father and brother once and his in-laws had not hidden their disapproval and dismay at seeing Efa marry a Roman. The suspicion on their faces had been clear as daylight.

Suddenly one of the horses snorted and with a start Corbulo opened his eyes. Had he fallen asleep? He peered around him but all seemed normal. How far had they come? Corbulo rubbed his eyes again. They had been on the road since before dawn, so they couldn't be far from Verulamium, *St Albans*. He leaned sideways and glanced back down the road from which they had come but saw nobody. That was good. There had been no sign of any pursuit since they had left Londinium. Maybe they had managed to get away after all.

A little noise behind him made him look round. Dylis and a little blond girl were clambering towards the front of the wagon and Corbulo recognised the Christian girl as the one who had spoken out in his house. The girl still had the leather satchel with the protruding doll strapped to her back.

"Christiana wants to ask you something, father," Dylis said quietly as the two girls placed their elbows on the wagon's wooden side just behind him.

"What?" Corbulo snapped tiredly.

"Why don't you like us?" a timid little voice said.

Corbulo fixed his eyes on the road and said nothing. Behind him the two girls were silent for a while.

"Where are my father and mother?" Christiana asked.

Corbulo shook his head. "I don't know," he said. "Now no more questions. Dylis, take your friend to the back."

Behind him Corbulo heard movement and when he glanced around he saw that Dylis had done as he had asked but when he caught his daughter's eye she refused to look at him.

***

With a sudden jerk Corbulo pulled on the reins and the wagon came to an abrupt creaking halt. He lifted up his hand to shade his eyes from the sun's glare. Yes there it was. In the distance a long column of thick black smoke was rising into the sky. Mesmerized he stared at the smoke and as he did so he remembered Falco's warning about the civil disturbance around Verulamium. Softly Corbulo swore under his breath. He had no idea how large or organised the trouble up ahead was but chances were that he wouldn't just be able to ride straight through it. For a moment he was seized by indecision. Then he turned to look back in the direction from which they had come. At his side Efa stirred and opened her eyes. Corbulo ignored her. What had Falco told him? Something about the Governor sending a company of soldiers up the road to crush the disturbance. He groaned. The soldiers could not be far behind him. Londinium was only twenty-five miles or so from Verulamium, so if the company had set out at dawn they would be here before nightfall. He was trapped. He couldn't go forwards and he couldn't go back and if he stayed where he was the soldiers' were bound to find him. Corbulo felt a bead of sweat trickle down his face. The Legionaries may not be searching specifically for him but it was still a hell of a risk. He glanced around at the fields and meadows and his eye came to rest on a thick wood a half a mile up the road.

"Why have we stopped?" Efa said, peering around her. In reply Corbulo pointed at the black smoke in the distance.

"Wo will hide in that wood until its dark," he murmured. "I need to get some rest."

Efa was staring at the smoke.

"What do you think has happened?" she asked quietly.

"Fuck knows, all I know is that we need to get off the road," Corbulo growled as he urged the horses' forwards. With a shudder, the wagon started forwards again. Nervously Corbulo glanced over his shoulder but the road behind him was empty.

"Are you still angry with me?" Efa said, laying a hand on her husband's shoulder.

"Yes, now shut up," Corbulo   snapped irritably.

As the wagon rolled into the wood the trees blocked out some of the sunlight and Corbulo felt the welcome cool air touch his skin. The forest floor was covered with thousands of blue flowers whose name he did not know. The road cut straight through the trees, disappearing over a small hill. Corbulo peered into the wood to his right and then to his left. The trees seemed to line the road like sentinels and the thick undergrowth made it impossible to see much further than ten or fifteen yards. Then he saw what he was looking for. A clearing between the trees that was wide enough to let the wagon pass through. He brought the horses to a halt and handed the reins to Efa before jumping to the ground and as he landed he groaned at the stiffness of his muscles. A quick glance up and down the road confirmed that they were alone. Then grasping the horses by their harness he led them into the clearing and down a rough muddy lane. Behind him the wagon rocked and jolted as the wheels rolled over the broken ground. The children had woken up and some of them were leaning over the front of the Carrus watching him. Up ahead the lane disappeared deeper into the forest. When they had gone forty yards or so Corbulo brought the horses to a halt and looked around. The trees and undergrowth and blue flowers crowded around him. He turned to look back the way they had come but he could no longer see the road.

"We will stay here until its dark," he called to Efa.

Efa said nothing and avoided his gaze as Corbulo clambered back up onto the wagon. Corbulo turned to look at the children. All ten were awake and all of them were staring at him as if waiting for him to say something. Corbulo took a deep breath and rubbed his eyes.

"Now listen, all of you," he said in a tired voice, "we will be safe here but none of you are to go anywhere near the road and you are not to make a sound. If people hear us they will catch us and I will be very, very angry. Is that understood?"

The children did not reply but   Corbulo saw a few nods.

"Dylis," Corbulo said sharply, "give everyone a cup of water and their day's ration of bread but no more than that. From now on we will only eat twice a day, once at dawn and once at dusk, understood?"

"Yes father," Dylis said moodily.

"Sounds like you are back in the army," Efa muttered as she stepped down onto the ground.

Corbulo ignored his wife. For a moment he studied the children and his eyes came to rest on the older boy who had offered him money for protection. The boy of around twelve with jet-black hair was staring at him with sullen indifference.

"You," Corbulo said pointing at him, "What is your name?"

"Petrus," the boy replied proudly, "I am named after the first disciple of Jesus and I know all of Gods commandments."

"I am sure you do," Corbulo growled, "But now your job is to find something for the horses to eat and drink. We don't have enough water to share with them. Do you think that you can handle that?"

Petrus gave a little defiant shrug as he hold Corbulo's gaze.

"Sure, I am no child," he said, "My father was a man of importance. I have money."

"Look I told you before, I don't want your money," Corbulo snapped tossing an empty water skin in the boy's direction, "Now get moving before I give you a smack around your ears."

Petrus shrugged and with an unconcerned look he jumped down onto the ground and picked up the water skin. Corbulo watched him vanish into the trees. Then he turned back to the children.

"If any more of you want trouble, just let me know," he glowered.

***

Corbulo woke with a start. How long had he been sleeping? Dazed he glanced around him. It was still light. Efa was at his side shaking his shoulder. She looked tense.

"Petrus is back," she said urgently, "He says that men on horseback are approaching along the road from the south. They will be here very soon."

Corbulo heaved himself up onto his feet and turned to look down the lane that led to the road. The children lay splayed about the wagon oblivious to Efa's news. Then he caught sight of Petrus hurrying towards him. The boy covered the final few yards in a run.

"How many? Are they armed?" Corbulo said quickly.

"I counted twelve but maybe there are more, I don't know," Petrus panted with large exited eyes. "But they are close Corbulo."

Without another word Corbulo ran up the lane. Ten yards from the road he veered into the trees and crouched beside a large oak. From his vantage point he had a good view of the road to the south. He turned as he heard a twig crack behind him. Petrus, his face flushed with excitement, came creeping through the undergrowth and knelt down beside Corbulo. Corbulo swore and was just about to tell him to go back when the first of the riders came into the view. The horsemen were still a couple of hundred yards away but Corbulo could see that they were armed. The men came on at a walk and they seemed in no hurry.

"Don't move or make a noise," Corbulo hissed as his fingers came to rest on the pommel of his sword.

Petrus did not reply. The boy's eyes were fixed on the approaching horsemen. Corbulo took a deep breath as he studied the men. There were twenty of them and they were all young and fit looking men, armed with Roman weapons, yet they didn't look like soldiers that belonged to any auxiliary unit he'd ever seen. Their horses looked in good shape but their clothes were civilian garb. They didn't look like local British farmers either. As Corbulo stared at the riders an uneasy thought started to grow. Then as the horsemen were only a twenty-yards away Corbulo's face went pale and he groaned in dismay.

The man leading the troop was Bestia. Corbulo stared at the small, wiry mercenary in horror as the group of horsemen drew level. How had Bestia managed to find them so quickly? He had been counting on Bestia wasting his time looking for him in Londinium. What was the man doing out here? How had he managed to guess their plan? As the riders passed by, Corbulo's dismay grew. Patiently he waited until the last of them had disappeared from view before rising to his feet.

"Fuck, fuck," Corbulo muttered.

"They didn't see us," Petrus said excitedly," who were they Corbulo?"

Corbulo shook his head.

"You don't know their leader like I do," he said tightly," He and those men are the ones who are hunting us. They won't give up so easily." He turned to look at Petrus and the boy's face seemed to lose some of his youthful excitement.

"Those men are working for the Governor," Corbulo said, "If they catch us they will take us back to Londinium and kill us. If you see them again you either hide or you run, understood?"

Chapter Ten - Verulamium

Carefully Corbulo made his way through the dense green foliage of the forest pausing now and then to listen but the only noises he could hear was the rustle of small animals in the undergrowth and a distant woodpecker. The air was growing cooler and the sun was just about to set. He looked up at the sky. The light would be completely gone in a couple of hours. To his right the billowing column of black smoke was still visible but Corbulo had seen no further sign of the rebels. He peered at the smoke for a moment longer. It looked like it was coming from about a mile away to the east, maybe from along the River Ver. Through the trees he could just about make out the road. He glanced behind him but he was alone. Petrus had decided not to follow him this time. That was just as well. The boy knew nothing about scouting and reconnaissance. He would just be a hindrance and a nuisance.

Corbulo quickened his pace and a few minutes later caught sight of the edge of the wood. He crouched beside a tree. Beyond the forest, the road cut through open fields and there, a half a mile away, he could see the earthworks and ditch that formed the defences of the town of Verulamium. The town looked peaceful enough and there were no obvious signs of any disturbances. Maybe the citizens of Verulamium were not involved in the uprising? The sight of the earthworks however brought on a surge of memories and for a few moments Corbulo was lost in the past. He had seen the devastation and the aftermath of the slaughter of the town's folk after Boudicca had raised the city to the ground. The sight was something that he would never forget. The Barbarian Queen had spared no one, not even the children.

As he sat watching, a couple of women emerged from the forest fifty paces from his position. They were carrying baskets and Corbulo guessed that they had been out searching the wood for forest fruits. The women disappeared up the road in the direction of the town and Corbulo was just about to do the same when he halted in mid-movement. Coming towards him through the gap in the earthworks were eight men on horseback. Corbulo grunted. It was Bestia. The mercenary raised his hand just beyond the defensive ditch and the riders came to a halt and spread out on either side of the road. Corbulo watched them dismount and tie their horses to a solitary tree. What was Bestia doing? Corbulo could feel his heart pounding in his chest. The mercenaries looked like they were settling down to wait for something. Then as he realised what they were doing Corbulo closed his eyes in dismay. Bestia had set up a checkpoint on the road. The man was not going anywhere. No doubt the other twelve riders were doing the same on the secondary tracks that led into the town. Corbulo turned away and leant against the tree. Now what was he going to do?

To the west the land seemed open but the fields ended in a dense looking forest that stretched away until it was out of view. Corbulo turned to look eastwards but beyond the fields and billowing smoke he noticed tall marsh reeds. From memory he knew that the river Ver was not far away and the only crossing point was within the city. He sighed. There was no way he was going to get a heavy four-wheeled wagon through a forest or across marshland and a river. That left just two options, forwards or backwards along the road. Corbulo rose to his feet and gave Bestia and his men a final look before wearily beginning to retrace his steps through the forest. He could abandon the wagon and slip away on foot but Deva was still a very long way away and he doubted that most of the children would be able to make it on foot. No, they needed the wagon. He would have to think of something else.

As he made his way back through the wood Corbulo suddenly heard the braying of a donkey followed by a man's cursing. Through the foliage he could see a solitary man approaching from the south. The man was leading a donkey on a rope and leather bags had been strapped across the animal's back. The traveller looked like he was in a hurry and he kept glancing over his shoulder. Corbulo studied him for a moment. Then boldly he stepped out of the forest just in front of him. The traveller halted

and stumbled backwards in alarm and Corbulo saw that he was an old man, a Briton with a white messy looking beard.

"It's allright friend," Corbulo said raising his arm in greeting. Then he pointed in the direction of the smoke.

"Say, do you know what is going on over there? I have heard that there is some trouble."

The man was studying him suspiciously but then as Corbulo made no further move he turned slowly to look towards the column of smoke.

"Yes Roman," the man muttered in a thick accent, "there is trouble allright and you had better keep well clear of it for Romans are not very popular around here right now. Some of the local farmers have attacked the Roman magistrates villa along the river. They are burning the whole place to the ground. The magistrate and his family managed to escape."

The man paused to spit onto the road.

"This trouble has been brewing for weeks ever since that druid arrived," he said eyeing Corbulo carefully. "They didn't want to listen to me, the fools. I told them that attacking the Magistrate was the wrong thing to do. They should have taken their grievances to the courts in Londinium. Now they are going to die. There is a company of Legionaries and cavalry on their way up here to restore order. When they get here there is going to be a bloodbath."

"Where are these rebels now?"

The old man raised his arm in the direction of the smoke.

"They haven't moved, they are still at the villa. The last thing I heard was that they had found the magistrate's wine supplies. Most of them are probably pissed out of their minds by now. The fools, fools."

74

The old man tugged on the rope and started up the road followed by his donkey. As he passed Corbulo he turned his head.

"Eh Roman," he said sourly, "You tell those soldiers when they get here, that the citizens of Verulamium had nothing to do with this. We don't want any trouble in our town. We are a peaceful community and we want to be left alone, understood? But if those Legionaries come into our homes, stealing and raping, then we will fight. We didn't burn that villa, it wasn't us – allright."

***

Corbulo leaned against the side of the carrus as he finished explaining his plan. Efa was watching him closely. He had expected her to argue with him but she had not uttered a single word of protest.

"Will it work?" she said at last.

Corbulo glanced at the children lounging about in the wagon. "I don't know," he muttered, "but I can't think of anything else. Just make sure that you lead the children around the town and wait for me along the road to the north. It's not far and it will be dark soon," Corbulo paused and fixed his eyes on his wife. "And if they find you, take Dylis and run," he said quietly.

Efa turned to look at the children and for a moment she was silent.

"How long should we wait for you?" she said.

Corbulo shrugged. "I should make it by dawn tomorrow. Just sit tight and wait. I will be there."

Efa nodded and looked down at her feet. Then she took a step forwards and wrapped her arms around him.

"You are a man, Corbulo," she said quietly, "You are the finest man I have known."

Corbulo nodded and was about to say something when he stopped himself. Carefully he loosened her embrace and turned to look at the children.

"Petrus, come here," he said sharply. Reluctantly the boy got to his feet and clambered over towards Corbulo and Efa.

"Listen," Corbulo said quietly, "You are the oldest so I am going to give you a task. This is really important, understood. If you fuck up, it may cost everyone their lives. Now whilst I am gone, Efa is in charge and you will do exactly what she tells you. Soon all of you are going for a walk. I want you to keep an eye on the others, make sure that they don't fall behind or get lost. Can you do that?"

Petrus looked serious. Then he nodded.

"Good lad," Corbulo said. Then he turned to Efa.

"Allright, after I am gone, wait for a few minutes and then head west. Keep the earthworks and the ditch to your right. You will be fine. It shouldn't be more than a couple of miles. I will see you shortly."

***

Corbulo had only gone a mile or so down the road when he caught sight of the column of Roman infantry marching towards him. He reined in the horses and the wagon came to an abrupt halt. He turned to stare at the smoke as he waited for the Legionaries to reach him. As the soldiers approached he saw that they were being led by a Centurion and a Signifer who was proudly holding up the unit banner on a wooden pole. The Centurion's red plumed helmet was easy to spot and the sight made Corbulo grin. When the infantry were a hundred paces away a squadron of Thracian cavalry thirty strong, came cantering towards him flowing along the flanks of the marching Legionaries. The men's armour, horses and weapons looked first class and Corbulo grunted in approval. The eighty or so

76

Legionaries and Thracian cavalry would be more than a match for a bunch of rebellious peasants. The old man with the donkey had been right. It was going to be a bloodbath. Corbulo did not move as the cavalry surrounded him, their spears lowered and pointed in his direction. His eyes remained firmly fixed on the Centurion.

"Are you in charge?" Corbulo called out as the infantry company reached him.

The Centurion raised his hand and the marching column came to a crashing halt.

"Move your wagon off the bloody road," the Centurion shouted. "You are blocking our way."

Corbulo raised his hand in the air. "I will Sir," he replied. "I will but I thought you would like to know where the rebels are. I have some information that could be useful to you."

The Centurion frowned and turned to look at the smoke.

"You are local are you?" the officer snapped.

Corbulo shrugged and grinned at the Centurion. "You will find your enemy at the magistrate's villa near the river. Some of the local farmers attacked it and burned it, fuck knows why, but that's where the smoke is coming from. The last I heard was that they had discovered the magistrate's wine supplies so they are probably all pissed as farts right now. If you march over there right now and attack them I don't think they will put up much resistance Sir."

The Centurion scratched his chin and glared.

"Who the fuck do you think you are? How do I know that you are not leading me into an ambush?"

Corbulo's grin widened. "I served twenty-five years with the Twentieth, Centurion. I have built camps all over this country. You can trust me."

The Centurion took his time as he examined Corbulo carefully.

"Everyone is a veteran these days," he muttered at last. Then he turned to look at the column of smoke.

"Allright, Decurion," he barked loudly," take ten men and reconnoitre the villa. Report back to me with what you have found." The Centurion turned to the column of infantry behind him. "The rest of you follow me."

"Sir," Corbulo called out, "I am coming with you. I can help you with my wagon."

The Centurion did not seem to have heard him. The heavily armoured Legionaries had lifted their rectangular shields from the ground and were already passing the wagon on both sides. Further up the road a section of ten Thracian cavalrymen were galloping away in the direction of the smoke.

***

The wagon swayed and jolted as Corbulo followed the Legionaries across the muddy fields. He could smell the smoke now. The horses snorted and strained as the wheels ploughed onwards. Gods don't let them get stuck, Corbulo thought as he anxiously looked down at the wheels. Half a mile from the road, in a dip in the ground between two shallow hills, the Centurion raised his hand and the soldiers halted. The ten Thracian riders were galloping towards them from the north. The Decurion reined in his horse in front of the Centurion. The cavalryman looked excited.

"He's right," the Decurion exclaimed in his strange foreign accent, "the villa is just over this hill, a few hundred yards away. The rebels are swarming all over it and some do look drunk Sir."

"What are their numbers?" the Centurion snapped.

"Around two hundred or so, men, women and children," the Decurion replied.

The Centurion nodded and glanced in Corbulo's direction.

"Allright," he growled, "we will form a single line and attack straight across the hill. No prisoners, I can't be bothered. Decurion, take your riders around the flank and when you see us driving the enemy before us, you are to storm into their rear, cut them down, I don't want any of them to escape. Understood?"

The Decurion nodded that he had understood and shouted something to his horsemen in a language that Corbulo did not understand. Then the riders were racing away, their horse's hooves throwing up clumps of mud into the air before the Thracians vanished behind a copse of trees. Corbulo did not move as the Centurion issued his orders in a quiet urgent tone. The soldiers dumped their marching packs onto the ground and ran to form a single line. The men placed their shields on the ground resting them against their legs as the Centurion, together with his Signifer, who was still holding the unit standard, strode off towards the extreme right of the line. On the extreme left Corbulo could see the Optio, the second in command, doing the same.

"Company will advance", Corbulo heard the Centurion roar. The Legionaries remained silent as they lifted their shields off the ground and started to advance up the slope of the grassy hill. Corbulo watched them vanish over the crest. Then he jumped down onto the ground and scrambled up the slope. By the time he reached the crest of the hill he could hear shrieks, screams and cries of alarm. He went down on one knee and took a deep breath at the sight that met his eyes. The villa was burnt out, a smouldering blackened ruin of tumbled stone and charred timber. The roof had crashed inwards and red roof tiles lay scattered about. Close by a barn was on the fire and the thick black smoke was billowing up into the sky. Another, smaller building behind the villa was on fire too and scattered around the farm and villa were dozens of cows, pigs and chickens, some dead and some alive. But Corbulo hardly saw the animals, his eyes were fixed on the dozens of figures frantically rushing to and fro between the burning buildings.

Mesmerized he watched as the line of Legionaries closed in on the villa complex. A group of rebels boldly surged towards the line but got no closer than ten yards before a hail of Pilum's, throwing spears brought them down. The sole survivor swiftly turned and fled back the way he had come. Corbulo looked up at the sky. It was getting late but the onset of darkness was still a little way off. The night was not going to save the rebels.

The Legionaries had unsheathed their short swords and were closing in at a steady walk and Corbulo grunted in approval. The Centurion was executing a perfect assault. The screams and cries from amongst the buildings seemed to grow more and more frenzied and panicked. Then when they were only twenty yards away the Legionaries raised a loud cry and stormed forwards. Corbulo watched the carnage that followed. The Centurion's men surged into the courtyard in a frenzy of swords and shields battering through everything in their path and killing everything that moved. A few people, thinking that they could surrender, went down on their knees but were mercilessly cut down. A woman held up a baby but a soldier stabbed her in the head and the baby disappeared from view. Round the back of the villa a large group of figures broke out and made a run for it, spreading out across the open fields towards the river, but just at that moment the Thracians burst into view. The cavalrymen came tearing across the fields screaming their foreign battle cries before swarming into the fleeing rebels. From his vantage point Corbulo could see the running figures scythed down and he heard the desperate, terrified screams of those still alive. A Thracian rider decapitated a running man with a single blow, sending the man's head sailing through the air. Inside the villa complex the remaining survivors darted here and there but there was no escape and soon the screams and cries died away so that the only noise was Roman voices shouting to each other and the mooing of the cows. Corbulo blew the air from his cheeks. The Thracians had met with no opposition and the fields around the river were littered with corpses. Stiffly he rose to his feet. The fight was over.

Corbulo found the Centurion resting against the stonewall of the well. The officer looked tired and his face was streaked in sweat but there was a grim satisfaction about him as he stared at the carnage his men had created.

"Sir," Corbulo said quietly as he glanced at the courtyard littered with corpses, "if you have any wounded men, I am happy to transport them into Verulamium on my wagon."

The Centurion did not reply immediately. He turned to look at the burning barn ignoring Corbulo completely. Corbulo glanced again at the corpses strewn across the ground. The Legionaries were looting the dead of anything of value.

"Optio," the Centurion barked, "Strength report, now!"

Corbulo waited patiently as the officer scurried off to carry out his orders. A few minutes later he was back with a party of Legionaries, some of whom looked wounded.

The Optio halted before his commanding officer and saluted. "Sir, four men lightly wounded, one serious and one of the Thracians fell off his horse and has broken his leg. No dead Sir."

The Centurion grinned and turned to two of his men.

"A Thracian fell off his horse, what a joke," he chuckled.

The Legionaries grinned.

Corbulo was about to open his mouth when the Centurion beat him to it.

"Allright veteran, I never did think much of the Twentieth but as you are here, take my wounded into Verulamium. I will send some of the Thracians to escort you." The officer turned to look at Corbulo with a faint smirk. "Well off you go, there is no point hanging around here. Our work is done."

Corbulo nodded and turned away. He knew why the Centurion did not want him hanging around. By morning everything of value that the villa and the dead had ever possessed would have found its way into the pockets of the soldiers. That was one of the perks of being a soldier.

***

It was dark when the wagon finally approached the earthworks that surrounded the town of Verulamium. Up ahead Corbulo could see torches blocking the road. It had to be Bestia and his men. He pulled the hood of his Pallium over his head and tightened his grip on the reins. In the wagon behind him the six wounded were silent apart from the soft moans of the seriously wounded man. The soldier had been stabbed in the groin and had lost a lot of blood. One of his companions was pressing a bandage to the wound. Further back four Thracian riders brought up the rear, their horse's hooves ringing out on the paving stones. Corbulo glanced sideways at the young Optio who was sitting beside him. In the gloom Corbulo could see that the officer looked annoyed. The man had after all missed out on the chance to loot the villa.

"Who are you and what are you doing here?" a voice suddenly cried out in the darkness. Corbulo lowered his eyes. That was Bestia's voice. The Batavian accent was unmistakable.

At his side Corbulo felt the Optio stir.

"We're the Legionary detachment from Londinium," the young officer replied irritably. "I have wounded men who need treatment."

82

There was no reply from the darkness. Then a number of flaming torches were coming towards them. Corbulo brought the horses to a halt and waited. Bestia appeared out of the gloom and thrust his torch up so that he could see the occupants of the wagon and as he did so Corbulo inclined his head to the ground. With a bit of luck the Batavian would not recognise him in the darkness and with a hood over his head.

"You driver," Bestia snapped, "Get down on the ground so that I can see you."

Corbulo readied himself to run but just as he was about to climb down onto the ground the Optio leaned forwards.

"Eh arsehole, maybe you didn't hear me," the officer said sharply, "I said that I have wounded men who need treatment. Why are we being held up?"

Bestia grunted and raised his torch so that he got a better view of the officer.

"Sorry to bother you," Bestia said without any sincerity in his voice, "But I have orders, directly from the Governor himself. We're looking for a man who is possibly accompanied by a group of children, Christian children. They have fled Londinium and we think they are heading north."

"Well do you see any fucking children in this wagon?" the Optio cried exasperated.

Bestia ignored the comment and moved along the wagon raising his torch so that he could see the occupants. A few moments later he was back.

"Allright, move on," he growled.

The Optio grunted something in reply and gestured for Corbulo to get moving. Without hesitation Corbulo urged the horses forwards and soon the carrus rolled past the seven-yard wide ditch, through an opening in the earthworks and into the town of

Verulamium. The town was quiet at this hour but the thatched strip houses that lined the streets looked very similar to those in Londinium. Corbulo guided the wagon down the street and after a couple of turns they reached the newly built Forum and basilica in the heart of the city. At the junction with the road that led towards the bridge across the Ver to the northeast the Optio called a halt.

"Thank you citizen," the young officer said, "Stay here whilst I take the wounded into the Forum. After that you can be on your way."

Corbulo nodded and clambered down onto the ground as the Optio barked out an order before he vanished into the night. In the wagon the lightly wounded men remained where they were. Corbulo glanced around him and the darkness hid the relief on his face. He had done it; once again he had outsmarted Bestia. He smiled and turned to look down the street that led to the river. It had been years since he had been in Verulamium but the city seemed to have recovered from the devastation wrought by the Barbarian Queen. He chuckled as he stared in the direction of the river wondering whether the old abandoned and ruined watchtower that had been built nearly forty years ago to guard the river crossing was still there. It had been inside that ruin that he had once managed to seduce a Tribune's wife. That seduction had nearly cost him his life after the Tribune had discovered the affair.

***

It was late when Corbulo at last made it out of the northwest gate. As he passed the earthworks and ditch he peered into the pitch-black darkness ahead. There were no stars or moon tonight. His earlier elation at having slipped through the checkpoint had been replaced by anxiety. Would Efa and the children have made it? He allowed the wagon to roll on for a little while before he halted. The road seemed deserted. To his left he could just about make out trees but it was impossible to see whether it was a wood or just a copse. To his right there was nothing but utter darkness. He got down onto the ground and gently stroked the noses of the horses. The animals too were exhausted and covered in sweat.

"Efa, Efa, are you there?" he called quietly.

There was no reply from the darkness. Corbulo took the harness of the horses and started to walk them down the road. After a little while he stopped again.

"Efa, it's me Corbulo, it's allright. You can come out."

This time he thought he heard a little noise in the darkness up ahead. Corbulo stood very still and turned to look up the road, listening. Then he heard it again. The soft footfall of someone coming towards him.

"Corbulo is that you?" a female voice whispered from the darkness. It was Efa. Corbulo closed his eyes in relief as a moment later a figure appeared out of the darkness. Efa gave a little yelp of joy and flung her arms around her husband. For a moment the two of them stood in the middle of the road holding on to each other. Then gently Corbulo loosened Efa's grip.

"The children, are they allright? Did they all make it?" he whispered.

"I didn't know you cared," Efa replied with a smile that went unnoticed.

"Are they allright?" Corbulo asked again.

"We got lost but we managed to find our way to the road eventually. They are all here with a few scrapes and bruises but don't worry."

Corbulo grunted in approval.

"Allright let's get out of here," he muttered.

***

It was a couple of hours later, deep into the night when Corbulo suddenly heard a cracking splintering noise. Behind him the wagon lurched and slewed across the road as the left side sank alarmingly towards the ground throwing the sleeping children on top of each other. The night was instantly rent with howls and screams. Corbulo forced the horses to a halt and jumped down onto the road and ran around the back of the wagon. Inside some of the children were crying.

"What's happened?" Efa called out in alarm.

For a moment Corbulo did not answer. Then he raised his head and rubbed his face with his hand.

"Oh Fuck," he muttered, "The rear axle has broken in two and we have lost a wheel."

"Can you fix it?" Efa called out.

"No," Corbulo muttered despondently.

Chapter Eleven - The Forest

Wearily Corbulo came to a halt as he noticed the movement in the distance. In his right hand he gripped the horse's harness. Up ahead the road stretched away until, a mile away or so, it disappeared into a large dark green and forbidding forest. It was late in the day and beside him the horse snorted and lowered its head to nibble at a tuft of grass. Corbulo turned to glance at Efa who was following him with the second horse upon which sat three children. His wife looked weary and her clothes were stained and dirty. The strain was telling on her too, he knew. Ten days had passed since they had been forced to abandon the wagon along the road. The axle had been beyond repair and the accident had forced them to continue on foot. They had followed the road, sometimes on it and sometimes parallel to it but never far from it. The road had become their lifeline, a guarantee of direction, news, progress and succour and from the farms along its course he had managed to purchase enough food to keep them all alive whilst his moral had been bolstered by the fact that there had been no further sightings of Bestia and his men. Maybe the mercenary and the Governor had at last abandoned the search? Corbulo glanced up at the three children who were sitting on his horse. They too looked exhausted and worn out but at least they didn't have to walk. The four eldest children, the ones he had deemed the strongest and fittest and the ones who had done the brunt of the walking, looked thin, miserable, hungry and ready to drop.

"What is it, why have we stopped?" Efa said quietly as she came up to him.

"Someone is coming down the road," Corbulo muttered, "Best if we wait and see who they are."

Efa stared up the road in sullen silence.

"How far do you reckon before we reach Viroconium," *Wroxeter,* she murmured.

"I don't know, maybe one or two more days. I think we have been doing around fifteen miles a day. The town can't be far away."

Beside them one of the children suddenly bent forwards and exploded in a fit of coughing. The child sitting behind him held on to him to stop him from falling off the horse. Efa closed her eyes, sighed and rummaged around in the satchel, she was carrying until she found the small clump of honey a farmer had sold to them three days ago. She broke off a piece and licked it to moisten it before forcing the honey down the sick child's throat.

"The boy is ill," Efa murmured turning to Corbulo, " he needs attention and medicines but I have neither. If he doesn't receive treatment soon he may die."

Corbulo looked away and shook his head.

"Can't you do anything for him, you know about these sorts of things Efa?"

It was Efa's turn to shake her head.

"He's been coughing for days and he's got a fever. There is something wrong with his breathing. I recognise the symptoms of the illness but this is beyond my skill."

"What do you need?" Corbulo said as his eyes remained fixed on the distance figures on the road.

"He needs to see a doctor," Efa said firmly, "a proper doctor like the men that the Legions employ. The boy needs Hyssop, rest and warmth. The Hyssop will stop the coughing. After that the gods will decide if he deserves to live or die."

"Well I can't give you any of that," Corbulo growled. "Maybe the boy is destined to die. Maybe it is the will of the Gods."

Beside him his wife shook her   head.

"Viroconium is a large town, they will have a doctor and supplies of Hyssop. Just get us there and I will give him a fighting chance. The gods do not own him yet."

Corbulo nodded without much enthusiasm as he kept his eyes on the figures approaching down the road.

"Stay here," he said at last, "I am going down to the road to speak with them."

***

The travellers were a large group of seven heavily laden wagons with attendant drivers, slaves, dogs and an escort of fifteen mounted and armed men. The goods within the wagons were hidden by large brown covers. Corbulo stood in the middle of the road and did not move as the vanguard approached. The foremost wagon came to a creaking halt a few paces away and three riders came galloping towards him with lowered spears. The horsemen looked unfriendly and suspicious. They circled around and surrounded him.

Corbulo raised his hand in greeting.

"Friends, I mean no harm," he cried. "Who is in charge here?"

The horsemen did not answer but a few moments later a tall bearded man clad in an expensive looking Pallium came striding towards the front.

"Who the fuck are you?" the man exclaimed in a self-confident voice.

"Just a fellow traveller Sir, I mean no harm," Corbulo replied. "I was just wondering if you good merchants would possess any Hyssop? I am prepared to pay for it."

The bearded man frowned.

"What the fuck is Hyssop?" he   growled.

Corbulo glanced away in embarrassment. He hadn't got a clue.

"Are you with that lot over there by the trees?" the merchant said glancing towards Efa, the children and the two horses.

Corbulo followed his gaze and nodded.

"One of my children is ill," he muttered.

"Well I can't help you," the merchant replied.

Corbulo shrugged and gestured, pointing up the road. "Well maybe you can tell me how far it is to Viroconium?"

The merchant turned to glance in the direction from which he had just come.

"The town is not far away, maybe a day and half by foot," he said with a sigh. "But I wouldn't advise you to take the road. See that forest, there are outlaws in that forest who will attack anything that moves on the road. It's a dangerous place. Stay away from that wood. Those robbers watch everyone who is travelling on the road. They will not let you pass without taking everything you possess."

Corbulo frowned and peered at the forest in the distance.

"Well you seemed to have managed to pass through unscathed," he retorted.

The merchant shrugged.

"They don't attack well defended convoys, that's all I can say." He paused and glanced in the direction of Efa and the horses. "But you, with just a woman and those children, they will swoop down on you like bees going for the honey. Take my advice; don't enter that forest. They will kill you, rape your woman and sell your children into slavery. They are scum. That's just the way it is these days. People just take what they want."

Corbulo took a deep breath.

"Do the authorities in Viroconium do nothing about this?" he exclaimed in a depressed voice.

The merchant chuckled.

"The Twentieth has moved up north so there are no longer any troops in the city," he said. "The local magistrates do sometimes try and flush these robbers out but these outlaws know that forest like the back of their hand. Whenever there is an attempt to find them, they just melt away. It's fucking annoying if you ask me but what can be done about it?"

Corbulo spat on to the ground. "I hate them already," he said moodily.

***

Efa was watching him closely as he strode up to the horse and grabbed hold of the harness. Corbulo glanced up at the sky. It was nearly dusk and on the horizon he could see dark ominous rain clouds.

"The road ahead is dangerous," he said wearily, "there is a band of outlaws lurking in the forest. We'll have to go around."

Efa turned to look at the forest that stretched before them.

"How long will that take us?" she exclaimed. "The boy needs treatment. He may die if we don't get to Viroconium soon."

"I don't know," Corbulo replied as he started to lead the horse away from the road, "but we have no choice. If those outlaws catch us they will most likely kill me, rape you and take the children as slaves."

After a moment's hesitation he heard Efa start to follow him. She had a good heart he thought and he did love her but Efa had never cared about the consequences of her actions. No, dealing with the consequences was his task, even when he had warned her about them in the first place. He grunted and shook his head. But then again maybe he was lucky to have her, for Efa had not known about the amber stone when they had married, and how many young attractive women would want to marry a broke old man with just five teeth?

Corbulo turned and glanced at the four eldest children, three boys and a girl who plodded on behind him. They looked exhausted with their dull eyes and shrunken faces. All of them had lost a lot of weight and one of the boys boots were no more than rags of leather and cloth.

"Keep your chin up lads," Corbulo growled, "Not far now."

Behind him on the horse that Efa was leading, the sick boy broke out into another coughing fit that had him nearly doubled up. Efa brought her horse to a halt and spoke a few soothing words until the fit passed. As he paused Corbulo caught Dylis's eye. She was sitting at the front of Efa's horse with her legs dangling down the beasts flank and directly behind her was Christiana still clinging to her satchel and straw doll. The two girls seemed to have become firm friends during their long journey. Dylis gave him a little smile and Corbulo grinned back at her and suddenly his daughter's smile seemed to fill him with renewed energy. He turned away to study the forest ahead. It was huge, stretching away towards the horizon. How far inland from the road would they have to go?

He was just about to start walking again when he noticed the wooden cross around Petrus's neck. It was dangling freely and in full sight of everyone.

"Petrus," Corbulo cried angrily, "What did I just tell everyone about those wooden crosses? If you have to wear it then do so out of sight, under your clothes. If people see that cross they will know who you are. You know that there are men looking for us. Put that thing away immediately."

Petrus looked up and glanced around the empty field with an insolent look.

"I don't see anyone here, so what is the problem?" the boy shrugged.

Corbulo let go of the horse's harness and strode towards the boy. Petrus backed away as Corbulo came up to him.

"Put the cross away before I take it from you," Corbulo said in a quiet voice.

"You are not my father, you can't tell me what to do. My father is an important man, I have money and I am educated," Petrus cried defiantly.

"Your father is dead and so is your mother. All these children's parents are dead," Corbulo shouted, "You are not going to see them again, don't you understand? I am trying to help you, you little shit. Now for the final time, put that damned cross away!"

"Petrus, put it away for now," Efa said sharply.

The boy turned to look at her and in the corner of his eye a tear was starting to build. Then slowly he stuffed the cross back inside his tunic.

"Corbulo, not another word, you are scaring them," Efa hissed furiously as she caught his eye and gestured at the children.

Corbulo glanced at the children. They were all staring at him, pale faced and some seemed close to breaking into tears.

"Sorry," he mumbled. Quickly he turned and strode back to his horse and grasped it by its harness.

"Come, we will go in this direction," he said in a loud voice.

***

93

It was dark when Corbulo halted beside a large oak. Behind him he heard Efa and the others come to a shuffling halt. Corbulo peered around him into the darkness but he could make out nothing apart from the dark shapes of the trees. He glanced up at the sky which was filled with twinkling stars. Thank the gods the rain clouds had been moving in the opposite direction.

"What's the matter? Why have we stopped?" Efa called out.

Corbulo took a deep breath.

"We're lost," he muttered, "I thought we were heading south but now I don't know where we are. It's too dark. I don't know in which direction we should be heading. We will have to rest here and start out again in the morning."

"Lost," Efa groaned as she ran her hand across her neck. "Viroconium cannot be far. It's been hours since we saw those traders. Can't we keep going?"

Corbulo shook his head. "I can't see in the bloody dark," he said. "If we stumble on like this we may end up going in completely the wrong direction. No, we will have to rest here and start out again at dawn."

Behind him the darkness was rent by another fierce coughing fit.

Efa appeared out of the gloom and laid a hand on her husband's shoulder.

"He's started to cough up blood," she said quietly.

Corbulo nodded and gave her an encouraging look that was lost in the darkness.

"I can help," a voice said suddenly.

Corbulo and Efa turned.

"What's that Petrus?" Corbulo said as he recognised the boy's voice. A moment later Petrus appeared at his side. His head was tilted and he was gazing up at the stars.

"It's a clear night," the boy said, "I can guide us using the stars. Look there is Polaris, the northstar. As long as I can see the stars I can tell you in which direction we should go."

Corbulo grunted in surprise. He looked up at the stars and then turned towards Petrus.

"You can navigate using just the stars?" he said.

"Yes," Petrus said confidently," my father taught me astronomy. I know all the constellations. When we left the road we headed south. I know this from the position of the sun. We carried on south until dusk; then I think we turned west. The road is to the north." The boy paused for a moment as he stared at the stars. "Which means that we must go in that direction," he said pointing off into the night.

Corbulo raised his eyebrows as he peered in the direction in which Petrus was pointing.

"What if you are wrong?" he said at last.

"I am right, the road is that way," Petrus replied in a self-assured voice. "The stars never lie."

Corbulo glanced at Efa but in the dark it was hard to see her face. The boy's confidence had impressed him.

"Allright, let's keep going," he growled starting forwards again. Behind him he heard his horse snort and whinny as he grasped hold of the harness.

***

Dawn was not far away and he could not sleep. In the east Corbulo could see the blackness of the night becoming dark blue. He lay against the bank of the V shaped ditch in the abandoned army marching camp. To his right in a single line the children lay on the ground, fast asleep, huddled in their clothes and the few blankets that Efa had brought with them from Londinium. A little way off the two horses stood tied to a tree. Brambles and plants had encroached into the ditch and the bottom was muddy and water logged but it was a safe enough place as any. The camp's wooden palisade had long ago been removed but the earthworks were still visible and so too were the gaps in the ditch where the camp's gates would have once stood. The night was quiet and peaceful and a cool breeze rustled in the young trees just beyond the ditch. The camp was old probably dating back twenty or thirty years when this part of the province had first come under Roman control.

Petrus had found the road two hours after he had first pointed them in the right direction and the boy's unswerving confidence and navigational skill had earned him Corbulo's silent respect. Maybe he had been wrong about the boy? Maybe he should not have been so hard on him. The boy had lost everything. All the children had lost their families and everything they had possessed. They were orphans now, orphans whom no one would want because they were followers of Christus. Corbulo sighed as he was reminded of what Efa had told him as they were settling down to sleep in the ditch. They have lost everything Corbulo, but some of them don't understand what this means, she had said. They are clinging on to what they have lost in the hope that it will come back. That's why Christiana will not be parted from her satchel and her doll or Petrus from his wooden cross. Those things were given to them by their parents; they are the last link that they have with their families. Don't force them to part with that.

Corbulo turned onto his side and ran his hand over the stubble on his chin. Viroconium *Wroxeter*, could not be more than a few miles away now and all they had to do was follow the road. He twisted round as he heard one of the children sobbing in their sleep. There was nothing more he could do for them right now. Efa would be lying there beside the sick boy holding him close to her so that at least he had her body warmth to see him through the night. The boy's condition had deteriorated steadily until he could barely cling to the horse's back. Corbulo had resorted to tying him to the horse with a piece of rope but if they didn't get him to a doctor soon the boy was certain to die. Corbulo turned onto his back and stared up at the night sky. Forty-eight years he had lived. He had seen the Empire, he had known utter fear and glorious euphoria, served the Legion and Jupiter, greatest and best. He had ventured alone into the wilds of Caledonia to rescue his son Marcus but maybe when his time came to pass across into eternity this would be what he would be remembered for the rescue of nine Christian orphans. In the gloom he grinned as he pictured his tombstone.

Here lies Corbulo, a soldier of the Twentieth Legion with twenty-five years service. This monument was erected by the nine he helped to save.

Chapter Twelve - Viroconium Cornoviorum

Corbulo smiled as he finally caught sight of Viroconium in the distance. He halted and gazed at the town. How long had it been since he had visited the old fortress, the Legionary camp where he had spent so many years of his service with the Twentieth? It was from here that he had taken part in the campaigns to subdue the Cornovii and the Ordovices, two tribes who had fiercely resisted the Roman advance. It was from Viroconium that Governor Paulinus had launched his campaign to destroy the druids in their strong hold of Mona Insulis, a campaign that had ended with the uprising led by the Boudicca, the Barbarian Queen. Corbulo took a deep breath as he remembered it all. The sight of the town had brought on a flood of memories and for a few moments he was lost in the past. Would the old camp still be there? Maybe he would recognise some friends on the street? Surely some of the veterans from the Twentieth would have returned to the town upon their retirement. On the horizon he could see the clear outline of the Wrekin. The hill soared a thousand feet above the plain, a lonely sentinel, and upon its crest were the ruined, burned remains of the Cornovii hill fort where Virico, last king of the Cornovii, together with a few hundred loyal followers had led a heroic last stand that had ended in a fight to the death. Corbulo had heard the story from soldiers in the Fourteenth who had told him how for three hours Virico and his men had fended off the assault by two Cohorts of the Fourteenth Legion before they were eventually overrun and slaughtered. The story had been told to every new recruit who had been posted to Viroconium; a reminder not to underestimate their Celtic enemies.

Corbulo was still staring at the town as Efa came up beside him leading her horse by its harness but she said nothing.

"Ten years," Corbulo muttered to himself, "That's how long I was here I think. Well I never expected to be back."

Efa remained silent as she started on down the road with the eldest children following close   behind her.

After a moment's hesitation Corbulo followed. It was an hour after dawn and no one was in the mood to speak. The calm quiet morning was interrupted by the sick boy's coughing fits and the cheerful birds singing in the nearby trees. Alongside the road Corbulo suddenly noticed a solitary gravestone with an inscription.

Here lies Valerius, son of Valentinian from Gallia Lugdunensis, a soldier in the Fourteenth Legion.

Someone had left a coin at the base of the stone. Corbulo looked away in sudden embarrassment. He had known that man. Valerius had been a veteran who had settled in the civilian town after his discharge. He'd had a daughter with whom Corbulo had had an affair. What was her name again? All he could remember was the tattoo on her arse. He took a deep breath as he tried to remember. Lucilia, yes her name had been Lucilia. He had been thirty and she eighteen. Valerius had discovered the affair and had threatened to kill him if he ever came near his daughter again and that had been the end of it. He glanced again at the tombstone as he led his horse down the road. If Lucilia had left the coin it meant that she was still living in Viroconium.

***

As they neared the earthen ramparts that marked the edge of the town Corbulo saw the Severn river and the island in its midst across whose southern tip a wooden bridge had been constructed. A detachment of armed men were lounging about at either end of the bridge and out on the water the occupants of a few Coracles were fishing and enjoying the fresh sunny morning. The crossing place across the river had been the reason why the fortress had been placed here, for to the west lay the wild rugged hills and valleys where the Ordovices had their homes. The men of the hills may have been defeated but their resentment against Rome still lived on, smouldering away in the hearts of each new generation. Those same wild hills had been found to contain rich deposits of lead and silver and the produce from the Roman mines was transported down the Severn all the way to the great estuary and the open sea where the cargo was transferred to ocean going ships that would transport it to destinations across the Empire. It was this trade and prosperity that had turned Viroconium into the fourth largest city in Britannia.

Watling Street led straight into the heart of the town and as he passed through the gap in the defensive earthworks Corbulo could see that the town had grown enormously. The narrow wooden strip houses with their thatched roofs lined the road in neat ordered lines and the town had been laid out in the distinctive Roman street grid pattern. Idly he glanced in the direction where the Legionary fortress had once been. The Twentieth had departed some years before and now resided at their base at Inchtuthil in Caledonia but the outline of the old camp was still visible even though most of it had been dismantled and the space converted to civilian use. Corbulo grunted as he recognised the rectangular earth embankment along whose very side, Watling Street now ran. The street was thronged with people and no one seemed to give them a second glance. Up ahead he noticed a half-finished bath-house complex. There were no workers to be seen on the construction site and the work looked like it had been abandoned. Opposite the baths was a newly constructed indoor market, which Corbulo had never seen before.

"We need to find a doctor," Efa said quietly as he drew level with her.

Corbulo nodded and looked around him.

"The Twentieth had many skilled physicians," he muttered, "But they will have departed with the soldiers."

"You were here for ten years," Efa said impatiently, "Surely you know someone whom can help us?"

Corbulo grumbled and muttered something to himself.

"There may be someone," he said at last, "but he was only a boy with dreams of becoming a doctor when I last saw him. He was an apprentice to one of the doctor's who served the army. He was only twelve years old. He could be anywhere by now."

"Where can we find him?" Efa said hastily as the sick boy bent over and burst out into another coughing fit.

"How the fuck should I know," Corbulo shrugged. Then as he caught the look on Efa's face he sighed.

"Allright, allright, stay here, I will make some enquiries," he grunted.

***

The doctor's house was on a street in the newly constructed northern section of the town. Corbulo thumped his fist against the door and turned to glance around at the children crowding behind him. They were watching him with anxious, nervous faces. He gave them a reassuring wink. The sick boy looked pale, weak and feverish as he leaned up against Efa for support and his eyes were closed. The door was opened by a young Briton in his twenties and Corbulo recognised him immediately.

"Hello Sawbones," Corbulo said cheerfully as he stepped past the doctor and into the man's house. Without a word the children silently followed Corbulo into the building, filing past the surprised and startled looking doctor. The young man said nothing and did not move. Efa, leading the sick boy by the hand, was the last to enter the dwelling.

"Are you the doctor?"she said peering up at the young man.

"I am," the doctor replied with a frown as he turned to look at Corbulo.

Efa stooped and picked up the sick boy and held him up before the doctor.

"My son is very ill, he needs treatment, will you examine him? It's urgent," she said.

"Well I was just about to go out," the doctor protested, "Can you not come back another time. I am rather busy."

"We'll pay Sawbones, I have money," Corbulo said, "Now be a good lad and take a look at the boy will you. He needs your skill, if you still have it."

The doctor was peering at Corbulo as if he was trying to figure out where he knew him from. Then suddenly he blushed in embarrassment.

"Please Sir, he has difficulty breathing and he has a fever," Efa pleaded.

The doctor turned to look at the boy. Then he sighed and nodded. "Allright, take him into the back room and lay him on the table," he said. "I will take a look at him but the rest of you must wait outside."

***

An hour had passed before the young doctor and Efa finally emerged from the back room. Efa looked tense and Corbulo quickly rose to his feet. For a moment the surgeon paused in the doorway as he carefully examined the children who were sitting on the floor. Then he turned towards Corbulo, raised his finger and pointed at him with a baffled look.

"I remember you now, you were a soldier with the Twentieth," the young man said smoothly, "No one has called me Sawbones in years, not since the soldiers departed for the north."

Corbulo nodded.

"The men had a bet that you would faint during your first amputation," he said quietly.

The young doctor shook his head as a faint smile appeared on his lips.

Corbulo gestured towards the back room. "So what about the boy, will he live? Did you manage to save him?"

The surgeon took a deep breath. "Well I have done all I can for him," he said, "Whether he lives or dies is now a matter for the gods."

"He needs rest, a warm bed and hot food," Efa interrupted, "If we keep moving him and sleeping outside he will certainly die. The boy needs a good rest or else he will never recover."

Corbulo shot his wife a sharp warning look.

"We cannot stay here Efa," he snapped.

"No, your wife is right," the doctor said, "The boy needs a proper rest. If you keep on moving him he won't stand a chance."

Corbulo was studying Efa. Then slowly he turned to look at the doctor. The room fell silent. He had a decision to make.

"Allright," he said at last, "we started out with nine and we will finish this journey with nine. How long will it take before he is fit to travel?"

The doctor shrugged. "Maybe a week, maybe two. He is very ill. It is hard to say."

"Great," Corbulo muttered, "Well the last time I was here in this town there were five taverns who rented out rooms to travellers." He glanced around at the children who were sitting on the floor and as he did so he took a step towards the doctor and lowered his voice. "The tavern's, doctor, are they all still brothels?"

"The Pink Elephant is decent," the doctor replied, "You will find it on the corner of the next block beside the clothes washers' house. I would have offered you accommodation here but I see patients every day and there is little privacy or space."

Corbulo nodded and reached into his pocket to pay the surgeon but as he retrieved his money pouch the doctor stepped forwards and laid a hand on his shoulder. "I love my work," the man said quietly, "Looking after the soldiers was what I always wanted to do and it was a sad day when you lot departed. Sure you ridiculed me and you weren't an easy bunch to get on with but you were my heroes. My all-conquering warriors. So I have some news, which I think you would like to hear. The Procurator, Classicus, arrived here in Viroconium yesterday from Londinium. He is staying at the Magistrate's house."

Corbulo did not reply as he straightened up and looked the doctor in the eye.

"What concern is that of mine?" he said carefully.

The doctor smiled. "There is no need to keep on pretending," the man said quietly, "I will not say a word, you can trust me on my oath as a doctor and as a freeborn man. I have heard that the Procurator is here because he is searching for a band of Christians who fled Londinium a few weeks ago. He thinks that they have come north."

"So what?" Corbulo growled as his fingers came to rest on his sword pommel.

The doctor turned and pointed a finger at Petrus. The boy was sitting on the ground with his arms folded across his chest and his back leaning against the wall. He looked sullen and in a rebellious mood. His large wooden cross-hung from his neck and over his tunic on full display for everyone to see.

"If I am not mistaken," the doctor said, "These are all Christian children. Maybe they are the Christians that our Procurator is looking for? I thought I would warn you before you happen to run into him and his thugs. There is talk that the Procurator is going to offer a reward for their capture."

Chapter Thirteen - The Pink Elephant

Corbulo cast a glance over his shoulder as he hastened through the street but there was no sign of anyone following him. The Pink Elephant had looked decent enough and they had a room, not a very large room, but it would have to do and he'd paid the tavern owner up front for a week's rent. He came to halt beside the doctor's door and idly turned to look around him. It was nearly noon but the sky was covered by a mass of grey clouds. What bad luck had brought the Procurator to this very town. Corbulo sighed as he struggled to make sense of it all. How had he managed to get himself into a position where the two most powerful men in the province were both out to get him? It was bad enough having the Governor of Britannia, through his agent Bestia on his trail but now the Procurator, the province's finance minister, had also joined the hunt. Corbulo spat onto the ground. The gods were stacking the odds against him.

Why had Classicus personally joined the hunt for the Christians? Was he working in cooperation with the Governor or against him? How had he known to come north? Had Falco talked? Had the banker betrayed him? But he'd told Falco that he was heading south and Falco did not know about the children. It didn't make sense. The doctor had promised to try and find out what was going on and Corbulo had decided to trust him. After all he didn't really have much choice. He could have murdered the man to keep him silent but that was something, which he really didn't want to do. He muttered something to himself and picked at one of his five remaining teeth. And as for Petrus and his wooden cross, the boy was beyond infuriating.

"Allright, it's fine, let's go," Corbulo muttered as the young doctor opened the door. The surgeon was silent as the first of the children slipped out onto the street. Corbulo waited until they were all there before marching quickly up the street in the direction of the tavern. The children followed obediently with Efa bringing up the rear carrying the sick boy in her arms. The boy seemed to be asleep. The passersby in the street hardly gave them a second glance but that did not stop Corbulo from dreading the sudden appearance of the Procurator. It was a short walk to the tavern and as they approached Corbulo noticed the washers' house. The owner had placed three large barrels at the front of the building alongside the street. The barrels were open and designed as public urinals for the clothes washers used the piss to disinfect the clothes they were washing. As Corbulo drew level a sturdy looking woman with long flowing red hair came out of the house and picked up one of the barrels. She was about to disappear indoors when she made eye contact. Corbulo blushed as he recognised her. It was Lucilia, his old girlfriend. The woman hesitated as she peered at him. Then as she recognised him she opened her mouth in shock.

"Is that you Corbulo, is that really you?" she exclaimed in a loud voice.

Corbulo could not move and for a moment he was unable to reply. Behind him the children and Efa came to a halt in the street. Lucilia placed the barrel of piss on the ground and came towards him.

"Do you still have that tattoo on your arse?" Corbulo said at last mustering a desperate grin.

"I do and its larger than ever," Lucilia replied with a laugh. For a moment she examined him in silence taking her time to absorb every detail. Then a broad smile appeared on her face and she raised her arms.

"Well are you going to give me a hug and kiss or what?" she cried.

Corbulo embraced her, giving her quick peck on her cheek. Then he quickly glanced up and down the street. A few people were looking in his direction.

Lucilia raised her eyebrows. "What, that's all I get, after all these years," she exclaimed. "I remember that you knew how to use your tongue once. Come here and give me a proper kiss."

Then she froze as she caught sight of Efa.

"So is this your wife?" Lucilia said giving Efa a careful and cautious examination. "The one who was not supposed to know about us?"

"No that was the other one, she died," Corbulo muttered uncomfortably.

Lucilia turned to look at the children, then back at Efa.

"So you are the new wife," she said with a little smile. "I can understand him," she said crooking a thumb in Corbulo's direction. He would never say no to sex but you, you look a bit young to have had ten children."

"You need to learn to mind your own business," Efa retorted looking Lucilia straight in the eye.

Lucilia shrugged, "You are right, it's none of my business darling."

She was about to say something else when a tanned man with a black eye appeared in the doorway to the washer's house.

"Who are you talking to?" the man growled glancing at Corbulo and the children with restless, suspicious eyes.

"Just an old friend," Lucilia said, "Corbulo here is a soldier in the Twentieth and this is his wife and family. I knew him when he was based here. Corbulo, this is my husband, Seisyll."

Seisyll stepped out of the house and into the street and Corbulo immediately sensed an aggression and hostility in his manner. A knife hung from the man's belt and the black eye looked to have been recently inflicted.

"So you are a Legionary are you?" Seisyll said in a thick Briton accent.

"I am retired," Corbulo replied stiffly.

Seisyll turned to glare at Lucilia, "So this was your boyfriend? You preferred to fuck this old man?"

Lucilia rolled her eyes and wearily shook her head.

"Forgive my husband," she said, "He can be such an arsehole sometimes."

"I saw your father's grave along the road," Corbulo replied turning to her and ignoring Seisyll.

Lucilia nodded. "Yes, he died a year ago." She gestured in the direction of the Wrekin. "He wanted to be buried with a view of that mountain over there, so that he could be with his mates who died during the assault." She sighed. "They are all the same these veterans," she sniffed, "They would rather be buried with their comrades than with their own families."

An awkward silence descended. Corbulo glanced at Seisyll. The man was looking at the children and Efa.

"Where are you staying Corbulo?" Lucilia said.

Corbulo hesitated and glanced at the Pink Elephant sign above the tavern door that was only a few yards away. He couldn't lie. Lucilia was bound to see them enter the place.

"We have taken a room in the Pink Elephant until my boy is better," Efa said icily. "After that we will be heading south towards Londinium. Come husband we must go, the children are hungry and tired."

Lucilia turned quickly to Corbulo.

"Come and say goodbye before you leave, Corbulo," she said quietly. "It will be good to catch up, it's been a long time."

***

Corbulo glanced out of the small window on the second floor of the tavern. The night was pitch black and moonless. The street outside was quiet and deserted but below him Corbulo could hear the noise of the tavern's revellers, the raucous laughter and the hum of dozens of conversations. He turned away from the window and noticed Efa mopping the brow of the sick boy with a cloth. The boy had his eyes closed and she was talking to him in a quiet voice just like she did when she was telling Dylis bedtime stories. The rest of the children lay slumped across the floor occupying every available inch of space. Most of them seemed asleep. They'd had a long and exhausting journey and it had taken its toll. Efa had spent most of her evenings soothing blisters and cuts, repairing shoes and clothes and fending off the endless stream of questions.

A solitary wall fixed oil lamp bathed the room in a dim reddish glow. Corbulo leaned back against the wall. The owner of the Pink Elephant had asked no questions when Corbulo had shown up with ten children in tow. The man, a retired veteran from the Fourteenth, had seemed uninterested in his guests but Corbulo had slipped him a few extra coins nevertheless with the request that he warn him if strangers came asking questions about the occupants of his tavern. The man had taken the money without saying a word.

Dylis lay huddled close to the door beside Christiana who was clutching her straw doll and resting her head on her leather satchel. The two girls were covered by a single mud stained blanket and were whispering to each other. Corbulo caught his daughter's eye and winked and received a wink in reply. The two girls seemed to have grown close friends during their journey north and it comforted him to think that Dylis had someone she could talk to, for he'd had very little time for her since they'd left Londinium. Corbulo sighed. Had that not been

110

the case with Marcus, his adult son? He'd never had any time for him either.

Carefully Efa picked her way across the room until she was beside him. She looked exhausted.

"How is he?" Corbulo muttered quietly gesturing at the sick boy.

"I don't know. He is resting, the doctor did all he could, we will have to wait and see what happens," Efa replied leaning her head against his shoulder.

"Maybe you should take Dylis and the other eight north to my father's village," Efa whispered, "I could remain behind with the boy until he is fit to travel. It would be safer for all of us. If what the doctor says is true, the Procurator is here to announce a reward for our capture. Everyone could give us away if they suspect that these are the Christians the Procurator is looking for. I don't trust anyone in this place."

Corbulo shook his head. "No," he whispered slipping his arm around his wife's shoulders, "We will stay together, I am not leaving you behind. We will sit it out and stick to the original plan. It will be allright."

Corbulo felt Efa's body relax.

"I don't understand," she whispered at last. "Why are they still looking for us? It's been weeks since we left Londinium. What does the Procurator of all people want with a group of Christian children? Hasn't he got more important things to deal with? What threat do these children pose? What harm can they possibly have done?"

Corbulo remained silent. It was exactly the same question he had been wrestling with all day.

A little knock on the door startled him and in an instant Corbulo was reaching for his sword. The room went silent. Then the knock came again.

"It's me, the doctor, it's allright. I have some news," a man said quietly.

Corbulo stepped across the room and opened the door and the doctor quickly slipped into the room. He was holding a small oil lamp. For a moment he looked around at the children on the floor before turning to Corbulo.

"So I made some enquiries," the young man said earnestly, "the good news is that the Procurator has left Viroconium. He and his staff are heading north up the road towards Deva, *Chester.*"

The doctor paused to catch his breath. "The bad news I'm afraid is that a reward has been issued for the capture of a band of Christian children. It's all over town but not only here, the Procurator and his men have been visiting every town in the province and instructing them about the reward. The whole province will know about it by now and it gets worse. The Procurator is looking specifically for nine Christian children. He is telling people to look out for nine children travelling together."

"How by Jupiter's cock do they know that there are nine of them?" Corbulo cursed.

The doctor shrugged. "You should also be aware that the local magistrate has posted armed men at each end of Watling Street where it enters and exits the town. They have orders to keep an eye on the traffic."

Corbulo muttered something to himself and turned away. For a moment he was silent. Then he turned to look at the doctor.

"Thank you, friend," he said quietly, "I will remember what you have done for us. I can pay you..."

But the doctor shook his head and a little smile appeared on his face.

"No," he said quietly, "I don't want your money." The doctor glanced around at the sleeping children and sighed with sudden emotion. "I never liked bullies who pick on the weak and the poor," he gasped, "These children deserve a chance, give them that chance, Corbulo, tell that pompous tax official to pick on someone his own size."

Chapter Fourteen - No Time for a Piss

The children were bored and restless. Three days had passed since the doctor had last come and during that time Corbulo had not allowed them to leave the room on the second floor of the tavern. It was just too dangerous he'd told them, but the confinement was beginning to tell. Corbulo sat slumped against the wall watching Efa spoon-feed the sick boy. The boy seemed to be recovering and his coughing fits seemed to have become less and less but the fever still persisted as did Efa's concern. His wife's devotion to the little boy was touching. Efa might be stubborn, pig- headed and have little regard for the consequences of her actions but she was an honest, loyal girl and she had a heart of gold.

A gentle but urgent knocking on the door brought Corbulo up onto his feet. The children's chatter ceased abruptly. Corbulo glanced at Efa as he strode towards the door and bent his ear against the wood. He could hear nothing. Then the knocking came again, louder this time. Corbulo opened the door. Beyond in the small landing beside the ladder leading down into the tavern he saw the towering bulk of the tavern owner. He opened the door wider and stepped out onto the landing.

The tavern owner was balding and slightly overweight. He looked at Corbulo with a perplexed expression.

"Your horse died during the night, heart attack I think," the man blurted out. "There was nothing that my stable hand could do about it. I am sorry."

Corbulo rubbed his forehead and sighed. "Ah fuck," he muttered, "which one was it?"

"The stud," the tavern owner replied. "He's in the barn. Do you want to have a look at him?"

Corbulo nodded and closed the door behind him. Despite the bad news the relief at leaving that room was intoxicating.

Without a word the two men descended the ladder. The tavern was empty at this hour and Corbulo followed the tavern owner out onto the street. It was morning and the sun was still low on the horizon. The barn was next to the tavern and consisted of a small simple stable that could hold up to four horses. Corbulo paused as he caught sight of the dead animal. The black horse lay on its side, its head half covered in hay. The brown mare stood beside the body. A nervous looking stable boy stood to one side. The boy had been crying.

"I am sorry," the tavern owner said," What do you want me to do with the carcass?"

Corbulo stared at the dead horse.

"The carcass is yours," he said quietly.

The tavern owner nodded and turned to look at the dead beast. For a long moment no one said a word.

"Which Legion did you serve in?" the tavern owner said at last.

"The Twentieth," Corbulo replied.

"Ah," the man said with a little smile," I served twenty-six years in the Fourteenth. I knew you were a veteran." He paused and gazed at the horse. "Were you there at that place along Watling Street when we defeated the Barbarian Queen?"

"I was," Corbulo said.

A distant look seemed to appear on the tavern owner's face. He turned to Corbulo.

"You don't need to pay for your stay or for your horses feed. It's on the house," the man said. "You and your woman and children are welcome to stay as long as you like."

And with that he strode out of the barn.

***

The tavern was beginning to fill up with customers. It was late in the afternoon and Corbulo sat alone with his back against the wall at a small corner table holding onto a half-finished cup of wine. The temptation had been too much after all the days cooped up in that room. It was a guilty pleasure for the children and Efa were still up there but hell, he deserved a drink and he was going to have it. He glanced at the two men across from him unable to stop listening to their conversation. One of the men, a sea captain was telling his companion, a master builder about his experiences upon the western ocean. Unable to resist any longer Corbulo leaned towards them.

"Sorry to interrupt lads," he said in a friendly voice, "I was just curious, if a man wanted to flee to Hibernia, how would he go about it?"

The conversation between the two men ceased abruptly and they turned to look at him.

"Why do you want to know?" the sea captain said.

"I have a friend," Corbulo replied, "He fled to Hibernia a few weeks ago. It's a long story."

The sea captain eyed Corbulo carefully. "Well," the man said at last in a deep voice, "the merchants at Deva make regular sea crossings to the trading post at Drumanagh. With a fair wind the crossing can be done in a day. From Drumanagh to the court of the High King in Tara will take another full day's walk, it's about twenty- five miles inland."

"Have you been there," Corbulo said quickly," have you been to Tara?"

The sea captain nodded solemnly, "Not a very welcoming place for a Roman," he replied, "the women bite, the dogs are lazy, the food is horrible and it rains all the fucking time."

Corbulo nodded as he remembered the two occasions when he'd accompanied his old commander Agricola on reconnaissance missions to Hibernia. The rain had been never ceased and the missions had accomplished little.

"Is it true that Elim the Hibernian High King is offering asylum to all refugees from the Roman Empire?" he asked.

The sea captain exchanged a glance with his companion.

"So they say," the captain muttered, "King Elim is a shrewd man. I saw many foreigners at Tara. Merchants come from as far away as Hispania and Africa to trade for slaves and those sleek Irish hunting dogs. Elim tolerates us for we pay in gold but he is no friend of Rome. He trades with us but at the same time his vassals raid our western shores. They take what they like. Just a month ago one of their raiding parties even dared to attack the shipping coming out of Deva. It's a fucking outrage. Mark my words mate." The captain nodded solemnly. "The western sea is dangerous. I am fortunate to have a fast ship but the insurance costs of my cargoes are unbelievable." The captain took a swig of wine and wiped his mouth with the back of his hand. "The Governor should do something about it I reckon, these Hibernian pirates are getting bolder by the day. It's got to stop."

"Why did your friend flee to Hibernia?" the master builder asked suddenly.

Corbulo took a sip of wine. "He had an argument with the Governor."

"Did you serve in the army?" the captain asked taking another sip from his cup.

Corbulo nodded. "Twenty-five years in the Twentieth," he replied.

"I thought so. That Gladius of yours is a bit of a give away," the captain grinned gesturing at the sword that hung from Corbulo's belt. Then he nudged his companion. "Go on Julius, buy the man another drink, were in the company of someone who has stories to tell."

The builder smiled, got up and moved across towards the bar.

"My name is Albinus," the captain said extending his hand. Corbulo grasped it and raised his cup in salute.

"The Twentieth you say," the captain murmured, "They are up at Inchtuthil in Caledonia aren't they?"

"Yes, that's right," Corbulo said before draining his cup in one go.

The captain leaned forwards conspiratorially. "I heard something recently," the man said lowering his voice, "From an officer on the Governor's staff in Londinium. Apparently the Second Adiutrix are being recalled and sent to the Dacian frontier. They have orders to depart before the summer solstice."

Corbulo placed his cup back on the table.

"Who are they sending to replace them?" he exclaimed.

The captain shook his head. "That's just it. No one. It looks like there will be just three Legions in Britannia from now on."

***

It was dusk and the sun had vanished over the hills to the west when Corbulo stepped out of the tavern and into the street. He had enjoyed the chat with the captain and his companion and although the men had been generous with their wine he had managed to refrain from any heavy drinking or revealing the real reason he was in Viroconium and if Efa asked him where he'd been he would say he'd been trying to find out what was going on in town which was partially true. Along the edge of the street

118

the three barrels were standing outside the clothes washer's house. Corbulo glanced warily at the entrance door to the building but there was no sign of Lucilia or her husband. In the fading light he strode towards the barrels, halted before the middle one and after a brief fumble he started to piss into the barrel. The release felt wonderful and Corbulo glanced up at the dark sky above him and emitted a satisfied sigh. Off to his right and coming down the street towards him he heard the sound of clattering horse hooves on the stone pavement. Idly he glanced in the direction of the noise and as he did so his eyes bulged in sudden horror.

A party of ten horsemen, in single file, were coming towards him. The men were armed and clad in long black mud-spattered cloaks and leading them astride a huge black animal was Bestia. The bounty hunter was staring straight ahead and he didn't seem to have noticed Corbulo. Quickly Corbulo turned and pulled the hood of his Pallium over his head and he did so the stream of piss swung wildly and splattered onto the ground. Corbulo did not move as Bestia and his men drew closer. He had to stay where he was and just act normally. If he ran now it would only attract Bestia's attention. The stream of piss was starting to slow. Corbulo tried to slow the flow. He could feel his heart pounding in his chest. He had to act as if he was just another citizen having an innocent piss. Behind him just a couple of yards away Bestia's horse clattered past followed by the riders behind him. Corbulo forced his bladder to release the last of his urine and the piss splashed noisily into the barrel. No one spoke as the horsemen past by. Corbulo fumbled with his tunic, then bent down to check his boots. When he straightened up he risked a quick glance at the riders. Bestia and his men had passed him but as they drew level with the door of the Pink Elephant Bestia turned and shouted at two of his men.

"Brutus, Honorius, go and check if the owner knows anything about the Christian children. They may have passed through here. Tell him that we are looking for a man named Corbulo. Give him the description. I will be in the Fat Lady down the road. The   rest   of   you   follow   me."

Chapter Fifteen - Nemesis

Corbulo watched in horror as the two men dismounted, tied their horses to a wooden post and disappeared through the Pink Elephant's door. For a long moment he stood in the street torn by indecision. Bestia's men knew his name and they knew what he looked like. If he followed them into the tavern there would be a good chance that he would be recognised. But if he didn't the thugs would question the tavern owner and if they found the children he would not be there to defend them. From deep within him an anger started to take hold, a cold murderous rage. If those men touched one of his children he would have them. His hand trembled as it came to rest on the pommel of his sword. He paused beside the entrance to the tavern. The door was slightly ajar and through the opening he had a view of the bar. Bestia's men had their backs to him and were talking to the owner. Corbulo however was too far away to hear what was being said. He shifted his gaze towards the corner of the common room where he could just about see the ladder leading up to the second floor. It was only a few yards away. Maybe he could slip inside whilst the men were at the bar. He was just about to push through the door when he noticed movement. The men had turned away from the bar and were coming straight towards him. Corbulo turned and ran into the stables beside the tavern. In the darkness he crouched and was just in time to see the two men leave the tavern. They looked bored as they untied their horses and casually led them away up the street.

Corbulo glanced at the tavern owner as he stepped back into the tavern. The big veteran was wiping the top of his bar with a rag. He looked up as Corbulo approached.

"I told them to fuck off," the veteran said quietly as he pushed the rag across the bar.

Corbulo nodded gratefully.

"This is my establishment," the veteran murmured, "I don't care what trouble you are in or what you have done. When I say that you are welcome, you are welcome and you can stay here until I say that you can't and there is nothing that anyone else is going to do about that. This is my place. I make the rules here."

Corbulo leaned forwards and gripped the man's shoulder. Then he turned away towards the ladder. As he entered the room the children shrunk back in fear until they saw who it was. Efa was beside him in an instant.

"Where the hell have you been?" she whispered furiously. "You have been gone for hours. What happened?"

Corbulo looked around at the children. They were watching him with nervous frightened eyes.

"The bloody horse died," Corbulo sighed, "I have given the body to the tavern owner and after that I decided to have a drink."

Efa raised herself up on her toes and sniffed his breath.

"You went to have a drink, wine?" she said irritably.

Corbulo nodded. "Listen," he said quietly, "Something has happened. Bestia is here. I saw him outside in the street. Two of his men came into this tavern just now. They were asking about the children. They know my fucking name and what I look like. The owner however didn't say a word. He's a good man."

"Bestia is here in Viroconium?" Efa said, as her face grew pale.

Corbulo nodded sourly, "It looks like he's searching every tavern in town. He will probably be checking the baths and doctor's houses as well."

"So what do we do?" Efa said quickly.

Corbulo took a deep breath. He really didn't want to do this but there was very little choice. "We only have one horse," he said quietly. "So I want you to take it and ride north to your family and ask them for help. You will go tonight. The watchers along the road will not be looking out for a woman on her own. I will stay here and look after the children. It's probably the safest place in town now that Bestia's men have checked it out. I will wait for you here."

Efa was staring up at him with large eyes. For a moment she did not speak. Then she turned to look at the children. Gently Corbulo pulled his wife towards him and embraced her.

"Follow Watling Street until you reach Deva," he said quietly, "After that you will know your way, you will be in your people's territory. You will be allright."

He felt her body tense as he held her. She was scared he knew. It was dangerous for a woman to travel on her own. Too often Corbulo had heard the stories of solitary female travellers who had simply vanished, been taken as slaves or raped and murdered and buried in unmarked graves. Women did not travel alone; that was just common sense. He felt her loosen his grip. A solitary tear had appeared in her eye.

"Allright," she sniffed, "I will go. Look after them Corbulo. The sick boy needs honey and to be kept warm. I will return as soon as I can with help, I promise."

Corbulo reached for something in his pocket and retrieved a few coins. He pressed them into her hand and closed her fingers over them.

"Go," he said quickly.

***

Corbulo sucked a mouthful of air into his cheeks and blew it out. He sat slumped against the wall of the room. It was a hot day and the room was stifling. A full day had passed since Efa had departed. He'd hated his decision but it was the right thing to do. It was more than a hundred miles to Efa's village on the coast north of Deva and with just one horse most of the children would have had to walk, something they were just not capable of. No, they needed help. He closed his eyes, struggling with his nerves and once more he did the calculation. If she rode fast, did not stop or run into trouble or get lost it would take her two or three days to reach her village. If her father came right away she would be back in maybe five or six days. He sighed. Five or six days. It didn't sound too bad. Idly he glanced at the sick boy. The boy lay in a corner with his eyes closed and Corbulo muttered a silent prayer of gratitude to Jupiter. The coughing fits had subsided and the fever was fading fast. Last night had been the first in which the darkness had not been disturbed by the boy's coughing.

The children however were growing increasingly restless and bored and he'd already been forced to break up numerous fights and squabbles and somewhere during this time his Pugio, his old army knife had gone missing. How the hell had Efa managed to keep them quiet for so long? Carefully he glanced around the room. The children were scattered across the floor keeping themselves busy with their little games. Corbulo suddenly looked thoughtful. Something had been bothering him for a few days now. How could nine Christian children possibly be of such interest to both the Governor and the Procurator? They had left Londinium weeks ago and the authorities were still actively hunting them. What threat to Roman rule could these children possibly pose? Did these officials have nothing better to do? The whole affair smacked of more than just simple religious persecution. No there was something else at work here. He sighed as he studied the children, one by one. There was something special about these children. Something had happened in Londinium, something he didn't yet understand.

***

It was evening when Corbulo suddenly heard the shouting in the tavern below him. The children froze and alarmed and frightened eyes turned to look at him. Quickly Corbulo rose to his feet and crossed the room to the door. As he reached it he heard another shout. He turned to the children and pressed his finger to his mouth. Then quietly he opened the door and stepped out onto the landing. An oil lamp had been fastened to the wall and in its light he saw the square hole in the floor down which a ladder led to the ground floor. Corbulo leaned forwards and glanced down into the hole. A man was staring up at him, grasping the ladder with both hands. It was Seisyll. For a brief moment the two of them made eye contact.

"That's him," Seisyll cried out, "He's up there, That's him! He said his name was Corbulo."

Corbulo stumbled backwards against the wall in horror. He'd been discovered. They had found him. Seisyll had betrayed him. Then he heard someone scrambling up the ladder. Moments later a head popped up out of the hole. Corbulo did not think. He lunged forwards and struck the head with his boot. He was rewarded with a sharp cry of pain. The head vanished and he heard a body tumble down the ladder and onto the ground. Corbulo's chest was heaving. He leaned forwards and peered down the ladder. A man was kneeling on the ground pointing a bow and arrow straight up at him. With a yell Corbulo flinched as an arrow narrowly missed him and embedded itself in the roof of the building. Then a voice was calling out to him from below.

"You are trapped Corbulo, you have nowhere to go. You should have listened to my advice in Londinium."

Corbulo recognised the voice. It was Bestia.

"I am a patient man," Bestia cried out, "All I have to do is sit here until you collapse from starvation or thirst."

Corbulo leaned against the wall.

"Or maybe we could just go outside and burn this place to the ground," Bestia cried. "Either way you haven't got a hope."

Desperately Corbulo glanced around him. There was the small window in their room but he was never going to get ten children out of that without being noticed. He looked around the landing but there was nothing but the straw roof. Bestia was right, there was no way out.

"Listen," Bestia cried out, "I know that you have the children up there. I will make a deal with you. Come down here with your daughter and wife and I will let you go free but the Christian children are mine. That's a good offer, Corbulo, the best that you are going to get."

Corbulo looked up at the roof. It was a good offer, more than he would have expected from a man like Bestia but the bounty hunter's promises were worthless. He had learned that a long time ago. From the corner of his eye he suddenly noticed Petrus peering at him from the doorway. Corbulo closed his eyes and then opened them again.

He wasn't going to give up on the children. They had come too far. The thought of handing them over to a man like Bestia was too revolting to contemplate.

"If you want them," he roared drawing his sword, "then come and get them you cock sucking son of a whore."

For a moment there was silence below him. Then an arrow flew through the hole in the floor and thumped into the roof. Corbulo took a step forwards but was driven back by another arrow. He could hear movement and the creaking of the ladder but the threat from the bowman was forcing him to stay clear of the hole. A shape suddenly appeared and before Corbulo could react a man thrust himself up through the hole and rolled backwards onto the landing. The man was quick, very quick and in an instant he was on his feet, crouching with a sword in his hand. It was Bestia. The bounty hunter grinned.

"You should have taken my offer," he panted. "Now you are going to die and when I am finished with you I am going to have my way with your wife."

Corbulo steadied himself as he eyed Bestia warily from across the hole in the floor. The landing was not large and there was not much room for manoeuvre. Only the hole in the floor separated the two men.

"How did you know about the children?" Corbulo growled as the two of them slowly circled the hole.

Bestia sniggered. "Can't you guess," he sneered. "After you and your bitch vanished in Londinium I went straight to the person I knew you trusted. Priscus, I believe he called himself. He was your business partner wasn't he? So I got him to tell me everything about what you were up to. He sang like a bird. He told me about the children. He told me about where you were heading. He even told me about the wagon that you bought from that banker. He was very cooperative."

Corbulo's face darkened. "What did you do to him?" he said quietly.

"I tortured him," Bestia sneered again, "Then he died so I dumped his body in the river. He should have chosen his friends more carefully."

With a cry Corbulo attacked but Bestia evaded his sword thrust and the two men crashed into the wall grappling with each other. Corbulo grunted and heaved as he struggled to contain Bestia's sword arm. Then with a howl Bestia head butted him and a searing pain exploded down Corbulo's face. He stumbled backwards as Bestia came for him. Desperately he parried the bounty hunter's sword and the noise of metal against metal rang out. With a roar Bestia pushed him up against the far wall as Corbulo grasped hold of the man's sword arm. Bestia's sword point was hovering close to Corbulo's chest as the two men strained and grappled with each other. Then with a mighty effort

Corbulo flung the younger man backwards and moved to place the hole between them again. He crouched, breathing heavily as Bestia readied himself for the next lunge.

"What does the Governor want from these children?" Corbulo gasped.

"I haven't got a fucking clue," Bestia snarled. "I am just doing my job."

The bounty hunter feigned a move to the left and smiled as Corbulo nearly fell for it.

"You are maggot, you always were," Corbulo panted, "You couldn't kill me in Caledonia and you won't kill me now. Do you know what happened to your friend, Vellocatus, do you know what I heard the Caledonians did to him?"

Bestia shrugged, "I couldn't give a shit," he replied.

Corbulo tried to slow his breathing. The fight was tiring him. Bestia was younger and fitter. The man was a professional killer. If it came to an endurance test, the bounty hunter would win. He had to do something and he had to do it quickly.

Bestia came for him feigning a move to the left before storming in from the right. The man aimed his stabbing movement directly at Corbulo's midriff and his movement was so fast it nearly succeeded. At the very last moment Corbulo however twisted his body away and wildly thrust his sword at Bestia but found only thin air. The two of them stumbled backwards against the wall beside the doorway in a melee of shrieks, groans and grunts as they struggled for control of each other's sword hands. Corbulo could feel his strength starting to fade. Bestia was stronger; there was no doubt. As he struggled to force the man's blade away from his chest he grimaced as he felt the blade inching towards him. With a desperate cry he tried to force the blade away but Bestia was remorseless. The bounty hunters face contorted as he forced the blade closer and closer. Then suddenly Bestia screamed and his head reared upwards and the pressure on Corbulo's chest ceased. Bestia staggered backwards and screamed again and this time he dropped his sword. Slowly he turned and Corbulo saw the look of surprise on his face. Blood was soaking through his tunic from the three places on his back where he'd been stabbed. Corbulo gasped as he caught sight of Petrus standing in the doorway. The boy was holding a bloodied Pugio, his knife, the army knife that he'd thought he'd lost. Petrus looked completely calm.

"You, a boy, a fucking child," Bestia gasped as he stared at Petrus before he crashed down onto his knees. "Killed by a boy."

"No," Corbulo said as he stepped forwards, grasped Bestia by his hair, yanked his head backwards and slit his throat in one swift movement. "That was for Priscus, you piece of shit."

Blood spurted from Bestia's throat and splattered the wall and the floor. As the body crashed to the ground Corbulo pushed it over the side of the hole and heard it tumble and crash onto the floor below. The noise was followed by a cry of alarm and shock. Then he heard what sounded like a soaking wet rag hitting paving stones. The noise was followed by a shriek that ended in a gurgling rattle. Once again the tavern fell silent. Corbulo risked a quick glance down the ladder. The bowman lay on the ground in a growing pool of dark red blood beside Bestia's corpse. The man's bow lay discarded on the ground. Corbulo took a deep breath and dropped down into the hole and half slid down the ladder and onto the floor. As he regained his footing he saw the tavern owner standing in the middle of the room. The big veteran had a knife in his hand and he was facing Seisyll who was cowering, trapped in a corner of the bar. Beside the door another of Bestia's men stood propped up against the wall with a knife sticking out of his head. The tavern owner turned as he heard Corbulo land on the ground.

"I told you once," the man growled in a deep angry voice, "This is my place. I make the rules here. No one presses a knife to my throat in my own place."

"Where are the others?" Corbulo gasped looking around at the deserted tavern.

The tavern owner shrugged, "No idea. There were only three of them and this worthless dog here," he said gesturing at the cowering Seisyll.

"Please, please I will say nothing, I promise," the man pleaded.

The big veteran seemed to consider the man's words for a moment. Then he shook his head and strode straight for Seisyll.

"Sorry Seisyll," the veteran muttered, "But you have seen too much. I can't take that risk. You are going to have to die."

And with that he thrust his bloodied knife into the man's head.

Corbulo remained silent as Seisyll collapsed into a bloody heap. The tavern owner retrieved his knife and wiped the blade on the dead man's tunic. Then slowly he turned to look around at the bloody carnage.

"What a fucking mess," the veteran grumbled, "what a mess." He turned to look at Corbulo.

"You and your children had better go now," he said. He paused and took a deep breath before wiping the sweat from his forehead. "I know about those children and who they are supposed to be but don't worry I am not going to give you up. You can hide in the stables next door for a few days until things calm down. I will have my boy bring you some food and water."

Corbulo nodded gratefully.

"What about the corpses, what will you tell the authorities?" Corbulo muttered.

"I will blame you," the tavern owner replied. "You are the one they are looking for."

Corbulo's face cracked into a little smile.

"Death to the Barbarian Queen," he said quietly.

"Death to the Barbarian Queen," the tavern owner said solemnly.

Corbulo sheathed his sword and climbed back up the ladder and as he poked his head through the hole in the ceiling he saw the children watching him anxiously from the doorway to their room. Petrus stood beside the door still holding the bloody knife. The boy had not moved.

"Was that the man who killed my family?" Petrus said in a strange voice.

Carefully Corbulo took the knife from the boy's fingers and as he did so it seemed to release Petrus from a spell for suddenly his whole body began to shake uncontrollably. Corbulo wrapped his arm around the boy and pulled him into an embrace as Petrus broke out into great sobs.

"I don't know lad, I don't know," Corbulo murmured ruffling the boys hair.

***

Corbulo was asleep when a hand gently shook him awake. Instantly he was awake and reaching for his sword but it was only Dylis. His daughter raised her finger to her mouth and pointed at the sleeping children who lay curled up in the hay on either side of him.

"She's back," Dylis whispered excitedly, "Mum's back and she's brought Grandfather and my uncle with her."

Corbulo blinked. Then he was up on his feet. Petrus was crouching beside the stables door staring out into the street and Corbulo knelt down beside him as Dylis hung back behind him. Outside it was dusk.

"What did you see Petrus?" Corbulo whispered.

The boy was concentrating on the street and didn't seem to have heard Corbulo for he remained silent. Four days had passed since the killings and Petrus had said little during that time, so little in fact that Corbulo had begun to worry about him. The boy was still too young to cope with what he'd experienced.

"What did you see?" Corbulo whispered again giving Petrus a gentle nudge.

"It's them, it's Efa, she was with two men, both armed" the boy said quietly. "They just entered the tavern. Have they come to rescue us?"

"They sure have Petrus," Corbulo whispered with sudden delight, "They sure have. We are going to be leaving very soon." He turned and grinned at Dylis. "You will never hear me say this again but for once I am really happy to see that miserable old bastard of your grandfather again."

Chapter Sixteen - The Inlaws

The sun was an orange ball on the horizon as the riders clattered down the road. To the north and south the monotony of the flat empty and muddy fields and meadows was interrupted by small woods and in the distance, smoke was curling upwards into the cloudless sky. Corbulo glanced at Efa who was riding beside him. They had not spoken much since they had left the Roman cavalry fort of Bremetennacum earlier that day. It was not like Efa to be so quiet he thought. He turned to look behind him at the two old battered chariots and the three sleek grey hunting dogs that ran alongside the riders. The chariots were being pulled along by a team of horses and their drivers. Efa's cousins stood bolt upright holding the reins. The men were in their early twenties and both of them looked stern and unfriendly. Across their backs they had strapped their hunting bows and a quiver of arrows and crammed in around them were the children. Somehow they had managed to squash five children into each chariot but despite the cramped conditions and their sullen drivers the children seemed to be enjoying the ride for they were all smiles and laughter. The sight brought a smile onto Corbulo's face too. He had faced these Briton war chariots in battle and the vehicles had proved utterly useless against resolute and well-trained infantry but now they were proving their worth.

Three days had passed since they had managed to slip out of Viroconium. Efa had returned with her father, brother and cousins. They had brought the two chariots, the dogs and spare horses and had left the town immediately. Corbulo had noticed a couple of men watching them as they had departed and headed northwards but no one had tried to stop the well-armed party. He turned to look at the two figures up ahead. He had only ever met Efa's father and brother once when he had brought Efa back to her village, after he and Quintus had freed her and Dylis from a life of slavery in Caledonia. He had stayed in her village for four days, just long enough for them to get married. That had been eighteen months ago now. Efa's father,

Aidan had not said a word to him since he'd arrived and the silence between them had led to a number of awkward moments. Corbulo however, was not surprised, for Aidan had also refused to speak to him the first time they'd met. Only once had he deigned to break his grumpy silence and that had been to ask about his age. Aidan had not liked the answer Corbulo had given him for it had turned out that Corbulo was older than his father in law. Later Efa had told him not to worry about it but to Corbulo it had become clear that her father did not approve of his daughter's marriage to a Roman; a foreigner. Logan, Efa's brother, however was friendlier and had provided much needed distraction.

The road led westwards into the setting sun. Corbulo glanced at Efa again and this time she gave him a little smile. She had done well he thought. It was over a hundred miles from Viroconium to her village on the coast and she had done the distance in two days and nights. He sighed and his thoughts wondered back to the events of the past few days. Bestia had not known why his patron the Governor wanted the Christian children so badly. The mystery unsettled Corbulo. The more he thought about it the more he knew he was missing something. What could possibly be of such interest to the Governor and the Procurator? What did these children have that was so important? Puzzled he shook his head. He hadn't gotten a clue. Suddenly his eye caught sight of movement on a small grassy ridge off to his left. Aidan too had seen the movement and raised his hand and the small party came to an abrupt halt on the road. Ten horsemen clad in armour and armed with spears came riding towards them. Corbulo peered at them.

"They are auxiliaries, probably on patrol," he cried urging his horse towards the front where Aidan and Logan had halted. His father in law ignored him and muttered something to his son in an accent so thick that Corbulo could not understand it. Logan immediately urged his horse forwards and rode off straight towards the riders. Corbulo came to a halt beside Aidan. Up ahead the horsemen had reached Logan and had encircled him. Corbulo looked on as Logan spoke with the auxiliaries. Then a few moments later the young man was riding back to his father and the horsemen were trotting off in the opposite direction. Logan pulled up beside his father and glanced quickly at Corbulo.

"Corbulo is right," he said with a thick accent, "They are a Roman patrol from their fort at Kirkham. I know their leader. He is the man I sell our honey too. They just wanted to check who we were. No harm done."

"Did he ask you for a bribe?" Aidan scowled.

Logan looked away. "I said I would bring him some extra honey when I next go to trade with them."

"Thieves, bloody Roman thieves, the lot of them," Aidan growled spitting angrily onto the ground. "They claim to protect us but all they do is rob us at every possible opportunity. It was better in the days before Rome came."

***

The sun had vanished beneath the horizon when, three miles beyond the small Roman fort on the hill, the road suddenly veered sharply northwards and as it did so Corbulo knew that they were close to Efa's village. A fresh western wind had picked up and rain clouds were closing in. To his right the marshlands stretched all the way towards the distant River Wyre. They were close to the sea now and Corbulo could smell the salt on the breeze. He glanced at Efa and noticed the sudden look of excitement on her face and as he did he sighed. This whole journey had been her idea. It had been her courage that had saved the Christian children back in Londinium and it was her determination that had helped save the sick boy's life. They had started out with nine and they were going to end it with nine. He was about to look away when, as if reading his mind, Efa turned to look at him.

"I have spoken with my father," she said quietly," and he has agreed to place the children with families in my village who want them. They will be safe here and they will be well cared for. These are my people. They will treat the children as if they are their own." A single tear had appeared in her eye. "But none of this would have been possible without you Corbulo. All of them," she said gesturing at the children, "They all owe their lives to you and one day they will realise that."

Corbulo was silent as his thoughts turned to his ruined business and as he pictured Priscus's dead body floating down the Thames and out to sea. There had been a cost to this whole affair.

"I need a drink," he muttered.

***

Portus Sentantiorum, the port of the Setantii clustered around a small shallow bay. The round houses had been built close to the sandy beach. As Corbulo approached along the road he could see a wooden jetty jutting out into the sea. A number of small Celtic fishing boats were bobbing up and down on the waves and further along the coast in the direction of the mouth of the Wyre River he could just about make out a fortified Roman signal tower in the fading light. The tower had not been there when he had last visited. They had just reached the first round house when a Carnyx, a boar headed Celtic war trumpet, emitted a long mournful blast. The noise was followed quickly by another trumpet blast. Aidan raised his hand as a few villagers emerged from their homes and returned his greeting. As the small party headed towards two round houses that stood close together at the edge of the settlement, three girls aged around ten came racing towards them. The girls had recognised Aidan and Efa and were shouting their names in delight but as the girls noticed the children in the chariots they came to an abrupt halt and fell silent. Aidan dismounted from his horse in front of the largest of the round houses and as he did so two women appeared in the doorway.

"Efa, you are back, thank the gods," the older woman exclaimed as Efa dismounted and embraced her.

Corbulo dismounted stiffly and glanced at the children. Efa's cousins had parked the two chariots underneath a tree and the children stood huddled together like a group of ducklings that had lost their mother. Corbulo handed his horse to one of the cousins and strode towards the children and as he did so he noticed the three girls watching the newcomers curiously.

"Listen," he said placing his hands on his hips, "I've got something to say to you all. This village, this place, this is going to be your new home. You will be safe here, the people who live here are good people." He paused as he made eye contact with each one of the children. "Now I want you to promise me something, all of you. I want you to promise that you will look after each other. Your parents are dead. They are not coming back for you. Learn to love this place and these people and everything will be allright. You are the nine who survived and when I come to visit you again I want to see all nine of you alive, understood."

The children were silent as Corbulo finished his little speech. For a moment no one said a word. Then the older woman who had greeted Efa came up and beckoned to the children to follow her into the large round house. Corbulo watched them go. Then he sighed. He was about to follow when Logan appeared. The young man had a strange expression on his face.

"You will sleep over there tonight," Logan said in his thick accent as he pointed at the smaller round house. "Efa says she needs you."

Corbulo raised his eyebrows and hesitated.

"Go," Logan said gesturing with his hand.

Corbulo muttered something to himself and strode off towards the hut. The round house was made of solid wooden posts interwoven with wood, straw, soil and clay and it had a thatched roof. He pulled aside the heavy leather sheet that hung across the doorway and stepped inside. In the middle of the earthen floor an open fire was burning and the smoke was escaping through a hole in the roof. Efa lay on a bed of soft animal skins. She was stark naked.

"I want to fuck," she said.

***

It was just after dawn as Corbulo strolled along the beach. He was alone as he gazed out to sea. The fresh sea breeze was blowing into his face and above him he could hear the screeching of the sea gulls as they dived and climbed in lazy swoops searching for breakfast. Out to sea a line of grey rain clouds were heading towards him but he hardly noticed them. Something was bothering him. What did the Governor and the Procurator want from these children? The question would not go away however hard he tried to forget about it. He paused beside a pile of stones and timber beams that had been dumped close to the old wooden jetty. The authorities seemed to have started on the construction of a solid stone harbour wall but the work had barely begun. A solitary fisherman was sitting at the end of the jetty. The hunched old man sat staring vacantly at the waves as Corbulo approached. He turned and looked up as Corbulo halted behind him.

"Ah, you are the Roman who married Efa," the old man said sourly as he recognised Corbulo, "I remember your wedding. Aidan didn't agree but you did it anyway. That's how you make enemies."

Corbulo ignored the comment and gestured at the fortified Roman signal tower.

"The Hibernian and Caledonian raiders, do they still cause you trouble?"

The old fisherman glanced at the signal tower and shrugged.

"Sure, there is always trouble," he replied, "and that little fort over there with its eight man garrison is not going to make any difference. The Hibernians and Caledonians will continue to raid and take what they want. It has always been so."

Corbulo shook his head in disagreement but said nothing. What was the point in trying to explain to this old fisherman the superb network of carefully planned and positioned Roman forts that spanned the whole western coast of Britannia. A signal from the watchtower at Portus Sentantiorum would be picked up by another tower further down the coast and so on until it reached the cavalry fort at Kirkham. Thirty auxiliary cavalrymen could reach Efa's family home within two or three hours of a raid and if the Hibernians and Caledonians landed in force a signal could be sent to the cavalry fort at Bremetennacum and five hundred mounted men from the 2nd Cohort of Astures could reach Portus Sentantiorum within twelve hours. Corbulo stared at the Roman watchtower. It had been Agricola who had been mainly responsible for the layout of the Roman forts and roads and the thought of his old boss brought a wry smile to his face. Despite the huge difference in rank and class Corbulo liked to think he'd got to know the man. They had shared the same boat during the river assault on the druidic strong hold of Mona Insulis and later when Agricola had risen to become Legate of the Twentieth he had come to Corbulo's rescue when Corbulo had refused to swear loyalty to the Legion's mutinous officers. Corbulo scratched his cheeks. What would Agricola be doing now? The last time he had seen him was in Rome when he'd gone to the famous general's house to inquire about the whereabouts of Marcus, his son. That had been over two years ago.

"Would you prefer that the soldiers were not here?" Corbulo asked turning to the fisherman.

"Yes," the fisherman nodded. "We do not fear the men from across the sea," he muttered. "They raid us and burn down a house and steal some of our women but houses and women can be replaced." The old man paused. "But no one listens to me, they think I am an old fool," he grumbled, "when I warn them that one day the sea will take our whole settlement." With his hand the man made a sign over the water as if to placate the waves. "We built our homes too close to the sea and one day the water spirits will have their vengeance for such disrespect. This is what I fear," he growled.

***

Logan was busy checking up on the beehives when Corbulo stumbled upon him later that morning. The wicker hives stood in a row some distance from the civilian settlement. Bees were everywhere but Logan seemed unconcerned as he went about his work. Corbulo however kept a safe distance. Just beyond the hives the marshland crisscrossed with water channels stretched away until it reached the Wyre. In the sky birds were swooping up and down as they hunted for food above their boggy nests. The scene was peaceful. Close by, one of Aidan's sleek hunting dogs lay stretched out on the grass gazing at Logan with it's red tongue hanging out of its mouth. Corbulo folded his arms across his chest as he too watched Logan work. The noisy buzzing of the bees did not fade as Efa's brother went down the line of hives carefully checking each one. When he was done he came up to Corbulo.

"Where will you take the honey?" Corbulo asked.

Logan turned to look at the hives. "Aidan has made me master of the bees," he said with a hint of pride in his voice. "Our village is famous for our honey. Sometimes I sell it to the Romans in their watchtower but tomorrow I shall go to their fort at Kirkham, the one we passed along the road. If the bees are productive I may even go all the way to Bremetennacum. The old men don't like it, but business has been very good since you Romans came."

"Well we soldiers do have a sweet tooth," Corbulo replied.

139

"We trade with Hibernia too," Logan said as he turned to look towards the sea. "They don't always come here to raid. They sell us dogs and we give them honey and Roman wine. It's a good trade. Red Tongue over there," Logan said pointing at the dog lying in the grass, "he came from Hibernia."

Corbulo glanced at the dog.

"Aidan, your father, he still hasn't forgiven me has he?"

Logan looked down at his feet as he poked his toes into the grass. "My father will never approve of you," he said at last. "If it wasn't for the fact that you brought back his only daughter he would have killed you long ago. My father fought against the Legions when Rome first came to our lands. He will not forget that. He remembers how it was before Rome came here."

"Fair enough," Corbulo said with a sigh.

The two of them were silent for a while.

"Did my sister keep you awake last night?" Logan said as an amused smile appeared on his face.

"She did," Corbulo nodded.

"Can you tell Efa to make less noise," Logan said abruptly, "the whole village heard her last night. No one could get any sleep."

Corbulo shrugged and looked away as a little colour shot into his cheeks. For a long moment no one spoke.

"So what will you do now Corbulo?" Logan asked.

Corbulo sighed and scratched his chin. "I don't know," he exclaimed. "I cannot return to Londinium and I have lost my business."

"I like you Corbulo," Logan said in a solemn voice, "You should stay with us here in our village. I could teach you how to look after the bees and you could take Efa down to the beach where she can make all the noise she likes."

"That's a fine idea but your father would not approve," Corbulo muttered sourly.

Logan raised his hand in a dismissive gesture. "I will speak with him. It was you after all who brought Efa and Dylis back to us. I will remind him of that."

***

It was noon when Corbulo entered the round house. The nine Christian children were sitting around the open fire eating their stew. Efa was serving them from a large iron pot that hung over the fire. She gave him a happy little smile as she moved around the circle. Corbulo said nothing as he took a swig of water from a water skin and leaned back against the wall of the house. They were just children he thought as he studied them. The Emperor Domitian had a reputation as a moderate when it came to the Christians. So why were the Governor and the Procurator so persistent in their attempts to find them? Had they really nothing better to do? No, this was more than just religious persecution. Corbulo stared at the children, willing himself to find the answer. Petrus was wearing his wooden cross over his clothes in full view of everyone. The boy had changed after the struggle with Bestia in Viroconium and Corbulo had noticed that he'd started to distance himself from the others. The boy had begun to crave solitude. Corbulo turned to look at Dylis. His daughter was eating and talking excitedly with the children beside her. She looked happy and full of life. He smiled. Maybe because Efa was happy, her daughter was as well. Then his eye came to rest on Christiana. The little blond girl was listening intently to what Dylis was saying. On her back she was wearing her satchel. Corbulo blinked. In all the time he'd known Christiana he had never seen her take that satchel off her back. She had clung to it wherever she had gone. He peered at her and then slowly he opened his mouth.

"Christiana," he said abruptly, "who gave you that satchel?"

The children fell silent and turned to look at him.

"Who gave you that satchel?" Corbulo repeated.

The little girl looked embarrassed by all the sudden attention and she refused to look up at Corbulo. The room fell silent until only the crackle and hiss of the wood burning in the fire could be heard.

"My father gave it to me," Christiana said at last in a timid little voice. "He said I should look after it and I have."

Corbulo strode across the space that separated him from the children and knelt down beside Christiana. He gave her a little smile.

"Will you let me take a look at your satchel," he said. "I just want to check something. I will give it back to you, don't worry."

Christiana nodded and Corbulo gently pulled the bag off her back. The satchel was small and the opening was secured by a leather strips that had been tied into a knot. Corbulo undid them and reached inside the bag. When his hand emerged he was holding five tightly rolled scrolls.

"What's this?" he exclaimed.

No one replied. Corbulo stared at the scrolls. They looked like letters. Then he noticed the wax seals that secured the parchment. He lifted one of them up and peered at it closely. Suddenly his face grew pale.

"Well fuck me," he murmured.

***

Corbulo sat alone in the round house staring at the five parchment scrolls that lay in his lap. He looked nervous and tense. Close by, the open fire crackled and spat and the lazy smoke drifted upwards towards the hole in the roof. He had just finished reading each scroll for the third time, just to make sure he had not missed anything but now as he finally grasped the full meaning of the letters he was stunned. He turned to look at the fire shaking his head in disbelief. So this was what the Governor and the Procurator had been so desperate to retrieve? Five letters, hidden in a leather satchel, carried by a seven-year old girl who'd had no idea of their importance or existence. Corbulo stared at the flames. He understood now, it all made sense. A sudden shiver ran down his spine. He, Efa, the children and Efa's whole village were all in mortal danger. The Governor and the Procurator would not give up the search, they could not for both had become desperate men.

The heavy leather curtain that hung across the doorway was suddenly pushed aside and Efa came in. She gave her husband an inquiring look and crossed over to sit beside him.

"It's already evening," Efa said, glancing down at the scrolls, "the children cannot stay outside forever. It's going to rain soon."

"I need to speak with Christiana, can you bring her here," Corbulo said abruptly.

Efa gave him a searching look. Then silently she rose and left the house. A few minutes later she was back holding Christiana by the hand. The little girl looked nervous as she shuffled towards the fire. Efa laid a reassuring hand on the girls shoulder as she turned to look at her husband.

"Christiana," Corbulo said gently, "who was your father? What did he do?"

The girl looked down at her feet and for a moment she did not reply. "His name was Alexander. He was an important man," she said at last. "He worked in the Governor's palace in Londinium. He took me there once. We met the Governor. I didn't like him. He was so fat   and ugly and rude."

143

Corbulo nodded. "And your father gave you this satchel?"

Christiana nodded. "He gave it to me just before Efa came to fetch me. He said that I should look after it very carefully and I have."

Corbulo managed a smile. "You did well Christiana, you did very well. Your Dad would be proud of you."

"He's dead isn't he?" Christiana said.

Corbulo glanced up at Efa and gestured for her to take Christiana away. A few moments later Efa returned alone and came to sit beside him. She looked concerned.

"What do the letters say?" she inquired.

Corbulo sighed. "These letters mean trouble, a lot of trouble, more than you can imagine." Corbulo gave his wife a tense glance. "This one here, "he said picking up a scroll from his lap, "is from Lucius Antonius Saturninus, Governor of the province of Germania Superior and commander of the Fourteenth Gemina and the Twenty First Rapax Legions who are based at Monguntiacum. The letter is addressed to Governor Sallustius Lucullus of the province of Britannia. This one here is from Marcus Ulpius Traianus, Legate of the Seventh Gemina Legion in Hispania and these other three are from leading Senators in Rome. They are all addressed to Governor Lucullus and from their seals, I would say that they are genuine."

Corbulo paused and stared moodily at the fire.

"The seals were broken when I found them," he murmured, "So we are not the first to have read these letters. I bet my life savings that Christiana's father managed to read them too and that it was he who stole the letters. In Londinium Falco, the banker told me that a Christian named Alexander had stolen a letter from the Governor's palace. Why Christiana's father stole them is beyond me, he must had had his own reasons, but it

144

explains the whole sudden pogrom against the Christians back in Londinium and it also explains why the Procurator is involved."

Efa was staring at him intently. "What do the letters say?" she said.

Corbulo sighed again and turned to look at his wife. "They are plotting rebellion," he said, "the letters are discussing a revolt against the Emperor in Rome. Saturninus is driving it but he has support from many Senators and it looks like Traianus and our own Governor Lucullus have joined him. They all hate Domitian. They want him dead. There is going to be an attempt on Domitian's life soon. They don't give details but it's clear that the Senators are going to try and murder the Emperor. After that Saturninus plans to march on Rome and proclaim himself Emperor. Together with Lucullus and Traianus he will control seven Legions. Saturninus even talks about bringing in some of the Germanic tribes from across the Rhine as allies." Corbulo paused. "You can understand why the Governor is so desperate to retrieve these letters. He is a dead man if the Emperor were ever to find out about this. He will do anything to keep this a secret."

Efa was silent for a moment as she digested Corbulo's words. Then she frowned.

"I understand why the Governor wants to get these letters back," she said, "but what about the Procurator? Isn't he just in charge of money and taxes?"

"The Procurator, Classicus," Corbulo replied patiently, "may be just in charge of raising taxes but he is also Domitian's man in the province. The Procurator reports directly to the Emperor and the Emperor alone. His loyalty is to the Emperor and any threats against Domitian are very much his concern. He is the Emperor's eyes and ears and it is part of his job to keep Domitian informed of threats against his person. Classicus must somehow have got wind of what is happening but without the

145

letters he has no proof. That's why he is after them." Corbulo paused. "If this rebellion succeeds and Domitian is assassinated then the Procurator is a dead man just by his close association with the Emperor. He knows this. He too is a desperate man. The Governor and he hate each other. Classicus will be the first man to be executed if the rebellion succeeds."

Efa was staring at Corbulo in alarm.

"So we are not safe," she muttered, "the children are not safe?"

Corbulo nodded sourly. "Powerful and desperate men are the most dangerous of all men. They are going to keep on looking for us," he said quietly.

"Then we should destroy the letters," Efa exclaimed, "Throw them into the fire Corbulo, let's be done with this evil once and for all."

But Corbulo shook his head. "No," he said, "Destroying the letters will not help us. The Governor and the Procurator will never believe us. They will suspect that we have read the contents, that we are hiding the letters. They will suspect that everything around us will know about the plot. The Governor will kill us all, just as a precaution, just to keep this secret and if the Procurator finds us, the Governor will kill him too if he gets the chance."

"Then what?" Efa said, with a hint of desperation in her voice.

Corbulo turned to stare at the fire. For a long moment he remained silent.

"I don't know," he said at last, "I need to speak with Marcus about this. I will go to Luguvalium, *Carlisle,* tomorrow to discuss the matter with him. Marcus, my son has a good head, he may know what to do."

Efa looked down at the ground. Then she nodded and looked up.

"Aidan wants to see you," she said quickly, rising to her feet.

***

Corbulo frowned as he stepped into the dimly lit round house. What did his father in law want? The summons to his home was highly unusual. His head was still spinning with what he had just learned from the letters and the interruption felt unwelcome but he could hardly refuse Aidan's request. A fire was burning in the centre of the hut and shadows were playing across the walls. Aidan and Efa's two cousins were sitting at a table. In the flickering light he could see their stern, unfriendly faces watching him. Then he noticed that they were all armed. He stopped and glanced around. There was no sign of the women or children who normally lived in this house. Behind him he suddenly heard a little noise. He whirled round and saw that Logan had moved to bar the doorway through which he had just come. Efa's brother too looked hostile and he was armed. Slowly Logan folded his arms across his chest. Corbulo turned quickly to face Aidan as his hand dropped to the pommel of his sword. What was this? Were they about to try and kill him after all?

For a long moment the round house was silent. Then slowly Aidan rose to his feet and Efa's cousins did the same. Corbulo stood rooted to the ground. Aidan nodded at one of the cousins who stooped to drag something out from under the table.

"Now we shall see what kind of man you really are," Aidan snapped, staring Corbulo straight in the eye, as the other cousin slammed five crude wooden cups onto the table. Corbulo blinked in surprise as he saw one of the cousins roll a large cask into the fire light.

"We are going to drink, you and I," Aidan growled as he handed Corbulo a stool, "and the man who cannot take his mead is going to spend the night with the pigs."

Chapter Seventeen - Luguvalium

To Corbulo the barren treeless mountains were breathtakingly beautiful. He glanced up at their jagged, rocky and lofty peaks, unable to look away as he rode his horse along the bank of the river. A yellow flower he'd picked up along the way dangled on a cord around his neck. It was morning and he was alone. Three days had passed since he'd said farewell to Efa, Dylis and the children. Efa had been nervous, constantly picking at her finger nails and Dylis had cried but he'd told them not to worry. Everything would come right in the end. As for Aidan, he'd not come to say goodbye but Logan had and that had been enough. Down in the valley the land was heavily wooded, lush and green and the river swollen and fed by the little streams of melting snow water that came down the steep slopes like white veins. He'd not seen a single person all morning and he'd lost count of the number of lakes he'd seen on his journey north. The last person he'd run into, had assured him that Luguvalium, *Carlisle* was only half a day's ride away. That had been yesterday. He wrenched his gaze away from the mountain peaks and glanced at the dark forest around him. The fir trees stood close together, an impenetrable maze, the perfect hiding place for an ambush and the terrain reminded him of Caledonia. He grunted. Had it really been nearly two years since he and Marcus had fled south pursued by that bloody thirsty Caledonian vixen? How time had flown.

Marcus, his son was twenty-two. Wearily Corbulo shook his head. Marcus and he were friends now but that had not always been the case and there had been a time, after his first wife's death, when the two of them had been estranged. Corbulo felt a sudden flutter of nerves. The estrangement had been his fault. The rawness of that time had still not fully healed and he wasn't sure what to expect when he reached Luguvalium. But despite that he was looking forward to seeing his son again. He sighed and urged his horse on down the forest path. Marcus, the bastard by his first wife, had wanted to follow him into the army but because the army would not allow active soldiers to marry,

Marcus had not inherited his father's Roman citizenship and therefore had been unable to apply for the Legions. Instead the boy had been accepted into the Second Batavian Auxiliary Cohort and had fought at the battle of Mons Graupius in Caledonia under the then Governor Agricola. The last news that Corbulo had received was that his unit had been posted to the fort at Luguvalium. Corbulo raised his hand to his mouth and picked at one his remaining teeth. It had been months since he'd last seen his boy. He tapped his finger gently against the tooth. He had missed Marcus's company. The last time they'd met, at the festival of Saturnalia in the midst of winter, had been far too short.

"Come on horse," Corbulo bellowed urging the beast on down the path, "Move your lazy four legs."

***

It was morning on the next day when Luguvalium finally came into view. Corbulo brought his horse to a halt as he studied the small settlement, the most north- westerly town in the Empire and four hundred and forty three thousand paces from Londinium. The fort and the little settlement that clung to it, nestled in between the Eden and a tributary river. The place looked tranquil and the surrounding fields and forests lush, fertile and promising. It was good land. Corbulo however looked grim. This was not the first time he'd been here and the memories weren't particularly pleasant. The local Brigantian tribe led by their leader Luguvalos had refused to accept Roman rule and during the winter of seventy-two they had broken out into open rebellion. The Brigantes had put up ferocious resistance, ambushing supply columns and patrols and conducting hit and run raids on Roman settlers until finally that following spring, reinforcements from the Twentieth had managed to crush them. Governor Cerialis had been ruthless, ordering the captured tribesmen to be garrotted and Corbulo had witnessed the execution of the prisoners and had seen the scores of bodies dumped into the Eden River. The only thing that seemed to have survived from that rebellion had been

149

Luguvalos's name. Corbulo glanced uneasily at the fertile fields and distant forest. Resentment against Rome still smouldered in the hearts of many Britons who had survived the Roman conquest and if they found the right leader that resentment could easily burst out into another rebellion. There was a reason why fifty two thousand Roman soldiers and auxiliaries were needed to keep the peace in the province of Britannia. How different to Gaul where not a single Legion was needed to keep the peace.

Corbulo urged his horse up the road towards the river. The Roman fort was clearly visible. It lay just north of a small tributary river and was surrounded by the customary V shaped ditch and a timber and turf rampart from which protruded four watch towers. Close to the southern gate-house a few huts and round houses marked out the civilian settlement that had grown up around the fort. Smoke was rising up from a few of them. As he approached along the road he could hear a blacksmith at work and the noise of children playing by the river.

The wooden gates to the fort were open and a detachment of Batavians, tall blond men clad in their typical auxiliary armour and helmets and armed with flat shields and long hastae thrusting spears, were lounging about around the gateway. They peered at him warily. Corbulo raised his hand in greeting and dismounted stiffly. The Batavians said nothing as Corbulo grasped his horse by its harness and led it towards the gate.

"It's allright lads," Corbulo said, "I am here to see Marcus. He's the only red haired man amongst you so you shouldn't have any difficulty in knowing who he is."

One of the Batavians, a giant of man with piercing blue eyes came towards him.

"You mean Marcus, the Decurion?" the soldier said in a thick guttural Germanic accent.

Corbulo raised his eyebrows. "Decurion?" he muttered to himself. "Well, well."

"Who are you?" the Batavian asked.

Corbulo gave the soldiers a cautious glance. "Tell Marcus that an old friend has come to pay him a visit," he replied.

The Batavian studied Corbulo for a moment. Then he turned and gestured to one of his comrades.

"Wait here," the Batavian said.

Corbulo turned to stroke his horse gently on its nose. He had to be careful. If the Procurator or the Governor's men had already visited Luguvalium then it would be dangerous for him to use his name. He pretended to busy himself with his horse as he waited for Marcus. He was oblivious to the man watching him from the doorway of the nearby round house.

***

Marcus looked annoyed when he finally came stomping through the gate holding his helmet tucked under his arm, but his expression changed to one of weary resignation as he caught sight of his father. He was tall handsome man of twenty- two, red haired and clad in armour and a long cavalry sword, a Spatha, hung from his belt. Corbulo grinned as they briefly embraced.

"Father," Marcus acknowledged him with a stiff little nod. "What are you doing here? They told me an old friend had come to pay me a visit. Why didn't you just announce yourself?"

Corbulo glanced quickly at the Batavians who were watching them. Then he took Marcus by the arm and led him away from the gatehouse.

"Keep your voice down son," Corbulo said gently, "It's best that people don't know that I am   here."

Marcus stopped and sighed.

"You are in trouble again aren't you," he said wearily.

"No," Corbulo said defensively but Marcus shook his head. "Oh yes you are, I can tell. It's just like the old days isn't it when we had to hide the Centurion's money and pretend we hadn't seen you for a week when he came to pay us a visit. That was a lot of fun."

Corbulo broke out into an embarrassed smile. He opened his mouth to say something. Then he hesitated.

"You are right," he said quietly, "I am in trouble but it's not what you think. Come let's go for a walk, I need to talk to you."

Marcus turned to look towards the fort with a thoughtful expression.

"I should have known something was going on," he murmured. "It's a pretty lonely and remote posting up here and apart from a few despatch riders and traders we don't get many visitors, so imagine my surprise when a few days ago Gnaeus Julius Agricola, ex Governor of Britannia arrived to pay us a visit."

Corbulo's face rapidly drained of colour.

"Agricola," he exclaimed, "The Agricola?"

"Yes," Marcus said cheerfully pointing towards the fort, "he's over there. He's been staying in the commander's quarters and guess what? On the first day that he arrived he came to find me, not to ask me about my experiences in Caledonia, but to ask me if I knew where you were. He seems very keen on finding you. I think that is the only reason he has come up here. He's planning to head back south tomorrow."

"Agricola?" Corbulo muttered looking puzzled. He turned to gaze at the Batavians lounging about around the gate. "So what did you tell him?"

"I told him that you were in Londinium. That's where you live, don't you?"

Corbulo raised his eyebrows. "So what was his reaction?"

Marcus shrugged. "He didn't say anything after that, apart from to tell me that he really wanted to speak with you as soon as possible and that I was to report to him if I saw you. He wasn't too polite either. I suspect that you have done something to piss him off. He told me that he'd come a long way to find you."

Corbulo's face darkened and he muttered something to himself. Then before Marcus could say another word Corbulo was dragging him away from the fort.

"Come let's go for a walk," Corbulo snapped. "Is she still here?"

"She is," Marcus replied lowering his eyes to the ground.

The two of them strode northwards meandering in between the huts and round houses of the civilian settlement. The dull metallic ring of a blacksmith at work merged with the shrieks of playing children and the smell of pig manure was strong and heady. A couple of old women, clad entirely in black sat on little stools outside the doors of their homes squinting silently at them as they passed by. Around the back of the last hut two men were trying to repair a broken chariot. A new wheel lay in the grass waiting to be fitted. The men paid no attention to Corbulo and Marcus other than to shout at the pack of barking dogs to be quiet. The beasts had been tied to a tree and obediently fell silent as their quick, eager eyes watched Marcus and Corbulo head out across the fields towards the bridge over the Eden River.

"Jupiter's cock," Marcus swore in astonishment as Corbulo finished telling him about what had happened in Londinium and on their journey north and the discovery of the plot against the Emperor.

153

Corbulo nodded as he picked at a tooth. "The Governor and the Procurator need those letters," he muttered. "They are going to keep looking for them. Efa and the children will never be safe and neither will I until this matter is resolved. I wish I had never come across those damned scrolls but now I am stuck with them. I have to find a way out of this."

"So you killed Bestia," Marcus said staring at Corbulo with an incredulous look.

"Well I needed a bit of help," Corbulo replied sourly.

"You just can't stay out of trouble can you," Marcus said shaking his head. "So now you want my advice? Isn't it supposed to be the other way around? Shouldn't it be the son coming to the father for advice?"

"Well you can always ask me if you want," Corbulo said defensively.

Irritated Marcus held up his hand and closed his eyes.

"It's allright," he said sharply, "I can manage." He paused. "I have a woman in the town and I have a son of my own now. The boy was born a few weeks ago. I have named him Fergus, after my mother's father. I thought you should know."

Corbulo came to an abrupt halt and turned to stare at Marcus in surprise.

"You have a son?" he said quietly, "You said nothing about this when I last saw you at Saturnalia during the winter."

"Are you not pleased for me?" Marcus replied.

Corbulo opened his mouth. "Fergus," he said the name out loud. "You decided to choose a British name then for your son?"

Marcus nodded.

Corbulo frowned and looked down at the ground. For a long moment he was silent. Then he looked up and slapped Marcus against his shoulder as a broad smile appeared on his face.

"Excellent news, congratulations, Fergus, it is a good name. I would like to see him."

Marcus looked relieved. "So you shall," he said quietly, "Soon."

"And they have promoted you to Decurion."

"Yes," Marcus said as a hint of pride appeared on his face. "We lost one of the officers to illness over the winter so there was a position that needed filling. I was just lucky."

"So you didn't have to..." Corbulo made a crude gesture with his mouth and hands.

"No, of course not," Marcus said with a horrified look. "What kind of unit do you think the 2nd Batavians are?"

***

The Roman bridge across the Eden was a sturdy looking pile bridge and the fort at Luguvalium had been built to protect this important river crossing. On the southern bank a fortified watchtower had been constructed and on its upper level two auxiliaries were on guard duty. Corbulo glanced up at the soldiers as they leaned out over the wooden balustrade, staring at the river with bored expressions. Their flat shields and spears stood propped up against the wooden tower wall. Corbulo felt a sudden cool breeze on his face as he stepped out onto the bridge. The river was swollen but it was not very wide and on the northern bank the dense forest came right up to the water's edge. The gravel road vanished off to the north in a straight line disappearing over a hill. Corbulo glanced at the fast flowing river water. The last time he'd seen the Eden it had been filled with floating corpses.

"There is something else that you should know," Marcus said breaking the silence. "We have received orders. The whole Cohort, all eight hundred and fifty of us have been ordered south to Deva. We are just waiting for the Ninth Batavians to arrive to take our place before we leave."

"Why, what's happening at Deva?" Corbulo said.

"I don't really know," Marcus muttered, "but there is a rumour that a battle group is being formed for an invasion of Hibernia. They say the 2nd Batavians are going to be part of it."

Corbulo grunted in surprise.

"Well well, maybe our Governor has got more balls than I thought," he replied. "It makes sense I suppose, we can't just allow Elim the Hibernian High King to mock us and freely grant asylum to the enemies of Rome."

"Apparently they want to teach the Hibernians a lesson," Marcus said, "The raids on our coast have increased in the past year. It's got to stop."

"Yes," Corbulo said, "I have heard talk of this."

They reached the northern bank and Corbulo paused to take a deep breath. For a moment he stared down at the ground. Then he glanced at Marcus but his son looked away. A strange tension seemed to settle over them as they silently started up the road. A little way from the riverbank beside a small rise in the ground Corbulo halted and turned towards the forest. A few paces from the roadside but still with a clear view of the river stood a solitary gravestone. Corbulo sighed as he knelt down beside the grave and gently touched the stone with his fingers. Behind him he could sense Marcus watching him. The sandstone had an engraving in it and Corbulo read it out loud.

"To the spirits of the departed. Here lies Alene a much-loved mother and wife. Like you are, I was. Like I am, you will be. This memorial was erected by Marcus and Corbulo."

Corbulo fell silent as he looked upon the grave of his first wife. He and Marcus had agreed that if they managed to escape from Caledonia they would erect a gravestone to her and Marcus had decided that it should be here at Luguvalium with a view of the river so that her spirit could find its way home. Corbulo reached inside his tunic and retrieved the yellow flower he'd plucked on his way to Luguvalium and placed it beside the stone. Then he rose to his feet and turned to look at Marcus.

"I am sorry," he said, "She did not deserve her fate. But I hope her spirit rests freely now and that she forgives me."

Marcus nodded silently and turned to look at the river.

The sudden snorting of a horse made both Corbulo and Marcus turn round. Two horsemen clad in long black cloaks sat on their beasts at the edge of the forest just across the road. Corbulo took a step in their direction, hesitated and laid his hand on the pommel of his sword. The two riders did not move. They looked like men who knew how to fight. Then more hooded horsemen emerged from the forest. One of the men urged his horse straight towards Corbulo. The beast's hooves clattered on the stone paving stones of the road and beside him Corbulo sensed Marcus reach for his sword. Quickly he raised his hand in warning.

"No, son," he said quietly.

"Well well so I was right after all," the hooded stranger said in perfect Latin, "find the son, find the father. So this long journey has not been a huge waste of time after all."

The man flung back his hood. "Remember me?" he exclaimed.

Corbulo stood his ground. For a moment he did not reply. "Yes Sir I do," Corbulo said at last, "You are still the same prick who nearly had us all killed at Mona Insulis and who sent my son into the trackless wastes of Caledonia."

"Good to see you too Corbulo," Agricola snapped with a faint grin. "But you forget that it was I as Legate of the Twentieth and your commanding officer who saved your hairy arse in the year of the four Emperors."

The ex Governor of Britannia and victor of Mons Graupius looked slightly fatter than when Corbulo had last seen him in Rome two years ago. The man was in his late forties with short black-hair, clean-shaven cheeks and his keen, intelligent eyes took in every detail. To his right and left, Agricola's men walked their horse's forwards until Corbulo and Marcus were surrounded.

"You are far from home Sir. What do you want from me?" Corbulo said.

"Oh I think you know what I want," Agricola snapped. "If it wasn't for you and that great bleeding heart of yours I would still be enjoying the sun on my estates in Gallia Narbonensis."

Corbulo shrugged and turned to Marcus.

"Do you know what the fuck he's talking about?"

Marcus did not reply. His hand was on the pommel of his sword as he was staring tensely at the riders around them.

"Stop playing games Corbulo," Agricola said, "We know you helped those Christian children to escape from Londinium. We know that one of those children was carrying letters stolen from Governor Lucullus's palace. We know that you have those scrolls. I want them back and I want them now."

"Well you have been busy," Corbulo snapped, "But how do you know all this? Who has been

158

feeding you all this information?"

"Governor Sallustius Lucullus," Agricola said as a note of anger entered his voice, "He told me everything. One of the Christians in the Governor's prison killed himself before he could be interrogated but Lucullus suspected that he had passed the letters on to his daughter. She was one of the children that you helped escape. The rest of the information was obtained by Lucullus's men. How they managed to do that is not my concern. I am just here for the letters. Now give them to me and you will walk away with your lives."

Corbulo stared at Agricola, his face suddenly emotionless.

"Well I am sorry but I can't do that Sir," Corbulo said quietly, "You see a good friend of mine, who had nothing to do with this, was murdered by the Governor's men, the same men who came looking for those scrolls. It's a matter of honour Sir. If I give you those letters without anything in return I will be spitting on his grave."

"So you have them," Agricola growled with a hint of triumph.

"Yes," Corbulo nodded angrily, "I have the Governor's letters, all five of them. Letters that talk openly about rebellion and assassinating the Emperor. But do you think that I am so stupid as to carry them around on me?" Corbulo took a step forwards and pointed an angry finger at Agricola. "If anything happens to me or Marcus and we do not show up within the next ten days a very good friend of mine has instructions to hand the letters personally to the Procurator. That's when the shit really starts to fly Sir. So you dare lay a finger on me and Marcus and the Governor and his pals are not going to be very pleased with you."

Agricola was staring at Corbulo. Then he frowned.

"Five letters you say," Agricola muttered, "Five not six? Are you sure? Six letters were stolen   from the Governor's palace."

Corbulo lowered his finger.

"Well fuck me," Corbulo muttered as the realisation finally dawned. He looked up at Agricola, his eyes sparkling.

"You are in on the plot against the Emperor," Corbulo gasped, "You wrote the sixth letter didn't you? That's why you are so desperate to get it back. That's why you have returned to Britannia. You are planning to join the rebellion against Domitian."

Agricola did not reply but as he stared at Corbulo a little smile appeared on his face.

"I remember that you were always a most loyal soldier," Agricola said. "Even when all your comrades were in open mutiny you did not join them. I wonder if you are still that same man Corbulo?"

Corbulo spat onto the ground. Then he looked up at Agricola.

"I am no longer a soldier," he replied. "I have a wife, a daughter, Marcus here has become a father." Corbulo paused and studied Agricola for a moment. "But despite being a prick you always treated me fairly and I can't say that I ever served a better general than you Sir. So now you and I are going to make an agreement. I will give you the five letters and I will promise you, on my honour as a veteran of the Twentieth that I will not reveal a word about your plot. In exchange you will speak with the Governor and he will agree to release any remaining Christian prisoners he still has in his jails and he will abandon the search for the children who I brought out of Londinium. Those children deserve to be left in peace. They have suffered enough. They are not to be touched, understood Sir?"

Agricola raised his eyebrows and glanced in the direction of Luguvalium.

"The Governor will also agree to pay a sum of one thousand Denarii to each child as compensation for the murder of their parents and families," Marcus interrupted.

Surprised Corbulo turned to look at Marcus. His son was staring at Agricola with a fierceness and anger that Corbulo had never seen before.

Agricola seemed to be considering the deal. Then abruptly he nodded.

"It seems fair," he said, "I shall speak with the Governor. Lucullus is at Deva over seeing the preparations for his Hibernian adventure." Agricola paused and suddenly his face darkened.

"So you are sure that you only have five letters?" he growled. "You wouldn't be lying to me would you now Corbulo?"

Corbulo shook his head. "I am telling you the truth," he replied.

"So who has the sixth letter, the one I wrote to Lucullus?" Agricola barked angrily.

Corbulo looked down at his feet. Then a little colour shot into his cheeks as it all began to make sense. He looked up sharply. Should he tell Agricola? His old generals life was at stake after all if the Procurator got hold of that letter. Suddenly Corbulo was torn between two competing loyalties. He rubbed his eyes and sighed wearily.

"Do you remember a Centurion in the Twentieth called Quintus?" he said.

Agricola nodded. "I remember him, he was a good officer."

"Quintus is a good friend of mine," Corbulo said. "and several weeks ago I discovered that he'd become a Christian. The Governor's men were out looking for him and I understand why now. The Christian community in Londinium was very small.

They must have all known each other. Quintus has your letter. The Christian druid, Alexander, the one who stole the letters in the first place, he must have given his daughter the five letters for safekeeping and given yours to Quintus. Don't ask me why."

"Where is he?" Agricola said quickly.

Corbulo blew the air from his cheeks and turned to look to the west.

"I heard he fled to Hibernia," he replied. "Probably because possessing your letter made it too dangerous for him to remain in Londinium. He would be a dead man if he had stayed."

Agricola turned to look west and for a moment he said nothing. Then slowly he turned to Corbulo.

"You will meet me at Deva in ten days," he said angrily, "and bring the letters or else you too are a dead man. I want those damned letters."

Then without waiting for an answer he signalled to his men and the riders cantered away towards the bridge. Corbulo watched them go. Then when the last of the riders had vanished he glanced towards Marcus. The young man was stroking his chin tensely.

"Well that didn't work out too bad," Corbulo said trying to sound cheerful.

"The Governor will never agree;" Marcus murmured, "He will kill you before he concludes an agreement."

"Well we shall see," Corbulo replied cheerfully fumbling for something inside his tunic. "Here, hold these for a moment will you," he said handing Marcus five tightly rolled scrolls.

Chapter Eighteen - Corbulo's Dilemma

Corbulo emerged from the tavern looking tired and grumpy. It was just after dawn and he'd had very little sleep. The timber ramparts of Deva Victrix, the Legionary fort housing the Second Adiutrix, were just down the street from the tavern where he'd managed to get himself a room. But as he made his way southwards towards the bridge across the Dee River, Corbulo gave the fortress scant notice. He had arrived around midnight, tired, aching and dirty after his long journey from Luguvalium and looking forward to a hot meal and a good sleep in a soft bed. Instead what he'd got was the tavern's leftover food and the noise of the whores at work. The noise had gone on for hours.

He strode on down the path between the huts and thatched round houses of the civilian settlement. Smoke was drifting upwards from a nearby hut and a little way off he could hear the barking of dogs and the crowing of a cock. He glanced at the faces of the civilians and Legionaries going about their daily business, hoping perhaps to catch sight of a familiar face but he recognised no one. Deva however was flourishing. He could see it in the number of new tradesman's shops and factories. It was still dawn but the shops were already open and from their crude advertising hoardings written in appalling Latin he could see what they were advertising. A few Legionaries were haggling with a wool trader. As Corbulo pushed on down the muddy track towards the river a slave girl came out of one of the round houses and dumped a pile of clothes into a washing vat. Close by a boy of around two, watched Corbulo curiously from a doorway and a little further along a man was lying beside the road snoring loudly and covered in his own vomit. Corbulo scratched at the stubble on his cheek. Five years he had spent living in this place and he knew the town like the back of his hand. It was here in their little wooden, turf and thatch house beside the river that Marcus had grown into adulthood. It was here too, soon after he had retired from the Twentieth, that his first wife had killed herself. He lowered his eyes and muttered a little prayer to rid himself of the memory of that horrible day.

The place he was looking for was close to the river. Just outside the town in a small copse of trees he halted and crouched, turning to look back the way he'd come but he could see no one. The path was empty. Behind him he could hear the murmur of the river and in the trees birds were in full song welcoming back the sun. He peered around him but saw nothing unusual. He seemed to be alone. Satisfied that he had not been followed he rose and picked his way through the trees until he came to a tangle of brambles. He muttered something to himself as he knelt down beside the simple white altar stone. The damn thing was still here. No one though had bothered to look after the stone for it was covered in bird shit and surrounded by weeds. He rubbed some of the dirt away and quietly read the inscription.

"To the guardian spirit of the Twentieth Legion, Corbulo fulfilled his vow."

A little smile appeared on his face. He had paid for and had erected this altar stone the day after he had been discharged from the Legion after twenty-five years-service. For a moment he stared at the stone. Then quickly he began to dig into the earth. When he had created a shallow hole he slipped his hand into his tunic and brought out the piece of brown leather, which he had wrapped around the five scrolls. Carefully he placed the letters at the bottom of the hole and then laid his money-bag beside them before covering them all with earth. When he was finished he rose and glanced about. He wasn't supposed to meet Agricola until tomorrow but it was wise not to take any chances.

***

The fortress of Deva Victrix stood on top of a stone bluff overlooking a sharp bend in the river. Corbulo took a deep breath as he paused to stare at the Legionary base. The fort had been named after the goddess of the River Dee. It was a good name he thought and it had been placed in a superb location, separating the Brigantes to the north from the Ordovices to the west and at the same time providing access to the sea through the river. The fortress was substantially larger than the other Legionary bases and Agricola had intended it to be the starting point for an invasion of Hibernia, which apart from a few reconnaissance missions, had never happened. The massive timber and earth ramparts, twenty feet wide were protected by a muddy waterlogged, V shaped ditch. A detachment of Legionaries, wearing their distinctive helmets with wide cheek guards and clad in Lorica Segmentata armour, were on guard duty outside the gate. Corbulo approached one of the men and hailed him.

"Say, friend," Corbulo said cheerfully, "how about you let a veteran from the Twentieth pass. I want to have a wash and you lot have the only decent baths in town."

The Legionary regarded him coolly.

"You can have a wash in the river," the soldier replied gesturing for Corbulo to move on.

Corbulo however refused to budge. After all the days spent in the saddle and on the road he needed a bath, a proper bath.

"Come on, do a favour for a veteran. I spent five years here," he said showing the man the coin that was stuck to the palm of his hand.

The Legionary looked away. Then he grasped Corbulo's outstretched hand taking the coin in the process.

"Allright go," the soldier murmured quickly.

Corbulo did not hesitate as he slipped through the gateway and into the camp. He had learned long ago that in the army, if you wanted something, all you had to do was bribe the right people.

165

The camp was full of activity and Corbulo immediately noticed that something odd was going on. The Legionaries, some clothed in just their plain white tunics were everywhere, preparing their breakfasts, doing their morning exercises and going about their business but parked along the side of the street was a long column of four wheeled wagons. The column seemed to stretch all the way to the ramparts at the far end of the camp some seven hundred yards away. As Corbulo strode on by he could see the men loading the wagons with supplies and kit.

"What's going on?" he asked a Legionary who was lifting amphorae into the back of one of the wagons. The man gave Corbulo a hurried glance.

"Haven't you heard the news," the soldier replied, "We're moving out. The whole Legion is being transferred to the Danube."

Corbulo grunted in surprise. Of course, he'd forgotten. So the sea captain he'd spoken to in Viroconium had been right. The Second Adiutrix was leaving Britannia.

"When do you go?" Corbulo asked as the soldier heaved another amphora into the back of the wagon.

"As soon as the Twentieth arrives to take our place," the man gasped. "They are already on their way south from Caledonia."

Corbulo moved on up the street in the direction of the Principia. So the Twentieth were abandoning their fortress at Inchtuthil. The camp must have been barely completed. He shook his head in dismay. It had been less than three years since Agricola had destroyed the Caledonian confederation and conquered their lands and now Domitian was giving it all up without a fight. The Emperor was undoing all Agricola's hard work. Corbulo spat into the gutter. No wonder his former commander wanted Domitian removed. The army too would not be happy about this. The strategic move could only embolden the Caledonian tribes.

On both sides of the street the long and narrow wattle and daub barracks blocks stood in ordered endless rows. Close to the Principia, the Legion's HQ and where the Legate had his quarters and the Legion's eagle was kept, he could see the Legion's granaries and a large and strange looking elliptical building. Corbulo frowned. He had not seen that building before. It looked odd and out of place amongst the familiar and standard army constructions. Corbulo shifted his gaze. Up ahead he could see the baths complex. It was a large square building made of stone and around eighty yards by eighty. A queue of Legionaries had formed at the entrance. Corbulo joined the end and waited patiently for his turn. As he glanced casually at the Legionaries around him he was suddenly overcome by melancholy. He had missed the army life. Grumpily he picked at a tooth. But this was no time for melancholy he thought. He had to plan for the future. He would meet Agricola, do the deal with the Governor, hand over the letters and then head back to Efa and Dylis and after that he would return to Londinium and try and rebuild his stone trading business. All he had to do was to stick to that plan.

***

The Caldarium, the hot room in the baths, was so steamy that Corbulo could not see the far wall. Stark naked he waddled over towards the edge of the pool. He'd left his sword and boots with the slaves at the entrance and he'd paid them the small sum to have all his clothes washed. The slaves had assured him that the job would be done by the time he emerged from the baths. Cautiously he poked a foot into the water. It was hot, very hot. He glanced around him and was surprised to see that there were only three others bathers. The Legionaries it seemed had other things on their mind than spending much time at the baths. The bathers were occupying three of the corners of the bath and did not seem to have noticed him. Corbulo felt the sweat starting to run down his face. He sat down at the edge of the bath and lowered his legs into the water. The heat was fantastic. For a moment, lost in thought, he stared at the fine mosaic that decorated the floor of the pool. Then he cupped his penis in his hand and frowned as he examined his balls. It was still there, a swelling on his scrotum. He had first noticed it at Portus Sentantiorum. He sighed and wiped the sweat from his forehead and slowly slipped into the pool until only his head was above the water. The steam was making him drowsy and he closed his eyes.

When he opened his eyes again the three bathers had vanished. He turned just as two men slipped into the pool along the far end and Corbulo's eyes widened in shock as he recognised one of them. It was Agricola. The ex Governor of Britannia splashed some water across his own face and leaned back against the edge of the bath as he fixed his eye on Corbulo. At his side his companion, a pale-faced man of around thirty with long flowing black hair examined Corbulo coolly.

"Good to see you again Corbulo," Agricola muttered, "don't worry no one is going to disturb us. I have a man outside the door. Come it's time to talk."

Corbulo peered towards the exit but the steam prevented him from seeing more than a few yards. He turned to face Agricola.

"We were supposed to meet tomorrow," he growled. "I haven't had a decent bath in weeks and now you show up."

"The Governor has agreed to the deal," Agricola said ignoring Corbulo's retort. "He will receive you tonight at his HQ. You will bring the letters and he will grant you and the Christian children an official pardon."

"And ten thousand Denarii, or else you get nothing," Corbulo interrupted.

Agricola's face darkened.

"We settled on one thousand per child, that's nine thousand," he retorted.

"Yes, well I have expenses," Corbulo snapped. "It's ten thousand or the letters go straight to the Procurator."

With an irritated gesture Agricola waved his hand in the air. "It's of no concern," he replied, "The Governor agrees to your terms," Agricola paused to mop the sweat from his face. Then he fixed his eye once more upon Corbulo and there was a sudden ruthlessness in his manner.

"The Governor may have agreed to your little deal but I do not," he said sharply. "The letter that I wrote to the Governor is still missing and I want it back. So here is what is going to happen. You, Corbulo, are going to go to Hibernia to retrieve my letter. I have arranged for you to have a position on the Legate's staff when his battle group sails for Hibernia. Officially you will be an advisor with no authority and no responsibility, exempt from all duties. Your sole task will be to find your friend, Quintus and bring him and my letter back to me here at Deva. I don't care if you bring your friend back dead or alive but I want to see his body and I want my letter, understood?"

Corbulo was staring at Agricola. For a long moment the Caldarium was silent. Then Corbulo wiped the sweat from his brow.

"And if I refuse?" he said quietly.

Agricola's eyes flashed dangerously. "You don't want to do that Corbulo," he hissed. "The 2nd Batavians will be heading south soon. When they get here I suggest that you ask your son Marcus where his woman and newborn son are?"

Corbulo felt a lump appear in his throat. He stared across the pool at Agricola.

"What have you done with them?" he said.

169

Agricola shook his head.

"They are under my protection, they are my hostages," he said. "But if you fail in your mission they will die. I will cut their throats myself. I want my letter back Corbulo and I don't care how many men have to die before I get it."

Corbulo felt a bead of sweat trickling down his neck. Agricola was not bluffing. He could hear it in the man's voice. Agricola was desperate. If the Emperor ever got his hands on that letter then Agricola and his entire family were dead. For a long moment no one spoke.

"Does Marcus know what has happened to his woman and son?" Corbulo said at last.

"No," Agricola replied.

"So why me?" Corbulo said angrily, "You could send a hundred men to Hibernia to look for Quintus. Why pick on me?"

"Yes I could do that," Agricola replied, "but you are his friend, his blood brother. If I sent a hundred men he would run and hide. But he trusts you. You are his friend after all. He has no reason to suspect you. Your friendship will allow you to get close and fulfil your mission."

"Quintus is not to be harmed," Corbulo said quickly, "If I can find him and persuade him to come back with me, he is not to be harmed."

Agricola shook his head. "I cannot make any promises," he replied.

"You are an arsehole, you know that, a complete dick," Corbulo grunted.

"I don't give a shit," Agricola retorted. "You are going to bring Quintus and my letter to me and don't think about playing games Corbulo. The Procurator has no army and Domitian is far away in Rome. You would do well to side with us. I advise you to choose your friends carefully."

Corbulo raised two fingers in the air. "Shove these up your arse," he snapped. "If anything happens to my son's family I will be coming for you Sir. There won't be a place in this world where you can hide from me."

"Just do your job," Agricola sneered, "You have a month. I will be waiting for you here at Deva." Agricola glanced at his longhaired companion. The man had remained silent throughout and was watching Corbulo with barely concealed contempt.

"This here is Tuathal Techtmar son of the deposed High King of Hibernia," Agricola growled. "He and his men are accompanying the expedition to Hibernia. Once you are ashore, you can come to him for anything you need. I am his patron. He is my man, understood."

Corbulo turned to stare at Tuathal and took an instinctive dislike to the man. There was something untrustworthy in the man's demeanour.

"That's right," Tuathal said in his strange Celtic accent, "But when we take Tara I shall be the new High King and you boy, should you need anything, will go down on your knees before asking for it."

***

His damp freshly washed clothes clung uncomfortably to his skin as he swayed down the street towards the river and harbour front. Corbulo however did not feel the damp cloth. There was a pained, sombre expression on his face. The western part of Deva, between the Legionary fortress and the river was heavily urbanised and the thatched homes had been packed closely together. He pushed his way through the throng of people coming up from the quays along the river oblivious to the advertising cries of the merchants, the haggling women, screaming babies and barking dogs. To his right he caught a glimpse of the small circular wooden amphitheatre where as a soldier he had spent so much time and money gambling on the cock fights but now as he passed by he hardly gave the place a second glance.

The cruel dilemma he faced was weighing on him. Agricola was forcing him to choose between his family and his friend. Quintus however was not a just a friend, he was a blood brother. The two of them had known each other since their first days with the Twentieth, over twenty-five years ago. They had shared an assault boat at Mona where Corbulo had saved his younger friends life and they had stood together in the line during the decisive battle against the Barbarian Queen. The comradeship between Brothers in Arms sometimes ran deeper than that between a man and his wife or a man and his family. In his time Corbulo had known many soldiers who had chosen to be buried with their comrades rather than with their own families. He sighed and glanced up at the sky. Grey rain clouds had appeared in the west. No, he could not betray Quintus's trust, he knew it in his heart, they had been through too much together. Corbulo emitted a little painful moan. But neither could he betray Marcus. He had already caused his son too much grief. The beatings he'd subjected Marcus too when he was younger and the way he'd treated his first wife had rent father and son apart for over three years. He had only just managed to restore that friendship and trust. No, he could not and would not be responsible for the death of Marcus's woman and baby son. If Marcus ever found out he would never want anything more to do with his father.

He started down the steep slope towards the waterfront and as he did so he gasped as he caught sight of the ships of all sizes that lay anchored along the river. There had to be over a hundred vessels. He stopped to stare at the galleys. Here then was the invasion fleet that would take Roman arms to Hibernia. As he approached the quayside he could see that the harbour was full of activity. Soldiers, sailors, labourers and slaves were everywhere loading supplies and horses onto the ships. Officers

172

and captains were supervising the loading and the whole harbour area was filled with voices, shouts, curses and commands. As he stood staring at the scene Corbulo's shoulders slumped. The invasion was going to take place and he had no choice but to accompany it. An overwhelming feeling of hopelessness came over him. Soon he would have to act and if Quintus refused to return with him or hand over the letter he would be forced to choose between a blood brother and family. He felt a bead of sweat run down his neck. Had it really come to this? Would he really have to force Quintus to return with him or worse kill him if he refused to go? How could he do such a thing? What wicked fate had made him face such a dilemma?

***

Corbulo had never been inside the military HQ of the Legionary fortress. The strange newly built elliptical stone building that he had noticed that morning was large, beautifully constructed and spacious and as he followed the guards inside the noise of his boots on the floor echoed off the walls. The high ceiling of the central hall rested on two intersecting arches and in the centre of thc hall were twelve alcoves containing stone images of Roman gods. A small group of men were waiting for him. Corbulo recognised Agricola and Governor Lucullus at once. Tuathal the pale-faced Hibernian Prince was standing beside his patron and another man, a stern grey haired officer of around fifty was at the Governor's side. From his armour and fine arms bands and rings Corbulo could tell that the man hailed from a wealthy family.

Lucullus was the first to speak. The Governor of Britannia was overweight and seemed to be trying to conceal the fact by wearing a large white toga. He gave Corbulo a terse examination.

"So you are the man who has caused me all this trouble?" he muttered. "Well do you have my letters?"

Corbulo said nothing as he handed over the five scrolls. The Governor took them eagerly and quickly examined each one. When he was satisfied he slipped the letters into the folds of his toga and shook his head.

"You could have avoided all of this unpleasantness," he said with a hint of irritation. He glanced across at Agricola. "I have however been informed that you served the Twentieth well, that you were a good and loyal soldier, so I am prepared to pardon you and your family and those Christian children whom you helped escape from Londinium. I personally have nothing against Christians but when a man's confidence is betrayed he must be harsh. I cannot be weak; if the people think that I am weak the whole province will explode into rebellion."

Corbulo was staring at the Governor.

"The money, the children were promised compensation," he said quietly.

Lucullus sighed, raised his hand and snapped his fingers. A few moments later a slave appeared holding a bag. He handed it to Corbulo who undid the leather bindings and peered inside.

"It's all there, you don't have to count it," the Governor said in annoyed voice.

Corbulo stared at the coins glinting at him from inside the bag. It was poor compensation for what the children had lost but it was better than nothing. He closed the bag and fastened the bindings.

The Governor was watching him as he looked up.

"So now that we have concluded our business," the Governor hissed pointing a finger at Corbulo, "I never want to see you again."

And with that Lucullus turned on his heel and strode away. Corbulo watched him leave. Then slowly he turned to Agricola and as he did so he shook his head.

"You are such a fucking prick," he said quietly.

Agricola's face seemed set in granite but it was Tuathal who spoke first. The Hibernian prince took a step towards Corbulo and with a speed that caught him by surprise he rammed his fist into Corbulo's stomach. Corbulo collapsed onto his knees in a moan of agony.

"Don't you ever talk to my patron like that again," Tuathal snarled, "By the gods, boy, when I reach Tara I am going to have your friend Quintus torn to pieces by my dogs if he doesn't reveal what happened to that letter."

Corbulo groaned as he clutched at his stomach. Tuathal raised his hand to strike Corbulo over the head.

"That's enough," the grey haired officer barked suddenly and the authority in his voice was enough to make Tuathal hesitate. On the ground Corbulo gasped and managed to stagger back up onto his feet.

"So you are the useless mouth that my friend Agricola here has lumped me with," the officer said glaring at Corbulo with a stern expression.

Corbulo groaned and gritted his teeth.

"Who the fuck are you?" he gasped.

"My name is Trebonius, Lucius, Metellus Trebonius, I am the Legate of the Twentieth and commander of the battle group that will shortly be sailing for Hibernia and you will address me as Sir," the officer said sharply. "As of now you are back in the army and subject to military discipline."

Then the grey haired officer leaned forwards and peered at Corbulo.

"Do I know you?" he said in an exasperated voice. "You look vaguely familiar."

Corbulo took a deep breath and massaged his stomach.

"Perhaps you saw my hairy arse in the line when we defeated the Barbarian Queen," he muttered, "I served the Twentieth for twenty five years Sir, third Cohort, Julius's century. I was the watch commander."

A look of grudging respect briefly appeared in Trebonius's eyes. Then the Legate looked away.

"So you were there on that day. So was I," he replied.

Chapter Nineteen - The Battle Group Trebonius

The harbour was packed with soldiers. Long queues of heavily laden Legionaries were embarking onto the troop transports. The men stood in single files weighed down by their armour, helmet, weapons, rations, supplies and personal kit as they waited patiently for their turn to board the ships. The soldiers had placed their large red rectangular shields against their legs and their Pilum's, throwing spears had been strapped to their back and each man was clutching two, six feet long, wooden stakes that had been sharpened at the end. The Legionaries were quiet and there seemed to be no appetite for the marching songs, which they had so lustily sung when the Twentieth had come marching into Deva Victrix a few days earlier. Beside the galleys the Legionary officers clustered together in small groups watching the embarkation. Further along the water front Corbulo could hear the shouts and nervous neighing of the cavalry horses as they were led onto the transports, one horse at a time. The journey across the sea towards a hostile coast seemed to be weighing on everyone's mind. Beyond the lines of Roman Legionaries, a queue of Syrian archers were boarding their galleys. The Syrians too were each clutching two sharpened wooden stakes and they had slung their bows and quivers over their shoulders. They were small men with olive coloured skin and black hair and they seemed to be keeping themselves to themselves. Corbulo peered at them keenly. These then had to be the men belonging to the First Cohort of Hamian Archers. Corbulo had never heard of this auxiliary unit before but the Legate's staff officers had told him that the Hamians were amongst the finest bowmen in the Empire and that they had only arrived in Britannia from their home province of Syria a few months ago.

Corbulo pushed his way through the throngs of Roman soldiers towards the section of quayside that had been reserved for the Second Batavian Cohort. Five large troop transports lay at anchor in the river, one next to the other, as if they were building a bridge across the Dee. The Batavians were shuffling onto the ships across the narrow deck planks that had been laid out in between the galleys. The sailors and rowers onboard the vessels were leaning over the sides of their ships watching the embarkation. Corbulo caught sight of a small group of Batavian officers and veered towards them. He recognised the commanding officer from his uniform and helmet.

"Sir," Corbulo said snapping out a quick salute, "I am looking for one of your Decurion's. His name is Marcus; he's got red hair. Do you know where I can find him?"

The Prefect of the Second Batavians was a tall thin man with a white scarf tied around his neck to stop his armour from chafing. He glanced at Corbulo and nodded.

"He's over there making sure those sailors don't mishandle my horses," the officer replied gesturing in the direction of the horse transports.

Corbulo saluted and strode away in the direction that the officer was pointing. He didn't have much time. Trebonius, the battle group commander had ordered his staff not to leave their galley but Corbulo had slipped ashore nevertheless. He had to see Marcus before they sailed. The Second Batavians had only arrived at Deva yesterday and there had been simply no time to see his son. He glanced up at the sky as he pushed his way through the queues of soldiers. It was an hour or so after dawn and a gentle breeze was coming up from the south. The four hundred and fifty or so cavalry mounts had been herded together into a makeshift pen with wooden fences. Slaves were leading the animals by their harnesses over the deck planks and onto the transports. Clumps of horse shit lay everywhere. The horses were nervous and a group of Batavians were trying their best to calm the beasts down. They were talking to them in their guttural native Germanic language and amongst them was Marcus.

"Decurion?" Corbulo said snapping out another salute.

Marcus turned, saw him and frowned.

"Father," Marcus said stiffly as he came towards him. "What are you doing here? Why are you in armour?"

Corbulo managed a little smile and the two men embraced briefly and awkwardly.

"Well believe it or not I am back in the army," Corbulo said looking away, "Agricola has managed to get me a position on the Legate's staff. So I am going with you to Hibernia. How about that son?"

Marcus shook his head. He looked exhausted and worn out and his face was blackened and covered in dust and grime.

"Why does Agricola want you to go to Hibernia?" Marcus said sharply.

Corbulo waved the question away. "Fuck knows," he murmured. "But I am sailing with the HQ Company." Corbulo paused and then patted Marcus affectionately on the shoulder. "Just wanted to see you before we sail. Is everything allright? The men seem to be in good shape and spirits?"

Marcus turned to glance at the horses.

"No, things are not allright," he said tensely. "After you left, something terrible happened. My woman and Fergus have vanished. I have looked for them everywhere. I don't know what has happened to them." Marcus turned to look at his father with a worried and worn out look. "How can they just vanish like that? I asked nearly everyone in Luguvalium, but no one knows anything." Marcus took a deep breath. "My woman, she is not the kind that will simply leave without saying anything. No, something has happened to her. I should be out looking for her but now I am on my way to fucking Hibernia. That miserable island is the very last place that I want to go to."

Corbulo lowered his eyes and   sighed.

"That's bad fortune, son," he murmured, "bad fortune but you will find her and your son. You know how women can be? She probably needs some time on her own. They can go a bit crazy after giving birth."

Marcus fixed Corbulo with an angry look.

"So you are an expert on women now are you," Marcus retorted. "No, I think someone has taken her and Fergus, I really do."

Corbulo scratched his cheek and glanced at the horses.

"You will find them both," he muttered, "I shall offer a prayer to the gods tonight for their safe return. I suggest that you do the same."

Moodily Marcus looked away. Then at last he nodded.

Corbulo was about to say something else when the harbour was shaken by a great trumpeting roar. Everyone turned to look in the direction from which the bellowing roar had come and there, striding down the steep slope from the Legionary fortress, surrounded by a gaggle of armed attendants, was a solitary elephant. As Corbulo and Marcus stared at the big grey beast, the elephant lifted its trunk high into the air and shook its massive ears and bellowed again.

"What is that doing here?" Corbulo exclaimed.

"We are taking it with us to Hibernia," Marcus said tersely," the officers think that the beast is going to scare the shit out of the Hibernians. It's pretty certain that they will never have seen such an animal. They will probably think it's a god."

Corbulo stared at the elephant for a moment longer. Then he turned and gripped Marcus by the shoulder and managed a faint smile.

"I will see you Hibernia," he said.

***

The prow of the Neptune rose and crashed back down into the waves as the galley ploughed through the choppy sea. The southern breeze had picked up during the course of the morning and now it filled the ship's sails until they were bulging and straining at their moorings. The ship creaked and groaned as the captain kept her heading due west. Corbulo stood beside the mast gripping it tightly with one hand. He took a deep breath as he steadied himself for the next pitching roll. Gods he hated ships and the sea. It was not a natural environment for a man, especially a Legionary laden down by eighty-five pounds of equipment. The sentiment seemed to be shared by most of the officers and men in the HQ company who stood crammed together on the deck with nowhere else to go. The stiff breeze could not extinguish the smell from the dozens of men who were being seasick. The crests of the waves were white and now and then a large rogue wave would slam into the galley sending a blast of freezing seawater cascading onto the deck. The galley's captain had ordered the oars to be brought inside the ship and the rowers were sitting and lying about on their benches chatting, eating and sleeping.

To either side of the Neptune the invasion fleet of over a hundred galleys, warships, troop transports, horse transports and supply ships had formed into three neat lines, one following the other. There was no sign of land and the skies were grey and overcast. Corbulo stared at the ships and their white bulging sails as they pitched and rose through the waves and despite his discomfort he felt a stirring of pride and admiration. Agricola had dreamed of invading Hibernia but had never managed it but now that long planned invasion was about to become a reality. Corbulo had attended the final council of war in Deva before they had sailed and had heard Agricola warn the assembled officers about the Hibernian High King Elim and his fierce hatred of Rome. Elim too had a personal grudge against Agricola for it was under his Governorship that the son of the deposed High King, Tuathal Techtmar had been granted Roman protection and the first plans to invade Hibernia had been drafted. Elim will defend his land and people with all his might and cunning Agricola had warned the officers. Do not underestimate him. He is a formidable warrior who loves to wage war by trickery, ambushes and ruses. Be on your guard. Nothing is what it seems in the land of mist and rain. From the staff officers Corbulo had learned that the battle group had been formed around a vexillatio from the Twentieth Legion consisting of the first and sixth Cohorts, thirteen hundred and fifty Legionaries plus the Legion's entire cavalry force of one hundred and twenty men. To this had been added the Second Batavian's, two hundred Hamian archers, a HQ company consisting of the Legate's staff, engineers and artillery, one elephant and eight hundred Hibernians and mercenaries loyal to prince Tuathal. The whole force consisted of around three and half thousand men.

Corbulo raised his hand to his mouth as he felt his stomach move. For a moment he struggled to stop himself from throwing up. Then the moment passed. He took a deep breath, filling his lungs with fresh sea air and turned to look at Trebonius. The Legate of the Twentieth and commander of the battle group was staring patiently towards the west lost in his own thoughts. Reluctantly Corbulo let go of the mast and pushed his way across the crowded deck towards him. The Legate did not seem to notice Corbulo as he squeezed up beside him.

"No sign of any Hibernian ships Sir. This is good," Corbulo said glancing out to sea. "But they must know that we are coming. You don't keep an invasion fleet of this size a secret for very long."

Trebonius glanced sideways at Corbulo.

"They know that we are coming," the Legate replied calmly, "but they don't know where we are going to land. That will keep them guessing."

"Where are we going to land?" Corbulo said boldly.

Trebonius pointed a finger directly towards the west. "We are heading for the trading post at Drumanagh. If this wind holds the captain has assured me that we will be there by nightfall. We are going to land there, fortify the place and secure it as our supply base. Then we will march inland to take Tara, defeat Elim and crown Tuathal Techtmar as High King of Hibernia. Tuathal will rule Hibernia as a client king of Rome and we shall remain at Tara to keep him in power. Those are my orders."

Corbulo grunted and steadied himself as the galley pitched alarmingly.

"Well that should probably stop the Hibernians raiding our shores," he said as he regained his footing. "I have been to Hibernia before Sir. Agricola always said that a single Legion and some auxiliaries could conquer and hold the whole island. So forgive my curiosity but why haven't they sent the whole Twentieth legion? Seems to me that we are a bit light on numbers Sir."

Trebonius shook his head and there was a hint of irritation in his voice as he replied.

"You do not need to concern yourself with that," he said sharply.

Corbulo nodded and fell silent.

"Yes, but about Tuathal Sir," Corbulo exclaimed, "I made it my business in Deva to find out a bit more about him and his men. It seems his father was not very popular amongst the Hibernian tribes Sir; that's why they got rid of him and as for the eight hundred followers he claims to have, most of them are foreign hired mercenaries, criminals and adventurers with no military training. They are nothing more than a rabble Sir. If I was you I wouldn't trust them."

"Is there anything else that you would like to advise me on?" Trebonius said icily.

"Well Sir," Corbulo said ignoring the tone in his commander's voice, "I mean, if we do manage to reach Tara and make Tuathal High King, do you think the Hibernian tribes are going to just accept him?"

"Well why not?" Trebonius retorted giving Corbulo a hard look.

"I don't particularly like the Hibernians Sir," Corbulo replied, "but they are not stupid. Tuathal is a dick. The Hibernians are not going to accept him. No one would accept a cock like Tuathal, the man's nothing more than a violent, whoring bully."

"Tuathal Techtmar has told me that he will be able to raise a force of five thousand loyal men if we can place him on the throne," Trebonius snapped. "He has the money, he has the name and the claim to the throne and he has us. We are going to succeed."

Corbulo sighed and turned to look out to sea.

"The man's a cock Sir," he said quietly, "Take my advice; don't count on any help from the Hibernians. We are invading their land. They are not going to forget that."

Trebonius growled angrily and turned on Corbulo.

"I think I have heard enough," he snapped, "You are not here to advise me. You are just a useless mouth who Agricola has dumped on me. Now go before I have you tossed overboard. I don't want to hear your voice again."

Corbulo saluted and started to move away. The deck was crowded with soldiers and supplies and it took him a while before he found an empty spot. He was just about to sit down when amongst the officers and men he suddenly came face to face with a man and as he recognised him Corbulo turned pale.

"You," the man cried out in shock.

Corbulo staggered backwards into a soldier as, horrified, he stared at Classicus, the Procurator Augusti of the province of Britannia.

Chapter Twenty - The Beach at Drumanagh

"Land, Land," the hoarse excited cry woke Corbulo up. Quickly he rose and turned to look out across the sea. Onboard the packed galley the Roman officers and men were rising to their feet eager to catch a glimpse of their destination. Corbulo rubbed his eyes. Then to the west he suddenly saw it, the grey smudge of a coast on the horizon.

"Not long now boys," a Centurion bellowed encouragingly. Corbulo turned to look across at the other ships. It was an hour after dawn and the neat ordered lines of galleys had become somewhat ragged. It was to be expected. The fleet had spent the short night at sea and during the hours of darkness the ships had lit signal torches to show their positions but it was inevitable that some of the galleys would have lost their way in the dark. The gentle southern breeze was propelling them straight towards the coast. Corbulo yawned and glanced up at the sky. The cloudy weather was still with them but the sea had been calm during the night.

"What did I tell you," a Legionary beside him said turning to his mate, "Sacrificing those sacred chickens to Neptune has worked. No storms, no sea monsters. We're nearly there, thank the gods."

Corbulo glanced around him but there was no sign of the Procurator on the crowded deck. He picked thoughtfully at one of his teeth. The shock of seeing Classicus onboard had worn off once he'd realised the official was not about to try and arrest him. No something else had brought Britannia's finance minister out here, where he had no business to be, and Corbulo had guessed what it was. The Procurator had the same task as himself, to find Quintus and the letter that Agricola had written to the Governor. How the man had managed to deduce this was a mystery. Someone must have talked or else the Procurator was one hell of a clever arsehole.

***

The small peninsula poked out into the sea like a solitary tooth. It was surrounded by water on three sides and Corbulo could see the waves crashing onto the dull grey rocks beneath the cliffs. It looked a dreary, unwelcoming place. He stood at the prow of the galley with its figurine of Neptune as the galley plunged and rose through the waves. From the corner of his eye he noticed the ship's captain suddenly point to the sea cliffs that surrounded the peninsula.

"That's the trading post at Drumanagh right there," the captain shouted triumphantly as he turned to the small cluster of Roman officers at his side, "I promised to land you there and so you shall."

Corbulo peered at the coast. Just to the north of the headland he could make out a long crescent shaped beach. They seemed to be heading straight for it. He glanced across the sea at the fleet. The others too seemed to be converging on the beach and for a moment Corbulo was struck by the scene of dozens of ships, their grey ornamented prows pitching and rising as they eagerly bore down on the enemy beach. Then suddenly he heard Trebonius's deep voice.

"Get the men ready," the Legate said turning to his officers as he placed his helmet on his head. "Once we are ashore I want the Sixth to form a defensive line across the landward length of the peninsula and I want three part mounted pickets a mile inland, one to the north, west and south. Understood?"

The officers around the Legate nodded eagerly.

Corbulo turned as he heard a Centurion bellow an order. The Legionaries on the crowded deck were all standing up now and craning their necks to catch a glimpse of the approaching beach. The tension on the men's faces was clearly visible. Corbulo scratched his cheek as he stared at the beach that was not far away now. There was no sign of the enemy, no blaring Carnyx's, nothing at all apart from the screeching sea gulls circling in the sky. The landing it seemed was going to be unopposed.

With a deep scraping judder and groan the galley came sliding up onto the beach.

"Overboard men," the vexillatio standard bearer of the Twentieth, clad in his wolf skin head and clutching the Vexillum standard, roared as he leapt down into the surf. He was followed moments later by the Legionaries as they jumped down into the shallow water and started to wade ashore. Corbulo slung his legs over the side of the galley and landed in knee-deep seawater. All along the beach the ships of the fleet were coming in to land. Corbulo staggered ashore. Along the length of the beach the Legionaries were storming onto the sand but their speed and progress was slowed by the heavy burden of equipment that they were carrying. Above the tumult he could hear the shouts of the Centurions and their Optio's as the officers tried to instil some order into the troops streaming ashore. Corbulo grunted as he saw that the standard bearer was already half way towards the peninsula. A ragged line of Legionaries were trying to keep up with him. Behind him Corbulo heard a man land in the surf. He turned and saw that it was Trebonius. The Legate had his eyes fixed on the headland.

"Well what are you waiting for," Trebonius roared at the troops as they struggled ashore, "Get your arses up onto that peninsula, move it, damn you!"

Corbulo started after the standard bearer. The headland was no more than a hundred yards away but the soft sand was slowing him down. Behind him he heard a trumpet blast. Then another. As he drew closer to the peninsula he could see a small cluster of huts and round houses. Smoke was billowing up from one of the huts. Then as he reached the foot of the cliffs he heard a woman's scream. The first of the Legionaries were already in amongst the buildings of the small trading post. Corbulo stumbled up the grassy slope and paused to catch his breath. Inland and a hundred paces away he could see figures fleeing towards a wood. The figures were sprinting as fast as they could. Corbulo turned and started towards the small settlement that occupied the centre of the peninsula. When he reached it the Legionaries were going from house to house, kicking their way into the huts and evicting anyone they found. A small group of women, men and children were cowering on the ground guarded by a couple of soldiers.

"So where is the enemy?" the standard bearer cried raising his standard in the air.

***

The rhythmic thud of a thousand pickaxes reverberated across the peninsula. It was late in the afternoon and it was raining. Corbulo stood sheltering in the entrance to one of the white tents watching the Legionaries at work. The men had already completed two V shaped defensive ditches, which stretched across the whole width of the peninsula, a distance of some two hundred yards and they were now starting on a third. In between the ditches were two earthen ramparts, the first of which had been fortified with the thousands of wooden stakes, which the soldiers had brought with them. The stakes had been pushed into the ramparts at an angle so that their sharpened ends were pointing at the main land. A line of Legionaries from the Sixth Cohort were guarding the first rampart. The men were kneeling down on one knee with their red rectangular shields leaning against their bodies and their pilum's lying on the ground beside them, whilst behind them, on the second rampart, Trebonius had positioned his two hundred Hamian archers. The Syrians looked a little bewildered and uncomfortable in the rain.

Down the remainder of the peninsula, swamping the small cluster of huts and round houses of the trading post, stood row upon row of white tents. The mooring lines of the tents had been fastened by long metal spikes, which had been driven into the grass and in between them were supply dumps, barrels, sacks and amphorae of all shapes and sizes. Most of the Batavian's and Hibernians were resting after their labours and at the far end of the peninsula, a few hundred yards from Corbulo, he could see the makeshift horse enclosure where the battle group's four hundred and fifty horses were being kept. Out in the crescent shaped bay the Roman ships had dropped their anchors and now rode the gentle swell. A long line of slaves was coming up from the beach loaded with supplies.

Corbulo was just about to leave the shelter of the tent when he heard a sudden trumpet blast. The dull rhythmic thud of the pickaxes seemed to miss a beat as the Legionaries straightened up and hesitated. Then Corbulo heard the trumpet blast again and this time he recognised the signal. The Legionaries too seemed to have recognised it for a murmur broke out and some of the men dropped their pickaxes and ran towards where they had left their weapons and shields. Down the whole peninsula men stumbled out of their tents, cursing and shouting as they hastened to fix their armour and grab their weapons. Corbulo looked around him and saw Trebonius surrounded by his staff officers hastening towards the ramparts. Quickly he ran over to join him. The rain was coming down in grey remorseless sheets but Corbulo hardly felt it. The trumpet blast had been signalling the approach of the enemy. Trebonius was standing on top of the first rampart beside a Scorpion bolt thrower when Corbulo clambered up the earthen bank to join him. The Legate was issuing orders to his officers in a calm and clear voice.

"Have the First Cohort line up behind the Hamian's but they are to stay out of sight until I order them up onto the rampart. The Batavians and Hibernians are to remain in the reserve." Trebonius turned quickly to another Centurion. "Bring the slaves inside the camp and tell the ships to remain out at sea. I also want those pickets brought back."

"I think they got the message Sir, look," a young Tribune exclaimed as he pointed inland. Across the open fields beyond the first ditch Corbulo suddenly caught sight of a small group of men racing towards the fort. Amongst them he recognised a

Cornicen, a trumpeter. The man was lugging his cylindrical trumpet and he was lagging behind his comrades.

"Sir, look over there," one of the Centurions said nudging the Legate. Three Roman Legionary cavalrymen came thundering towards the fort from the north. The slaves plodding along from the beach seemed to mistake them for the enemy for instantly the neat ordered column dissolved into chaos as the slaves panicked. The horsemen did not care. The leader catching sight of the group of officers up on the rampart urged his horse towards them. He halted beside the ditch as clumps of earth flew from his horse's hooves.

"Sir," the rider cried, "there is a large group of Hibernians coming this way. Most seem to be infantry but a few are mounted and they have war dogs."

"What are their numbers?" Trebonius shouted.

The cavalryman shook his head. "Hard to tell Sir but they are making a lot of noise. Maybe a few thousand, that's a guess Sir."

"Get your men inside the fort," Trebonius replied as he turned to stare at the distant wood. The cavalryman saluted and cried out to his two companions to follow him as he galloped on towards the fortified gateway. The Roman infantrymen were still racing across the fields towards the fort when Corbulo saw the first of the Hibernian cavalry appear from amongst the trees. The Hibernians were riding small shaggy looking horses and they looked un-armoured and were clutching spears and small round shields. They caught sight of the fleeing Romans and with a wild joyful cry set off in pursuit. The Roman's were running for their lives now. From the ramparts the Legionaries suddenly started to shout and holler urging their comrades on. In the fields one of the soldiers dropped his shield. Corbulo stared at the flight. It was going to be close. The Hibernians were charging and closing the gap fast.

"Come on, come on," Corbulo heard the Legate mutter. All eyes were now on the running men as the Hibernians closed with them.

"Soldier, when you have the range, open up," Trebonius said calmly turning to the crew of the Scorpion. The bolt thrower mounted on its tripod was already loaded with an iron tipped yard long bolt. In the fields another Roman dropped his shield as he raced towards the ditch. The soldiers on top of the ramparts were yelling and shouting at their comrades. With a sudden twanging noise the soldier manning the Scorpion released his bolt. The aim was good and in the meadows one of the Hibernian riders was punched from his horse with such velocity that it sent him hurtling backwards several yards. From the ramparts a great cheer rose up. The first of the fleeing men reached the ditch and flung themselves into it. The Hibernians seeing the ramparts suddenly shied away and from the earth embankment another great roar rose up. The roar was quickly overtaken by a cataphony of excited shouts. The Cornicen, lugging his trumpet was still racing towards the fort. The soldier had lost his shield and helmet and seemed to be doing his best but just as he was about to reach the safety of the ditch a Hibernian launched his spear and struck him in his back. From the ramparts the Legionaries fell silent as they watched the Cornicen collapse face down into the grass, just yards from the ditch.

The Hibernian riders had retreated to a safe distance when the remaining slaves came scrambling over the rampart and to safety.

"What's happened to the southern picket?" Trebonius frowned as he turned to his officers. "Did they make it back?"

One of the Tribunes shook his head.

"No Sir, they must still be out there, maybe they are hiding."

"Maybe," the Legate muttered   sourly.

On the fringe of the wood the Hibernian riders had gathered together and were watching the ramparts. Among their ranks were packs of sleek grey Hibernian hunting dogs and their baying and barking was incessant. The Hibernians however seemed to be waiting for something. From amongst the trees Corbulo suddenly heard the mournful blare of a Hibernian Carnyx. It was followed by another blast and then another. Armed men began to appear along the tree line; more and more of them until the whole forest was bristling with shields, axes and spears. The Hibernians were singing and the noise of their strange language mingled with the barking dogs as it carried across the open fields to the Romans on their ramparts. Then from amongst the massed Hibernian ranks a solitary war chariot pushed out into the fields and came cantering towards the Roman fort. The chariot was pulled along by a two white small shaggy horses and in it stood three men. The vehicle came to a halt beside the Hibernian rider who had been impaled by the Scorpion. Two of the occupants got down onto the ground and Corbulo's face darkened as he noticed that the man who had remained standing in the chariot was wearing a black eye patch over one eye. Corbulo peered at him with a sudden sense of foreboding. The man was tall and thin and had a white beard that reached to his ears and a bald- head. He looked like a druid.

"Hold," Trebonius snapped as the Scorpion crew swivelled their weapon in the direction of the chariot. "Looks like they want to talk."

The Legate turned and was about to start off in the direction of the gateway when Corbulo cleared his throat.

"Sir," he said stepped forwards, "Why don't you let me talk with them. I know something about these Hibernians. They are an untrustworthy lot. Maybe this here," he said, gesturing towards the three men beside the chariot, "is just a ruse to identify and kill you. The Hibernians train their warriors to prioritise and kill the leaders of their enemy. It's how they fight."

Trebonius hesitated and glanced at Corbulo with a wary mistrustful look. Then he turned to stare across the fields at the solitary chariot. For a moment he said nothing as he made up his mind.

"Allright," he said sharply, "Go and find out what they want and you," the Legate said pointing at a young spotty faced Tribune of no more than eighteen, "will accompany him."

As Corbulo made his way along the lines of Legionaries towards the main gateway he was suddenly conscious of the young aristocratic Tribune by his side. The youth was nervous.

"What's your name?" Corbulo growled.

"Galba," the Tribune muttered. The youth was silent for a moment. "Do they really train their men to go after our officers?" he said at last.

"Do you think I made it up son?" Corbulo replied.

The Tribune did not reply but his face grew more and more serious. He did not seem to notice the faint smile that appeared on Corbulo's lips.

***

Corbulo could feel the hundreds of Roman eyes staring at him as he strode across the open muddy field towards the three Hibernians and their chariot. The relentless rain was still pouring down from grey skies. Galba plodded along at his side in tense silence. As they moved away from the fort three Roman Legionaries slithered down the earthen rampart to retrieve the body of the Cornicen and his trumpet from where it lay in the grass. The instrument after all was a valuable piece of military equipment.

As he approached the waiting men Corbulo could not take his eyes off the tall thin bearded man with the long white cloak he'd spotted earlier and as he did so his mood darkened and his mouth seemed to dry up. The man was in his thirties and he was gripping a wooden staff and he definitely looked like a druid. Corbulo clenched his hand into a fist as the sight of the druid brought forth memories of the battle for Mona Insulis, the strong hold of the druids, the sacred isle, where the druids, mad with blood lust and vengeance, had sacrificed and tortured captured Roman soldiers in order to appease their alien gods. Corbulo had seen the aftermath of their work and he had never forgotten the utter depraved barbarity of it all. Every Roman soldier hated and feared the power of the druids and their closeness to the gods but the druids were still just men and they could die like men too he thought with growing anger.

Corbulo came to a halt before the chariot and its small horses. The three hostile Hibernians stared at him in silence. The two veteran warriors were older men of around Corbulo's age and they were clad in dark leather armour and were wearing golden and silver torques around their necks. They did not look very different to the wild Brigant tribesmen Corbulo had fought in his youth. Their long dark wild hair fluttered gently in the breeze and numerous tattoos disappeared up their arms and they were leaning on their spears. The men looked as hard as nails and Corbulo folded his arms across his chest as he waited for the warriors to speak. But it was the druid who spoke first and his fluent command of Latin took Corbulo by surprise.

"I am Faelan, eldest druid of Tara," the tall man with the bald head said in a deep powerful voice, "This is Finn and his brother. They do not speak your language but I shall translate. This land does not belong to Rome, it belongs to Finn and he wants to know what you are doing here, Roman?"

The druid fixed his eye on Corbulo and Corbulo felt a sudden shiver of unease pass down his spine. Could this druid read his thoughts? At his side Galba had thrust his chin into an aggressive confident look but it was all just show. The young Tribune was as tense as a newly wed virgin on her wedding night. Slowly Corbulo wiped the rainwater from his forehead and ignoring Faelan, he turned to the two warriors who were watching him with hostile eyes.

"We have come to support the claim of Tuathal Techtmar to the High Kingship of Hibernia," Corbulo said grandly. "If Finn will promise his support to Tuathal then he and his people will be left in peace."

A hiss escaped from Faelan's mouth. "We already have a High King at Tara," he snapped.

Corbulo kept his eyes fixed on Finn and his brother.

"But I don't see him here." he exclaimed looking around the small gathering.

Faelan was silent as the two brothers muttered something to each other in a dialect that was too difficult for Corbulo to understand.

"King Elim is in the north but he will be returning to Tara soon," Faelan growled. "Tuathal Techtmar is not welcome here. Take your soldiers, board your ships and go home Roman, no one here wants you, nor will they support you."

Corbulo sighed and turned to look at the earthen ramparts of the Roman fort. For a moment he was silent.

"I agree with you," Corbulo said as he turned back to face the Hibernians, "Tuathal is a dick and I don't blame you for not wanting him but he does have one thing that you and your men don't have." Corbulo grasped his hand around his cock. "He's got balls gentlemen. He is waiting for you over there. If you are such brave warriors, then why don't you come and try and kill him?"

At his side Corbulo sensed Galba stiffen. Finn and his brother too did not seem to need a translation to understand what Corbulo had just said. They broke out into an angry muttering and one of the warriors took a threatening step towards

Corbulo. But it was Faelan who replied first and there was anger in his voice.

"Do you think that we are that stupid?" the druid cried. "If you have come to fight then tell your cowards to come out from behind their walls and face us like real men."

Corbulo ignored Faelan and shook his balls with his hands.

"Have you got any of these Finn?" he cried turning from one brother to the other. "Shall I check just in case?"

Faelan stepped down from the chariot and called out something to his two companions that Corbulo could not understand but the warriors were not listening. One of them spat onto the ground beside Corbulo's feet and without a word stepped up onto the chariot. He was swiftly joined by the second warrior who grasped hold of the reins and with surprising speed the chariot was rolling away towards the lines of waiting Hibernian tribesmen. Only Faelan remained. The druid was staring at Corbulo with sudden wariness. Then he shook his head and raised and pointed his staff at Corbulo.

"You should remember my name," Faelan said quietly, "for I am the son of Queen Boudicca, last rightful ruler of the Iceni and I have seen what is to come. If you do not leave by tonight, then we shall take no prisoners and I promise you, those that fall into our hands will have their hearts ripped out whilst they are still alive. Lugh does not want you to survive. By the next full moon you will all be dead and the ravens will feast on your corpses. Fear the one eyed man, fear the coming of the black ravens on the northern wind."

"Oh fuck off," Corbulo snapped angrily. Then he turned and strode off back towards the Roman fort calling for Galba to follow him. A few moments later the young Tribune caught up with him. He was breathing rapidly and blushing despite the cold rain.

"Walk, don't run lad, show them that you are not afraid," Corbulo muttered.

Galba nodded quickly and tried to slow his pace. Up ahead the lines of Legionaries on top of their fortified ramparts were still down on one knee with their large red rectangular shields leaning against their bodies.

"What was all that about?" Galba gasped at last unable to contain himself. "You insulted them."

"I certainly hope so," Corbulo murmured grimly, "That was the whole idea. Let's hope Finn is really annoyed for I want him to attack us."

"Why, I don't understand, those were not the Legate's instructions," Galba said in alarm.

"Maybe not," Corbulo said with a sigh, "but if they attack us, they are going to get slaughtered."

Chapter Twenty-One - The Stained Earth

"Well what did they want?" Trebonius cried as Corbulo followed closely by Galba clambered up the earth rampart towards him. Corbulo straightened up as he reached the top and rapped out a quick salute.

"They wanted to know what we were doing here Sir," Corbulo replied, "So I told them about Tuathal but they didn't seem very keen on him so then I invited them to attack us."

Trebonius opened his mouth and then closed it again. His eyes narrowed.

"You did what?" the Legate exclaimed.

"I told them," Corbulo said patiently, "That if they were real men, they should come and try and kill Tuathal."

Trebonius shook his head in bewilderment. Then before he could say anything else a great roar of voices rose up from the Hibernian lines followed by the blaring of a dozen Celtic war trumpets.

"Fuck," the Legate muttered as he quickly turned to his staff officers, "Have the Hamian's prepare to shoot on my signal. If they attack we will hold them on the first rampart. Go!"

Across the fields the Hibernians were shouting and banging their weapons against their shields and the din was growing in volume.

"Looks like they are going to attack Sir," a Centurion from the 6th shouted as he came hurrying towards Trebonius.

The Legate ignored the officer and turned to Corbulo and Galba.

"I know what you are trying to do," he said angrily pointing a finger at Corbulo. "But I never told you to provoke the enemy."

"Yes Sir," Corbulo said quickly, "but there is something else." Corbulo caught Trebonius' eye. "Elim, the High King, he's not here. The druid said that he was in the north. I find that rather odd Sir, considering that he must have known we were coming. Maybe the Hibernians are not as united as they would like us to believe. If Elim is dealing with a local rebellion then there must be friction amongst the Hibernian tribes."

"I will deal with that and your insubordination later," Trebonius growled as the noise from the Hibernian lines grew more frantic. "Look at the fine fucking mess you have created."

Corbulo turned to stare across the fields towards the Hibernians. The Celts were working themselves up into a rage. The ranks of Legionaries from the 6th Cohort were staring at the enemy impassively and suddenly from amongst their lines Corbulo heard a booming voice and saw a huge bear of a man, the Cohort's senior Centurion striding down the line behind his men. The officer was wearing a red plumed helmet.

"The first man to break ranks without my permission is a dead man," the Centurion roared at his troops as he passed along behind them tapping his vine stick against his leg. "There will be no retreat from this position. The boys from the 1st Cohort behind us think that we are not up for the job. They think they are going to be needed today. Well let them play with their cocks. The 6th Cohort is going to hold the enemy, not one of those Celtic bastards is coming over our wall. We know how they like to fight boys. Don't be scared by the fierceness of their charge; it's all they've got. Stand up to them and they will quickly give up. They have no armour, their shields are small and their weapons are of wretched quality as for their dogs, we will eat them for supper."

Corbulo's attention was wrenched away by Galba's sudden cry. The young Tribune was pointing at something across the fields. Out in the meadow two Hibernians were dragging something along across the slippery wet grass. Behind them, striding towards the Roman fort, with calm confident steps, came Faelan holding his wooden staff in one hand and a short gleaming scythe in the other. The druid's long white cloak fluttered in the breeze. Corbulo wiped the rain from his face as he tried to see what the two Hibernians were dragging along. Then he groaned. The Hibernians halted and in between them, forced up onto his knees was a Roman Legionary. The soldier was facing the fort and his hands were tied behind his back. Slowly Faelan came up behind him, paused, then grasped the man's hair, jerked his head backwards and swiftly slit his throat with his scythe. Even from where he was standing Corbulo could see the blood spurting from the soldier's throat. Faelan allowed the corpse to flop forwards before one of the warriors stepped forwards and decapitated the Legionary with a single blow of his axe. Amongst the small group of officers who clustered around the Legate not a word was said. The silence continued as Faelan picked up the Roman head and raised it high in the air. The gesture seemed to release the Hibernians for suddenly their bloodthirsty shouts, screams and yells reached a climax. Then they were coming, storming towards the ramparts in a great howling surging mass of grey led by their packs of war dogs.

"Hold, wait for the order," Trebonius bellowed at the trumpeter. Along the earthen rampart the Legionaries from the 6th Cohort lifted up their spears as they awaited the enemy onslaught. Corbulo stared mesmerized at the flood of Hibernians that was surging towards them. There had to be thousands of them. The Celts were armed with swords, spears, axes and clubs but the Centurion had been right. Their small round shields of wood and hide and their body armour of stiffened hide were going to offer them little protection from what was to come.

"Now," Trebonius said turning to his trumpeter.

The soldier raised his trumpet to his lips and a second later a short blast reverberated across the headland. For a few moments nothing happened. Then from behind the ranks of the 6th a volley of arrows arched gracefully into the air before plunging straight into the mass of running warriors. The Hibernians were too closely packed together and their shields too small and here and there men plunged to the ground whilst others shrieked and cried out in pain. A second volley was already in the air even before the first had struck home and the arrows mercilessly slammed into the enemy ranks. Despite the carnage the Hibernian charge showed no sign of wavering. The war dogs, grey sleek beasts were the first to reach the outer ditch. Some of the animals crashed straight into it, howling and barking in their eagerness to reach the Romans, whilst others leapt across it with mighty bounds but the steep earthen rampart and sharpened wooden stakes were not easily climbed. Here and there a Legionary rose to his feet and jabbed his spear at a dog that had managed to work its way past the defences.

Trebonius was staring at the advancing Hibernians. The foremost warriors had nearly reached the ditch. At the Legate's side the crew of the Scorpion were hastily fitting another bolt into their machine as the thin line of Legionaries protecting the rampart in front of the group of officers rose to their feet and raised their spears. Corbulo could clearly see the faces of the enemy now. He was suddenly conscious that he did not have a shield.

"Hold them, hold them!" a Roman voice screamed.

As the Hibernians came piling down into the ditch they were greeted by a volley of spears flung down at them from the Romans on top of the rampart. At such short range it was hard to miss and the bodies of the dead and dying tumbled back onto those coming on behind. The shrieks of wounded men mingled with the barking howling dogs and the cries and screams of the Hibernians as they sought to force their way up the rampart.

Corbulo unsheathed his sword as the fighting drew closer. Along the entire length of the rampart the surging tide of Hibernians had got stuck in the ditch. Men were trying to scramble up the steep embankment, trying to find a way through the rows of sharpened wooden stakes whilst above them the legionaries had risen to their feet and were hacking and stabbing at the enemy with their short swords and pushing them back with their large rectangular shields. Here and there a small group of Hibernians had managed to fight their way up onto the rampart but their existence was short lived as the Legionaries drove them back with their shields. The vicious hand to hand combat rippled along the rampart and the air was rent with screams and cries. Close by a Hibernian grasped hold of one of the stakes and tried to pull it from the earth. A Legionary brought his shield down on the man's hand and was rewarded by an agonising scream. Corbulo snatched a quick glance at Trebonius. The Legate had not moved and his sword was still in its scabbard. The officer was staring at the fighting with a calm calculating eye. Then he noticed Corbulo and a brief knowing look passed between the two of them.

The 6th Cohort seemed to be holding the enemy. The ditch, rampart and sharpened stakes seemed too great an obstacle for the Hibernians. They milled about at the base of the defences, seemingly without a plan as the unrelenting hail of arrows continued to slam into their rear most ranks. The Legionaries manning the ramparts suddenly seemed to sense that victory was theirs for they started to become bolder, venturing out from behind their defences to close with the enemy.

"Tell those men to hold their positions," Trebonius cried as he caught sight of the rising confidence amongst his men.

"Shall we order the 1st to counter attack Sir?" one of the Tribunes said hurriedly. "The enemy look like they are ready to break."

"No, we can't afford the casualties," Trebonius barked.

A spear suddenly embedded itself in a Centurion standing beside Trebonius and the soldier groaned as he doubled up and collapsed.

"Get him to the rear," the Legate yelled at a pair of slaves who wore crouching nearby.

Just in front of the group of officers the line of legionaries defending the rampart suddenly seemed to fall back and as they did so a group of Hibernians squeezed past the wooden stakes and clambered up onto the rampart. With a quick practised movement Trebonius drew his sword and with a hoarse cry threw himself into the fight. Corbulo spat onto the ground and ran to join him. The Hibernians were few in number but they seemed to know what they were doing. The men stood back to back as they fended off the Roman blows and jabs. Corbulo ducked under a wild axe swing and thrust his sword into a man's unprotected belly. He was rewarded by a groan of pain as his opponent staggered backwards. Close by a Hibernian throwing axe embedded itself with a thud into the shield of a legionary. Corbulo staggered backwards in fright and as he did so he tripped over a dead dog and went tumbled onto his arse. A huge Hibernian clad entirely in black sheep skin came roaring towards him holding a spear in both hands. Corbulo's eyes bulged and desperately he tried to roll away but at the last moment a Roman sword cut the Hibernian down and the man tumbled down the rampart and into the ditch. Corbulo caught sight of Galba. The boy's sword was stained with blood. Then he was struggling back onto his feet, panting from the exertion.

"They are fleeing, look at them run," a Roman voice suddenly cried out. Corbulo turned to stare into the fields beyond the ramparts. The Hibernians seemed indeed to have had enough and were retreating in disorder towards the forest from whence they had appeared. The Hamian's had not stopped shooting and their arrows were now slamming into the backs of the fleeing enemy sending men plunging and spinning to the ground. A victorious roar rose up from the Roman lines. Then Corbulo saw Trebonius. The legate's face was streaked with rain and mud.

"Hold. Tell the men to hold their positions; there will be no pursuit. Let them run!" Trebonius roared as he kicked the body of a dead Hibernian down into the ditch. His orders were quickly followed by a solitary trumpet blast. Corbulo staggered to the edge of earthen embankment. Close by a Hibernian hung impaled on one of the wooden stakes and down at the base of the rampart the dead lay everywhere, filling up the ditch. A few wounded men were trying to crawl away, one of whom was trailing his entrails behind him and the groans and cries of the wounded and dying were everywhere. Corbulo was breathing rapidly as he stared at the scene. A wounded Hibernian was clawing at the earth as he tried to rise to his feet and a few paces away from him a man was clutching his throat as he slowly drowned in his own blood.

Across the meadow in front of the fort the ground was a scene of utter devastation. Hundreds of corpses and wounded men littered the ground. The grass seemed to have been peppered with arrows. Corbulo straightened up and took a deep breath. Suddenly he became aware of someone at his side. It was Galba. The young Tribune was staring out across the fields.

"You were right," the boy muttered, "We slaughtered them."

"Well don't get too cocky," Corbulo replied, "These are not the High King's men. We haven't faced their main army yet and those boys won't make the same mistake as this lot did."

"How do you know?" Galba frowned.

"Because King Elim would not be High King if he was that stupid," Corbulo growled.

Galba wiped the rain from his face and blew the air from his cheeks.

"Do you believe what the druid told us," he said, "About being Queen Boudicca's son?"

Corbulo shrugged, "Maybe, it's possible, he is of the right age."

Corbulo turned as an Optio came hurrying up to Trebonius. "What are your orders Sir?" the soldier said. The Legate glared at the junior officer. Then he half turned to stare at the last of the Hibernians as they vanished amongst the distant trees. For a moment he was silent.

"Have the Batavians take the place of the 6th," Trebonius snapped at last, "tell the 1st and 6th to stand down and get some rest. Tomorrow at dawn we march on Tara. I want the men to be ready to leave at dawn. Tell the Centurions that I want every unit to give me their strength reports within the hour and get the slaves to clear those bodies from my ditch."

The Optio nodded and saluted before hurrying away.

"Are you allright Sir," a Tribune said offering Trebonius a water skin. The Legate took a long swig and handed the skin back to the Tribune without a comment. Then his eye fell on Corbulo.

"Quartermaster," Trebonius snapped as he glared at Corbulo, "that man over there shall no longer be entitled to his ration of wine and inform the Batavians that he will be spending the night outside the ramparts for disobeying my orders." Trebonius turned to look at the officer at his side, "Is that clear?"

The officer glanced quickly at Corbulo and nodded. "Yes Sir, outside the ramparts. I will inform the watch that he is not to be allowed back in until dawn."

"Just like old times," Corbulo said trying to sound cheerful.

Trebonius was staring at him. Then the Legate sighed. "I don't know what business you and Agricola are up to," he growled, "but I will not tolerate disobedience under my command. You are lucky that I don't have you whipped in front of the men."

From the corner of his eye Corbulo noticed another figure coming towards the small group of officers. It was Tuathal Techtmar and he looked annoyed.

"Legate," Tuathal cried as he clambered up the rampart followed by a few of his men. "Why was I prevented from joining you? Why did you have to fight? I am the rightful High King of Hibernia; these are my people. I could have talked with them and persuaded them to join us. Now you have slaughtered them. This is madness."

"This is my command," Trebonius said sharply as he turned to face the Hibernian. "You follow my orders. You and your men were held in reserve and your place was with your men. I did not need you."

"But there was no need to fight," Tuathal said angrily.

"Well blame him then," Trebonius said gesturing at Corbulo as he pushed past the Hibernian prince and down into the Roman camp, "He's the one who invited them to attack us."

Tuathal watched the Legate as he strode away followed by his staff. Then he turned and glared at Corbulo.

"You did what?" he exclaimed.

Corbulo stooped to wipe his sword on the back of a dead Hibernian. Carefully he glanced up at Tuathal.

"Galba here and I went out to speak with them," he said. "One of their leaders is a man called Finn, the other a druid called Faelan. They didn't seem to like you very much. So I invited them to come and try and kill you. Maybe they will succeed next time."

Tuathal's face darkened and his hand shot out as he pointed a finger at Corbulo.

"Be careful, be very careful," he hissed, "for when I am High King you are not going to get away with this insolence. You may think that I am just another ambitious Hibernian exile but I am Tuathal Techtmar, rightful king of this land and you will remember that."

Corbulo finished cleaning his sword and carefully returned it to its scabbard.

"You are Agricola's creature, nothing less, nothing more," he said sharply, "You think you are the High King of this land but you are just a puppet that dances to Rome's command. If you were a true king you would have been fighting on the opposite side today together with those dead men down there in the ditch."

Tuathal's face broke out into a blush. For a moment he stared at Corbulo. Then abruptly he turned and stormed off without saying a word.

Chapter Twenty-Two - The March on Tara

The night was pitch black as Corbulo lay in the grass leaning on one elbow. The corpses of the slain Hibernians lay scattered across the meadow around him and some of them were starting to stink. Corbulo could not sleep. The rain had finally stopped but the changing weather had not managed to lighten his bad mood. His situation had not been improved either by the cheerful band of Batavians up on the ramparts who had insisted on calling out his name every few minutes inquiring whether he was still alive. He had thrown a stone in their direction but the calls had not ceased. It wasn't the first time either that he had suffered this form of punishment. Many years ago during the year of the four Emperors when the loyalty of the Twentieth had been dubious he'd found himself tied to a tree and forced to spend the night outside the protective embrace of the Legionary camp. On that occasion it was the new legate of the Twentieth, Agricola who had come to his rescue. There wasn't much chance of that happening now he thought sourly.

A sudden noise in the darkness had him reaching for his sword. Something had moved in the darkness. Carefully Corbulo rose to his feet with his sword in his hand. Had the Batavians come down to play another joke on him or had some of the Hibernians returned to retrieve their dead? He peered into the darkness from whence the sound had come. Then he heard it again. A little jingle and rattle. Someone was out there. Corbulo crouched ready to thrust his sword into whatever came for him.

"Father," a voice whispered, "are you there? It's me Marcus."

Corbulo rolled his eyes as he relaxed and lowered his sword.

"I am here," he said.

A few moments later Marcus appeared out of the gloom.

"They told me that the Legate had ordered you to spend the night outside the fort," Marcus said with a voice that hinted at a smile. "Thought you may like to have some company."

Corbulo sat down on the grass. "Well the dead don't make very good company so yes I am glad you are here," he said grumpily.

Marcus chuckled and sat down. "For what it is worth my men, the Batavians think you are a hero. None of them like Tuathal and his mercenaries. Most of Tuathal's men are not even from Hibernia, they are the scum of the earth, the lot of them. Murderers, rapists, thieves, runaway slaves." Marcus paused. "Everyone has heard about how you invited the Hibernians to kill Tuathal." Marcus sighed. "There are quite a few who wish the Hibernians had succeeded for then we could abandon this expedition and go home. The man is a complete prick."

"Well they can't," Corbulo growled, "we march on Tara at dawn or have you forgotten?"

In the darkness Marcus was silent for a moment.

"Trebonius is leaving most of my Cohort behind to defend the fort," Marcus said at last, "only us mounted troopers will be coming with you. The infantry is staying to fortify and defend the fort. Trebonius wants to secure his supply lines."

"You mean he wants to secure his line of retreat," Corbulo snapped.

Again Marcus was silent. Corbulo looked up at the sky but there was no sign of the usual stars or the moon.

"What are you doing here father?" Marcus said quietly.

Corbulo lowered his eyes. "Agricola ordered me to go," he said. "He wants me to find Quintus and bring him back. Quintus has a letter that belongs to Agricola, an important letter. That's my mission."

"Yes, but why should you give a damn about Agricola and a letter? What has it to do with you? This is a dangerous expedition; you should be with Efa and Dylis. You saved those children and you got the money. You are too old to be serving in the army."

"I know where I should be son," Corbulo said quietly, "but matters are not as simple as that."

"Why not?" Marcus shot back.

Corbulo sighed and scratched at his cheek.

"It's just something that I have to do," he said wearily.

From the darkness there was no immediate reply. Then Corbulo heard Marcus shift position.

"Does this have anything to do with the disappearance of my woman and my son?" Marcus said quietly.

Corbulo closed his eyes. Then he sighed.

"No," he replied, "This is between me and Agricola."

***

When dawn finally came Corbulo was standing outside the main gateway into the fort as the Legionary cavalry began to emerge. As the horsemen trotted out of the camp he snapped to attention. The riders peered at him curiously as they rode past. They were followed by the two hundred and fifty mounted Batavians and amongst them Corbulo saw Marcus. His son snapped out a quick salute as he trotted past. Corbulo watched him vanish from view across the corpse-strewn field. The next to pass him were the solid ranks of Legionaries from the 6th and 1st Cohorts, thirteen hundred and fifty men in all. The boots of the heavily armoured Legionaries reverberated on the soil. The men were singing a marching song and the gusto of their voices told Corbulo that the soldiers were in good spirits. They were followed by the two hundred Hamian archers. The Syrians were silent and tense and Corbulo noticed that their quivers were filled with arrows. The next to pass were a long column of supply wagons pulled along by oxen, horses and slaves. Some of the slaves had hitched a ride on the wagons and stared at the solitary figure curiously as he stood to attention as the column passed by. Then it was the turn of the two hundred and fifty men from the HQ Company. The part mounted Company including the solitary grey skinned elephant. As he stood to attention waiting to be relieved from his punishment he suddenly caught sight of Trebonius mounted on a horse. The Legate caught his eye and shook his head. One of the men accompanying him peeled off from the column and Corbulo saw that it was Galba. The boy was leading a second horse.

"Here you go Sir," the boy said.

"You don't have to call me Sir," Corbulo growled as he tried to mount the horse. The beast backed away nervously but on his second attempt he was successful.

"If it allright with you," Galba said quietly, "I will call you Sir. A man who fought against the Barbarian Queen deserves that respect."

"How the fuck do you know about that?" Corbulo said as he joined the column.

"Everyone knows about you Sir," Galba said urging his horse on with a tight smile.

***

Soon the sea was left behind and the Roman column began to move inland across bleak empty fields. Here and there the open gently rolling hills were interspersed with small woods and ring forts. There was however no sign of the Hibernians. Corbulo peered at a distant ring fort perched on top of a hill as the rhythmic thud of the Legionaries boots and the soldiers singing

212

filled the cool dawn air. The gates to the fortified farm house were firmly closed and there was no sign of life. The Hibernians it seemed had fled en masse and had taken their animals with them for across the bare grassy hills he could not see a single cow, horse or sheep. He turned to look back in the direction of the headland fort but it had already vanished behind a screen of trees. Trebonius had left the bulk of the 2nd Batavian Cohort, some six hundred men, behind to strengthen and defend the newly constructed fort.

As his eye fell on the eight hundred Hibernian and foreign mercenaries who were bringing up the rear of the column Corbulo grunted in disgust. Tuathal's men seemed to have no discipline or leadership for they were strung out in small individual disorganised groups and seemed to be lacking any kind of discipline. At their head rode Tuathal surrounded by a band of Hibernians on horseback. There was a proud look on his face.

"When we reach Tara," Galba said as he noticed Corbulo watching Tuathal, "they will crown him High King of Hibernia. Tara is their capital, the place where they have crowned their kings for hundreds of years. Apparently there is a standing stone right in the centre of the place. The Hibernians call it the Stone of Destiny. The would be king must touch the stone and if he is the rightful heir the stone will scream and the noise will be heard in all corners of this island."

Corbulo glanced across at Galba as the two of them rode across the muddy field.

"It's a load of bollocks," he muttered.

Galba shrugged. "Maybe," he replied, "But it makes a good story and I think here, in this land of eternal winter, a man needs good stories. The weather and the bleakness of this place are enough to drive a man insane."

"It's no different to Caledonia or the land of the Brigantes," Corbulo grunted. "But you should be more concerned with the whereabouts of King Elim and his army than with fancy stories. Do you think the High King is just going to let us take Tara without a fight?"

Galba was staring ahead at the long column of heavily armed Legionaries that was vanishing over the crest of the next hill.

"The Legate says Tara is only twenty five miles away so we will reach it before nightfall. Trebonius has ordered a forced march. Maybe the speed of our advance will take King Elim by surprise. You said yourself that he was in the north."

"So I did," Corbulo admitted.

As the morning wore on Corbulo started to notice a river to the north meandering its way through the green country. Soon their progress began to slow as the column started to encounter bogs, desolate soggy looking fields of coarse heather that seemed to go on and on. Tuathal's Hibernian scouts however kept the column from losing its way and there was a constant coming and going as the riders and scouts reported back to Trebonius and his staff. Corbulo, riding just behind the Legate, was in a good position to hear their reports and the news the riders brought was promising. There had been no sightings of Elim's army.

It was noon with a fresh westerly breeze blowing into his face when Corbulo suddenly saw Classicus, the Procurator riding towards him. The Finance Minister was accompanied by a Turma of thirty mounted Praetorians. It had been the first time he'd seen the Procurator since they had bumped into each other on the ship and Corbulo's heart sank and he groaned. Classicus gave Corbulo a hard, cold glance as he came up and slowed his horse to a walk.

"And so we meet again," the Procurator exclaimed, "I can't seem to get rid of you, Corbulo. Everywhere I go, I seem to run into you."

"Well you can always fuck off," Corbulo replied avoiding the man's gaze. At his side Galba blushed in embarrassment.

The Procurator shrugged and looked away with an annoyed expression.

"I see that you still haven't learned to show respect to your superiors but maybe one day I shall teach you some manners," he replied.

Corbulo did not answer as he rode on along the trail.

"What are you doing here in Hibernia?" the Procurator said suddenly. "Aren't you a little old to have rejoined the army?"

"I am here for the same thing as you are," Corbulo said sharply.

"Ah yes," Classicus's eyes glinted and a little smile appeared on his lips. "When I last saw the Governor he was looking pretty pleased with himself so I suppose that you struck a deal and he got his letters back." The Procurator paused as he glanced down the column of marching soldiers. "I know everything Corbulo," he said at last in a quieter voice, "I know about the letters and I know about those Christian children you smuggled out of Londinium. You did well to evade me and those thugs that the Governor sent after you. I didn't think you would make it but you did. The Emperor wants to know what was written in those letters and who wrote them. Don't take me for a fool. You are here because Agricola arranged it. He has persuaded you to go and find your Christian friend Quintus. Agricola wants his letter back too but the bad news for him is that it is still missing." Classicus chuckled and glanced over at Corbulo. "You don't want to go up against the Emperor, Corbulo, one word from me and you and everyone close to you will die. If Domitian wants something, he gets it."

"Well why doesn't the big hero come here himself then?" Corbulo muttered keeping his eyes on the column of men ahead of him.

"It doesn't have to be this way," Classicus said carefully, "If you were to help me retrieve Agricola's letter, if you were to find your friend Quintus, the Emperor would look favourably upon you. It could turn out to be quite a lucrative move and I know that you are a businessman. Why don't you think about that?"

Corbulo lowered his eyes and was silent for a moment.

"I think," he said slowly, "that the time has come for you to fuck off."

The Procurator's face darkened. "What's this? You dare defy the will of the Emperor," he hissed. "You had better be careful Corbulo for you are making some very powerful enemies and don't think they all wear Roman clothes. I have allies amongst the Hibernian tribes, men who hate Agricola, men who long for the chance of revenge. You had better watch your back, you Christian loving son of a whore. When I want something, I get it."

And with that Classcius called out to his men and urged his horse up the column. Corbulo was silent as he watched him go.

"That was the Procurator Augusti, wasn't it?" Galba said suddenly as he watched Classicus and his men ride away. "What a fucking prick. When I want something, I get it," Galba grinned as he imitated the Procurator's voice. The young man turned to Corbulo. "What strange company you keep, Corbulo," he said.

***

It was early evening when a Roman cavalryman came charging down the flank of the marching column. The man was crying out for the Legate. Trebonius seeing the rider urged his horse towards him.

"What's going on?" the Legate cried out in a loud voice.

The rider veered towards him. Sweat was streaming down the flanks of his horse. The soldier looked excited.

"Sir," he said snapping out a quick salute, "The Batavian cavalry are at the gates of Tara. They want to know what your orders are?"

Corbulo joined the Legate and his staff and turned to look west towards where the sun was a large fiery ball of orange on the horizon. Trebonius too had turned to stare at the dying sun.

"What about their defences, did the Batavians get a look at the defenders?" he said sharply.

The soldier's eyes glinted with feverish excitement.

"The place in unfortified and it looks lightly defended Sir," he blurted out.

Trebonius nodded as a mutter arose amongst his staff officers. "What about King Elim, is there any sign of him and his army?" the Legate snapped.

The rider shook his head and a grin appeared on his face.

"Nothing, there is no sign of him. The Hibernians have scouted the land for miles around and they report no sign of the enemy. Tara awaits to be taken Sir."

"Could it be a trap Sir?" a Centurion said as he turned to look at the Legate.

Trebonius was looking thoughtful and for a moment he did not reply. Then he turned to the rider.

217

"Very good," he snapped, "Ride back to the Batavians and tell them to hold their positions until the Legionaries reach them. Go!"

The cavalryman saluted hastily and with a little cry he was away racing back up the column towards the west. Trebonius turned to his officers.

"We are going to take Tara tonight," he said abruptly, "prepare the men. I want the 1st and 6th to attack as soon as they reach the hill."

The officers glanced at each other and there was a sudden excitement in their eyes.

"Boys," Trebonius said calmly, "Today we are going to set foot where no Roman soldier has ever been before."

Chapter Twenty-Three - The Fort of the Kings

The hill of Tara was not what Corbulo had expected. It was low and not very imposing but nevertheless it dominated the surrounding countryside. Corbulo grunted as he came to a halt and stared up at the mile long bleak and treeless ridge. The sun had vanished behind the horizon but it was still light enough to pick out the individual features of the capital of Hibernia. Dominating the hill-top was a prominent circular fort enclosed by an earthen rampart. From the top of the rampart a wooden pole had been driven into the earth and from it, flapping in the westerly breeze, was a black flag. As he peered up at the ramparts he suddenly caught sight of men staring back down at him.

A sudden trumpet blast wrenched his gaze away from the ramparts and towards the lines of Legionaries who were forming up at the base of the hill. The rattle and jingle of the men's armour and weapons mingled with the neighing of the cavalry horses and the urgent cries and shouts of the Centurion's and officers. Corbulo urged his horse towards the southern end of the hill where the Batavian cavalry squadrons stood drawn up ready to protect the Legionaries flank. The Batavians were silent and disciplined as they stared up at the defenders on the earthen rampart. Corbulo came to a halt beside one of the squadrons and turned to gaze back at the Legionaries. The infantry companies had formed up in tightly packed wedge formations with their Centurions at the very point. He glanced up the slope at the defenders on the embankment. There seemed pitifully few of them and Corbulo grunted in reluctant admiration. The Hibernians who had remained to defend their capital were brave men. They had not abandoned their posts even though they could have fled. Another trumpet blast rent the evening air and moments later the Legionaries began to move up the hill. The men's progress was slow but steady as they sought to stay in formation and as they came into missile range the Legionaries in the centre of the formations raised their shields over their heads to form a testudo. Corbulo was staring at the defenders up on the ramparts. The Hibernians had still not moved but he could hear their shouts and cries. The defenders were cursing and insulting the Romans.

As the Legionaries reached the base of the earthen embankment their formations suddenly surged forwards and with a great roar the Romans stormed up the grassy embankment and within a few moments the few Hibernian defenders were overrun. Corbulo watched mesmerized as the foremost assault companies vanished over the top of the rampart. Here and there a body tumbled down the embankment and the screams of the wounded rung out into the gathering darkness. A sudden stir beside him made him turn. The Batavians were moving. The foremost squadrons were peeling away southwards around the base of the hill. Corbulo followed and in the fading light he saw that the leading troopers were making for the gateway into the fort. The wooden gates were closed but as the troopers approached a trumpet blast erupted from within the hill top fort. The blast was followed by a great cheer. Then the gates started to open and a few Legionaries appeared in the entrance and raised their swords and shields in triumph. A little smile appeared on Corbulo's face. The Legionaries had taken the place in the first assault. The battle had lasted just a few minutes. Tara had fallen. The Batavian cavalry needed no further invitation as the troopers surged through the gate and into the fort. As he approached the gateway Corbulo could see now that the fort was large and oval shaped. The Legionaries beside the gateway raised their weapons and cried out in triumph as Corbulo passed in between the earthen embankment and across a narrow wooden bridge that spanned a deep waterlogged ditch. The ditch seemed to follow the circumference of the ramparts before it vanished from view behind a few Hibernian round houses. Corbulo slowed his horse to a walk as he gazed around him. The settlement was filled with Legionaries and their rough cries and shouts filled the evening air. Some of the soldiers were still struggling to cross the inner ditch but others had spread out amongst the cluster of round houses and were kicking in doors and vanishing into the buildings. Close by a woman screamed and further away he could hear a baby's cries and the barking of a dog. There were very few Hibernians to be seen and Corbulo sighed with sudden disappointment. Had he really expected Quintus to be here, waiting for him with open arms? A few terrified looking prisoners, old men, women and children were kneeling on the ground in a line with their hands clasped behind their heads as a squad of Legionaries searched them stripping them of anything of value.

Up ahead Corbulo caught sight of two smaller circular enclosures. As he approached he saw that they were two linked ring forts. The forts were enclosed by a ditch and an earth rampart and Roman Legionaries were swarming over the embankment and around the narrow entrance passage. Corbulo peered down the path that led into the complex but he couldn't see what lay beyond the earthen walls but it surely had to be an important place. He skirted the side of the two small ring forts and turned to gaze about him in disbelief. Two women were on their knees in front of a house with their hands clasped behind their heads. They were trembling with fear as inside the house Corbulo could hear the noise of male voices and of pottery being smashed.

"Where is everyone, where are the people of Tara?" he cried looking down at the women. The girls were too frightened to raise their heads and look up. Corbulo repeated himself but this time in a calmer voice.

"They have fled, they have gone," one of the women said quickly, "but we serve the goddess, we will not leave her."

Corbulo stared at the women for a long moment. Then he urged his horse onwards. Of course Quintus would have fled too. The Roman March on Tara had caught no one by surprise and there had been ample time to flee. Corbulo's shoulder sagged. His friend could be anywhere in Hibernia by now. How was he going to find him in this vast hostile and unknown land? He sighed and stared around him with mounting desperation. Then he blew the air from his lungs as he felt his resolve stiffen. It had been an unrealistic hope to find Quintus in Tara but he would think of something. He would find a way. There would be clues. He would find his friend. He had no choice.

A sudden scream caught his attention. Twenty paces away close to the outer ditch and rampart a Hibernian had set himself on fire. The flames were tearing away at his clothes and body as the man staggered towards a group of Legionaries. His terrible high-pitched screams rent the evening air. The Romans shouted at him as they stumbled backwards in alarm. Then a soldier threw a spear at the flaming figure and the screams were cut off as the man collapsed to the ground. Corbulo stared at the burning corpse as the flames continued to burn. Agricola had often talked about taking Tara but he had never managed it. But today Rome had conquered. There was no doubt about that and he Corbulo had been part of it. This would be a worthy tale to tell Efa and Dylis. Corbulo wrenched his eyes from the burning corpse and turned to stare at the deserted and abandoned round houses that had been packed tightly into the fort. Something felt wrong. It was clear now that the majority of the Hibernian population had fled and had even had time to take their precious cattle with them. Corbulo picked at one of his teeth as he stared at the corpse of a man lying beside the door to a house. The fight had been too easy. The Hibernians had made no serious effort to defend their capital. But he knew these people. They never gave up without a fight.

He urged his horse down the narrow alleys between the houses until he reached the end of the smaller linked ring forts. A commotion to his right caught his attention. Close to the outer rampart he spotted a small mound of raised earth. A passage way led into the mound ending in a solid looking wooden door a yard or so high. As Corbulo approached he saw Tuathal and a group of his men were kicking and hacking at the door. Some of Tuathal's men were holding burning torches and the reddish light gave the whole scene a hellish appearance.

"What is this place?" Corbulo cried at one of Tuathal's Hibernians who was standing back from the rest. The man glanced up with a triumphant, excited look.

"This is the Mound of the Hostages," the Hibernian replied in a thick accent. "The tomb beyond that door is as old as the Lugh himself. It was built by the ancients to honour their dead but now we use it to imprison hostages."

Corbulo turned to stare down the narrow passage at the wooden door. Tuathal was cursing and shouting a name as he repeatedly swung an axe into the wood. The door was starting to buckle and give way.

"Is there someone in there?" Corbulo said.

"He was there yesterday," the Hibernian hissed, "so let's hope he is still there and wasn't allowed to flee with the rest of them. If he's still in there then Tuathal is going to have him tortured and executed."

"Why, what has he done?" Corbulo inquired with a frown.

The Hibernian shook his head in disgust. "That's Eochaid Ainchenn in there. He is the man who murdered Tuathal's father, the rightful High King of Tara. Tuathal has waited years for this revenge."

"Who?" Corbulo said raising his eyebrows.

The Hibernian's eyes remained fixed on the door.

"Eochaid Ainchenn," he said with a hint of irritation, "one of the four kings who led the rebellion against Tuathal's father. Elim was one of them too but he and Eochaid quarrelled some years ago and Elim had him locked up in the Mound of the Hostages. With their King held hostage, Eochaid's people will remain loyal."

223

Corbulo turned to stare at the wooden door. Tuathal was hammering away at it in a flurry of blows as if he had gone berserk. Then with a howl Tuathal launched his foot against the wood and with a splintering noise the door gave way. Tuathal took a step back, grabbed hold of a flaming torch and tossed it into the dark narrow passageway beyond.

"If you are in there Eochaid, then come on out. Tuathal Techtmar has business with you tonight," Tuathal roared.

The party of men around the tomb fell silent as they waited for a reply. Then from inside the narrow passageway something moved. A man appeared and stooped through the doorway and calmly tossed the burning torch onto the grassy roof of the mound. Then he folded his arms across his chest and turned to look at Tuathal.

"I am Eochaid and I am here Tuathal Techtmar, there is no need to shout," the man said in a calm, quiet voice.

Eochaid was a big man with long straight black hair and a broken nose. He was clad in simple white sheepskin clothes and a wild black grey beard covered his cheeks and chin. He looked around fifty.

Tuathal's eyes sparkled as he stared at him. The silence lengthened. Then Tuathal took a step towards Eochaid and lifted his axe so that the sharp edge rested against Eochaid's neck. The hostage however did not move. Instead a proud little smile appeared on his lips as he looked at Tuathal.

"Go on then, do it, avenge that arsehole of a father of yours," Eochaid said calmly. "I am not afraid to die."

Tuathal's body started to tremble and a tortured whine escaped from his mouth. He lifted his axe away from the man's neck and prepared to strike.

"Wait!" Corbulo shouted as he urged his horse through the party of Hibernians and towards Tuathal. "Do not strike that man. The Legate will want to question him. He may have useful information about the enemy. Do not harm him!"

The Hibernians who clustered behind Tuathal turned and hastily stepped aside as Corbulo and his horse forced their way up the narrow passage. Both Tuathal and Eochaid were staring at him in surprise.

"You again," Tuathal snarled as he recognised Corbulo, "Why don't you fuck off, this is none of your business. This man belongs to me."

"No he doesn't," Corbulo snapped, "Like I said, the Legate will want to question him. He is coming with me. Trebonius will decide what to do with him."

Tuathal raised his axe in the air and for a moment a murderous look passed across his face as he stared at Corbulo with a wild aggressive look.

"I wouldn't do that," Corbulo said quietly, "killing a Roman soldier will not go down well with the Legionaries, nor with Agricola, your patron."

Tuathal's face darkened and he muttered a string of curses the like Corbulo had never heard before.

"You shit," he hissed at last. "Why are you doing this? This man means nothing to you. This man murdered my father."

"You shouldn't have hit me," Corbulo retorted. Then he turned to look at Eochaid. "You," he said pointing his finger at him, "will come with me."

***

Trebonius had established his command post in the northern most of the two small linked ring forts. The tumult amongst the civilian section of the fort was dying down as Corbulo, still mounted on his horse, and preceded by Eochaid rode up to the narrow entrance into the two small ring forts which he'd spotted earlier. They were closely followed by Tuathal and his men who strode along in sulky silence. A squad of eight Roman Legionaries were guarding the entrance across the ditch. The soldiers eyed Eochaid curiously.

"I need to see the Legate," Corbulo said, "This man here," he said gesturing at Eochaid, "has information that may be useful."

"No he fucking hasn't," Tuathal growled from the back.

The Optio in command of the section peered at Eochaid and then up at Corbulo. Then he nodded.

"Allright, the Legate is in King Elim's palace," the soldier sniggered as he said the word palace and some of his men joined in, "it's a fine palace for a king," the officer continued. "You will find it over there beside the tethered goat. You can't miss it, it's the only building within the walls."

Corbulo dismounted and handed the reins of his horse to one of the Legionaries. Then he gave Eochaid a shove as they started out across the bridge and into the passageway between the steep earthen embankments. Eochaid remained silent but behind him Corbulo could hear Tuathal muttering and cursing.

The Royal Seat, the official residence of the High King's of Tara was enclosed not only by an outer ditch and earthen rampart but by a second ditch as well. As they emerged into the ring barrow Corbulo could see that the fortification was small. In the middle of the enclosed space the earth had been raised by a couple of yards and standing on top of the artificial terrace was a solitary round house. The wooden wall posts had been set in a circle and in between them the wickerwork walls were stained white while the conical roof finished in a small smoke hole at the top. The thick low slung straw roof came down to a yard above the ground. A Legionary was standing guard outside the doorway and beside him tethered to a wooden post was a goat. The animal turned to look at Corbulo.

"Forty seven men, women and children, that's the final number of those who did not flee?" Trebonius was saying as Corbulo pushed Eochaid through the doorway and into the house. The Legate had been addressing his staff but he turned sharply at the intrusion. Corbulo cleared his throat and saluted.

"Sir," Corbulo said, "I found this man locked up in some kind of passage tomb. He seems to be of royal blood so I thought you may want to speak to him. He may have some useful information for us."

Trebonius frowned and glanced from Corbulo to Eochaid. The big Hibernian with his broken nose calmly stared back at the Legate.

"Well who are you? Why were locked up?" Trebonius snapped switching to the Celtic language.

"My name is Eochaid and I am King of Leinster," Eochaid replied with a little humorous smile, "and as for being locked up, it's a long story and you look like a busy man."

Trebonius did not look amused. He glanced briefly at Corbulo and was about to speak when he was interrupted.

"This man belongs to me," Tuathal hissed as he took a step forwards, "He murdered my father. I have the right to take revenge."

"You are not the High King yet," Trebonius said sharply, "I am in charge here and I will decide what happens to him."

Tuathal sneered and muttered something under his breath but did not reply. Trebonius turned to Eochaid.

"So do you have anything useful to tell me?" he said.

Eochaid smiled again. "Let me explain," he said cheerfully, "I have been locked up in the Mound of Hostages for a long time and all I know is darkness and the tone of the old man's cough when he brought me my food. I know nothing."

"You know nothing?" Trebonius said wearily. His remarks were followed a sharp muttered hissing noise from Tuathal. Corbulo scratched his cheek and looked down at his boots.

"Get him out of here," Trebonius said wearily gesturing at Corbulo, "Find him a dark place and lock him up but do not harm him."

"He is mine," Tuathal burst out no longer able to contain himself, "When I am High King he belongs to me."

The Legate did not reply as Corbulo grasped Eochaid by the arm and pushed him out through the door. Darkness had fallen and the skies were covered in a multitude a brilliant stars. It was a beautiful sight. Corbulo grasped Eochaid's arm as they descended the steps from the raised terrace and headed for the exit. They were closely followed by Tuathal and his men. Torches had been erected close to the passageway through the earthen berm and in their flickering light Corbulo could see a few Legionaries staring at him. The firelight reflected off their armour and metal helmets.

"Cormac's house would do," Eochaid said suddenly as they passed down the passageway, "It's a good place to lock me up in. It's dark and hard to escape from. Why don't we go there Roman? I have always wanted to spend a night in Cormac's house."

Corbulo grunted. "Where is that then?"

Eochaid pointed at the southern of the two linked ring forts.

"Planning to enjoy your last night in this world?" Tuathal snarled from behind them. "Tomorrow I shall be High King of Tara and you Eochaid Ainchenn will belong to me. Think about that tonight when you try to sleep."

Corbulo ignored Tuathal as they passed back over the outer ditch and turned in the direction of the second ring fort.

"I came here hoping to find a friend," Corbulo said quietly as he steered Eochaid in the direction of the entrance to Cormac's house. "We know that there are many Roman refugees who came to Tara to seek asylum. My friend's name was Quintus, he is a follower of Christus and a retired Centurion from the Twentieth, an old warrior like myself. He spoke your language." Corbulo paused. "What happened to these Romans, were they killed or did they flee with the rest?"

In the darkness Eochaid's eyes glinted and for a moment he remained silent.

"I know nothing," he said quietly.

Chapter Twenty-Four - The High King of Tara

It was morning and in the pale blue cloudless sky the sun was steadily climbing to its highest point. The Stone of Destiny stood just north of the Mound of the Hostages and around it a crowd of several hundred men had gathered. The Hibernians and Romans, split into separate groups and proudly holding up their unit and battle standards, stood on either side of the stone facing one another. They looked serious and solemn and not a man uttered a word. A patch of grass beside the stone looked disturbed as if an animal had been doing some digging. To Corbulo, standing with Trebonius and the Roman officers, the stone looked like any other standing stone he'd seen and it reminded him of the great circle of stones he'd once seen in the land west of Londinium. The druids had claimed that the standing stones contained magic and had been erected thousands of years ago but some of the army surgeons he'd spoken too had told him the great circle of stones was an ancient place of healing. Eagerly Corbulo peered at the Stone of Destiny. Whatever its original function the stone was being treated with the utmost respect by the Hibernians.

A breeze was coming in from the west and the wind tugged and played with the long wild beards and rough cloaks of the Hibernian mercenaries. From the direction of the main fort Corbulo suddenly caught a glimpse of movement and saw Tuathal Techtmar striding towards him down the narrow space between the Romans and the Hibernians. The Hibernian prince was closely followed by a group of his supporters and he looked calm and composed as he marched up to the stone and stopped before it. Corbulo could see that he was naked from the waist up and he had dark blue tattoos across his back and chest. Still no one spoke. Then Tuathal got down on his knees and opened his arms wide and bowed his head.

"See father," he cried, "Witness the return of your son and watch him claim his birthright. See me now father as I become High King of Tara and take back what is rightfully ours."

230

And with that Tuathal leaned forwards and kissed the Stone of Destiny. Corbulo took a step forwards and grunted. The stone had not screamed. There had been no noise. From the corner of his eye he noticed Galba staring at him from his position beside the Legate. The Tribune gently shook his head as if in warning and the worried look on the young man's face suddenly made Corbulo smile. Beside the stone Tuathal had risen to his feet and had turned to face the Hibernians.

"Swear your loyalty to me, your true High King!" Tuathal shouted and as his voice faded the Hibernians raised their weapons and battle standards and roared their acceptance. Then they did it again and there was no mistaking the enthusiasm in their voices. Slowly Tuathal turned to face the Romans and for a few moments he looked at Trebonius in silence as behind him the Hibernians started to recite and shout out their individual oaths of loyalty. The Legate, clad in his splendid parade ground armour and wearing a red cloak was flanked by the vexillatio standard bearer of the Twentieth who was wearing the head of a wolf and holding the battle group's standard in his right hand. Trebonius looked stern and dignified.

A satisfied smile appeared on Tuathal's face as he waited for the tumult behind him to die down. Then as the Hibernians fell silent Trebonius stepped forwards and saluted.

"Emperor Domitian accepts you as a friend and ally of the Roman people," the Legate said in a clear voice. "Rome wishes for peace with the people of Hibernia and their rightful king."

Trebonius snapped his fingers and Galba scurried over and handed him a tightly rolled scroll of parchment. The Hibernians began to mutter as Trebonius took his time and carefully unrolled the parchment before holding it up with two hands. He glanced at Tuathal. The High King of Tara was beginning to look a little resigned and impatient as if he knew what was coming.

"I have here," Trebonius cried, "a treaty of friendship between Rome and Tuathal Techtmar, High King of Tara and of all

231

Hibernia, rightful king, friend and ally of the Roman people. This treaty states that Hibernia shall remain an independent land, governed by its own laws, free from imperial taxes or occupation but shall solemnly pledge to forever stop raiding Roman land and ships and to stop giving aid to the enemies of Rome. The High King of Tara shall also agree to stop offering asylum to all enemies of Rome and shall open its land to Roman traders who shall pay no tax to the High King or his vassals." Trebonius rolled up the parchment and looked Tuathal straight in the eye. "Do you agree to this treaty?" he said sharply.

Tuathal smile was cold and fake.

"I agree to it and everything in it," he replied. "I give you my solemn oath."

Corbulo turned away and started to make his way through the ranks of the curious Roman soldiers pressing in behind him. He had seen enough. The whole show may have excited the Hibernian and foreign mercenaries but it was clear that the coronation had been planned long in advance. He sighed. No one had bothered to mention the other High King. Elim still had an army and it was fairly certain that he would not surrender his crown without a fight, which meant that the Romans were going to be staying at Tara for some time to come. As if to confirm his thoughts he caught sight of a work party of Legionaries up on the earthen ramparts of the main fort. The men were building a wooden palisade on top of the embankment and another work party were strung out in a line digging a new defensive ditch. Trebonius it seemed had come to the same conclusion and was wasting no time in preparing his defences.

Corbulo climbed up the embankment of the Fortress of the Kings and set off in the direction of Cormac's house. He would have to hurry if he was to beat Tuathal and his desire for vengeance.

***

The round building within the ring fort that the Hibernian had called Cormac's house was large and sturdily built. Corbulo paused in the entrance and for a moment he allowed his eyes to adjust to the gloom. In the centre of the room a long wooden pole rose up to support the conical straw roof. The house was empty and he guessed that the previous owners had taken their belongings with them, when they'd fled for all that was left were a couple of dirty and worn looking animal skins on the cool earthen floor and a broken table. Corbulo's nose twitched. The previous occupants must have shared the house with their cattle and pigs for the place smelt of shit. He took a step forwards and turned to look at the prisoner who was sitting beside the central pole. Eochaid gave him an enquiring look and Corbulo noticed that his hands were bound behind his back and fastened to the pillar. Another rope bound his ankles together and a third dug into his chest and he was gagged by a piece of cloth. Corbulo pulled the cloth from the man's mouth.

"Remember me?" he said quietly.

Eochaid nodded as he gave Corbulo a wary glance.

"Why did they gag you?" Corbulo said gesturing at the piece of cloth.

Eochaid shrugged and turned to look towards the entrance to the house.

"The soldiers outside, the ones guarding me, they told me they didn't like my singing. They told me to stop singing but I like singing. So they gagged me."

Corbulo did not reply. Then slowly he sat down in front of the prisoner and looked Eochaid straight in the eye.

"So you are Eochaid Ainchenn, King of Leinster," Corbulo said quietly as he examined the prisoner, "one of the four kings who successfully rebelled against Tuathal Techtmar's father. After your victory you must have had it all but somehow you still ended up being a hostage and a prisoner in your own capital. Some men may call that bad luck but others may think that you are just plain stupid."

Eochaid drew a sharp draw of breath and for a moment his eyes glinted. Then with an effort a smile appeared on his face.

"Why have you come here Roman?" he said.

Corbulo raised his fingers to his mouth and prodded one of his teeth. Then he fixed his eyes on Eochaid.

"I spent my whole life surrounded by men like you," he said slowly. "I was a watch commander in the Twentieth Legion and I know every soldier's trick and excuse. To get to the point, I know when someone is lying to me."

Eochaid's eyes widened in mock horror.

"You must be a very wise man," Eochaid replied, "But as you know, I am off to meet my gods soon so please remind me why I should give a fuck?"

Corbulo was gazing at the prisoner with a serious expression.

"Yesterday I asked you whether you knew or had heard about a Roman called Quintus, a retired Centurion and follower of Christus," Corbulo said speaking slowly and carefully. "He was one of the Roman refugees who came to Tara. I think you know the man whom I am talking about."

Eochaid was staring at Corbulo. Then abruptly he looked away.

"Like I said before, I know nothing," he muttered.

"Come on, stop the fucking bullshit and tell me the truth, one old warrior to another," Corbulo said calmly.

For a long moment the room remained silent. Then Eochaid stirred and a strange look   appeared in his eyes.

"You are a foreigner," he said quietly, "so I don't expect you to know the laws of hospitality in my country but I think even in Rome a man does not do something without getting something in return."

Without a word Corbulo drew his sword from its scabbard, leaned forwards and cut the ropes that bound the prisoners ankles.

"Tell me about Quintus, tell me what has happened to him?" Corbulo said.

Eochaid looked down at his ankles. Then he looked up at Corbulo and smiled.

"Cut me free and I will tell you everything I know," he said quietly, "but until then you won't get a wet fart out of me."

"I can do that," Corbulo nodded, "but what about the guards outside? You will never get past them. No," he shook his head, "tell me what you know and I will give you an honourable death, a warriors' death. That will be better than what Tuathal Techtmar has in mind for you."

Eochaid eyes gleamed and for a moment it seemed as if he was considering Corbulo's offer. Then a little smile appeared on his lips.

"I like you Roman," he said at last, "you tell it as it is but you do not know Cormac's house like I do. Don't worry about me. There are secrets in this place, secrets that you do not need to know about. Cut me free and I will tell you everything I know. I swear it on my family's good name."

Corbulo raised his eyebrows as he turned to look around the empty and deserted room.

"You can get out from this place without being seen?" he said quietly.

235

"I can get out," Eochaid nodded.

Corbulo looked down at the earthen floor. If Eochaid was indeed speaking the truth then there had to be a hidden tunnel somewhere in the room.

"Well?" Eochaid said glancing towards the entrance of the house.

Corbulo rose to his feet, stepped around the back of the Hibernian and swiftly cut the ropes that bound the prisoner to the central pole. Eochaid grunted in relief and rubbed his wrists as the ropes came loose. Quickly he got to his feet and turned to Corbulo with a sudden grateful and curious look.

"My apologies," he said in an urgent whispered voice as he dipped his head. "There was a Roman called Quintus, just like you described him. He and I spent some time together in the Mound of the Hostages. Your friend told me that Elim had welcomed him at first but then had him thrown into my prison for being rude. His time with me was brief, just a few days for Elim must have sobered up and forgiven him but I was glad for the company even though he was a Roman."

"That sounds like Quintus. He was always rude," Corbulo said quickly. "What happened to him? Where did he go?"

Eochaid took a deep breath.

"Your friend had a woman in Tara. She was high born and quite a catch. She came from Dun Aengus on the Forbidden Islands. The place is the capital of the Druids, for it is there that the druids teach and pass on their knowledge to the next generation. Dun Aengus can be found on the Aran islands far to the west where there is nothing but the endless ocean. He will have gone there. He has nowhere else to flee to."

"Dun Aengus," Corbulo frowned as he turned the name over in his mouth. Then he looked up sharply."How can you know this for sure?"

Eochaid shrugged. "I can't be certain but I too know something about men's hearts. He will have followed that woman when everyone fled. He lost his heart to her. That's my best guess."

"Why do they call them the Forbidden Islands?" Corbulo asked.

"The druid's call them this," Eochaid said with a serious face, "They say that no foreigner may land on the islands. They don't want foreigners coming and learning what they know. It is death for anyone caught breaking the rules."

"A strange place for Quintus to flee to?" Corbulo said with a frown.

"Yes," Eochaid muttered, "but maybe they will treat him differently. His woman is high-born; she has influence. The druids are not the only power in my country. We kings have our swords and the loyalty of our warriors."

Corbulo's mind seemed to be racing and for a moment he was silent.

"How far is it to Dun Aengus?" he said at last.

Eochaid chuckled quietly. "It's at least a hard three day ride on a good horse if you know the way, which you don't. After that you will have to brave the ten mile ocean crossing to the islands and Roman, the seas around those islands are like nothing you have ever experienced before. A single wave is enough to sink a boat and the druid's of Dun Aengus will kill you if they find you or have you forgotten that already?"

Corbulo was silent as he stroked his chin with a thoughtful look. Then at last he turned to Eochaid with his mind made up.

"There is one more thing I need from you," Corbulo said quietly.

Eochaid raised his eyebrows enquiringly.

"Be my guide and take me to the islands. I will get us two horses and some provisions. We shall leave tonight."

Eochaid was staring at Corbulo in surprise. Then slowly he shook his head.

"You are mad, you are completely insane," he whispered.

Chapter Twenty-Five - In Search of Quintus

Hastily Corbulo strode down the narrow paths that separated the densely packed round houses from each other. There were few people about and most of the Hibernian homes looked empty and deserted. Close by a dog was barking and up on the ramparts a Centurion was bellowing at his men but Corbulo paid them no attention. He was looking thoughtful. He was taking a gamble by trusting Eochaid but he had very little choice. The King of Leinster was the only one who seemed to have an idea of where Quintus had gone. There was no one else to ask. If the man was lying he would find out soon enough but he had to try. There was no way he would ever be able to look Marcus in the eye again if he didn't at least try to find Quintus. He'd agreed to meet Eochaid beside the river that flowed a couple of miles north of the Fortress of the Kings. The Hibernian had promised to be there. Baffled, Corbulo shook his head. How the man was going to escape from Cormac's house and just walk out of the fortress remained a complete mystery but when he had pressed Eochaid for an answer the Hibernian had just smiled. Corbulo had shrugged and left Eochaid to it. All that he needed now was a spare horse and some extra army rations.

Galba would hopefully be able to help. The Tribune was on the Legate's staff but that was no guarantee. The battle group needed every one of its horses and the Roman officers were sure to look dimly on any request for one of their valuable beasts. Corbulo groaned. If Galba could not help then he would have to go to Tuathal. Agricola had told him that he should approach Tuathal if he needed help but the thought of asking the newly crowned High King for assistance made him feel sick.

From the corner of his eye Corbulo noticed movement to his right. A man came out of the doorway making straight for him. Corbulo blinked. The man was a Praetorian. What was he doing here? Then from behind him a violent shove sent Corbulo careering into the wooden wall post of a house. His forehead slammed into the wood and he cried out in pain and shock as he staggered backwards from the impact. A boot struck his calf and then another shove sent him bouncing once more into the wall of the house. Corbulo yelled in pain as blood poured down his face. Vainly he reached for his sword but it was too late. Two pairs of hands had grasped his arms and were pinning them behind his back. A man appeared in front of him and with a vicious kick he struck Corbulo in the groin with his boot. Corbulo sank to the ground with a low moan. Then the world went dark as someone pulled a leather hood over his head.

"Get him inside the house," the Procurator snapped.

It took Corbulo a while before he was able to speak. The pain in his groin had become a dull throb that extended to his stomach and he could feel the blood caking his face where it had dried and congealed. His captors had forced him down on his knees and his hands had been bound behind his back and his ankles too had been tied up. Without warning the hood over his head was pulled away. Slowly he raised his head. He was inside one of the deserted Hibernian round-houses. The earthen floor around him was bare and it stank of the usual combination of animal piss and shit. Standing before him bearing a smug little smile was Classicus and beside him was one of his Praetorian guards. Corbulo turned round and saw two other Praetorians standing behind him. The men were armed and clad in full armour.

"Does it hurt?" the Procurator said.

"Fuck you," Corbulo muttered as he looked away.

"I told you to be careful," Classicus replied drawing a vine stick from his belt. Slowly he moved round behind Corbulo slapping the vine gently into the palm of his hand. "I warned you not to cross me." The blow came in fast and furious and the vine stick caught Corbulo on his kidneys. He cried out in pain.

"Now I am going to teach you to show a little respect to your superiors," the Procurator gasped. A second blow struck

240

Corbulo across his back and he groaned. Then a third blow lashed his head sending him toppling over onto the ground.

"Get him up on his knees," Classicus hissed.

Corbulo grimaced with pain but he was silent as the Praetorians dragged him upright. Classicus slowly circled and then came to a halt before him. Impatiently he tapped the vine stick in his hand.

"What do you want?" Corbulo groaned.

Classicus was staring down at him.

"Bring the Hibernian inside, I want him to see this," he said turning to one of the Praetorians. The guard moved towards the doorway and poked his head outside. A few moments later the animal skin that covered the entrance was flung back and a tall bearded man with a black eye patch over one eye stepped inside. Corbulo's eyes widened in shock as he recognised the man.

"You," he gasped.

Faelan did not reply. Slowly and silently he came up to Corbulo. There was a faint mocking expression on his face and he was holding his wooden staff. Without a word the druid carefully sat down on the earthen floor and turned to stare at Corbulo with his one good eye. The silence lengthened and grew uncomfortable and then unnerving.

"Did a fucking raven pick your eye out?" Corbulo muttered as a fresh trickle of blood slowly made its way down his forehead.

Faelan remained silent, staring intently at Corbulo.

"What is he doing here?" Corbulo gasped turning to Classicus in sudden exasperation, "This man is a fucking druid. He's our enemy. I saw him at the battle of Drumanagh. He has promised to have every Roman prisoner executed. What are you doing

241

with such a man? He will tell the Hibernians everything that he has seen here. How did he get inside our camp?"

Classicus chuckled. "What simple men you soldiers really are, believing that the only enemy is the one in the opposing army. What simple lives you lead. Tell me Corbulo, who do you think our real enemies are? Do you think it's the Hibernians, do you think its King Elim and his army or even the druids?" The Procurator shook his head. "No, there is only enemy and that is the traitorous scum who are plotting rebellion against the Emperor. Those men are our real enemies Corbulo. They are the men we must stop."

"You are mad," Corbulo shouted angrily, "You have allowed a spy to enter our camp. The Legate will have you executed for that!"

One of the Praetorians behind Corbulo struck him over the head with his fist and once more Corbulo crashed sideways onto the floor with a yell of pain.

"I am growing tired of you," the Procurator said wearily as Corbulo was hauled back up onto his knees. "So now we are going to talk you and I." Classicus paused as he started to circle Corbulo tapping his vine stick against his hand. "Let me start from the beginning," he said patiently. "My position as finance minister for the province of Britannia means that I am here to protect the Emperor's interests. We have known for some time that there has been a plot against the Emperor's life and we have a list of suspects involved in this treason. Those Senators in Rome are being taken care of but it is a lot harder and more dangerous for us to accuse and confront military commanders who have the loyalty of their legions behind them. So I have to act carefully for starting a civil war is not a desirable outcome. I need absolute proof of their involvement before we can move against them." The Procurator paused as he came full circle and looked down at Corbulo. "Now earlier this year I thought I finally had that proof when my spy within the Governor's palace managed to steal six highly incriminating letters addressed to the Governor from a number of military commanders of Senatorial and Equestrian rank. But I seem to have underestimated my spy's loyalty to his own kind for instead of passing the letters on to me as I had ordered him to do, he hid them amongst his own community."

Corbulo lifted his head and looked up at Classicus. One of his eyes was badly swollen and his face was caked in blood.

"Your spy was the Christian," he mumbled, "the man called Alexander, Quintus's friend."

"Yes," Classicus nodded sternly, "he was a Christian and I made the mistake of trusting him and those religious zealots. So before I could find out where Alexander had hidden the letters, the Governor tried to arrest him but Alexander killed himself before he was captured." The Procurator shrugged, "You know the story from there. By all rights I should stick a knife in your back right now for all the damage you have done to my interests. You helped those damned Christian children escape from Londinium and then you handed those letters back to the Governor." The Procurator raised a single finger in the air as his whole body shook with sudden anger, "You Corbulo may yet cause the downfall of the Emperor, but I assure you that you will not live to see what comes afterwards."

Corbulo closed his eyes and then opened them again. Slowly he raised his head to look up at the Procurator and there was a grim smile on his lips.

"What did Alexander demand from you?" he whispered hoarsely, "What did he want in return for the letters?"

Classicus restrained himself with an effort.

"That is something you don't need to know," he said firmly, "but we are not finished yet. There is one letter that is still unaccounted for. By torturing Alexander's Christian friends in Londinium I learned that Alexander gave one of the letters,

Agricola's letter, to your friend Quintus, a recent convert to Christus who promptly disappeared." The Procurator took a step towards Corbulo.

"So where is he, Corbulo? Where is our friend Quintus? I would very much like to meet him."

Corbulo looked down at the ground and did not answer.

"You know where he is," Classicus said quietly; "the Hibernian King. Eochaid, you went to visit him just now and he told you didn't he?"

"Why don't you go and ask him yourself?" Corbulo muttered.

"Well I would," Classicus retorted, "but he's gone. He's vanished. They are looking for him everywhere. You let him escape didn't you? So what was the plan, take a couple of horses and let him guide you to where Quintus is hiding? It's over Corbulo, you are not going anywhere."

Corbulo stared down at the dark earth. The pain in his head was coming in waves.

"If you kill me, you will never find him," Corbulo mumbled.

The Procurator grunted contemptuously.

"I thought you would say that," he snapped, "but if you refuse to cooperate, it won't be you who will die. My men tell me that you have a son serving amongst the Batavian cavalry. So let's put it bluntly and plainly, either you tell me where Quintus is or else your son Marcus will end up lying in the mud with his throat cut. The choice is yours, make it now."

Corbulo closed his eyes and his head drooped. For a long moment he was silent. Then at last he looked up at Classicus and as he did so Faelan stirred and rose to his feet. The druid had not said a word since he'd entered the house.

"Allright," Corbulo nodded, "Eochaid told me it was likely that Quintus had fled to a place called Dun Aengus. It's on the west coast. Eochaid said that Quintus had a woman who came from there. That's all he told me. Leave my son alone. He has nothing to do with this."

"The Forbidden Islands," Faelan exclaimed in alarm. "No foreigner is allowed to set foot on those islands."

Corbulo glanced up at the druid. Faelan looked shocked.

The Procurator was staring at Corbulo intently. Then abruptly he turned to Faelan.

"You know what, I think he is telling the truth," he said. Quickly he snapped his fingers at the Praetorians. "Get the men ready, we are leaving. You two shall stay here with him. Keep him here for a couple of days and then hand him over to the Legate and tell Trebonius that it was him who allowed the prisoner to escape. The guards at Cormac's house will back you up. He was the last man to see Eochaid."

The Procurator turned to look down at Corbulo.

"You see Corbulo, when I want something, I get it. I believe the punishment for a soldier aiding the enemy in war time is death, " he said gleefully.

***

Corbulo woke with a start. A hood had been placed over his head and he could see nothing. How long had he been out? He lifted his head and groaned as he turned to look in what he thought was the direction of the doorway. The Praetorians had left him lying on the floor with his hands and ankles bound together and a gag wrapped around his mouth, but his ears had not deceived him. In the darkness he had heard something. Close by he sensed someone move.

"Lucius, is everything allright?" a Roman voice called out.

Corbulo lowered his head back onto the cool earth. The man's voice belonged to one of the Praetorians left behind to guard him. He was calling to the other guard. There was no answer from outside and the Praetorian cursed quietly and drew his sword. The metal blade made a faint noise as he pulled it free.

"Lucius," the Praetorian called out again, "Don't play games with me now. Are you allright? I heard something."

For a moment all was silent. Then violently the animal skin covering the doorway was flung aside and Corbulo heard men's harsh guttural cries. The Praetorian cursed loudly as men's boots thudded across the earth. A flaming torch landed on the ground beside Corbulo and he felt the heat start to burn his skin. Desperately he rolled away from the flames. Close by someone was straining and groaning as if involved in a fight. Then a single high-pitched cry rose rent the darkness and a body tumbled to the ground beside him. Corbulo froze as the hut went quiet. In the darkness he could hear men's laboured breathing. The silence lengthened. Then someone stooped down and pulled the hood from his head. Corbulo blinked and tried to adjust to the light. Outside through the open doorway he could see the stars in the night sky. The hut itself was lit by three or four flaming torches; but in their flickering light it was hard to see the faces of the men holding the torches. Slowly Corbulo turned to glance at the body of the Praetorian. He was dead. Then a man was kneeling down at his side and removing the gag that had been wrapped around his mouth.

"No one touches my dad," Marcus growled as he used his Pugio, to cut the rope that bound Corbulo's hands and ankles. Corbulo felt the ropes ease and stiffly he moved his hands and sat up.

"Is that really you son?" he muttered.

Marcus lowered his torch so that Corbulo could see his face.

"Yes it's me," Marcus replied, "and I brought some of my Batavians with me. You are allright now Dad, we took care of the other guard outside. You are free. Unfortunately that arsehole Classicus left Tara a few hours ago."

"How did you find me?" Corbulo said as he stiffly rubbed his wrists.

Marcus did not reply immediately. Instead he rose to his feet and handed his torch to one of the Batavians. Then he sighed. "Let's say that I suspected that you would get yourself into trouble, so I had one of my men follow you, discreetly, just to make sure that you were allright. He told me what happened. I am sorry that I could not have come sooner for the Procurator's head would be on a spike by now. Look at what that bastard did to you."

Corbulo grunted as he got up on his feet.

"Where's my sword?" he muttered casting about around the hut. The house remained silent as Corbulo stumbled around until he had retrieved his sword and had slid it back into his scabbard.

"Thank you," Corbulo said wearily turning to look at his son. "I was foolish, I should have seen them coming."

Marcus spoke quickly to the Batavians in their own language and one of the auxiliaries stooped to light the hearth in the middle of the round room as his comrades silently exited through the doorway. The wood fire took a while to catch but then it grew rapidly bathing the round room in a reddish glow.

"Yes you should have seen them coming," Marcus said as he sat down beside the flickering, crackling fire. "But then again you have been busy." Marcus looked down at the flames as Corbulo slowly sat down on the opposite side of the hearth. "They say that you went to see the Hibernian King and that after you left, the prisoner simply vanished." A little smile appeared on Marcus's face. "Some of the men think that you possess magic."

"And what do you think?" Corbulo muttered.

Marcus looked up. "I think you know much more than you are telling me," he said quietly. "I am not stupid father, I know something is going on with you and Agricola and I know that it is somehow connected to the disappearance of my woman and child. I want you to tell me the truth?"

Corbulo was staring into the flames moodily and for a long moment he said nothing.

"Ah fuck it," he exclaimed at last, "you have a right to know." He looked up at Marcus. "Your woman and son are allright. Agricola has taken them. He is holding them hostage until I manage to find Quintus and retrieve a letter from him that belongs to Agricola. That's why I am here. I went to talk with the Hibernian King because I thought he might know where Quintus had gone and he does."

Corbulo took a deep breath and shrugged.

Marcus was watching him closely as an awkward silence descended. The crackle of the fire and the smell of smoke filled the room.

"Were you afraid that I would desert my unit and go looking for Agricola?" Marcus said with a tight voice. "Desertion is punishable by death."

Corbulo refused to look his son in the eye. He shrugged. "Maybe," he muttered. "I would have thought about it if I were you."

Marcus looked away. Then swiftly he rose to his feet.

"Well I am not going to desert," he said calmly, "because I have faith in my dad. Go on, find Quintus and give Agricola what he wants. Sort this thing out."

Corbulo looked up at his son in surprise. Then slowly a little smile appeared on his lips.

"I am going to need two good horses and some extra rations," he said.

Chapter Twenty-Six - Into the West

Corbulo glanced up at the full moon as he led the two horses towards the dark outline of the forest. The beasts snorted uneasily and stamped their hooves. The night was silent and cold and a western breeze was tugging at his cloak and hair. Would Eochaid keep his promise? Would the Hibernian be waiting for him as they had agreed? At the edge of the forest Corbulo paused and turned to look back in the direction of Tara. The royal fortress was shrouded in darkness and he could hear nothing apart from the gentle moaning wind and the breathing of the horses. He sighed. This was a journey into the unknown. Few Romans had ever ventured this far into the interior of Hibernia. In the barracks blocks and army tents he'd often heard the Legionaries discussing Hibernia, the land of eternal winter, the land at the edge of the world and the tone of the men's voices had been cautious. Corbulo turned away and entered the forest. The trees closed in around him and his pace slowed. After a while he stopped again as in between the trees he suddenly caught sight of the river. In the moonlight it looked placid and tranquil and it was not very wide. For a moment he did not move. In the cool night he could hear the splash of the water and saw the moon's reflection in the river. Then he turned and started to follow the river upstream. Down at the river bank an animal splashed noisily into the water and in the forest an owl hooted.

The abandoned ring fort had been built beside the river and Corbulo paused at the edge of the forest as he studied the fortified farmhouse carefully. The place looked deserted and he could see no lights nor could he hear anything. With a gentle tug on their harnesses, he led the two horses towards the gateway into the farm. As he approached he could see that the walls had collapsed in places and that the roof of the main building had fallen inwards. Weeds were growing out of cracks between the stones. At the gate he paused and turned to look around him.

"Eochaid, it's me Corbulo," he called quietly.

From the darkness there was no reply.

"Eochaid you prick," Corbulo called quietly again, "I am here like we agreed. Come on out, I have horses and food."

From amongst the rubble strewn entrance to the ring fort, something moved. Corbulo peered into the darkness. Then close by, a shape appeared. The horses snorted and whinnied in fright.

"You didn't think I would keep my word did you?" Eochaid said with the hint of a smile as he came up to Corbulo. "But I always keep my word. You should not doubt me. I am your friend Corbulo. Without you I would be fertilizing the earth by now." Eochaid paused and his eyes glinted in the moonlight. "You took your time about getting here though. I have been waiting for hours and I am hungry. Haven't eaten in days."

Corbulo looked un-amused. He handed the reins of one of the horses to the Hibernian.

"Do you know the way?" he asked quietly.

Eochaid nodded as he turned to inspect his horse with a keen eye.

"Fine beast, a fine foreign beast," he muttered as he slid his hand approvingly over the horses flank. "At least you know something about horses Roman."

Then in one smooth movement he lifted himself up onto the horse's back.

"I ran into some trouble after I left you," Corbulo said as he prepared to mount his beast, "We are not the only ones who are looking for Quintus. There is a Roman called Classicus who is after him as well. Classicus has Praetorian guards and he's allied himself with one of your countrymen, a druid called Faelan. They too are heading for Dun Aengus."

251

"That will be the men I saw riding away this afternoon then," Eochaid said cheerfully. "I know Faelan, his loyalty however is to King Elim. He's dangerous."

Corbulo hoisted himself onto the horse's back and for a moment he clung on awkwardly. The horse snorted impatiently. With an effort Corbulo managed to right himself and sit up properly.

"We need to reach Dun Aengus before Classicus," he muttered ignoring Eochaid's amused look. "Which means we rest only when it's strictly necessary. I have enough food to last us four days and if you have to piss then you piss whilst riding. It's really important that we reach those islands before our competition."

"I think I understand," Eochaid said raising his eyebrows, "Classicus has a head start of several hours and Faelan knows the way but they move like fat well fed cattle." Eochaid chuckled to himself. "Don't worry Corbulo. We shall be like hungry wolves. I am the finest tracker the world has known and we have got good horses. What can go wrong my friend?"

Corbulo sighed and turned to look in the direction of Tara.

"How long will it be before King Elim arrives with his army?" Corbulo said.

Eochaid turned to look in the direction in which Corbulo was staring. For a moment he was silent.

"I don't know," he replied at last, "but soon. Elim is a proud man, he will not allow his capital to remain in Roman hands for long." Eochaid turned to Corbulo with a sudden smile. "I am surprised that you haven't realised the truth yet?"

"What truth?" Corbulo snapped.

Eochaid slowly drew his finger across his throat. "I was not present at the High King's Councils but I suspect that your soldiers have walked into a trap. They will never leave Tara alive. Elim will surround you and cut you off from your supplies.

252

He will strangle you in Tara and starve you to death. He has a large army and he has the loyalty of nearly all the kings."

Corbulo cleared his throat. "Tuathal Techtmar has promised that he will raise a force of five thousand Hibernians to fight for him," he exclaimed. "With such number's we will defeat Elim."

At the mention of Tuathal's name Eochaid spat onto the ground.

"The only thing that Tuathal Techtmar will raise is his cock," he snorted derisively.

***

Corbulo could hear the boom of the surf on the beach. He sat on his horse staring at the village, a small cluster of white stone and thatched round houses that huddled beside the sea. It was morning and a strong westerly breeze was blowing into his face as if willing him to turn back. The grey ocean stretched away to the horizon and out in the bay he could see white tipped waves. High above him circling lazily on the air currents he could hear the screech of the white-sea gulls as they hunted for their breakfast. Corbulo looked exhausted. His eyes were tinted red and dark wrinkles had appeared under them from a lack of sleep. The stubble on his chin and cheeks was several days old and his face was stained with dust and streaked with sweat. Slowly he turned to look at Eochaid who was sitting on his horse. The Hibernian too looked tired as he squinted at the cluster of huts along the shore. Eochaid caught his glance and grinned wearily.

"The Forbidden Islands are beyond that headland to the north," he said gesturing with his hand. "They are no more than a day's sail but the wind is against us."

Corbulo nodded as he stared at the sea.

"Thank you Eochaid," he said at last, "You kept your promise and here we are. There is no need for you to travel any further. Go home to your people. I will go on alone."

Eochaid turned sharply to look at Corbulo and shook his head.

"No Roman," he said firmly, "You saved my life in Tara and when a man chooses to save another's life he owns that life. I am coming with you to the islands. We shall not be equal until I have saved your skin."

A faint smile appeared on Corbulo's face. "You already did by guiding me here," he replied but again Eochaid shook his head.

"No, we will not argue about this, it is the way of things." And with a small cry he urged his horse forwards in the direction of the village. "I am going to see if I can get us a boat, stay here Roman," he shouted as he trotted away.

Corbulo did not reply. Instead he turned to look around him at the green meadows. What a journey they'd had. Three days and nights they had ridden with barely a halt. Eochaid had been an expert navigator, always seeming to know which way to go. They had crossed vast tracks of flat, bleak and uninviting bog lands dotted with coarse colourful heather and pools of water and Corbulo had gotten thoroughly sick of the smell of the marshes and the relentless mosquitoes. Eochaid had kept the horses on the network of winding sand and gravel ridges that crisscrossed the land. Eskers he had called them and they had proved to be a much-used highway for they had overtaken many travellers. The people had all been going in one direction, away from Tara and they were accompanied by their cattle. The refugees had cast hostile and suspicious glances at Corbulo but amongst them Corbulo had also noticed a few men dressed in Roman clothing. The Romans, all of them men, had not been easy to talk to and had strayed off the path as soon as they caught sight of Corbulo. There had been no sightings of Quintus or Classicus but Eochaid had spoken to some of the Hibernians and with his easy charm he'd managed to barter water, a sword and news. From the travellers they'd learnt that High King Elim had issued a call for all able-bodied men to join him on his march on Tara and that Tuathal Techtmar was doing the same by calling on his supporters to rally to his defence.

Wearily Corbulo leaned forwards on his horse as he waited patiently for Eochaid to return. The western wind was strong and constant and out to sea the white tipped waves looked fierce and violent. A sandy beach stretched away southwards from the village and inside the small settlement he could hear a dog barking. Then at last he spotted Eochaid coming towards him from across the windswept field. The Hibernian was without his horse and he was carrying a large oval shaped object on his back that reminded Corbulo of a large Greek style shield. Corbulo peered at Eochaid curiously as he trudged towards him. Then his eyes widened in surprise. The object on Eochaid's back was not a shield; it was a boat.

The Hibernian halted beside Corbulo and with a groan lowered the oval shaped boat to the ground before rubbing his hands together with a satisfied look.

"It's a good bargain," Eochaid said cheerfully, "The man who owns this Curragh will get the use of our horses for as long as we get the use of his boat. We bring the boat back, we get our horses back."

Corbulo was staring down at the flimsy looking craft in dismay. It looked barely large enough to hold two men. The sides and hull seemed to be made of wickerwork over which brown animal hides had been stretched and fastened.

"That is a boat," he gasped in alarm, "You want to cross to the islands in that?"

Eochaid nodded. "It's sturdy and light," he replied, "And I have two paddles. The man from whom I loaned it says that the currents will help us out to the islands."

Corbulo was still staring at the Curragh in alarm. Then slowly he dismounted from his horse and gave the oval boat a gentle prod with his boot.

"And there is something else," Eochaid said quietly, "the villager I spoke with claims to have seen a Roman who fitted Quintus's description. The man was on a boat that sailed for the Forbidden Islands four days ago. The villager said that the Roman appeared to be in chains."

Corbulo looked up sharply. "Chains?" he exclaimed, "Why would they put him in chains?"

"I don't know," Eochaid said looking away.

Corbulo was silent as his mind raced to make sense of things. Then he shook his head and turned his attention back to the Curragh.

"Allright, let's see how well this thing floats," he growled moodily.

Chapter Twenty-Seven - The Forbidden Islands

In places the sandy beach was covered in dark green seaweed that clung to rocks and stones. Out in the sea, white tipped waves came rolling in onto the beach sending foaming seawater hissing and speeding over the sand. Without hesitation Eochaid strode straight into the surf and dumped the Curragh into the water holding onto it with one hand as the waves pulled and pushed at the flimsy looking craft. Corbulo looked on doubtfully. Then muttering to himself he waded out into the surf and grasped hold of the side of the boat. In the sky the white clouds were drifting eastwards as the full force of the western wind plastered Corbulo's face with stinging salty spray. Eochaid grinned at Corbulo as he clambered into the craft and retrieved the two oars from the bottom of the boat.

"Get in," Eochaid shouted, "We need to make the islands before nightfall or else there is a chance we will be swept out into the ocean."

Corbulo said nothing as he clambered awkwardly into the craft. The waves buffeted and slammed into the Curragh sending it spinning and bobbing up and down. Corbulo grunted in relief as he finally managed to right himself. There was just enough space for the two of them to sit, one behind the other but as he looked about him at the waves Corbulo suddenly groaned. How were they ever going to get Quintus off the island in this craft? There simply wasn't enough space for three men. He opened his mouth and cried out to Eochaid but the Hibernian sitting in front of him did not seem to have heard him, for all he did was hand Corbulo an oar.

"Now we row!" Eochaid cried as the wind sent a sheet of spray blowing into their faces. "Let's get clear of the beach."

Corbulo dug his oar into the sea as Eochaid did the same on the other side of the boat and to his amazement Corbulo sensed the light craft begin to move. He turned to look back at the beach and noticed a man watching them from the shore. He was too distant to make out his features. A wave slapped up against the side of the Curragh and Corbulo cried out in shock as he was drenched in icy cold seawater. He shook his head sending water droplets flying in all directions. Eochaid half turned to look back at him. The Hibernian was laughing.

"I love the sea," he cried. "I fucking love it!"

Corbulo spat some water from his mouth and silently dug his oar into the waves with grim determination. The boat surged up and down on the waves and to his right Corbulo noticed that the shoreline ended in a rocky headland. Eochaid seemed to be steering the craft straight towards it. Another wave slammed into the craft drenching Corbulo and making him gasp. Grimly he dug his paddle into the water and as he did so he defiantly stared down into the green boiling sea. It was what so many Legionaries had feared the most. Being lost at sea, drowned by the weight of one's armour, pulled down into the murky depths where the body would never find a final resting place, where a man's spirit would wonder forever, lost, confused and alone. He had witnessed whole companies refusing to board ships because the omens had been bad. Not even the fear of severe punishment had been enough to make the men change their minds.

A noise made him look up. Eochaid was singing and his voice was growing in volume as they ploughed on across the waves. Corbulo shook his head as he grimly stuck to his task. When this was over he was never again going out onto the sea. Not for the love of money or anything else.

The sky was overcast but the wind was as strong as ever when they finally rounded the headland. Eochaid paused and with a cry pointed towards the west and there a few miles away Corbulo caught sight of an island.

"There are three islands in all," Eochaid cried, "This is the smallest one, Dun Aengus is on the largest one, further out to sea. Come on Roman, put your back into it. We still have some way to go."

Corbulo peered at the distant island. It looked bleak, rugged and uninviting.

"When we were locked up together," Eochaid shouted, "Your friend Quintus told me about his god. He had such faith that his god would come and rescue him but this Christus is strange and he doesn't seem to be a very powerful god. Are you one of his followers, do you believe in Christus, Roman?"

Corbulo paused to wipe the sweat from his brow and catch his breath. Around him the waves came on surging forwards in straight lines as they headed for the shore. The craft bobbed up and down.

"No," he cried, "Jupiter has always been the patron god of Rome, Jupiter and the guardian spirits of the Twentieth will protect us. I have kissed their statues so many times and left them enough donations to last several lifetimes. They owe me!"

In front of him Eochaid boomed out in laughter.

"The gods owe us nothing," he shouted as a wave broke above them drenching the two of them in green hissing seawater.

"They do and today I am collecting," Corbulo roared defiantly.

***

It was early evening when Eochaid suddenly stopped rowing and raised his hand. A couple of hundred paces away the sheer, rugged and beautiful cliffs rose up from the sea towering over the little Curragh and its occupants. Corbulo stopped paddling and turned to look up at the cliffs. They reminded him of the cliffs he'd seen south of Rutupia but these were not white and they were marked by the ceaseless violence of the ocean, for here and there huge boulders had broken free and had tumbled into the sea and dark cracks in the rock hinted at the presence of caves. Eochaid twisted round and his eyes twinkled in excitement.

"We're here," he whispered, "Dun Aengus is on the other side of the island about a half a mile away."

Corbulo said nothing as the Curragh bobbed up and down on the gentle waves. They were in a bay and the island seemed to be shielding them from the rough ocean waves further out. He glanced up again at the cliffs. The grey and yellow slabs of stone seemed to be set in layers with clearly defined lines running along them and he guessed the cliff height at roughly a hundred yards. A few sea gulls had made their nests amongst the rocks and the screeching white birds rose and dived on the air currents. Close by a piece of dark driftwood floated aimlessly on the current. Corbulo peered up at the cliff tops but he could see no sign of human habitation.

"I am going to land us on that beach over there," Eochaid said quietly, "We will have to climb our way up to the top of the cliffs from there."

Stiffly Corbulo dug his paddle into the water as Eochaid starting to guide them towards the shore. The beach was small and narrow and strewn with tumbled rocks, seaweed and flotsam, that the sea had washed ashore. The roar of the waves as they broke onto the sand and rocks mingled with the screeching sea gulls. Then with a grating shudder the waves pushed them onto the shore and Eochaid leapt out of the boat and knelt down in the surf. Stiffly Corbulo rose to his feet and half staggered, half collapsed overboard into the water. His muscles were stiff and cold from the long hours sitting in the cramped boat and for a moment he stood in the surf unable to move as the water surged and retreated around his knees.

"Your gods heard you," Eochaid said with a weary but triumphant grin as he boldly lifted the Curragh out of the water and held it over his head. Then without waiting for an answer he started up the beach towards the cliff face. Corbulo blew the air from his cheeks and wiped his brow. Then slowly he followed Eochaid onto dry land. The Hibernian was stowing the oval Curragh into a gap between the rocks when Corbulo caught up with him. Wearily Corbulo sat down on a boulder as Eochaid finished stowing the craft and started to hide it with rocks and jetsam from the beach. When he was done the Hibernian came and sat down beside Corbulo.

"So I got you here, now what?" Eochaid said glancing up at the sky.

Corbulo closed his eyes. Then he opened them. "If these are the Forbidden Islands then I am not allowed to be here," he said slowly, "Anyone can see that I am a Roman so I am not going to be able to walk straight through the gates of Dun Aengus and ask them where Quintus is. No, you will have to do that. Go now before it's too dark and find out if Quintus is here and if so where he is being held."

"I knew you would say that," Eochaid replied with a sigh, "see Roman, if you had left me on the mainland you wouldn't have a hope."

Corbulo turned to look at the Hibernian. "If we can get Quintus off this island, you will have saved two lives Eochaid, two lives that mean a lot to me."

A little smile appeared on Eochaid's lips as he rose to his feet. "I know," he replied, "Two lives you say, well it must be worth it then. It will be you Roman who will owe me in that case."

He was about to walk away when he paused and looked up at the sky. For a moment it seemed as if he was doing a calculation in his head. Then Eochaid turned to Corbulo and raised his eyebrows.

"I nearly forgot," he exclaimed, "Tonight is the summer solstice, the longest day of the year."

Corbulo looked puzzled and shrugged.

"Dun Aengus is the capital of the druids," Eochaid said quietly, "They will be out celebrating tonight. No doubt it will be a great feast. Keep an eye open for their fires. I may not be back until the morning."

Corbulo's eyes narrowed suspiciously. "What do you mean?" he muttered as he rose to his feet.

Eochaid grinned and grasped his own balls with his hand. "I haven't had a chance to use these for a while, it's about time that I did," he replied.

***

Corbulo watched Eochaid disappear up the path leading to the cliff top. It was the right decision to send the Hibernian ahead as a scout but Corbulo could not get rid of the feeling that he should have been doing that job. Exhaustion was trying to close his eyes and force him to sleep. Stubbornly he shook his head and slapped his cheek. Then he rose and strode out into the surf, knelt down in the sand and thrust his head into the seawater. The water was still shockingly cold and he rose rapidly sending drops flying in every direction. He turned and started up the beach in the direction that Eochaid had taken. One thing he could do at least before it became too dark was to get a good look at Dun Aengus.

The sun had already vanished below the horizon when Corbulo crouched down beside the boulder. It hadn't taken him very long to climb up to the cliff top and cross the narrow neck of land that separated the beach from the other side of the island. The first thing that had struck him as he'd made it up onto the top of the cliffs was the sheer rugged, barrenness of the island. There was not a tree to be seen and the ground was featureless and covered by rocks. In the dying light the only sign of vegetation was a strange looking yellow moss that grew in the cracks between the rocks. Corbulo grunted in amazement as he caught sight of Dun Aengus. The settlement was larger than he had expected and much more impressive. The oval shaped inner wall stood on a small promontory jutting out into the sea with its walls ending at the cliff edge and its rear protected by sheer hundred yard high cliffs. Corbulo grunted respectfully. He could see why there had been no need to extend the wall all the way around to complete the oval shape. The cliffs at the rear looked formidable. Curiously he turned to peer at the dry stonewall a hundred paces away. Inside the enclosure beyond he could see a large herd of cattle, cows and sheep. The animals were guarded by three boys, armed with sticks. who were moving about the herd. He grunted and shifted his gaze. Beyond the herding enclosure was a field of upturned stones that created a maze of sharpened obstacles. Corbulo recognised it immediately for what it was, an anti cavalry defence and once more he grunted with growing amazement. This was no ordinary Celtic settlement, this place was a fortress, carefully designed and constructed. No wonder the druids had made it their capital. The place looked impregnable. He glanced up at the sky. Darkness was not far away. He turned back to stare at the fortress. There was another dry stone wall beyond the maze of upturned stones and maybe more behind it but he couldn't see any further. The walls looked like they were at least six yards high and it was impossible to know how thick. Corbulo grunted as he traced the walls to the single gate into the fortress. This place had never fallen; this settlement had never been captured. However old this place may be he was certain of that. Did anyone in Roman Britannia know that this place existed? As he stared at Dun Aengus, a solitary bonfire sprang into life. Corbulo turned to look at it. The fire was coming from the inner enclosure, from a raised rectangular platform that overlooked the sea and the sheer cliffs that jutted out into the ocean. As he stared at it he suddenly saw an answering light appear out on the ocean to west. Corbulo frowned. The light on the ocean had to be from a ship. What was a boat doing out there after dark?

It was a few hours later when Corbulo heard something move on the path leading up to the cliff tops. Instantly he was up on his feet, his sword in his hand. Close by a stone clattered down onto the beach and in the darkness he heard a soft muffled curse.

"Roman, are you there, it's me Eochaid," a voice whispered in the gloom.

Corbulo relaxed as he peered into the darkness. Then a shape appeared and he could hear a man's breathing.

"I am here," Corbulo said impatiently.

Another muffled curse erupted from the darkness. In the faint moonlight Corbulo caught a glimpse of the figure of a man.

"What are you doing here?" Corbulo whispered as he held onto his sword, "You said that you wouldn't be back until the morning."

"I know," the voice in the darkness replied, "and I am as disappointed as you are. I got the date wrong. The summer solstice is tomorrow. Must have missed a day when I was locked up in Tara. Shit happens, sorry."

A smile appeared on Corbulo's face as he slid his sword back into its scabbard.

"Did you get inside Dun Aengus? What did you find out about Quintus?"

In the darkness there was no immediate reply. The silence lengthened. Then Eochaid cleared his throat.

"I saw him," he said, "He's here allright and he's alive."

"Well?" Corbulo said impatiently.

"Well," Eochaid said sheepishly, "I may have gotten things wrong when I told you he had a woman here in Dun Aengus. I am sorry, I was locked up in Tara and may have gotten things mixed up."

"Just tell me what you saw," Corbulo said.

Eochaid sighed. "I saw him," he replied, "They have him tied up to a slaver's ring beside the raised platform that overlooks the sea, the platform the druids use to honour the gods. They say that when the bonfires are lit on that platform they can be seen from tens of miles away." Eochaid paused. "There is certainly a woman involved," he said wearily," but it's not what you think. Quintus is not her lover; he's her slave. She owns him. That's why he's tied up."

Corbulo opened his mouth, then closed it before opening it again.

"A Centurion of the Twentieth will never be a slave," he said at last. "He's not going to be a slave for much longer. It's a disgrace."

"There is more," Eochaid said patiently, "whilst in the settlement I saw Faelan, the druid. He was alone and he didn't see me but I have learned that he arrived today and that he has made it known that he wants to buy Quintus. He has spread the word around that he is willing to pay a good price."

"What about Classicus and his Praetorians? Did you see them?" Corbulo gasped.

"No," Eochaid said sharply, "these are the Forbidden Islands, no foreigners are permitted to land here or have you forgotten. I think Classicus and his men have remained on the mainland waiting for Faelan to return with Quintus."

Corbulo was silent for a moment. Then he looked up.

"So has Faelan's offer been accepted?"

"I don't know," Eochaid replied from the darkness. "His mistress will return to Dun Aengus tomorrow. I expect she will agree to the price then. Faelan can be a very persuasive man when he wants to be and he has gold. He did not hide that fact."

Corbulo was silent as he turned to look out to sea.

"Fuck, we are running out of time," he murmured.

"What do you want to do?" Eochaid said gloomily. "I have to warn you Roman, Dun Aengus is a fortress. You will never get inside without being spotted. There is only one gate and the inner walls are always manned and they have dogs guarding the space between the inner walls. I saw them. They are war dogs. They will tear you to pieces if they catch you."

Corbulo was silent as he stared out to sea.

"Can you get hold of some strong rope, a long rope," he muttered at last.

Eochaid frowned. "Why, what do you need it for?"

Corbulo was still staring out to sea. Then abruptly he turned to face Eochaid.

Tomorrow," he said quietly, " we will enter Dun Aengus and free Quintus. He is my friend and I owe him this. I will not leave him here to rot as a slave. Tomorrow we are going to break him out of that place."

In the darkness Corbulo did not see Eochaid shake his head.

"I said it once before," the Hibernian murmured, "and I shall say it again. You are mad Roman, stark raving mad."

Chapter Twenty-Eight - Beacon of the West

It was noon and the sky was a brilliant blue. Corbulo crouched beside the rock and peered at the outer wall of Dun Aengus and the stone field beyond. A yard to his right the cliff edge fell away in a sheer drop to the sea, a hundred yards below. Dimly he could hear the waves crashing onto the rocks. A stout looking rope was tied around his chest and coiled over his shoulder and a second shorter rope was bound around his waist and tucked into his belt. He'd stripped off all his armour and was clad in his simple white army tunic. His Pugio a short knife hung from his belt but apart from that he was unarmed.

Dun Aengus was full of activity. From his vantage point Corbulo could see the men preparing a large bonfire on top of the rectangular raised stone platform that abutted the cliff edge. It was for the summer solstice and Eochaid had told him that the fire they were about to light was called the Beacon of the West. The druids were busy preparing for their solemn seasonal ritual, which was to be followed by a great feast. Corbulo sighed as he tried to calculate the distance to the platform. It was maybe two hundred to three hundred yards away but it was difficult to tell. His gaze wandered inland and towards the entry gate into the middle enclosure with its cluster of tightly packed thatched round houses. Eochaid was in there somewhere waiting for him as they had discussed. In his mind Corbulo went over his plan one final time. Eochaid had told him that he'd seen Quintus tied up to a slaver's ring set in stone just beneath the raised stone platform but that had been yesterday evening. The Hibernians could have moved him by now or worse sold him to Faelan. He would have to hurry.

Stiffly he moved towards the cliff edge and peered over the side at the white waves as they crashed into the rocks far below. The cliff side was not smooth and straight like it was on the other side of the island. Here years and years of continuous exposure to the ocean and wind had left and created gashes, cracks and outcrops that formed an uneven jumble of rock. Slowly Corbulo lowered himself over the edge of the cliff and planted his feet on a thin ledge as he tried not to look down. Then slowly he started to move sideways along the cliff face, hugging the rock with his body as he grasped hold of the stone and tested the cracks and ledges with his feet. The traverse was not as hard as he had expected for in this section of the cliff, the rocks provided numerous hand holds and places for him to put his feet but his progress was slow and tiring. At last he paused to rest, standing on a thin exposed ridge with his face pressed into the rock. Close by a seagull swept past him and its screech echoed off the cliffs. Corbulo took a deep breath and looked up. The cliff top was only a few yards above him and he was suddenly reminded of the time in Caledonia when he'd leapt from a cliff and into the sea, but that cliff had not been as high as this one. Carefully he twisted his head to look in the direction of Dun Aengus but from his position clinging to the cliff face he could not see the fortress.

With a grunt he started out again on his traverse. Here and there green moss and small plants had found a niche between the rocks and once his foot slipped and sent a small avalanche of stones tumbling down into the sea far below. Corbulo paused and pressed his nose into the cliff as he steadied his nerves and struggled to contain the panic that threatened to overwhelm him. It was no use going backwards, he had to keep going. Grimly he started sideways once more, his fingers stretching and searching for the next grip before his foot followed, testing the cracks, outcrops and ledges gingerly. Once he startled a nest of birds in a crack in the rock and the outraged animals flew away squawking and screeching leaving their young behind. At last, after what seemed hours, he paused to rest and risked a quick look up at the cliff top. Suddenly he heard voices. They were coming from up on the top of the cliff and Corbulo felt a shudder of excitement. Had he made it? Had he reached the cliff below the raised stone platform? The next moment a stream of yellowish liquid came hurtling down the side of the cliff and splattered over his head and clothes. Corbulo closed his eyes and groaned. Someone had just pissed on him. As if to rub it in he heard the voices above him break out into laughter and move away.

Carefully he glanced down the cliff at the sea. It looked a long way down. Then he raised his head and looked up. The top of the cliff was not too far away. With a grunt he raised his arm and his fingers scrabbled around for a hold and found one in a protruding stone. With an effort he pulled himself up the face as his feet desperately searched for something to stand on. Then he found it, a crack in the slabs of rock. His arms were trembling with fatigue as he finally made it up to the edge of the cliff top. Flattening himself against the cliff face he cautiously raised his head above the rock and as he did so his heart leapt in joy. The raised stone platform was just a dozen yards away. He had it made it. He had traversed the cliff. Quickly he lowered his head and stared at the naked rock that was so close it touched his nose. How long had the traverse taken him? It was impossible to tell. For a few moments he waited allowing his aching body a rest. Then slowly he raised his head again and peered at the platform. The stone slaver rings in the ground were there just as Eochaid had said they were. He ducked back down as up on the platform he saw two men dragging a large piece of wood up onto a pile. That had to be for the fire that the druids were going to use to celebrate the solstice. As he clung to the rock he heard the men's voices as they called out to each other. At last they fell silent and Corbulo risked another glance and this time his gaze was fixed on the edge of the rectangular platform. If Eochaid was right, Quintus would be tied up just around that corner. A surge of excitement coursed through him but he managed to restrain himself. He shifted his gaze towards the wall that marked out the inner enclosure. The space between the platform and the wall was as empty and flat as the top of the platform. Corbulo bit his lip. Come on Eochaid, where are you, he thought. The Hibernian should have been waiting for him here. Why was he not here?

Corbulo hugged the rock as he waited but every time he raised his head there was no sign of the Hibernian King. Then suddenly he heard movement above him and a small stone came rattling and tumbling passed him. It was followed by a stream of liquid that spread out into a spray of droplets.

"Are you down there Roman?" a quiet voice said cheerfully.

Corbulo looked up and shook his head in disgust as he caught sight of Eochaid.

"You pissed on me," he hissed.

"Sorry," Eochaid replied as he fumbled with his clothing, "but that's why people come to the edge of this cliff. This is where they piss." Eochaid lowered his voice, "The druids are here, are you allright?"

"Is Quintus here," Corbulo gasped as he looked up at the Hibernian standing above him.

"He is," Eochaid replied quietly as a grin appeared on his face. "Tied up to a slave ring just around the corner. I think he's asleep."

"Good," Corbulo nodded as a wave of relief swept over him. "Then do what you have to do. I will meet you back at the boat as discussed."

Eochaid smiled sadly as he turned to look out to sea.

"The gate is heavily guarded and I have seen Faelan. I think he is about to conclude his purchase. You will never get out through that gate. You two will stand out like sheep amongst wolves. They will burn you alive if they catch you."

"We're not going out through the front gate," Corbulo hissed. He paused to catch his breath. "How will I know when you start your diversion?"

Eochaid raised his eyebrows and sent a stone flying out into thin air and down into the ocean below.

"You will know," he muttered turning away, "You won't be able to miss it and when this is over Roman we are equal."

***

Corbulo watched Eochaid disappear from view. Then his attention was suddenly drawn to the raised platform. The bonfire had been lit and a trail of smoke was rising up into the pale blue air. As he stared at the smoke a line of silent white robed druids appeared and slowly formed a circle around the bonfire. Corbulo lowered his head so that his eyes were barely above the cliff edge. The druids had clasped hands and were facing inwards towards the blazing fire. Then they started a steady chant that slowly grew in volume and power. Wildly Corbulo stared at the scene as the sight of the druids brought back a flood of memories, dark painful memories of dismembered corpses, headless bodies and bloodied hearts and testicles cut from bodies. The chanting reached a feverish pitch and abruptly died away but the circle of druids remained intact. Corbulo's mouth had gone dry and he had difficulty swallowing. The sight on top of the platform terrified him, but then a feeling of bitter hatred steadied his nerves. He wrenched his eyes away from the white clad figures and stared at the inner wall. What had Eochaid said? That he would not be able to miss the diversion he was about to create? What was keeping the Hibernian? He bit his lip and stared at the wall but nothing seemed to be happening. Carefully he lowered his head below the cliff face. His legs and arms were growing tired. He wouldn't be able to stay on this narrow ledge for much longer. Then suddenly he heard a cry. It was followed by a woman's scream; then another. He raised his head. Beyond the inner enclosure wall smoke was rising up into the sky, great billowing clouds of black smoke. It was coming from the closely packed round houses in the middle enclosure. Corbulo's eyes widened in shock. This was it. This was Eochaid's diversion. The Hibernian had set fire to Dun Aengus.

On top of the raised platform the druids had turned to stare at the smoke. From within the civilian section more screams and cries of panic rose up. Corbulo reached up with his hand and heaved himself up over the edge of the cliff and rolled onto the flat stone. Then he was on his feet and scuttling towards the side of the raised platform a dozen paces away. The druids were horribly close but none was looking in his direction. Then he was beside the platform wall. He tried to steady his breathing as he crouched in the lee of the wall. The platform was around two yards high. The druids were out of view but all one of them had to do was to take a step to the edge and look down and the game would be up. The shouts and cries beyond the inner wall continued to grow and so too did the billowing clouds of black smoke that drifted up into the blue sky. Corbulo edged sideways and grasped hold of one of the iron slaver's rings that had been set into the stone. It felt sturdy and quickly he slipped the coil of rope from his shoulder, found the end and tied it to the ring as securely as he could. Gingerly he edged along the side of the platform until he came to the corner. Above him he could hear the startled and alarmed cries of the druids as they stared at the inferno that was growing beyond the inner wall. Corbulo risked a quick peek around the corner. A figure was sat leaning against the wall just a few yards away. He too was staring at the smoke. Corbulo's heart jumped. It was Quintus. His friends legs were bound together and so too were his arms and the ropes were fastened to a metal slaver's ring.

Corbulo drew back and leant against the rock as he steadied his nerves. Then with a single grunt he went around the corner, crawling on all fours. Quintus turned as he heard him coming and his eyes bulged in shock. He was a big powerfully built man in his mid forties with a broken nose. Corbulo raised his finger to his mouth as he caught Quintus's eye. Without a word he crouched beside him and drew his Pugio from his belt. Swiftly he sliced through the bonds that bound his friend's hands.

"Tie this around your waist, quickly now, make it a strong knot," Corbulo whispered as he handed Quintus the short length of rope that was tucked into his belt.

Quintus stared at the rope that was tied around Corbulo's waist. Then he bent down and hastily started to wrap it around him.

272

Corbulo snatched a quick look up at the platform above his head. The druids were still calling out in dismay at the scenes beyond the inner enclosure wall. They were so close that he could hear the crackle and hiss of their bonfire.

"Have you got the letter?" Corbulo whispered as he bent forwards and cut the bonds that bound his friend's ankles. "Agricola's letter."

Quintus looked up and frowned. "You have come for that?" he hissed.

"No you prick," Corbulo whispered, "I am here for you. This is not how a retired Centurion of the Twentieth ends his days."

Quintus finished fastening the rope around his waist. Then a broad excited grin appeared on his face. "Thank fuck you are here Corbulo," he whispered, "I could kiss you right now but I am not going to."

"The letter, you know what I am talking about, do you have it?" Corbulo snapped.

Quintus squinted at his old comrade and for a moment he did not reply.

"So you know about that," he whispered, "well I don't have it. I don't have that cursed piece of parchment."

Corbulo's shoulders sagged with sudden defeat and he groaned.

"I don't have it with me," Quintus said urgently, "I put it in a leather satchel and buried it beneath the Stone of Destiny when I first arrived in Tara. I thought it would be safer there than with me."

Corbulo looked up and stared at his friend in dumbfound silence. Then he shook his head in bewilderment. "Now I want to kiss you," he whispered as a great big smile slowly appeared on his face. "You are a fucking genius!"

"What now?" Quintus said quietly, "How do we get out of here?"

Corbulo was about to answer when a cry from above him made him freeze. As he turned to look up he saw a druid standing on the edge of the platform staring down at him.

"Oh shit," Corbulo muttered.

"Trespassers," the druid cried out in a shrill voice as he raised his staff in the air, "We have trespassers in our midst!"

"It's time to go," Corbulo cried as he rose to his feet dragging Quintus with him. On the platform the druids had turned and were staring at him in shock. Then one of them took a step forwards. She was young, pretty and in her early twenties, with short black hair and as he saw her, Corbulo's eyes widened in shock.

"You," the druidess cried as she recognised him.

For a moment Corbulo stood rooted to the ground in utter shock. The druidess up on the platform was the girl who had chased him and Marcus half way across Caledonia.

"Time to go Quintus," Corbulo yelled, "for fuck's sake Quintus hold on to me."

And with that he turned and started running towards the edge of the cliff trailing the rope out behind him. Quintus cried out in protest as he was yanked along. Then his cries of protest turned to gasps of terror as he saw what Corbulo had in mind. Linked together by the rope Corbulo ran straight over the edge of the cliff and with flailing arms and legs he soared out into thin air. A split second later Quintus came leaping and yelling after him and somehow managed to collide with him in mid air and grasp him by the waist. With a hoarse cry of terror the two of them tumbled down the cliff towards the sea a hundred yards below as Quintus desperately clung on. Then just as they were about to hit the water, the rope that bound Corbulo to the slavers ring snapped taught and broke their momentum with a jarring jolt. With a wild swing they careered straight into the rock and Corbulo screamed in pain as the collision sent a jar of pain cutting through his body. The collision sent them bouncing out across the crashing waves and with a sharp crack the rope suddenly snapped and the two of them plunged straight into the sea. Corbulo cried out as he went down into a green, icy cold world filled with bubbles. For a moment he seemed to be suspended in the water, then he was rising to the surface. He broke through the surface coughing, spluttering and screaming with pain. A wave crashed over him, pushing him towards the tumbled mess of rocks at the base of the cliffs. Wildly he looked around him. Then he caught sight of Quintus's head poking out of the sea. Quintus looked in shock as he gasped and spluttered and tried to keep his head above the waves.

A wave of adrenaline surged through Corbulo and despite the aching pain in his ribs he hit the water with his hand and screamed in triumph.

Chapter Twenty-Nine - The Cave

Corbulo spluttered as another wave crashed over his head. With his hands he grasped hold of the rock at the base of the cliff. It was wet and covered in green slimy seaweed. The tide pulled him back and then the next wave pushed him up and out of the water. He squatted down on the rock panting from the exertion and turned as the green ice-cold seawater flooded around him. Quintus was bobbing up and down close by. Corbulo wiped the water from his eyes and stretched out his hand to his friend. Quintus grasped it and with a groan Corbulo pulled him up onto the rock. Quintus nearly slipped but managed to steady himself just in time. Then he vomited up some bile, staggered and gave a heartfelt cry as he embraced Corbulo. Quintus shook with sudden emotion.

"It's fucking good to see you Corbulo," he gasped, "I thought I was a goner. I thought I was going to end my days as a slave. I prayed to god for deliverance and then you came, the lord sent you Corbulo, he sent you to free me."

Corbulo gave Quintus a cautious little glance as the big retired Centurion released his grip and collapsed onto the rock. Then he looked up towards the top of the cliffs but his view was blocked by an overhang. Around him the waves came rolling in and crashing onto the tumbled jumble of jagged stones, boulder and rocks that formed the base of the cliffs.

"We are not free yet," Corbulo said grimacing as he turned to inspect his ribs. Blood was seeping through his white tunic.

"How bad is it?" Quintus muttered as he saw the bloodstains.

Corbulo shook his head and grimaced again. Then he opened his mouth and hurriedly inspected it with his fingers.

"Well at least I still have all my teeth," he said in a relieved voice.

Quintus nodded, leaned forwards and was sick again.

"How did you become a slave, Quintus, how did it come to this?" Corbulo said as he cut the rope away from his waist and dropped it into the sea.

"It's a long story," Quintus groaned wiping his mouth, "If you know about the letters then you may know some of it but it all started in Londinium with my Jewish friend Alexander. He is the one who persuaded me to become a follower of Christus. One day he came to me and told me he'd stolen six letters from the Governor's palace, six highly incriminating letters. He had his reasons. He gave me one for safekeeping. It was the letter Agricola had written to the Governor. Alexander gave me that letter because he knew that I had served under Agricola. He asked me what I wanted to do with it. If I handed the letter to the Procurator I may as well kill Agricola myself so I decided to leave and take the letter with me to Hibernia. It was not safe for me to stay in Londinium and I had heard that they welcomed Romans in Tara. I thought I would be able to build myself a new life there. The farm outside Londinium was not profitable anyway. I am no farmer, Corbulo, I am still a soldier but without a Legion. Soldiering is all I know."

"Your friend Alexander, the Christian, he's dead," Corbulo replied.

Quintus nodded, "I thought so," he murmured, "He picked a fight he was never going to win. He was a brave man and the Lord will honour him."

Corbulo blew the air from his cheeks.

"Agricola can be a complete prick," he snapped as he slotted his Pugio back into his belt. "He sent me here to bring you back home. He wants his letter back." Corbulo paused as he grimaced in sudden pain. "So what will it be, Quintus," he said softly, "will you come back with me to Britannia?"

Quintus rubbed his face with both hands. Then he glanced at Corbulo. "What would happen if I said no?" he gasped.

"I don't know," Corbulo said wearily as he gently massaged his ribs, "Agricola has taken Marcus's woman and son as hostages. He is threatening to kill them if I don't return with you and that letter."

Quintus turned to look out to sea and for a moment he was silent.

"They will kill me if I return," he replied at last, "The Procurator, the Governor, Agricola, they cannot afford to let me live, I know too much."

"So do I," Corbulo said, "but I need your decision old friend and I need it now."

A gentle smile appeared on Quintus's lips. "You have the knife," he replied. "But I will not force you to choose between me and your family. We have been through too much together for that." Quintus sighed. "Allright, Corbulo, let's go back home, I will take my chances, I am not such an easy man to kill."

Corbulo nodded and stretched out his hand and pulled Quintus onto his feet. Then he started out clambering over the jagged rocks with the sea to his right.

"There is something strange about this island," Quintus exclaimed suddenly as he scrambled after him. "I have seen some odd things."

"Like what?" Corbulo replied as he slid down a massive slab of rock and started clambering up the other side.

"Well like fruit that I have never seen before," Quintus frowned, "and they seem to have plenty of gold and silver. They are bringing it ashore by the sack load."

"I wouldn't mind some of that," Corbulo growled.

***

Corbulo paused as he suddenly caught sight of the large sea cave and heard shouts. He crouched down behind a rock and behind him Quintus did the same. The sea cave was wide and high, a great gash in the solid cliff face and large enough to sail a small galley into but it was impossible to see how deep it was. He turned to glance at Quintus. The big man was peering at the cave intently. Corbulo turned to look up at the steep sheer cliffs that towered above him. They were so high he could not make out the top.

"If there are people in that cave," he said quietly," then they must have come by boat or else there must be a landward exit. Come on, let's have a look."

"It would be better if I had a weapon," Quintus muttered and in reply Corbulo picked up a loose stone and tossed it to him, "You can bash their heads in with this if it comes to it," he said grimly.

Carefully Corbulo crept towards the cave. He paused beside a boulder that had fallen free from the cliff face long ago. The shouting had ceased and the eerie silence was only broken by the crash of the waves on the rocks. Slowly Corbulo slipped his Pugio from his belt and holding the knife in his hand he scuttled towards the edge of the cave mouth. Quintus was behind him in an instant. Corbulo pressed up against the cliff and then slowly poked his head into the cave. The cavern was huge and he grunted in surprise. On the far side someone had placed a series of torches and in their flickering light he caught sight of a large ocean going Curragh with a mast. Corbulo took a deep breath. Someone had managed to sail the ship right into the cave but why? What was it doing here? He crouched and listened but the only noise seemed to be gentle slapping tide as it moved in and out of the cave. The place looked deserted.

"What the hell?" Quintus whispered as he caught sight of the ship.

Slowly Corbulo slipped into the water and as silently as he could started out towards the boat. The water inside the cave was not deep and his feet touched the bottom. The sea swell was much less in the cave and beyond the anchored ship he caught sight of a mass of rocks and a dark passageway leading away from the water. Gently he caught hold of the hull of the ship and slowly edged around it until he was in between the shore and the boat. A man was slouched on a rock beside the dark entrance to another much smaller cave and in the torch light Corbulo caught sight of solid metal bars barring the entrance to the cave. For a moment he did not move as he stared at the figure. From his clothing the man looked like a druid and he seemed bored as he aimlessly flicked pebbles into the water. He had still not noticed Corbulo in the water.

Corbulo glanced left and then right but there was no sign of anyone apart from the solitary druid. Slowly he edged towards the shore and then boldly rose from the water and waded onto the rocky beach. The druid seeing him at last cried out in fright and stumbled to his feet. Without saying a word Corbulo strode towards him clenching his Pugio. The druid too drew a knife and shouted something that Corbulo did not understand before he backed away as Corbulo came for him. With nowhere left to retreat to the druid lunged at Corbulo but the man was no warrior and Corbulo deftly caught hold of his knife arm and rammed his knee into the druid's crotch. A great cry of agony echoed through the cave. Corbulo flung the man up against the cave wall and forced him to drop his knife. The metallic noise rang out through the cave as the weapon bounced on the rock and vanished into the water. With the side of his arm pressed up against the man's throat he pinned the druid's head up against the rock. The druid was groaning and whimpering in agony but he made no further effort to resist.

"What is this place? What is this boat doing here? Where are the others?" Corbulo hissed as he pressed the point of his knife into the man's ribs.

The druid groaned and his eyes flickered open. The man looked terrified and Corbulo suddenly saw that he was still young, barely eighteen.

"This is the harbour," the druid whispered hoarsely, "The ship has just arrived from the great voyage. We were unloading it but there is fire in Dun Aengus. The others have gone to help put it out."

Corbulo's eyes narrowed. "What do you mean, a great voyage?" he muttered.

The druid emitted another groan of pain and Corbulo pressed his knife a little deeper into his ribs.

"Well?" he snapped.

The druid was staring at him in terror. "The great voyage," he gasped, "To the new world that lies on the other side of the ocean. We have been going there for years."

Surprised Corbulo released the pressure on the boys throat and withdrew his knife and the druid slid slowly to the ground.

"What new world?" Corbulo said with a frown.

The druid was half curled up in a ball and he was sobbing.

"It's where the gold and silver comes from," he cried. "They have plenty of it over there. We trade with them. We druids control the trade but it's a dangerous journey. It takes weeks to cross the ocean but we do it. We know the way, we sail north and then west into the dying sun."

Corbulo was staring at the youth in stunned silence. "So that is why they call it the Forbidden Islands?" he muttered at last. "The druids don't want anyone finding out about their little secret." He turned to look at the large Curragh with its animal hide bound hull. Then he stooped and grabbed the boy and yanked him onto his feet.

"How do we get out of here boy?"

The druid sniffed and coughed and then gingerly pointed in the direction of the dark passageway that led away into the side of the cliff.

"Follow that and it will take you up to the top of the cliffs," he mumbled. "I can show you the way but let me live. I don't want to die."

Corbulo peered silently at the boy. Then he gave him a rough shove in the direction of the passageway.

"Allright show us the way," he growled.

The boy stumbled and turned to face Corbulo and as he straightened up a large figure suddenly loomed up behind him and with one swift movement of his hands Quintus snapped the boys neck. The boy did not utter a sound as he flopped down onto the stony beach.

"Why did you do that?" Corbulo exclaimed in an annoyed voice, "he was going to show us the way out of here."

Quintus's eyes glinted in the torch-light, "Have you forgotten Mona Insulis, brother," he growled, "Have you forgotten what these druids did to our comrades? Thirty six men from the Legion had their hearts ripped from their bodies whilst they were still alive."

Corbulo sighed and looked away.

"I thought this Christian god you now follow was a merciful god who forgives his enemies," Corbulo said tiredly.

Quintus shook his head as he stooped to clean his hands in the water. "Not when it comes to the druids," he muttered, "I came to Tara seeking asylum and King Elim granted it to me but the druids turned him against me. They threw me into a pit in the ground with some stinking Hibernian who claimed to be a King of Leinster. After that they sold me as a slave to a noble woman and that is how I ended up here."

Corbulo glanced towards the dark passageway leading away into the rock.

"No more harsh words about that king," he said, "His name is Eochaid and it is he who helped me find you. I couldn't have done it without him. You will meet when we get back to our boat."

"Why don't we take this boat......" Quintus's words trailed off in mid sentence and slowly he rose to his feet as he stared at the anchored ship. "Corbulo..." he said in a tight voice, "Look."

Corbulo turned to look at the ship. Onboard a figure was standing beside the hull. The man was staring straight at them and his head was adorned with a magnificent white and red-feathered crown.

Corbulo stared at the figure in stunned silence. He had never seen anything like it. Slowly he opened his mouth and closed it again. On the ship the figure did not move nor did he make a noise.

"Leave him. Let's go," Corbulo whispered at last as he stumbled towards the passageway. Quintus was still staring at the stranger. Then hastily he turned and followed Corbulo into the tunnel.

Chapter Thirty - Brothers in Arms

The tunnel was just high enough for them to stand up in and after a few paces it started sloping upwards at a steep angle. Corbulo spread his arms wide and touched both sides of the passageway. The rock felt cool and damp. Up ahead a torch had been fixed to the wall and the glow provided a faint light. Corbulo ran his hand over the surface of the rock as he heard Quintus halt behind him. The tunnel felt like it was man-made.

"What was that back there in the boat?" Quintus said uneasily.

Corbulo was silent as cautiously he started up the tunnel. "I don't have a fucking clue who that was," he whispered at last, "but now is not the time Quintus. We are not off this island yet. The druids will be looking for us."

Quintus fell silent as they hurried through the tunnel. They passed the torch and soon they plunged into utter darkness. Corbulo slowed his pace and raised his hand out in front of him as he picked his way up the slope. Then abruptly the tunnel twisted to the right and he nearly tripped over a sack that had been left on the path. Corbulo's arm banged into the side of the wall and he cursed. Behind him in the darkness he heard Quintus chuckle.

Corbulo straightened up and started forwards again. Soon his boot knocked into another sack and gingerly he stepped over it. Up ahead the tunnel seemed to be growing less dark.

"I think the exit is just up ahead," Corbulo whispered.

Quintus did not reply but Corbulo could hear him close behind him. Slowly he started up the tunnel. There were more sacks beyond and as he carefully stepped over them he looked down, trying to see what was in them but it was too dark to see their contents.

"This must be the cargo that they were unloading from that ship," Quintus said quietly. "What do you think they are going to do with all that gold and silver that they are bringing ashore?"

"Whatever their purpose, it won't be good," Corbulo growled.

Up ahead the darkness was growing less and as he rounded a corner Corbulo caught sight of the tunnel exit, a round circle of light. He paused, crouched and peered down the passageway. Behind him he heard Quintus's breathing.

"Give me your knife, I am a better fighter than you," Quintus whispered.

"Not a chance," Corbulo replied.

He straightened up and started out towards the exit. As he approached it he caught sight of another sack that seemed to have been hastily discarded in the tunnel. The contents had spilled out onto the rocks and curiously he stooped and picked up one of the strange roundish brown looking objects. He raised it to his mouth and sniffed.

"Looks like it's edible," Corbulo said quietly as he sniffed it again and then slipped the strange fruit into a pocket within his tunic.

The tunnel narrowed as he approached the entrance. Corbulo paused and went down on one knee, just before reaching the light of day and gave his eyes a moment to adjust to the brightness. Beyond the passageway and about a mile away he could see dark plumes of smoke rising up over Dun Aengus. He stepped forwards and poked his head out of the tunnel. The passageway emerged from the rock and to his left it sloped steeply down towards the cliff edge a dozen paces away. A dry stone wall of piled rocks shielded the entrance from the east but it was open to the north. Hastily he glanced around but he could see nobody.

"The fortress is on fire," Quintus exclaimed as he emerged into the light, "Well that's a stroke of luck, it must be..."

"It's not the work of your god," Corbulo interrupted. "Eochaid, the Hibernian with whom you shared a dungeon in Tara, set fire to the place as a diversion to get you out. Thank him when we get back to the boat."

Corbulo started towards the stone-wall but before he could reach it Quintus called him back.

"I am grateful Corbulo, I truly am. The Lord will reward the righteous."

Corbulo did not look back as he waved the comment away.

"Don't mention it," he replied, "Without your help Efa and Dylis would still be slaves up in Caledonia. We are Brothers in Arms, Quintus, don't let any god get in the way of that."

***

It was getting dark when they made it back to the small cove where Corbulo had landed only yesterday. They had crossed the neck of the island and the only living creatures they'd seen were a couple of sheep and a sea gull standing on a rock. As he waded into the water Corbulo peered around him but there was no sign of Eochaid. Grimacing he rubbed his hand over his ribs. They ached painfully and the blood on his white tunic had stained it red but at least the wound seemed to have stopped bleeding. He raised his head and stared up at the cliff tops, then he turned to look out to sea but the Hibernian was not there.

"What do we now?" Quintus said as he looked out to sea.

Corbulo waded back up onto the rocky beach. "We will wait for him," he said firmly. Without another word he picked his way towards the spot where Eochaid had hidden the small Curragh. The boat was still there and carefully Corbulo pulled it free and laid it down on the rocks beside the water. Quintus came and stood beside him and stared down at the flimsy craft.

"You are joking right?" he said with a doubtful expression.

Corbulo chuckled. "No I am not. I crossed the sea in this thing and now it will take us back to the mainland."

"I have seen shields that are larger than that," Quintus said contemptuously.

Corbulo looked down at the little vessel. "You are right, it is too small to fit three," he replied. "One of us will have to hold onto the side. We will take turns."

Quintus shook his head and sat down on a rock.

Corbulo stooped and from the boat he retrieved his Gladius and strapped it to his belt. Then he took his Pugio, knife and tossed it at Quintus's feet. The big man looked up.

"Take it. You need a weapon in case we run into trouble," Corbulo muttered.

Quintus picked the knife up and examined it carefully.

"You've had this thing for a long time," he exclaimed. "I recognise the dents and the handle." Quintus looked up sharply. "You never told me. How did you end up getting involved in all of this?"

Corbulo stood examining his bruised ribs.

"It's a long story," he replied, "I will tell it to you one day over a pitcher of wine. Gods I could do with a drink right now."

"That woman, the druid up on the platform," Quintus said looking straight at Corbulo, "She seemed to recognise you?"

Corbulo nodded as his fingers examined his bruised and bloody skin. But the bones did not seem to have broken. Satisfied he straightened up.

"Yes she chased me and Marcus half way across Caledonia. Marcus said that her name was Emogene and that she was the daughter of a druid. The bitch wanted to kill us because we had discovered the amber cave. I never went up there for the damned amber, I went there for my son."

"I don't think she liked you," Quintus said with a faint smile.

"I know," Corbulo muttered. Then he turned to look at Quintus with a perplexed expression.

"So why the fuck did you become a follower of Christus?" he said in annoyed voice, "Were the guardian spirits of the Twentieth not good enough for you?"

Quintus looked away in sudden embarrassment. For a long moment he refused to look at Corbulo.

"It is hard to explain," the retired Centurion muttered, "but somehow I know that our Lord is the one and only true god. I feel a stronger man when I think of him."

It was Corbulo's turn to look away.

"Twenty seven years I have known you," he said, "For twenty seven years we were loyal and faithful to Jupiter, greatest and best and he protected us and now you do something like this. The guardian spirits will be angry, Jupiter will be angry Quintus and we cannot afford their displeasure right now."

Corbulo shook his head and turned to look Quintus straight in the eye. "Don't," he said pointing a finger at his friend, "you dare try and convert me to become a follower of your god or else we shall no longer be friends."

288

Slowly Quintus rose to his feet and turned to look at the rocky and boulder-strewn path that led up to the cliff top.

"I don't think your friend is going to come," he said, "We should leave now. It will be dark soon and by morning these seas are going to be crawling with Hibernian ships out looking for us."

***

The sun had long since vanished and it was getting late. Quintus stood in the surf holding onto the flimsy Curragh as the waves came crashing ashore. Corbulo stood on the beach a few paces away peering up the steep rocky path that led to the cliff top. Eochaid had not shown up. Something must have held him up for he should have been here hours ago. Corbulo sighed and glanced up at the cliffs. It felt wrong to leave the Hibernian behind but Quintus was right. Soon it would be too dark to see the mainland and if they waited until the morning the Hibernians would surely be out on the sea looking for them. If they were going to get off the island they would have to go now. Eochaid knew how to survive and he was amongst his own people.

"He's not coming," Quintus cried, "Come on Corbulo we have to go. There is a storm coming, can you not see those clouds."

Wearily Corbulo cast a final glance at the path. Then he turned and waded into the water and grasped hold of the Curragh.

"Let's go," he said as he clambered into the craft.

The Curragh slid up and down across the waves as they paddled clear of the cliffs. To the east Corbulo could see the faint outline of the mainland. It was still several miles away at least. He glanced up at the dark storm clouds building up in the west. Quintus was right; a storm was coming. They would have to hurry if they were to avoid being caught out on the open sea. Quintus too was looking up at the clouds and without a word being uttered between them they both dug their paddles deeper into the water and with more urgency. A wave came surging towards them and its crest broke over the tiny boat swamping them with icy cold seawater. Quintus gasped in shock and stared at the waves in mounting horror. The sea seemed to be growing wilder and more violent. Grimly Corbulo dug his oar into the sea as behind him he heard Quintus start to mutter a prayer.

"I told you Jupiter and the guardian spirits of the Legion were angry," he growled. From behind him there was no response. Silently they pushed on as around them the swell seemed to grow sending the hide bound craft pitched and plummeting down into the waves. Corbulo shivered as he felt the wind starting to pick up. It was coming from behind them and it seemed to be driving them eastwards. Then the rain started to come down streaming in at an angle. Corbulo snatched a quick glance up at the sky. The clouds were dark grey and covered the sky and far away he heard the ominous rolling crack of thunder. Behind him Quintus had not stopped muttering his prayers.

"Now we row, we row," Corbulo cried.

The wind came rushing over the sea sending spray flying into the air as the waves grew and grew. Another crashed over the two men in their small boat swamping them completely in salty boiling green sea-water. Quintus cried out in rising panic as the water poured away over the side of the animal skin hull.

"Keep rowing you prick," Corbulo roared as he twisted round, "We're not going to die here, not today. Row, row!"

He turned to look ahead of him as the little craft shot up the side of a huge wave. For a moment it seemed as if they would not make the crest as they hung precariously at an angle but then the moment passed and immediately they were plunging down into the trough of the next wave. Behind him Quintus choked and threw up over Corbulo's back. There was no time to protest. The next wave was upon them. Wildly Corbulo dug his oar into the sea and they surged upwards and downwards again. The rain and sea-water had drenched him and the wind was cold and making him shiver but in the battle to stay alive all that was forgotten.

"We're going to make," Corbulo screamed above the fury of the sea, rain and wind. "We're going to make it Quintus. Stay with me."

There was no reply from behind him but he could feel Quintus's oar plunging into the water. Corbulo dug his paddle into the sea as the boat was lifted up once more and thrown down into the boiling green sea. How long could it withstand this sort of punishment? He snatched a glance at the bottom of the craft and gasped. His feet were half submerged in seawater.

"Now is the time to turn to our Lord Jesus Christ," Quintus screamed as another long roll of thunder broke in the clouds. "Do it Corbulo. Convert. If we die here at least you will go to paradise for all eternity."

Corbulo swept the water from his face as he powered his oar into the sea with a stubborn angry look.

"If you mention that again you are going overboard right now," he roared furiously as around him the waves came rolling in towards him and in the sky a bolt of lightning arched through the mass of dark grey clouds. "We're going to make it. I am not letting the sea take us."

***

In the east the sun had started to rise on the horizon. Corbulo lay stretched out on the stony beach. The storm had blown itself out and he could hear the gentle crash of the waves as they broke on the shore. Exhausted and pale he raised his head a little and felt the warming rays of the sun on his face. How long had he been out? All he could remember was the pitching and plunging movement of the Curragh and the endless, huge and terrifying waves. He coughed and brought up some bile and turned over onto his back and stared up at the sky. A solitary bird was circling high above him and the rain had stopped. With a groan he sat up and looked about him. He was on a stony deserted beach. Further inland he could see low lying green meadows and a small copse of trees.

Quintus lay a dozen paces away stretched out on the beach like some great big piece of drift wood that had been deposited there by the ocean. Alarmed Corbulo stumbled to his feet and staggered towards the old Centurion. Quintus was not moving. Corbulo stopped beside him and gave the body a kick with his boot. There was no reaction and Corbulo kicked him again, harder this time and he was rewarded by a muffled groan. Quintus opened his mouth, blinked and looked up at Corbulo with large wild looking eyes as if he had just woken from a horrible dream.

"Come on, get up," Corbulo said giving him another kick.

Without waiting for an answer Corbulo stepped over Quintus and walked over to where the small oval pointed Curragh lay upturned on the rocks. The boat looked intact and as he turned it upside down Corbulo grunted in respect. The craft may have looked small and flimsy but it had proved to be surprisingly resilient. He lifted it up in one hand and walked back to Quintus. The retired Centurion was up and brushing the sand from his arms and legs.

"Leave it here," Quintus said as he caught sight of the Curragh. Corbulo shook his head as he turned to look up and down the shoreline. "No, I need it," he replied, "The man from whom we borrowed this boat has our horses. He will be expecting his boat back."

"That's great," Quintus muttered as he too turned to look around him, "But how the fuck do we know where we are?"

Corbulo shrugged. "The village where we got the boat from was on the coast so we either head in that direction or in the opposite direction."

Quintus was silent for a moment. Then he looked up at Corbulo.

"It's your choice," he said solemnly as he lowered his gaze, "You were right, we survived the sea. I was a fool to think otherwise."

A little smile appeared on Corbulo's lips.

"You were afraid that's all, but don't worry Quintus I won't tell anyone."

***

Corbulo cried out in delight as he caught sight of the small cluster of houses beside the beach. They had taken the right direction after all. He turned to Quintus. The big man too looked relieved. He was carrying the Curragh on his back and the boat towered over him like a large shadow. It was late in the afternoon and they had been walking for nearly half the day. Above them in the sky the clouds were heading east. Corbulo's hand came to rest on the pommel of his sword as he peered at the Hibernian village. It looked peaceful enough but he could see no one about. Smoke was rising from the holes in the low hanging conical thatched roofs that nearly touched the ground. Close by, a dog started to bark. As he approached the house of the man who had lent them the boat, Corbulo saw their two horses grazing peacefully in the field behind the round house. He paused and gestured for Quintus to lower the Curragh to the ground. Then just as he was about to call out a man emerged from the doorway into the house. It was the owner of the Curragh and he did not look pleased. He was swiftly followed by another man and Corbulo's mouth opened in dismay.

"Surprised to see me?" the Procurator said in a triumphant voice.

A Praetorian appeared from behind one of the houses to Corbulo's left and then two more appeared to his right. The soldiers were clad in full armour and helmets and were clutching spears and shields as they calmly moved to surround Corbulo and Quintus. Behind him Corbulo heard Quintus curse and reach for the Pugio he'd lent him.

Classicus was staring at Corbulo.

"Did you think you would outwit me so easily?" he cried taking a step forwards.

"Fuck you," Corbulo snarled defiantly as he glanced tensely at the Praetorians. The soldiers had started to close in on them. There only seemed to be three of them but they were heavily armed.

"Your friend Eochaid should have been more cautious," Classicus said as his lip curled in contempt, "When they told me that a Roman had been spotted hiring a boat and setting off towards the Forbidden Islands I knew it had to be you. So then it was just a matter of time before you came back to retrieve your horses and I see that you have brought your friend Quintus straight to me. You have proved to be an excellent messenger boy, Corbulo."

Corbulo grunted as he remembered the figure on the beach as he and Eochaid had set off in the Curragh for the Forbidden Islands. Faelan's spies were everywhere it seemed.

"Where are the rest of your men?" he growled as he drew his Gladius. In response the Praetorians raised their spears into a throwing position as they inched closer and closer.

"They are out patrolling the shoreline, just in case you decided not to retrieve your horses," Classicus replied, "but these three are my best men. They are more than a match for you and your friend. So now you have a choice. A clean quick death if you tell me where Agricola's letter is, or a long painful journey of torture and then death if you don't. Well, what is it going to be?"

"If we die then you will never find the letter," Corbulo said as he went into a crouch. Behind him Quintus too was bracing himself as his eyes flicked from one Praetorian to the other. The big man was clutching his Pugio but the knife looked pathetically small and puny compared to the weapons the Praetorians were holding.

"Where is that letter?" Classicus roared.

The owner of the Curragh suddenly bolted, vanishing like a rabbit across a field.

Corbulo stood his ground. His eyes were fixed on the Procurator. Then slowly he opened his mouth.

"I ate it," he said with a defiant smile, "You have failed Classicus. All the evidence is gone. The Emperor is not going to be pleased with you."

A deep red blush appeared on the Procurator's face. For a moment he seemed to struggle with what to say. Then his voice was shrill and full of fury. "You bastard," he screamed, "Kill them, kill them both."

"Corbulo," Quintus managed a warning shout. Corbulo flung himself to the ground as a spear flew through the space where he'd been standing. The weapon ploughed into the wall of a house. Behind him Quintus screamed but there was no time to see what had happened. Corbulo rolled over as another spear narrowly missed him and thudded into the ground. The third Praetorian was charging towards him with a loud intimidating cry. The soldier was pointing his spear at Corbulo as if he was going to impale him onto the wall of the round house. Corbulo scrambled to his feet and at the last moment he jumped aside and jabbed at the Praetorian with his sword but the soldier managed to block the blow with his shield. Warily the Praetorian backed off a little as he prepared for the next assault. From the corner of his eye Corbulo saw Quintus a few paces away. A Praetorian came screaming towards him with a raised shield and sword in hand but as he thrust his sword at Quintus, the big man twisted away and in a single fluid and astonishingly fast movement he rammed his knife into the Praetorians eye. The blow was followed by a sickening crunch and a high- pitched squeal and the soldier was lifted boldly backwards off his feet.

In front of Corbulo the soldier with the spear shouted and charged. The man feinted to the left and then thrust his spear forwards aiming for Corbulo's stomach. Corbulo twisted aside and the soldier swung his shield at him and missed. Corbulo jabbed at him with his sword but the Praetorian easily deflected the blow. Close by Quintus was rolling over the ground as he and the third Praetorian grappled with each other in a rolling and writhing mass of legs and arms. The two men were howling like two demented animals as they struggled to end each other's life.

Corbulo felt a sudden spark of panic as the Praetorian in front of him turned and shouted at the Procurator to help him. If Classicus acted now he would be able to finish Quintus off easily. There was nothing he could do to help. The big man was horribly vulnerable as he struggled with the soldier but the Procurator was staring at the fight with mounting unease and he seemed paralysed by indecision.

The Praetorian jabbed his spear at Corbulo and then charged. Corbulo stumbled backwards against the wall of a house as the soldier flung his spear at him and drew his sword. The projectile slammed into the wall and Corbulo yelled in fright. Then he danced away as the soldier tried to batter him with his shield. The Praetorian was breathing heavily as he moved to corner Corbulo against the wall. Suddenly a terrified shriek of pure panic rent the air. It was followed by a horrible gurgling noise and silence. Corbulo's eyes widened in horror as he stared at the two struggling men on the ground. One of them was no longer moving. The Praetorian too, twisted round to see what had happened. For a moment the two bodies did not move. Then slowly Quintus staggered to his feet. His face was covered in blood and he had been stabbed in his leg. Grimly he picked up the dead Praetorian's sword, straightened up to his full height and with a fierce wild looking eyes he slammed his fists against his chest in a primeval roar that sent a flock of birds soaring away into the air. The big man had gone berserk.

"Twentieth, Twentieth," Quintus roared as he limped towards the remaining Praetorian. The soldier facing Corbulo hesitated, faltered and started to back away as he caught sight of his two comrades lying dead on the ground and as he did so Corbulo sprang forwards. The Praetorian twisted round to face him but he was a fraction too slow and with a cry Corbulo drove his sword straight into the man's exposed throat. The force of the blow sent the two of them tumbling to the ground. Corbulo screamed in pain as the collision jolted his ribs and a fountain of blood splattered across his face. He rolled free and staggered to his feet. His sword had punched through the Praetorians throat impaling him to the ground and the soldier's body and legs were kicking and shaking. Then slowly the movement ceased. Corbulo stepped forwards, placed his boot on the corpse and pulled his sword from the soldier's throat. Then he looked up.

Quintus was limping purposefully towards Classicus. The Procurator had not moved. He was staring at his dead men in confusion and growing panic. Corbulo started towards him holding his sword and as Classicus saw him coming his face went white and he started to back away. Desperately he raised his hand as if to ward off a blow.

"I didn't mean for this to happen," he gasped, "I am sorry, I am not a soldier, I was just doing my job, I had instructions which I had to obey, please."

Corbulo said nothing as he strode towards the Procurator forcing him backwards.

"Please, I don't want to die," Classicus screamed in mounting panic. The scream was cut short as Quintus caught him in a bear hug and sliced open his throat. Blood poured out down the man's tunic and as Quintus released him the Procurator flopped to the ground like a rag doll.

"That was for Alexander," Quintus hissed, "He was my friend."

Chapter Thirty-One - In Defence of the High King of Tara

Quintus reined in his horse and pointed at something in the distance. A piece of cloth was bound around his leg. It was stained with dark dried blood and a purple bruise surrounded one of his eyes. Strapped across his back was a spear and from his belt hung a Gladius, which he'd taken from one of the dead Praetorians. Corbulo rode up to his side and stared in the direction in which Quintus was pointing and there standing proudly on top of its hill, like a crown on a head, he saw the Fortress of the Kings. He turned to Quintus and silently the two men grinned at each other. They were back in Tara. It had taken them four days to cross Hibernia on their hundred and fifty mile journey. Corbulo had tried to follow the eskers that he and Eochaid had taken a few days before. He had tried to navigate using the sun but it had not stopped them from getting lost on the second day. Only the intervention of a friendly villager had put them back on the right path. The Hibernian villages they had passed had looked half deserted and in settlement after settlement they had noticed that only the women, children and elderly remained. All the men of fighting age seemed to have vanished. The villager who had helped them had said that the men had gone to join High King Elim and his army who were now advancing on Tara.

"Looks like we are not too late," Quintus said gesturing at the earthen embankments that protected the royal fortress. A work party of Legionaries were out extending a wooden palisade on top of the berm and a wagon filled with wooden stakes stood at the base of the ramparts. Another work detail was busy digging a trench around the fortress. The men's shovels were throwing up small clumps of earth into the air and the soldiers armour glinted and reflected in the bright morning sunlight.

Corbulo nodded. His cheeks were unshaven and he looked dog tired. A spear was strapped to his back and he was clad in torso armour and there were greaves along his shins. He glanced in the direction of the Stone of Destiny but from his position it was impossible to see the stone itself. He looked up. Over his head a formation of black ravens came flying past in a tight V. The birds seemed to be coming from the north and Corbulo's face suddenly darkened.

"What is it?" Quintus muttered as he noticed the change in expression.

Corbulo shook his head, as he watched the ravens vanish from view. "Just something a druid once told me," he murmured, "Beware of the ravens upon a northern wind, beware of the one eyed man."

"It's all crap," Quintus replied uneasily.

"Yes," Corbulo said staring up the hill at Tara, "The druid said that not a single Roman was going to leave this island alive."

Quintus did not answer and the two of them fell silent.

"Let's go," Corbulo muttered at last as he urged his horse out of the wood and up the open grassy slope towards the fortress. Quintus followed on close behind but they had only gone a few yards before Corbulo heard the thunder of hooves. He turned as a squadron of Batavian cavalry came galloping towards him. There were thirty riders in all and they were armed with spears, which were pointed straight at him. Corbulo reined in his horse and raised his hands as the Batavians swarmed around him. Beside him Quintus hastily did the same. The Germanic horsemen were staring at him suspiciously.

"Who are you? What are you doing here?" their Decurion a tall blond haired man cried in Latin as his horse snorted and edged sideways.

"We're Romans," Corbulo replied keeping his hands in the air, "my son serves in your Cohort, his name is Marcus, he's a

Decurion like you, he's got red hair and can't handle his wine. You must know him."

The young officer looked very serious and his expression did not change and for a long moment he said nothing as he carefully inspected the two newcomers. Then he turned to one of his men.

"I will take them to the Legate," he said, "You will remain on patrol."

The remainder of the squadron turned their horses and started to trot away leaving the Decurion and four of his men behind. The young officer gave Corbulo a stern look and then gestured for him to follow. Silently the small group of riders started out towards the southern entrance into the fortress.

"He's a bit of a serious minded lad isn't he?" Quintus said as he nudged his horse alongside Corbulo.

The young blond officer must have heard the comment but he said nothing and Corbulo shook his head warning Quintus against making any further jokes. As they rode alongside the outer ramparts of the fortress Corbulo could see that the Roman garrison had not been idle whilst he'd been gone. Sharpened wooden stakes had been rammed at an angle into the earthen rampart just like at the headland fort at Drumanagh and in places along the top of the ramparts they formed a continuous palisade. Close to the southwestern corner of Tara, a crude wooden watch tower had been erected and on its upper level two Legionaries were on guard duty. As they rode passed the Legionaries paused from their labours to look at the riders. The outer approaches to the southern gate were barred by anti cavalry-barriers, spiked wooden obstacles and a whole company of Legionaries seemed to be on duty. The Decurion raised his hand and the small party of riders passed into Tara without a single challenge.

Corbulo dismounted outside the earthen embankment that surrounded the Royal Seat. Two Legionaries were standing guard outside the narrow entrance into the ring fort. The Decurion beckoned for Corbulo to follow him and without a word Corbulo and Quintus crossed the outer ditch and stepped through the gap in the earthen rampart that protected the inner sanctum of the fortress.

***

Galba was on duty outside the round house that was serving as the Roman HQ. The house stood on an elevated bank of earth in the centre of the ring fort and a solitary goat stood tied up to a post beside the entrance. The door to the house was closed and two Legionaries were on guard on either side of it. Hastily Galba got to feet as he saw the small party approach. The Decurion saluted smartly.

"Sir, I found these two skulking around outside the fort. They claim to be Romans but I thought the Legate should see them."

Galba turned to look at Corbulo and Quintus in surprise. Then he grinned sheepishly.

"You did well to bring them here Decurion," he said, "I know this man. He is a friend. You can leave them in my care. That will be all."

The Decurion saluted and giving Quintus a final quizzical look he and his men turned and started to retrace their steps.

"Decurion," Corbulo called out, "Tell Marcus that his father has returned and is waiting for him here. Tell him that I have news, important news."

The Decurion paused, half turned and then without a word continued on his way. Corbulo turned and caught Galba's outstretched arm and gripped it in the Legionary manner.

"Is Trebonius inside?" Corbulo said gesturing at the closed door.

Galba nodded and the smile faded from his lips, "They are having a council of war," he said, "all the senior officers are present. We received word this morning from Tuathal's scouts. They say that Elim is marching on Tara with a huge army. He will be here by nightfall."

Corbulo looked down at his boots.

"Quintus," he said sharply, "go and retrieve that letter and bring it to me. I will wait for you here."

The big man nodded and quickly slipped down the embankment and made his way out of the ring fort.

"Where have you been?" Galba exclaimed in a puzzled voice.

Corbulo sighed and glanced up at the closed door. "I have been to the end of the world Galba," he said wearily.

www

Corbulo rose to his feet as he saw Quintus come through the passageway in between the earthen wall. The big man refused to look at him as he strode towards the round house but in his hand he was holding something. Silently he climbed up the steps towards the doorway and came to a halt.

"Here it is," Quintus said offering Corbulo a dirty leather satchel. Corbulo took it, opened it and retrieved a tightly rolled parchment letter. For a moment he peered at the seal. It looked genuine. Hastily he placed the letter back in the satchel.

"So many people died for that thing," Corbulo muttered, "When I return it to Agricola I am going to tell him not be so stupid next time. If it wasn't for these cursed letters, I would still have my business in Londinium. I worked hard for that business and now it's all gone and my business partner is dead."

303

"Maybe it was god's will," Quintus said quietly, "If you had not got caught up in this mess, those children that you rescued would be dead too."

Corbulo raised a warning finger and Quintus fell silent. Just then they heard voices inside the house and a moment later the door was flung open and the Roman officers started to troop out. The first one out, a Centurion halted in surprise as he caught sight of Corbulo and Quintus.

"Quintus," he bellowed as he recognised him, "By Jupiter cock, what are you doing here, I thought you were retired?"

The officer clasped Quintus by the shoulders in greeting whilst the other Centurions also seemed to recognise Quintus. Corbulo raised his eyebrows. He'd forgotten that these men had once been Quintus's fellow officers in the Legion.

"It's a long story," Quintus beamed, "but I am sure glad to see all you bastards again. It's been too long. Valour and victory, gentlemen."

"Valour and victory," the Roman officers cried as they passed by gripping his arm and punching him on the shoulder. As they departed Corbulo caught sight of the Legate standing in the doorway.

"What are you two doing here?" he snapped.

Corbulo, Galba and Quintus snapped to attention.

"I have returned from some private business, Agricola's business, Sir," Corbulo replied smartly.

The Legate muttered something to himself as he stared at them. "Agricola's business," he said contemptuously, "Sometimes I think that is the only reason they sent me to this cursed place. Well come on in, do you have any news?"

Corbulo and Quintus stepped into the round house and paused beside the doorway. Across from them on the other side of the dirt floor and the wooden post that held up the roof, a chair had been placed on a small raised platform and sitting in the chair was Tuathal Techtmar. The Hibernian High King was resting his head on one elbow but he straightened up as he caught sight of Corbulo.

"Kneel," Tuathal said sharply, "You are in the presence of the High King of Tara."

"My officers do not kneel for anyone," Trebonius replied sharply as he sat down in another chair and poured himself some water from an earthenware jug.

Tuathal hissed and looked away moodily.

Corbulo took a step forwards, gave Tuathal a little smile and then turned to the Legate.

"We have spoken with the locals Sir and they say that Elim has called on all men of fighting age to join him and his army. If this is true we are going to be seriously outnumbered."

"It isn't true," Tuathal bellowed in an annoyed voice, "I too have been calling upon the clans loyal to my father. My people will come to our rescue, it's just a matter of time."

Corbulo ignored Tuathal's outburst.

"I have travelled right across this land and I have seen village after village that is empty of men. I don't think it's an idle story. Elim will be here by nightfall and will surround us. All he has to do is starve us into submission."

"It's bollocks," Tuathal roared.

Trebonius raised his hand and turned to Tuathal, "You promised us that you would raise a force of five thousand men," he snapped, "And how many have come, not a single man, not a single warrior."

"They will come, give them time," Tuathal growled bad tempered.

Trebonius shook his head, "I don't have time, Corbulo is right, by nightfall Elim will have us surrounded inside this fortress."

"Sir," Corbulo said clearing his throat, "We have no hope of receiving any reinforcements, we are far from home, we have limited supplies and we are going to be heavily outnumbered. They are going to massacre us. You should give the order to abandon Tara at once and retreat to the coast. There is still time if we go now but we are doomed if we stay here."

"You are filthy coward," Tuathal cursed as he stared at Corbulo with bitter eyes, "I will never abandon my birthright. I am the High King and Tara is my seat, my fortress. None of my men will be leaving. We are going to fight for what is ours."

Corbulo turned to look at Trebonius. The Legate was looking down at the ground. Then he sighed.

"I cannot do that Corbulo," he said in a resigned voice, "My orders are to defend the High King and to hold Tara. We are going to stay here. The decision has already been taken."

Corbulo saluted stiffly and turned for the exit. As he stepped outside into the bright light he caught sight of Marcus hastening towards him.

"You are back," Marcus said in a relieved voice as he embraced his father. Corbulo smiled warmly and lifted up the leather satchel.

"I got it," he grinned, "with a little help from my friend Quintus here."

A smile appeared on Marcus's face as he turned and stretched out his arm to Quintus. "So where did you go, where did you find the letter?"

Corbulo raised his hand to his forehead and looked away.

"It was in Tara all along," he said awkwardly, "The idiot beside me hid it beneath the Stone of Destiny when he first arrived here."

Chapter Thirty-Two - The Valorous and Victorious

It was dark and in the sky not even the moon had dared to appear. Along the earthen ramparts of Tara burning torches of pitch bathed the defences in a reddish glow. The long lines of Roman Legionaries were quiet and disciplined as they manned their positions, kneeling down on one knee with their shields leaning against their bodies. The soldiers looked tense as they stared out into the darkness beyond the sharpened stakes. The night too was silent and warm. Corbulo strode along in the rear of the party of officers led by Trebonius, as they inspected the defences. The Legate seemed relaxed and cheerful as he paused here and there to speak with his men and offer them words of encouragement. They had reached the eastern part of the ramparts when a Hibernian Carnyx blared out, shattering the silence. Trebonius paused and turned to look out into the darkness. Then he turned to his officers and in a low urgent voice he issued his orders and with quick salutes, the Roman officers hurried away to their units.

Corbulo paused just behind the line of Legionaries and turned to stare out into the night. The enemy had finally arrived. Elim had come to claim his capital. In the darkness he could hear the faint cry of men's voices and the whinnying of horses. He squinted, trying to see through the darkness but it was impossible. Then a lone cry rent the night. To his right Corbulo caught sight of a Hibernian as he came screaming out of the darkness towards the Roman line. The man was completely naked and covered in tattoos and he was utterly alone. The man leapt across the ditch and ploughed into the earthen embankment. He managed to rise to his feet just as a Roman spear slammed into his chest sending him flying backwards into the ditch. Corbulo's hand dropped to the pommel of his sword but the man's solo assault was not backed up by a general attack for no more figures appeared from out of the night. The warrior seemed to have acted on his own.

Along the Roman line the Legionaries were silent as the noise in the darkness continued to grow. Corbulo got down on one knee and blew the air from his lungs. There was nothing else he could do but wait. Quintus crouched beside him and peered out into the darkness.

"What a fucking mess," the big man muttered. "Thirteen hundred Legionaries, four hundred cavalry, some Syrian archers backed up by a bunch of Hibernian and foreign mercenaries who will run at the first sight of a Hibernian blade. There must be thousands upon thousands of Hibernians out there. We're in trouble Corbulo and the men know it."

"Are you feeling nervous?" Corbulo said quietly as he too peered into the darkness.

"Not a chance," Quintus replied, "This is what I have done all my life. I was there when we defeated the Barbarian Queen."

"So you were," Corbulo nodded as a sudden image of the two of them as young men appeared to him. He shook his head to clear the image. "I am confident that our men will hold them if they attack, but if they starve us out we are all going to die."

"Best keep that opinion to yourself," Quintus murmured.

***

Corbulo was woken by the blaring of multiple Hibernian war horns. Dawn had come and the darkness of the night was lifting. Quickly he rose to his feet and turned to look at the country beyond the ramparts and as he did his face turned pale in shock. Quintus too had risen to his feet.

"Oh shit," the big man muttered as he caught sight of the massed ranks of Hibernian warriors a couple of hundred yards away. The enemy ranks stretched away into the forest. There had to be thousands upon thousands of them.

"Looks like the entire country has come," Quintus murmured. Along the ramparts the Roman officers had started yelling and shouting orders and the Legionaries were hastily scrambling into their positions. Quickly Corbulo turned to Quintus. "If something happens to me make sure that Agricola gets that letter. The lives of my son's family depend on it. Promise me."

Quintus nodded as a great and menacing cry rose from the Hibernian lines. The cry was followed by the blaring of dozens of Hibernian trumpets as along the Roman front line a voice was suddenly heard. Corbulo turned to see the senior Centurion of the 1st Cohort striding along the Roman line. The officers plumed helmet was unmistakable and he was followed closely by the standard bearer of the Twentieth clad in his wolf skin and holding up the vexillum standard. The Legionaries in the line were down on one knee, shields resting against their bodies and had their spears pointed at the enemy.

"We are Romans," the Centurion, a grizzled looking veteran was shouting, "We are the finest soldiers the world has ever known. The first Cohort is the pride of the Twentieth Legion and today we will remind the world why. Don't be afraid of the enemy boys, you are better than they are. Jupiter is watching us. Show him that the first Cohort honours him. Valorous and Victorious!"

Along the Roman line the cry was taking up by Legionary after Legionary.

"Here they come," Quintus gasped lifting his spear up as the massed Hibernian warriors came storming towards the fortress. Corbulo raised his spear into a throwing position and raised his shield off the ground.

"Where are the Hamians, where are our archers?" he cried as the Hibernian warriors came surging and yelling towards the ramparts.

"Trebonius has concentrated them around the southern gate," Quintus snapped, "They must be attacking us from all sides."

There was no time to look. The first of the Hibernians had reached the defensive ditch and were swarming across it like a wave surging up a beach. On top of the ramparts the Legionaries rose to their feet lifted their shields off the ground and flung their spears straight down at the enemy. The volley struck home bowling men backwards and cutting a swathe through the enemy line as the Hibernians were so tightly packed together it was impossible to miss. But the enemy numbers were huge and the volley did little to stop their momentum. Corbulo flung his spear straight into a half naked warriors chest and saw the man stagger backwards under the impact before collapsing to the ground where his body was trampled on by his comrades as they surged up the embankment. Hastily Corbulo drew his sword as the Hibernians reached the rows of sharpened-stakes that pointed outwards from the earth wall and for a moment their momentum slowed as the Hibernians hacked and weaved their way passed the obstacles.

A Hibernian armed with a spiked club managed to clear the stakes and with a scream flung himself at the Legionaries in front of Corbulo. One of the Romans raised his shield and took the man's blow before stabbing him in the stomach. With a groan the Hibernian went down onto his knees his hand pressed to his torso. All along the ramparts the Hibernians were breaking through the rows of sharpened stakes and the Legionaries, huddling behind their red rectangular shields were already engaged in fierce hand-to-hand combat. Their screams and yells rent the morning air as the Romans tried to drive the enemy back down the embankment with their shields. To his right one of the Legionaries collapsed as he was hit by a spear and a small gap opened up in the Roman line. Immediately three Hibernians battled their way into the gap. Corbulo scrambled down the Roman line and thrust the boss of his shield into a Hibernian's face. The man cried out and collided with his comrade. Then with a roar Quintus was upon them ramming his sword into a Hibernian face and driving the second man back down the embankment where he was swiftly impaled by a spear thrown from his own side. The third Hibernian swung his sword at Corbulo but the weapon broke as it smashed into Corbulo's shield. For an insane moment the Hibernian stared at the broken weapon in his hand. Then a Legionary knifed him from behind and the man collapsed.

"Throw them back, throw them back. This is our wall," a Roman voice shouted. The senior Centurion of the first Cohort was striding up the line. The officer was armed with a shield and he had drawn his sword. Corbulo gasped as he saw that the entire embankment was engulfed in a writhing, hacking, stabbing, shoving and screaming mass of men fighting for their lives. The Roman line however was just about holding. Corbulo staggered backwards as a stone hit and bounced off his shield. Beyond the mass of Hibernian infantry pushing up the embankment he caught sight of a line of Hibernian slingers. Close by a Legionary cried out and toppled backwards as he was struck by a stone.

"Cowards," Quintus roared as he shoved a Hibernian back down the slope with his shield, "Come and fight like proper men. Come on. I am here you filthy lying whores!"

Corbulo raised his shield as another Hibernian came at him clutching a spear. The man's face was covered in blue woad. Corbulo braced himself as the man crashed into him and for a moment the two of them groaned and strained as they tried to push each other backwards. The Hibernian stronger and younger seemed to be gaining the upper hand when Corbulo's sword sliced into the back of his leg. With a shriek the Hibernian went down on his knees as Corbulo stepped back and kicked the man in the head with his hobnailed boot. The blow sent the man spinning and tumbling into the ranks of his comrades. A sudden shout and commotion behind Corbulo made him twist round in alarm. Had the enemy managed to break through behind them? A Roman officer came running along the top of the embankment. He was closely followed by a column of Hamian archers running along in single file. The Syrian uniforms and equipment were unmistakable. The officer rushed passed Corbulo and as he did the Hamians began to form a line behind the hard pressed Legionaries. There was no time to stand and gawp however. Another Legionary close by collapsed from a stab wound and instantly the Hibernians tried to scramble through the gap. Corbulo sprang forwards and charged straight into a Hibernian who had managed to reach the top of the embankment. With a cry his shield battered into the man sending him flying backwards through the air and the force of his charge was so great that it nearly propelled Corbulo down the slope with him.

A Roman trumpet suddenly blasted away and behind him Corbulo sensed movement. With a taught twang, a volley of arrows shot up into the air over his head and hurtled towards the Hibernian slingers. The first volley had not even struck before a second was arching gracefully into the air. Shrieks and cries rose up from the Hibernian slingers. The enemy had no armour and no shields to protect themselves and the arrows slammed into them with ruthless efficiency. A Hamian was suddenly standing beside Corbulo with his bow trained on the enemy on the slope below. The archer's peaked helmet and exotic chain mail made him easily distinguishable from the Legionaries. Without a word the man released his arrow. Then he reached for another from the quiver on his back and released it. At such close range it was impossible to miss. Along the entire eastern rampart arrows began to fly straight into the Hibernian ranks, hammering into the lightly protected enemy with ruthless intent. Volley after volley hurled down the slope as the Hamians began to pick up their firing rate. Corbulo panting with exhaustion as he stared at the growing carnage below him in morbid fascination. The discipline and training of the Hamian archers was highly impressive.

To his right a strange trumpeting noise suddenly broke out. Corbulo snatched a look in the direction from which the noise had come. That had not been a Roman army trumpet. Then screams and yells of panic could be heard coming from the Hibernians near the southern gate and a moment later an enraged and bellowing elephant came ploughing through the Hibernian ranks. The animal's tusks flung aside everything in its path as it desperately tried to flee from the battle. Two spears were sticking from its thick hide. At the sight of the strange beast the Hibernians in front of Corbulo started to panic and run. The rout spread with amazing speed and within seconds the entire Hibernian assault was in retreat. Corbulo felt a wild surge of elation as the Hibernians began to run for their lives. Of course none of them had ever seen an elephant before. From the Roman lines there was little reaction to the sudden Hibernian retreat, for the men seemed too exhausted to celebrate. Corbulo sank down on one knee as he watched the enraged and terrified elephant vanish off into the forest. The battle was over. Down below him hundreds upon hundreds of corpses filled the ditch and littered the embankment and blood, entrails, discarded and broken weapons and arrows were everywhere. As he looked at the battlefield a few Roman Legionaries slithered down the slope and began to mercilessly finish off the Hibernian wounded.

Corbulo glanced across at Quintus. The big man was tightening the bandage around his leg and his torso armour was smeared with someone else's blood. He looked up and grinned.

"That wasn't too bad," he muttered.

From the corner of his eye Corbulo caught sight of a young officer hastening along the top of the rampart. As he drew closer he saw that it was Galba. The Tribune's face was ashen and he seemed to be looking for someone.

"Corbulo, Corbulo," Galba cried as he caught sight of him. Corbulo rose to his feet as he felt a sudden sense of unease.

"I am here," he replied searching Galba's face for clues. "What is it?"

Galba hastened over to him. The young man's face was covered in sweat.

"It's Trebonius," Galba gasped, "He has been badly wounded in the fighting around the southern gate. He's calling for you. I am bringing you to him right now."

Chapter Thirty-Three - The Commander

The door to the Roman HQ inside the Royal Seat was unguarded as Corbulo followed by Quintus and Galba barged through the entrance. Several men were standing around an army camp bed on which lay a body. The Centurion's looked up sharply as Corbulo strode towards them. One of the officers had a bloodied bandage wrapped around his head and the others were covered in sweat, mud and blood. Everyone of them looked worried and anxious. Corbulo pushed his way towards the bedside and looked down at the Legate. A slave, clad in a simple white tunic was mopping Trebonius's forehead with a damp sponge. Trebonius himself had his eyes closed and was groaning in pain. Dark red blood was seeping out through a bandage that covered an ugly looking gash in his abdomen.

"He was hit by a spear, the wound is grave," the army doctor tending to him said, as he caught sight of Corbulo.

"Is he going to die?" Corbulo said hastily.

The doctor lowered his gaze and nodded. "Soon," he muttered, "I can do nothing more for him, I am sorry."

"Corbulo is that you?" Trebonius murmured weakly as his eyes flicked open.

Corbulo took hold of the Legate's hand and gripped it.

"It's me Sir, I am here," he said quietly.

Slowly Trebonius turned his head and looked up at him. "Good man," he murmured, "I knew you would come but it's the end of the line for me."

"You should rest Sir," Corbulo said gently.

"No," Trebonius replied as he suddenly groaned in pain and for a moment he was unable to speak, "No, you have not been wrong before, don't start now Corbulo," he continued in a hoarse voice as his eyes closed.

"I want you to do something for me, promise me that you will do it," the Legate whispered. "I want you to take command of the battle group," Trebonius's eyes flickered open once more and he stared up at Corbulo, "See that my boys get home alive. They don't deserve to die out here. Promise me Corbulo, lead my boys back home."

Corbulo's eyes widened in shock. He was about to protest when he saw a faint smile appear on the Legate's lips.

"Just promise me," Trebonius whispered.

For a moment Corbulo was unable to reply. Then he took a deep breath.

"Yes Sir, I promise you that I will do my best," he muttered, "But why me? There are many here who can assume command."

The smile on Trebonius's face lingered as he looked up at Corbulo.

"I want someone," Trebonius whispered, "who stood in the line and faced the fury and might of the Barbarian Queen," the legate coughed and a trickle of blood ran down his chin, "That was a day wasn't it?"

Corbulo blushed, "Yes Sir, that was a day to remember," he said quietly.

"Take command Corbulo, you are the right man," Trebonius gasped as he suddenly tried to raise his head. Then his eyes closed and his head flopped back and rolled to one side. Hastily the doctor pressed his fingers to the legate's neck. For a moment he was silent. Then he looked up and shook his head.

"He's gone," the doctor said wearily.

Corbulo was staring down at the dead man as he silently muttered a prayer. Then at last he looked up and turned to the assembled officers. They were watching him with tense, worried faces.

"Where is the senior Centurion from the 6th?" he said.

"He's dead Sir," Galba replied quickly, "He was hit by a stone and the senior Centurion of the 1st is badly wounded. His men are looking after him but he's in a bad way."

Corbulo swore softly to himself. The battle group had lost all its senior commanders in a single fight. He turned to look at the company Centurion's.

"So this is it? This is all the officers we have got?"

Galba nodded.

Corbulo straightened up.

"Well you all heard the Legate," he said clearing his throat, "he has put me in command but if any of you want to dispute this or think another should take over, then speak up now."

Corbulo tensed. This was the moment when the Centurions would either accept him or kill him. At his side Quintus too seemed to have sensed the mood for idly his hand came to rest on the pommel of his sword. The officers glanced at each other but no one spoke and as the silence lengthened the tension grew.

"Well?" Corbulo said looking around him.

The Centurion with the bloody bandage around his head was the first to speak.

"What should we do now Sir?" he said.

317

Corbulo looked thoughtful. Then he scratched his cheek and glanced at Galba.

"Fetch my son Marcus and the other Batavian Decurion's and bring them here."

Galba saluted smartly, turned and vanished out of the door. Corbulo pushed his way through the group of officers and paused in the middle of the room and looked down at the brown earthen floor.

"Get me the casualty reports as soon as you can," he said.

One of the Tribunes, another young aristocratic youth stepped forwards. "I already have them Sir," he said smartly as he produced a small rolled parchment. "The First Cohort has thirty-seven dead and a hundred and six wounded, eight sick and six hundred and ninety-one men ready for duty. Sixth Cohort, four Centurions are dead as are fifty- two men and ninety wounded, one man is sick leaving three hundred and forty men ready for duty. The Hamian's suffered one fatality, our Batavian and Legionary cavalry were not engaged and report no losses and twenty Hibernian mercenaries are reported missing. We also lost the elephant Sir."

Corbulo nodded, "Thank you," he muttered.

"What are we going to do Sir?" the officer with the bandage repeated.

Corbulo turned to the man. "Tonight," he said calmly, "we're going to break out and retreat to the coast. That's what Trebonius wanted."

The officers exchanged glances with each other and a few of them broke out into muttered conversation.

"Gentlemen," Corbulo said sharply, "I am in command and have made my decision. We stand no chance of defeating the enemy. Their numbers are too great and we cannot expect any reinforcements. All we can do now is save the lives of our men. We will break out tonight during the hours of darkness."

"You had better tell Tuathal Techtmar then," one of the Centurion's said, "He will not be happy with that decision. We are leaving our ally to the wolves."

Corbulo nodded and gestured to one of the Tribunes. "Bring Tuathal to me, I will speak with him now."

"And what about our wounded?" the Centurion with the bandage said, "We have over two hundred wounded and sick men. Some will be able to walk but there are a lot who can't and they will slow us down. What are we going to do with them Sir?"

Corbulo felt all the officer's eyes turn on him as they waited for his answer. For a long moment he did not reply.

"Well I am not going to leave them behind," he snapped, "We will take everyone with us who wants to come. Trebonius told me to lead his boy's home and that's what we are going to do. That will be all, tend to your men and report back here when I call you. I will explain my plan to you then."

The officers saluted and started to file out of the doorway leaving Corbulo's small staff of Tribunes, signallers and the standard bearer behind. Corbulo watched them go. Then he turned to Quintus.

"Will you watch my back Quintus," he said quietly, "These are difficult days and I may need a bodyguard."

In reply Quintus drew his sword half out of its scabbard showing Corbulo the steel blade. Corbulo nodded gratefully.

Just then a man stepped through the doorway into the round house. It was Tuathal and he was accompanied by two of his men. Tuathal paused as he caught sight of Corbulo.

"Where is Trebonius? What's going on?" the High King growled uneasily.

In reply Corbulo gestured to the camp bed and the blanket that had been draped over the Legate's body. Without saying a word Tuathal marched across the room and pulled back the blanket and stared down at the corpse. For a long moment he stood there with his back to Corbulo.

"I have taken command of the battle group," Corbulo said quietly, "It was Trebonius's final wish and all the officers have now agreed."

"Why did you call me here?" Tuathal said as he refused to turn round.

"To tell you that we are leaving. I am taking my men back home. We are going to break out. You and your men are welcome to come with us."

Tuathal was silent, then slowly he turned round to face Corbulo and there was a resigned look on his face.

"I knew this day would come," he said quietly, "So you have done well for yourself Corbulo, I salute you, one moment you were an arrogant nobody and now you are in command of a force of men; that's quite a feat."

"Will you come with us?" Corbulo said folding his arms across his chest.

Tuathal shook his head. "No, I and my men will stay here. I have been a refugee for nearly all my life and I will not run away again. You once told me that a true king does not take orders from anyone. Well I am the true High King of Tara and this fortress is my home. My clansmen will come; they will not leave me here to die. You will see."

Corbulo nodded, "Well then that is settled," he said, "We are going tonight."

Tuathal turned to look at Trebonius's corpse and for a long moment he was silent.

"There is one final matter," Tuathal said with a hint of sadness in his voice, "When you get back to Deva, tell your scribes about me and how I returned home to Tara to claim my inheritance for I wish that my name be remembered."

And with that Tuathal strode straight across the room and out of the doorway without another word or glance in Corbulo's direction.

***

Corbulo walked up to the doorway and leaned idly against the door post. As he stared out into the sunny courtyard that surrounded the Royal Seat he caught sight of Marcus and a group of Batavians hastening towards him.

"Father, is it true?" Marcus cried as he hurried up the steps towards him, "Have you really taken command of the battle group?"

"Is it not customary that an officer should salute his superior," Corbulo snapped.

Marcus blushed and rapped out a quick salute as behind him the Batavian Decurion's did the same.

"Yes it's true," Corbulo said glowering at the auxiliary officers. "And I am promoting you to command of all my Batavian horsemen with immediate effect."

"Yes Sir," Marcus replied as his blush deepened.

"And we're leaving tonight," Corbulo muttered, "So see to it that your men and their horses are well rested, watered and fed. There will be a council of war when the sun goes down and I need you to be there. I have a plan that is going to involve your men. Is that understood?"

"Yes Sir, " Marcus said.

"Good, then report back to me at sun down."

Marcus saluted and turned away just as a Legionary came running up.

"Sir," he cried as he caught sight of Corbulo, "You need to come to the northern rampart. The Hibernians have sent an envoy and he is demanding to speak to you."

Corbulo glanced at Quintus. Then without a word they set off down the steps.

As he strode through the fortress towards the northern fortifications Corbulo and Quintus were joined by Galba and Corbulo's staff. The small party clambered up the embankment and Corbulo paused at the top. The Roman Legionaries were down on one knee resting their shields and spears against their bodies. The men were staring across the meadows at the Hibernian line. Down below in the ditch and strewn across the earthen slope the bodies of the dead lay scattered far and wide. Large black birds were swooping and crowing in the air and a few of the animals had already landed to inspect the dead. Beyond the worst of the bloody carnage stood a solitary Hibernian holding a flag of truce. He was staring at the Romans on top of their fortifications. Corbulo stepped passed the line of Legionaries and grasped hold of one of the sharpened wooden stakes as he peered at the man. Then his face darkened as he recognised him. There was no mistaking the black eye patch over the druid's face. It was Faelan.

"What do you want?" Corbulo shouted.

Faelan took a step forwards. "I want to speak to Trebonius," he cried.

"You can talk to me," Corbulo shouted back.

The druid took another step forwards. "Is that you Corbulo," he shouted. "Yes, it is. So you managed to escape. Classicus was not as smart as he thought he was. What happened to him by the way?"

"He's dead," Corbulo cried, "Now tell me what you want. I am busy."

Faelan was silent for a moment.

"High King Elim, rightful ruler of Tara and Hibernia has instructed me to offer you terms," he cried. "You and your men are completely surrounded and we outnumber you. Elim offers to spare your lives if you surrender immediately and hand over the bastard pretender that is Tuathal Techtmar. What is your answer?"

Corbulo turned and looked up at Quintus and his staff. Along the ramparts the Legionaries stared impassively at their enemy.

Corbulo turned back to face Faelan. "You once told me that not a single Roman was going to leave this island alive so my answer is no, now fuck off."

And with that Corbulo clambered back up the embankment and as he did so he heard Faelan's enraged voice behind him.

"You will regret this Corbulo," the druid screamed, "When I get hold of your corpse I am going to have you cut into four pieces and buried in the four corners of Hibernia so that your spirit will wander lost and alone forever. We are coming for you Roman, we are coming to kill you all."

Corbulo did not deign to look behind him as he regained the top of the rampart.

"That's the man who tried to buy me in Dun Aengus," Quintus said as he stared at Faelan, "He would have bought me if you hadn't shown up."

"I know," Corbulo muttered, "He was also one of Classicus's allies. Nothing is what it seems in this country."

Chapter Thirty-Four - Breakout

Corbulo stood looking down at the earthen floor of his command post inside the Royal Seat. Gathered around him in a large silent circle were all the principal officers of the battle group, some thirty-five men in all. Slowly Corbulo stooped and using a Centurion's vine stick drew an oval shape in the earth and marked the southern section with a small pebble. Then he drew a circle around the oval shape and straightened up. "Allright," he said quietly, "here's our position within Tara," he said tapping the centre of the oval, "and here is our enemy," he said tapping the circle. "The pebble is the southern gate. This then is my plan. We are going to break out in the deepest part of the night and we are going out through the southern gate here. The Hibernians seem to be weakest at this spot. With a bit of luck we will catch the enemy asleep and unprepared. The Legionary cavalry will lead the way. They will clear a path through the enemy line and will form our advance guard. Following them will come the infantry of the 6th and 1st Cohort's and the Hamians." Corbulo paused to look around at his officers. The men were watching him carefully. "Speed and surprise are going to be vital gentlemen," he said. "The aim is to break through the enemy line as fast as possible, heading due south and then once we are clear," Corbulo drew a line in the earth, "we will change course and head east towards the sea and the Batavian garrison at Drumanagh. It's twenty-five miles to the sea, a day's march but we will be going at a trot." He paused and cleared his throat. "The Legionary infantry will move in company sized groups. Each unit will be escorting a wagon upon which we will place our wounded. Tell your men to cover up their armour and secure their arms and belongings so that they minimize the noise. They are to travel light. Everything that is not needed for a fight will be left behind. We are to stop for nothing. We must be clear of the enemy before Elim realises what is happening."

"A night march is going to be difficult Sir," one of the Centurion's said, "Units and men can easily lose their way and get lost."

"I know," Corbulo said, "That's why we are going to have a burning torch fixed to each wagon. The men will have to follow the torches. It's the best that we can do."

"So let's assume that we break out successfully and start marching to the coast," another Centurion said staring down at the plan in the earth, "It will still take us most of the day to reach Drumanagh. We will be strung out in the open. What will stop the Hibernian cavalry from cutting us off and holding up our retreat?"

Corbulo turned and glanced at Marcus.

"That brings me to the final part of the plan," he said. "The Batavian cavalry, all two hundred and fifty men will break out from the north and create a diversion. They will lure Elim and his cavalry away from our main breakout to the south. Then once they have completed their task they will wheel round and rejoin us." Corbulo paused as his gaze came to rest on Marcus. "The Batavian cavalry will have the most dangerous job. Once we are clear and they have rejoined us, the Batavians will form a mobile screen for our troops. They will protect our rear and drive off the Hibernian cavalry if they attempt to intervene."

The officers were silent as Corbulo finished talking.

"How many riders do the Hibernians have?" a Tribune asked suddenly.

Corbulo cleared his throat. "It's difficult to tell but we think they may have five or six hundred mounted men."

A murmur ran through the assembled men.

"Gentlemen," Corbulo said quietly, "We are all Roman officers and we are going to succeed. Trust in your companions, follow your orders and all will be well. That will be all, see to it that your men are ready to go when I give the signal," Corbulo said sharply," We are going to do this and we are going to do it well."

The officers nodded as the gathering broke up. Corbulo watched the men leave. Then suddenly Marcus was at his side. There was a concerned look in the young man's eyes.

"Five to six hundred riders," Marcus said quietly, "If that is true it means that the enemy will outnumber my men by two to one."

"Well it's better than three to one," Corbulo said patting Marcus on the shoulder.

***

It was night and a gentle rain was coming down from the sky. Corbulo sat on his horse and looked up at the moon. The pale light would help his men. Jupiter had responded to his prayer for help. He turned to glance around him at the massed ranks of Legionary and Batavian cavalry who sat silently on their horses before the closed southern gate, waiting for the order to go. The men had blackened their faces with mud and had muffled their equipment but their camouflage could not hide the tension on their faces. Behind the cavalry and stretching off into the heart of Tara, the depleted Legionary formations clustered around the fifteen horse drawn wagons that were crammed with wounded men. Torches had been fixed to each wagon and the flames flickered and hissed in the gentle rain.

"Everything is ready Sir," Galba said as he rode up to Corbulo and saluted. The Tribune too had covered his face in mud. Corbulo nodded. Where was Marcus? Suddenly the urge to embrace his son for a final time before he rode out became overwhelming but Marcus had for some reason decided to stay away. Corbulo allowed himself a deep draw of breath. Marcus would be allright he told himself. Hell, the young man had after all survived months of captivity in Caledonia. He wrenched his thoughts away and glanced up at the ramparts. Tuathal had agreed to take over the positions vacated by the Legionaries and keep up the appearance that the walls were still manned. As he stared up at the earth embankment he suddenly caught sight of Tuathal. The High King of Tara was looking down at the

327

massed Roman troops and there was something tragic about his posture as the rain pattered onto his head. Corbulo eyed him for a moment and then raised a clenched fist in the air and after a moment's hesitation the Hibernian King returned the salute. Corbulo turned to his mounted staff as they clustered around him. The officers, tribunes and signallers were clad in their hooded pallia, cloaks and amongst them was Quintus and the standard bearer proudly holding onto his precious vexillum standard.

"Give the signal," he ordered, "Let's go."

Up ahead the Batavian Decurions, whose men would be first out, pumped their clenched fists in the air and the horsemen stirred as the gates swung open. Then with a soft cry the first riders charged out through the gate and into the night. Corbulo watched the Batavians as they poured out of the gate, turned sharply and vanished into the gloom. The next out were the hundred and twenty Legionary cavalry. The four squadrons led by their Decurion's charged forwards and straight towards the enemy lines a hundred and fifty paces away. They were followed by a handpicked group of a hundred Legionaries who stormed after the cavalry.

"Follow me," Corbulo cried as he urged his horse out through the gate. As he emerged onto the dark barren grassy slope Corbulo caught sight of the Hibernian camp-fires ahead. Suddenly he heard cries and shrieks and he grunted grimly. The Legionary cavalry had fallen on the enemy. Behind him he heard the thunder of hooves of his staff HQ Company. Corbulo passed a running Legionary and charged towards the campfires. Then he was in and amongst the enemy. Dead and wounded were everywhere and in an instant Corbulo knew the cavalry had caught the Hibernians completely by surprise. A man, stark naked came rushing towards him holding an axe. He was screaming but before he could strike, a Roman cavalryman struck him with his long cavalry sword and the man went tumbling to the ground head over heels. Amongst the campfires the Hibernians were fleeing in all directions. Corbulo wheeled his horse round and looked back at Tara.

"Move, move, keep going," he shouted at the Legionaries as they came storming through the abandoned Hibernian camp. "Where are those damned wagons?"

"There they are Sir," one of the Tribunes at his side called out. Corbulo blinked and then he saw it too. A convoy of burning torches was heading straight towards him. As the first overloaded wagon came rolling passed he saw the anxious crowded faces of the wounded men in the glow of the campfires.

"Come on, come on," Corbulo muttered impatiently. A sudden roar erupted to the north and he turned his horse in the direction from which it had come. Anxiously he peered into the darkness as the roar grew in volume. That had to be Marcus and his Batavians. They must have made contact with the enemy. He looked up at the moon and muttered a short prayer. Then a second wagon rumbled passed and in the glow he caught sight of the Legionaries as they half walked and half ran alongside it.

"Move it, move it," he shouted.

A warning cry in the darkness to his left suddenly rent the night. A man screamed. Then In the faint light Corbulo caught sight of figures running and leaping towards him.

"Here they come," a Roman voice cried out. Corbulo drew his sword and with hoarse cry he charged straight towards the running men. The two sides met in a whirl of movement, thuds and screams. Corbulo's horse shying away from a boulder, crashed headlong into a Hibernian, knocking the man to the ground. Corbulo slashed at the man but missed. Then close by a Hibernian came leaping through the air clutching a spear that was aimed at the exposed flank of his horse. Corbulo cried out in panic but just as the man was, strike Quintus came charging out of the gloom and sent the Hibernian spinning with an ugly cut to his neck. Corbulo looked around him wildly. In the darkness everything had descended into chaos and he no idea where his own men were. A party of Legionaries came rushing past a campfire with drawn swords before vanishing into the gloom.

"To me," Corbulo roared as he caught sight of a line of torches, "To me, fall back." He thundered back through the Hibernian camp towards the convoy. Around him horsemen appeared in and out of the darkness racing to keep up with him. As he reached the line of moving torches he wheeled his horse round and stared into the darkness from whence he'd just come. Quintus appeared at his side and slowly his staff gathered around him. Nothing moved in the darkness ahead. Corbulo turned to look at another wagon as it trundled past with its human cargo. The Legionaries did not look up as they jogged past. Anxiously Corbulo turned in the direction of Tara. The last of the torches was close by and coming towards him.

"That's the last one," he shouted, "When it's past us we follow. The HQ Company will form a rearguard. Follow my voice, follow my voice."

***

Dawn found the Roman column strung out on a path heading due east into the rising sun. The rain had stopped and there was a fresh western breeze in the cloudy sky. Corbulo, surrounded by his staff, walked his horse alongside one of the wagons loaded with wounded. The men in the wagon were staring vacantly out over the rolling fields. A long single file of Legionaries trudged along the path on the opposite side of the wagons. The men's faces were blackened with dried mud and they were carrying their shields and spears. No one spoke but in the wagons the soft cries of the badly wounded could be heard. Corbulo looked tense. He'd lost one of the wagons when its axle had snapped. Some of the wounded had managed to stagger along with the help of their comrades but he'd been forced to leave many of them behind beside the wagon. Their desperate pleas for help had haunted everyone who had heard them but there was nothing he could do for them. The wagons were already dangerously overcrowded.

Anxiously Corbulo turned to watch the horizon to the north. So far his plan was working, they had managed to break out and leave the Hibernian infantry behind but where was Marcus and his Batavians? With the light it would not be long before the Hibernian cavalry found them and if the Batavians were not there to protect him the whole column was going to be overrun and cut to pieces. Quintus nudged his horse alongside and gestured at one of the wagons up ahead.

"That one's axle is about to break," he muttered.

"Well what do you want me to do about it?" Corbulo grunted irritably.

Quintus's face grew sheepish. "You need to show the men that you know what you are doing Sir," he said quietly, "They are looking to you for leadership. Show them that you know what to do even when you haven't got a clue. Sometimes leadership is about pretending that you are in command."

Corbulo looked over at Quintus and for a long moment he remained silent.

"You can be one annoying prick sometimes," he muttered as a faint smile appeared on his lips. Their banter was interrupted by a shout from one of the Tribunes. "Look Sir," the officer cried, "over there. Horsemen."

Corbulo and Quintus turned in the direction in which the officer was pointing. Then Corbulo saw them too. A line of horsemen riding straight towards them about half a mile away.

"Batavians or the enemy, come on man," he cried at the Tribune, "You have better eyes than me, what is it?"

The Tribune was peering intently at the riders.

"Batavians Sir, they are our men," he cried out.

"Jupiter's cock," Corbulo muttered as he stared at the approaching riders in relief. "Marcus did it, I knew he would."

The Legionaries too had spotted the riders and a few men nervously lowered their shields and readied their spears.

As the Batavians came trotting towards him Corbulo caught sight of Marcus. His son's face was grim and streaked in sweat. Catching sight of the battle group standard Marcus veered towards it and seeing Corbulo he trotted towards him.

"I carried out my orders Sir," he said stiffly and without a smile, "We took the enemy by surprise and scattered them but they are stronger than we thought. Their cavalry is on our trail. They will be here within the hour."

"Good man, good man," Corbulo muttered awkwardly avoiding his son's gaze, "How many of them are there?"

"I think about six or seven hundred mounted men. They are accompanied by slingers who run alongside the horses and I counted one pack of war dogs." Marcus turned to look at the slow-moving wagons. "Did you get them all out?"

"We did but we lost one along the way, a broken axle," Corbulo replied.

Marcus nodded and sighed.

"What about casualties?" Corbulo said glancing at the line of Batavian horsemen.

"Thirty or so dead and missing," Marcus replied, "I lost some men in the confusion and in the darkness, you know how it is Sir."

Corbulo grunted as he turned to look to the north. "I am going to bring the Legionary cavalry from the advance guard to reinforce you. When those Hibernians get here you and your men are going to have to keep them at bay. Nothing must hold us up. We need to reach Drumanagh before their infantry has a chance to catch up. If we are caught out here in the open its going to end in a massacre."

"I know," Marcus replied.

***

It was an hour later with the Roman column heading east across the green open rolling hills when the first Hibernian riders appeared to the north. A warning trumpet blast rang out as the Legionaries ran to form a line. Corbulo with his staff officers close behind came galloping down the Roman column.

"Keep moving, keep moving," he yelled at the Legionaries, "Which arse gave that signal? The infantry is to keep moving. We can't stand still." Angrily he turned to one of the Tribunes, "See to it that every officer understands those orders. We keep moving; we don't stand still. Got it?"

The Tribune saluted nervously and nodded before galloping away down the column. Corbulo turned quickly to stare at the Hibernians. The enemy was closing in at a rapid pace and in the distance he heard the unmistakable noise of barking dogs. He turned to his trumpeter.

"Order the Batavians to intercept them," he said quickly.

"Yes Sir," the soldier said hastily and bringing his mouth to his instrument he blew two short blasts. Corbulo glanced back down the column of wagons and marching men. The rear most wagon had started to lag behind. The cart looked desperately overcrowded and a string of walking-wounded were moving alongside it. Some of the Legionaries were pushing the wagon up the slope.

"Oh shit," Corbulo muttered as he caught sight of the advancing Hibernian cavalry. The wagon and its occupants suddenly looked horribly exposed and vulnerable. What had happened to the rear guard, who were supposed to be protecting them?

As he stared at the wagon he heard the wild cries of the enemy horsemen as they rapidly closed in on the Roman column. Then a group of about a hundred Hibernian riders broke away from the main force and charged straight towards the rear most wagon. The Legionaries seeing the enemy surging towards them broke and scattered. Corbulo swore and was about to urge his horse towards the stranded men when he heard the thunder of hooves and a moment later a V shaped formation of Batavian and Legionary cavalry came galloping passed. Concentrating on the struggling and fleeing Legionaries the Hibernians were too slow to notice the sudden threat to their flank and too late they turned to face the Batavian charge. A volley of spears slammed into them and men went crashing and tumbling to the ground as a cry of panic and terror rose up from amongst the Hibernian ranks. Then the Batavian cavalry were in amongst their foes, slashing at the remaining riders with their long cavalry swords. The fight was over within seconds as the surviving Hibernian wheeled round and fled for their lives across the field.

"Get those men back into the column," Corbulo roared as he pointed at the scattered Romans around the rear most wagon, "and get a proper company down here to protect our rear."

"Sir look they are sending in their slingers and dogs," one of the Tribunes shouted. Corbulo turned and sure enough a line of figures was advancing towards him and in amongst them he could see and hear the war dogs.

For a moment Corbulo was struck by indecision. He glanced at the Batavians and Legionary cavalry who had fallen in at the rear of the column. The slingers could be lethal and he knew what those dogs could do. Some of the Hibernian war dogs were big and strong enough to bring down a horse. The

Batavians could rout both if they charged in formation but the presence of the main body of Hibernian cavalry made that unwise. As he stared at the approaching Hibernians he saw that the enemy cavalry were staying close enough to give their slingers the protection they needed. Corbulo frowned and scratched his cheek uneasily.

"They will be in range soon Sir," one of the Tribunes shouted.

Corbulo turned to look up the moving Roman column. "Get the Hamians down here, all of them, tell them to hurry," he shouted at one of messengers. The soldier nodded and galloped away up the line of wagons.

Close by, a stone clattered onto a rock and came to rest in the grass. Corbulo cursed under his breath. The enemy were getting the range. "Protect yourselves boys," he cried as he peered helplessly at the advancing slingers. He could clearly see the Hibernians darting and jumping towards him and whirling their slings over their heads. Then a volley of stones came hurtling into the Legionaries and the air was filled with clangs and cries as the stones struck armour, shields and flesh. A Legionary toppled from one of the carts and tumbled onto the ground bleeding from a wound to his head. Close by, one the Tribune's heads suddenly jerked backwards as he was struck and he tumbled from his horse without making a sound. Corbulo felt a stone whizz passed his head.

"This is fucking outrageous," he shouted, "Where are the Hamians?"

Quintus raised his shield as he tried to cover Corbulo from a second volley of stones. "Here they come Sir," a Legionary shouted as he huddled behind the protective cover of his shield. Corbulo turned to look up the column and sure enough the Hamians in their exotic uniforms and armour were running towards him. "Get them in formation and tell them to take out those fucking slingers," Corbulo roared.

Along the column the rear most wagons had come to a standstill as the Romans took shelter behind their shields from the hail of stones that was hurtling through the air. "Keep moving, keep moving," Corbulo screamed as he noticed the development. But despite his order the Legionaries refused to budge. Corbulo bit his lip. It was no use, the enemy had them pinned down. The barking of the war dogs was drawing closer and as he snatched a glance at the enemy he saw the dog handlers struggling to hold the dogs on their leashes.

Suddenly a volley of arrows went flying through the air in the direction of the slingers and immediately the hail of stones slackened. Cries rose up from the Hibernian ranks as here and there a man was hit. Then like a blast of sparks from a fire a second volley of arrows hammered into the slingers mowing a swathe through their ranks. The Hamian archers had formed a tightly packed formation and were pounding the Hibernians with arrow after arrow and as he stared at the developing missile duel, Corbulo felt a rising respect for these oriental bowmen. They were by far the finest bowmen he had ever seen. With a cry the dog handlers released their beasts and the ferocious dogs bounded away barking loudly as the pack surged straight towards the Hamian's. Corbulo opened his mouth in dismay. The dogs would tear the archers to pieces if they could close the range. Snarling and yelping the pack of dogs raced towards the archers. Corbulo turned to look around him but there was nothing he could do. Then as the dogs closed in for the kill with just yards to go the Hamians lifted their bows and sent a ferocious close quarters barrage of arrows straight into the dogs. The result was carnage as animal after animal was mown down and killed. Corbulo stared at the scene in utter fascination. The Hamians had not taken a single step backwards.

"They are retreating Sir," one of the Tribunes shouted. Corbulo turned to look and across the field the remaining slingers were indeed beating a hasty retreat. Quickly he turned to the stalled wagons and the Legionaries.

"Get those wagons moving, I want everyone on their feet, this is no time for a rest," he shouted. "Come on boys, we are going to make it. We're going home."

Corbulo turned to stare at the Hibernian cavalry. The riders had made no further hostile moves as they shadowed the Roman column from a safe distance. As he watched them however Corbulo grunted in surprise as he suddenly saw the Hibernian force split into two groups of roughly similar size. His surprise turned into alarm as one group began to race away towards the front of the Roman column.

"They are splitting their force," Quintus cried.

Corbulo watched as the second group of riders remained behind as they shadowed the Batavian and Legionary cavalry. The two groups looked about equal in numbers.

"They are going to try and slow us down," Quintus said, "Those riders at the front are going to make it difficult for our men to keep moving. They are going to pick us off one by one. They are using their superior numbers. Clever bastards."

Corbulo turned to stare at the Batavian cavalry who were bringing up the rear. Then he cried out to the trumpeter.

"Order the Batavians to attack the cavalry that is shadowing us. Order them to annihilate them."

"They have equal numbers," Quintus called out in alarm, "It will be a straight fight. The Hibernians will see them coming. Can we afford to waste our men like this? We need the Batavians Corbulo."

"Give the order," Corbulo snapped ignoring Quintus. A moment later the trumpet rang out and Corbulo turned to stare at the Batavian and Legionary squadrons. At first the cavalrymen did not seem to react, then slowly the horsemen started to turn towards the enemy and form into a V shape formation. Swiftly the walk broke into a trot and then as they closed with the enemy it became a charge. The Hibernians too had formed into a V formation and as the Batavians charged, they too charged. The two cavalry forces smashed into each other and the shock of the collision sent men catapulting from their steeds and crashing to the ground. Horses screamed in terror and collapsed to the ground crushing men beneath their weight. Grimly Corbulo stared at the fight as the two sides lashed and stabbed at each other with their spears and swords. From where he stood Corbulo heard the screams and yells of the struggling writhing mass of horses and men.

"This is a mistake Corbulo," Quintus hissed, "We need those horsemen."

"Have a little more faith in our Germanic allies," Corbulo snapped, "I have never seen them being beaten in a straight fight."

Quintus shook his head but said nothing as he stared at the vicious confused brawl. Then suddenly the Hibernians seemed to have had enough as en masse they broke, turned and started to scatter and flee. With a loud roar the Batavians set off in pursuit leaving the dead and dying behind in a mass of bodies, blood and gore.

"Sound recall," Corbulo shouted and a moment later the trumpeter blasted out the signal. Across the field the ragged ranks of Batavian and Legionary cavalry reluctantly abandoned the chase and began to trot back towards the column. A few riderless horses cantered passed. Corbulo was staring at the Batavians as they came towards him. They had lost nearly half their number. Anxiously he cast about for Marcus and saw him on the extreme right of the line. He looked tired but unhurt. Many of the Batavians and Legionary cavalry were covered in blood and flesh wounds but here and there the wounds were worse and the rider's half hung from their beasts as they clung on with the last of their strength.

"Get the wounded from those horses," he cried, "and find some space for them on the wagons. Keep moving boy, keep moving."

Corbulo turned as Marcus came riding up to him. The young man had been cut across his arm but the wound did not look deep.

"We drove them off as ordered Sir," Marcus said wearily.

"You did well, your men did very well," Corbulo muttered, "I shall see that it gets mentioned to the Governor when we get back to Deva."

Marcus nodded and looked up the column. "I have enough men to keep that other group from slowing our advance," he muttered, "But don't ask us to do another one of those frontal attacks. The men are close to their limit."

"I know," Corbulo said, "The enemy won't hold us up. They no longer have the numbers. We are going to make it thanks to you."

"No Sir," Marcus shook his head grimly, "We are going to make it because of you father."

Chapter Thirty-Five - Home

Stiffly Corbulo stood to attention as Sallustius Lucullus, Governor of Britannia flanked by Agricola came towards him across the smooth stone floor of the Legionary HQ in Deva Victrix. As the Governor approached, Corbulo saluted smartly. The Governor shook his head and frowned.

"How by Jupiter's cock did you," he said pointing a finger at Corbulo, "end up being placed in command of an entire battle group. You are not even an active soldier anymore, you are supposed to be retired."

"Did you read my full report Sir," Corbulo said keeping his eyes fixed on the floor.

"Yes," the Governor sighed, "I read your report and I must say I was impressed. You may have abandoned Tara, but you brought back the bulk of your men and it seems that all the officers whom I have spoken to have a high regard for you. It is of course a great shame that Trebonius did not make it and that our plan to pacify the Hibernians has failed but considering the circumstances, you did well Corbulo."

"Trebonius was a first-class officer Sir," Corbulo said, "He should receive any honour that is due. I was just carrying out his final order."

"Is that so," the Governor said quietly. Lucullus shifted his weight and pushed his left leg forwards. "No Corbulo," he said, "Trebonius had orders to hold Tara and to make sure that Tuathal Techtmar was installed as High King. He failed. He failed me. No, his family will not be compensated for his loss and he will not receive the honour that you demand for him."

Corbulo did not move as he stood rigidly to attention. For a moment, the Governor of Britannia studied him carefully. "But as to your other two requests," he said slowly, "I have given these some careful thought and I will consent to them. Your son

Marcus showed remarkable leadership during the retreat and I will confirm his promotion. When the commander of the Second Batavians retires, Marcus will take over command of the Cohort." The Governor coughed and cleared his throat. "And as for the matter of Quintus, retired Centurion of the Twentieth, he shall be pardoned on condition that he renounces his faith in Christus."

Corbulo saluted as the Governor turned away with a little shake of his head. "Get some rest and spend some time in the baths Corbulo," he said as he strode away, "You stink like a sewer rat."

Corbulo remained standing to attention as Agricola watched him in silence. The two men were alone.

"So do you have it?" Agricola said at last.

Corbulo nodded slipped his hand into his tunic and retrieved a tightly rolled piece of parchment. Agricola took it and carefully unrolled it before reading it. When he was finished he looked up at Corbulo.

"I suppose I should be grateful to Quintus for not handing this to the Procurator," Agricola said carefully, "The man's loyalty to me and the Legion saved his life but if he or you breathe a word of this to anyone, you will find me an implacable enemy. I mean it Corbulo, make sure that Quintus understands that."

"Yes Sir," Corbulo barked.

Agricola paused to study Corbulo for a moment.

"So what happened to Classicus, the Procurator?" he asked.

"He is dead Sir," Corbulo replied.

"How did he die?" Agricola looked surprised.

Corbulo hesitated, "He drowned whilst crossing the sea, it's all in my report. I have a witness, Quintus, Sir."

"He drowned," Agricola repeated to himself. "Well that is a stroke of luck isn't it? The man has many powerful friends, who will want to know what happened to him so maybe being drowned is convenient. It would of course not do if the man was found to have been murdered. The killers may be subject to retaliation but, as Classicus was my enemy, I think that drowning is a fitting end for him."

An amused look had appeared on Agricola's face.

"I want my son's family released at once," Corbulo said quietly.

Agricola nodded. "I will arrange for them to be released. They are here in Deva. Your son will be reunited with them tonight."

Corbulo looked up at Agricola, "Thank you," he muttered, "And next time take better care of whom you write letters to. That one in your hand has cost the lives of too many people including a good friend of mine Sir."

Agricola's eyes glinted as for a long moment he stared at Corbulo in silence. Then abruptly he looked away.

"Yes I heard about your business down in Londinium," he said, "It's a shame you lost it. So I have a proposal for you Corbulo. I want to offer you a job. I own a number of businesses here in the Britannia, a couple of farms, a bakery and a bank and I need a manager to look after them all for me whilst I am not here. You would be based in Londinium. What do you say?"

***

Corbulo emerged into the bright sunlight. At the gate into the Legionary HQ he suddenly heard an excited squeal and saw a little girl jumping up and down. Corbulo gasped in sudden emotion as he recognised Efa and Dylis. The guards at the gate swung the gate open for him and, as he stepped out, Dylis rushed into his arms followed moments later by her mother. Corbulo gasped as he embraced both of them in a tight hug. Then he caught sight of Marcus and Quintus leaning against the wall on the other side of the street. He nodded at Marcus and the young man's face lit up in relief and he pressed his fist into the wall. Corbulo caught Quintus's eye as Efa and Dylis refused to let go of him.

"You have been pardoned but you must renounce your Christian faith," he called out.

A broad grin appeared on Quintus's face. "No problem, it's just words," he replied slipping a small wooden cross out from underneath his tunic, "How are they ever going to know?"

Corbulo ignored the big man.

"Come on, let's go home," Corbulo said as he wrapped one arm around Efa and the other around Dylis, "I have some stories to tell you that you won't believe." As the three of them strode down the street, Corbulo felt something pressing against his chest and he slid his hand into his tunic and retrieved the strange brown looking fruit that he'd taken from the cave on the Forbidden Islands. The fruit had not tasted very good and it had been too hard to bite into. Idly he chucked it into a small altar fire that stood in the street beside a statue of Neptune.

"Oh," he exclaimed turning to smile at Efa and then at Dylis, "did you know that I have got a new job?"

Author's notes

Hibernia is a work of fiction but some of the characters like Agricola and Domitian are historical whilst others such as Tuathal Techtmar, Elim and Eochaid are mentioned in early Irish texts. In this novel I have tried to describe the places, people, towns and forts of Roman Britain and Celtic Ireland as accurately as possible but of course landscapes do change over the course of 2,000 years.

The question of wherever the Romans did land in Ireland is an eagerly contested one with arguments for and against. Tacitus writes that his father in law Agricola retained an Irish prince in his retinue and Irish legends talk of a Tuathal Techtmar who returned to Tara to claim the High Kingship around the end of the first century AD. To me it seems likely that the Romans would have carried out suppression and retaliatory raids on Ireland from time to time just as they did when they punished the Germanic tribes across the Rhine. There is however no evidence to suggest that the Romans "conquered" Ireland or built any permanent forts or roads. Recently the discovery of the remains of a "Roman fort" at Drumanagh has rekindled the debate but wherever Drumanagh was a proper military installation or just a trading post remains unclear. What is certain is that numerous Roman objects have been found right across Ireland.

The plot against Emperor Domitian was real. In AD 89 Lucius Antonius Saturninus commander of the Fourteenth Gemina and Twenty First Rapax Legions at Mainz on the Rhine rebelled against Domitian but his revolt was swiftly crushed and Saturninus was killed together with many co-conspirators whose heads were displayed on the Rostra in Rome. Curiously Domitian's General, Lappius who crushed the revolt burned all Saturninus's personal papers before Domitian could arrive on the scene, therefore raising the suggestion that he was protecting others who had known about the rebellion. In that same spring of AD 89 the Governor of Britannia, Sallustius Lucullus was put to death on Domitian's orders and there is speculation that he too, had been involved in the plot. Agricola too would be dead within four years from the date of the rebellion but whether this was Domitian's work, remains unclear. Another account has it that it was the future Emperor Trajan who burned Saturninus's personal letters.

In writing Hibernia I am grateful to Vittorio Di Martino's excellent book "Roman Ireland" and the London Museum's brilliant online reconstructions of what Roman London would have looked like. Finally thanks must go to Guns & Roses, Enya, Dire Straits, Bill Joel and the theme song from Gladiator for getting me into the mood to write.

William Kelso, London, September 2014